Leah's head spun. She should be so out of there. This was nuts. Insane. Completely unbelievable. But she was a cop, and cops followed the evidence. Right now, the evidence—if she could believe her own senses, anyway—was telling her there was something seriously whacked going on. Logic—and what she knew about how the world worked—said none of this was real. But if it wasn't real, how did she explain what'd just happened to her?

Her options seemed to be limited to: A) magic existed, and she'd gotten caught up in something way outside her comfort zone; or B) magic didn't exist, and she'd been kidnapped, nearly drowned, and then boffed a total stranger.

She squeezed her eyes shut, trying to slow the spins, trying not to freak right the hell out and start screaming at the dark-haired man. "And here I was last night thinking you were a fantasy, and how that was better than your being a doomsday nut."

"Last night?"

She realized her mistake too late, and backpedaled. "I meant just now."

"No, you didn't. Which means you dreamed about me."

Everything inside her went still. "Why do you say that?"

Heat kindled in his dark blue eyes. "Because I sure as hell dreamed of

NIGHT KEEPERS

*

A Novel of the Final Prophecy

JESSICA ANDERSEN

A SIGNET ECLIPSE BOOK

SIGNET ECLIPSE
Published by New American Library, a division of
Penguin Group (USA) Inc., 375 Hudson Street,
New York, New York 10014, USA
Penguin Group (Canada), 90 Eglinton Avenue East, Suite 700, Toronto,
Ontario M4P 2Y3, Canada (a division of Pearson Penguin Canada Inc.)
Penguin Books Ltd., 80 Strand, London WC2R 0RL, England
Penguin Ireland, 25 St. Stephen's Green, Dublin 2,
Ireland (a division of Penguin Books Ltd.)
Penguin Group (Australia), 250 Camberwell Road, Camberwell, Victoria 3124,
Australia (a division of Pearson Australia Group Pty. Ltd.)
Penguin Books India Pvt. Ltd., 11 Community Centre, Panchsheel Park,
New Delhi - 110 017, India
Penguin Group (NZ), 67 Apollo Drive, Rosedale, North Shore 0632,
New Zealand (a division of Pearson New Zealand Ltd.)
Penguin Books (South Africa) (Pty.) Ltd., 24 Sturdee Avenue,
Rosebank, Johannesburg 2196, South Africa

Penguin Books Ltd., Registered Offices:
80 Strand, London WC2R 0RL, England

First published by Signet Eclipse, an imprint of New American Library,
a division of Penguin Group (USA) Inc.

First Printing, June 2008
10 9 8 7 6 5 4 3

Copyright © Jessica Andersen, 2008
All rights reserved

SIGNET ECLIPSE and logo are trademarks of Penguin Group (USA) Inc.

Printed in the United States of America

To the other Jess, my road trip partner on the writing highway—speed bumps, roadkill, and all. Thanks for bringing me along, and yes, you'll probably always have the cooler car.

AUTHOR'S NOTE

The Nightkeepers' world is well hidden within our own; bringing it to light wasn't always an easy process. My heartfelt thanks go to Deidre Knight, Kara Cesare, Claire Zion, Kara Welsh, and Kerry Donovan for taking this book from a dream to a reality; to J. R. Ward for critiques and help each step of the way; to Suz Brockmann for being a mentor and an inspiration; to Angela Knight for early reads and encouragement; to Marley Gibson and Charlene Glatkowski for being there for me every day without fail; to Sally Hinkle Russell for keeping me sane; and to Brian Hogan for too many things to name in this small space.

Just as the few surviving Nightkeepers live among us today, their ancestors lived with the ancient Egyptians, Olmec, Maya, and Hopi; they left their imprint on each of these civilizations, and were influenced in turn. Thus, while their culture is best reflected in the myths and beliefs of the Maya, the parallel is not absolute.

That being said, I drew upon a number of sources to understand the Nightkeepers' world. These include the excellent hieroglyphic dictionaries of John Montgomery, Allen J. Christenson's translation and annotation of the *Popol Vuh*, Miller and Taube's illustrated dictionary of Mayan gods and symbols, and the vast online resources of the Foundation for the Advancement of Mesoamerican Studies, Inc. In addition, I used various resources to understand the cataclysm predicted for 12/21/2012; these included works by Patrick

Geryl and John Major Jenkins. Finally, works of Erich von Däniken, Kenneth L. Feder, Stephen Williams, and Charles Pellegrino were used for their discussions of Atlantis, alien influences on prehistoric cultures, and other so-called pseudoscientific theories. For a full list of references and recommended reading on the ancient Maya and the 2012 doomsday prophecy, please visit www.JessicaAndersen.com.

Every twenty-six thousand years, the earth, sun, and moon align at the exact center of the Milky Way . . . and all hell breaks loose.

During the last Great Conjunction, in 24,000 B.C., the earth's magnetic poles reversed, sunspots torched half the planet, tsunamis drowned the other half, and terrible, bloodthirsty demons broke out of the underworld and destroyed the civilization that would later become known as Atlantis.

The few survivors of the devastation, powerful warrior-priests called Nightkeepers, managed to band together and kick the demons' asses back to the underworld, sealing them behind a barrier of psi energy. Ever since then, the Nightkeepers and their servants, the winikin, have had one imperative: to stay alive until the next Great Conjunction, when the magi will be the only power standing between mankind and the demons' return . . .

. . . on December 21, 2012.

For tens of thousands of years, the Nightkeepers have walked among normal humans, teaching them math, science, writing, and an intricate polytheistic religion based on blood sacrifice and sex. They lived first with the Egyptians and then with the Maya, influencing the development of ancient legends and prophecies, and the backward-ticking Mayan Long Count calendar that will end on the day of the Great Conjunction, signaling that there is no more time to count. On that day, mankind will either enter a new time cycle, one of enlightenment . . . or humanity will cease to exist. It will be up to the Nightkeepers, guardians of the night and protectors of the barrier between the earth and the underworld, to make sure time continues past the zero date and mankind is enlightened, not annihilated.

Within the Mayan Empire, however, arose the Order of Xibalba, a group of demon-worshiping dark magi who believed that when the zero date came and humanity was destroyed, they would become the leaders of the new earth.

The Maya had no knowledge of the wheel or metal tools, yet they produced thousands of soaring stone temples and pyramids, serving a population that eventually topped thirteen million. They worshiped time and their three calendars, one of which was a set of daily prophecies used to plan everything from marriages and the naming of children, to wars and sacrifices. There were also larger prophecies repeating on a longer cycle that still holds today. One such prophecy, set for the Gregorian date of Easter Day 1521, spoke of a white man coming from the east. The Nightkeepers warned that he brought death and destruction. Members of the Order of Xibalba, however, convinced the Maya that this heralded the coming of the god Kulkulkan (later known as Quetzalcoatl).

When Cortés and the Spanish conquistadors appeared on precisely this day, the Maya welcomed them into their lands and hearts. Over the next thirty years, pre-Columbian civilization was decimated by disease, war, and the efforts of the conquistadors' missionaries, who slaughtered the priests and burned tens of thousands of written texts in their zeal to convert the "heathens" from the Mayan pantheon to the missionaries' one true God. A handful of Nightkeeper children survived the slaughter, protected by their winikin . . . *but most of their traditions and all but a few of their spellbooks were lost.*

The Order of Xibalba went underground, over time becoming a rumor, and then a myth. The surviving Nightkeepers fled north and took shelter with the Hopi for several hundred years, then eventually liquidated many of their artifacts and used the money to build a training center deep in the Chacoan territories of New Mexico. Each year the warrior-priests gathered at the training center to celebrate the equinoxes and solstices, the four cardinal days when the barrier was thinnest and the magi were sometimes able to speak to their gods and ancestors. They collected the remaining spells, along with their theories on the end date and interpretations of the ancient prophecies, in a hidden archive. They trained. They raised their children. And they waited for the Long Count to run out, signaling the time for war.

Then, nearly thirty years before the zero date, the Nightkeepers' king had a vision unlike any other—one he believed was sent by the gods. Even though prescience was never granted to Nightkeeper males, King Scarred-Jaguar saw himself leading an attack on the intersection of the earth, sky, and underworld and sealing the barrier forever, using a spell that was burned into his mind when he awoke . . . a spell that hadn't existed on earth since the fifteen hundreds. A spell given to him by the gods.

This intersection, located in a sacred underground chamber beneath the Mayan ruins of Chichén Itzá, was the one place the gods and demons could access the earthly plane. While sealing the intersection would rob the Nightkeepers of their magic and forever separate them from their gods, it would also prevent the coming apocalypse.

Or so the king believed.

PART I

✳

SUMMER SOLSTICE

*The first day of summer has the longest day
and shortest night of the year,
and the sun seems to stand still in the sky.*

PROLOGUE

June 21
Twenty-four years ago

Two big clocks hung high at one end of the great hall, counting time. One ran in reverse, measuring out how long was left until the end-time: almost exactly twenty-eight years and six months. The other was a normal clock, and it was creepy-crawling to nine fifty-three p.m., the moment of the summer solstice. The moment King Scarred-Jaguar and two hundred other Nightkeeper warrior-priests would take their places in the sacred tunnels beneath Chichén Itzá and cast the king's spell, sealing the intersection of the earth, sky, and underworld.

Three minutes and change to go.

Scarred-Jaguar's loyal servant, Jox, stood guard, along with fifty other *winikin*, all spaced around the edge of the huge hall, watching the seconds tick down. The Nightkeeper children who were too young to fight were gathered in the center of the room. Some of them were watching a Michael Jackson video on the big screen.

The rest were watching the clock.

"Nothing yet," Hannah said from beside Jox. The pretty brunette glanced down at the marks on her right inner forearm, rows of tiny lizard glyphs, each representing a member of the bloodline she was sworn to protect.

The *winikin* weren't magic users, but the marks themselves were magic. Every time a member of the blood-line died, one of the glyphs disappeared.

So far, so good. Two minutes to go, and nobody had lost a glyph.

"You should be with the baby," Jox murmured. "Just in case."

"I know." Hannah glanced down at the infants' area, where she'd gotten her best friend, Izzy, to watch her tiny charge for a few minutes. Instead of hurrying away as the countdown continued, though, she took Jox's hand and pressed his palm to her cheek. "Be safe."

His heart tightened in his chest, heavy with the knowledge that he couldn't put her first, not when he was blood-bound to the king's son and daughter. But when she released his hand, instead of letting it fall away from her soft, warm skin like he knew he should, he slid his grip to the back of her neck and drew her closer.

"Maybe after," he whispered, and touched his lips to hers.

She hesitated for a fraction of a second, as if wondering whether he actually meant it after all this time. Then she returned the kiss with a sharp edge of fear. Of hope.

Maybe after. It was what they were all saying—Nightkeeper and *winikin* alike—if not aloud, then in their hearts. Maybe after the intersection was sealed, they'd be able to break away from lives ruled by ancient roles and prophecies. If the end-time could be prevented from ever beginning, then the Nightkeepers wouldn't need to protect mankind anymore. The *winikin* wouldn't need to serve anymore. They could all disband, disperse, go off to live as they chose. Jox figured he'd start his own business, maybe a garden center. He could run the front with Hannah while their rug rats played tag in the shrubbery.

And he was so getting ahead of himself.

As the final minute began to tick down, he broke the kiss and gave her a little push. "Go on. Get back to work."

He didn't watch her go. He watched the clock. Forty-five seconds. Twenty-five. Fifteen. Five. Three. Two. One. There was a collective indrawn breath when half the wristwatches in the room went off in a chaos of digital bleats as the solstice came. . . .

And absolutely nothing happened.

The second hand on the big clock swept past the critical moment and kept going. Thirty seconds. One minute. Two. Three.

After five minutes there was a collective exhale and a few cheers, and the kids in the middle of the room started talking, only a few at first, then more and more, the volume building as the tension released and excitement took hold.

The *winiken* to Jox's immediate left, a sturdy guy named Kneeland who was bound to the ax bloodline, said, "Hannah, huh?" He elbowed Jox in the ribs. "Rock on. We didn't think you had it in you. Ever since the prince was born, you've been so caught up in— *Shit!*" Kneeland went dead pale and clawed at his arm, pushing up his sleeve. "Oh, no. No! Please, gods, *no!*"

Screams ripped through the *winikin*, echoing at the perimeter of the hall, then in the middle as the kids reacted to their protectors' alarm.

A second later, pain seared along Jox's arm. Cursing, praying, he shoved up his sleeve and stared at the black tattoolike marks on his right forearm.

There was a ripple of motion as the jaguar glyphs disappeared one by one.

Blood red washed across his vision and his pulse stuttered. Agony vised his body. Fear. Disbelief. Crushing, awful grief.

No! He wanted to scream for his people, for himself, but instead clamped his teeth on the cry as tears ran down his cheeks. Then, like a switch had been thrown, the pain was gone. So were almost all of the glyphs, including two of the four royal marks.

The absence of the pain echoed like silence. Like sorrow.

The king is dead, he thought. *Long live the king.*

The hall was in chaos. The girls—most of whom had the sight to one degree or another—screamed at the things they saw in their minds, or wept for their parents, or both. Most of the boys were shouting, running around, banging on the gun cabinet and hammering at the locked and warded exterior doors, ready to fight the enemy, the demons called *Banol Kax*.

Kneeland grabbed Jox's arm, his fingers digging down to the bone. "We've got to do something! They're dying! What do we do? What do we—"

"Focus!" Jox grabbed the other man and shook him hard. "The kids are the priority. We're safe here. The hall is protected, and if we batten down—"

Yellow light flared all around them as the protective wards fell. Jox's heart froze in his chest. *Impossible*, he thought. The wards had been set by blood sacrifice from the strongest of the Nightkeepers. The only creature capable of breaching them was one of the *Banol Kax*, or their lava creatures, the—

"*Boluntiku!*" shouted a *winikin* named Olivar as a dark shadow rose from the floor, radiating terrible magma-borne heat that set the parquet aflame. The creature coalesced out of a nightmare, rising up from the bowels of the earth, a swirling image of red-brown scales that remained translucent as it formed a six-fingered hand tipped with razor-sharp claws, and swung.

In the moment before it touched Olivar, the thing flared bright orange and turned solid. Blood geysered and Olivar's body arched like a crossbow strung too tightly, suspended from the *boluntiku*'s six-clawed grip.

A chatter of gunfire rang out, sounding loud even through the screams. Olivar's body jerked with the impact of bullets fired by a terrified-looking *winikin*, who'd unlocked the gun cabinet and grabbed an autopistol loaded with jade-tipped bullets.

Jade was to the *Banol Kax* as garlic was to the mythical vampires, or silver to the werewolves of legend. While the demons and their ilk were impervious to most other nonmagical weapons, jade could pierce their psi armor and do some damage.

The bullets had to hit to work, though, and these didn't. The *boluntiku* puffed to vapor so the jade-tips passed harmlessly through, and Olivar's limp body dropped to the floor. Then the lava creature turned on the shooter, going solid in the moment before it attacked.

Seconds later, the *winikin* was dead and the weapons cabinet was a mass of shattered wood and twisted metal. And the floor nearby was aflame.

Jox was moving before he'd even processed what was happening, running toward his charges, nine-year-old Striking-Jaguar and his fourteen-year-old sister, Anna-Paw.

Scarred-Jaguar's attack must have failed. The Nightkeepers were all dead and the intersection was wideopen. The *Banol Kax* had sent their creatures to kill the children, to wipe out any chance of resistance when the Great Conjunction arrived. And it wouldn't matter if the *winikin* got the kids out of the training center and hid—the *boluntiku* could smell magic.

They could also smell royalty.

Acting in concert, the *boluntiku* zeroed in on Anna, who was fighting her way toward Strike through the crush piled up near the exit, where children struggled to unlock the doors and *winikin* scrambled to get to their charges, everyone screaming as more *boluntiku* erupted from the floor.

"No!" Jox shouted, his voice breaking as he fought his way toward the king's children. Terrified cries rose up around him, and the floor was slick with blood, but he was entirely focused on the prince and princess he was blood-bound to protect.

Then a huge *boluntiku* rose up from the middle of the crush, rearing up and flaring its claws to swing at Anna, who was trying to shield her little brother.

Too late, Jox thought, desperation pounding in his veins as he struggled through a sea of panic and gore. He was going to be too late.

The creature went solid, killing everyone who'd been inside the confines of its vapor body. But in the second before the six-fingered claws raked the children, gunfire chattered and jade-tipped bullets struck home.

The *boluntiku* jerked back with a shriek that sounded like a thousand fingernails scratching across a giant blackboard, and spun toward its attacker. Jox turned, too, and saw Kneeland standing in front of the big-screen TV, holding a dented autopistol while tears rolled down his cheeks. When the *winikin* caught Jox's eye, he flashed his forearm.

It was bare. His protectees—and their bloodline—were gone.

With nothing left to live for, Kneeland lifted the weapon in salute, then ran across the raised platform and leaped straight for the huge *boluntiku*. The thing stayed solid and caught him in midair with its claws, hoisting him to its gaping, hundred-toothed mouth.

The moment before it bit down, Kneeland let loose with the autopistol, emptying the clip. The back of the creature's head blew out in a spray of blackish blood and rust-colored scales. But, still, its jaws closed with an audible crunch.

Kneeland's body went limp, then fell to the ground in a bloody heap when the *boluntiku* vaporized in death, opening up a corpse-filled hole in the panicked mob. Retching, Jox hurdled the bodies and tried not to think of them as people who'd been alive only seconds earlier.

Around him the screams and fingernails-on-blackboard howls continued and the air smelled of blood and death. Then he was at the doors, and Anna grabbed him, and she was hanging on to Strike, and all Jox could think about was getting the hell out of there.

Someone must've hit the panic release—shit, he should've thought of that—because the doors weren't locked anymore; they were wide-open and survivors were running out into the starlit crevasse where the training center was hidden, deep within Chaco Canyon. *Winikin* were dragging their children away from the carnage, running for their lives, but the *boluntiku* pursued with single-minded ferocity, their vapor bulks partially submerged beneath the ground as they gained strength from the magma flow at the earth's mantle.

"Jox, come on!" Anna pulled him toward the door. "*Jox!*"

Three *boluntiku* were closing in on them, drawn by the smell of royalty.

"Not that way." Most of the escapees were headed

toward the forty-car garage, or for the barns and the high canyon trails beyond. Jox's heart hurt with the knowledge that they'd never make it to the vehicles or horses. More important, it wouldn't matter if they did, because distance was nothing to the *boluntiku*. Only smell mattered.

He had to get the children to the secret blood-warded room beneath the archives, which only the royal *winikin* knew of.

"This way," he said, making the only call he possibly could, though it nearly killed him to turn away from everyone else he'd ever known.

Making sure Anna was right behind him, he grabbed a dazed-looking Strike by the waist and arm, half carrying, half dragging the boy across the great hall to the covered walkway leading to the mansion. It'd been locked all night, but now the doors stood open, one hanging halfway off its hinge. "Don't look," he ordered as their feet slid in the bloody wetness that seemed to be everywhere. He lifted Strike higher and the boy trembled and clung to him like a limpet, pressing his face into the *winikin*'s chest.

Jox heard fingernails on blackboard behind them, heard an infant's wail and a familiar feminine voice screaming a battle cry. Something deep inside him wept— *Hannah*. But he didn't turn back to help her.

He took the king's children and ran for his life.

CHAPTER ONE

June 21
The present

The glowing green numbers of the Crown Vic's in-dash clock ticked from eleven fifty-nine to midnight, signaling the start of a new day. Detective Leah Ann Daniels let out a slow breath, trying to settle her nerves. "First day of summer used to be a good thing."

"That was before the locals started drinking the Kool-Aid," her partner, Nick Ramon, said, then winced. "Sorry."

"Don't be." *It's not your fault my brother joined a cult and drew the short straw.* Battling the churning in her gut, Leah scanned the dark, cluttered alley outside the car, looking for Itchy Pasquale, the scrawny gangbanger—and occasional snitch—who'd called her for a meeting, claiming to know where the Kool-Aid was being served this time around.

She and Nick were parked only a few streets over from Miami's chichi Wynwood Art District, but the alley could've been in another world—one peopled with sallow-faced junkies rather than glitterati and run by gang rule rather than art critics. The Miami-Dade PD made regular sweeps of the buildings on either side of the alley, and the raids turned up pretty much every crime on the books, and occasionally some that weren't.

Like human sacrifice.

The bodies had started turning up eighteen months ago and had followed every three months like clockwork: two at each equinox, two at each solstice. The victims were beheaded, their hearts cut from their chests. The news vultures had dubbed them the Calendar Killings and hauled out all the old favorites—Buono and Bianchi, Dahmer, Kemper, Gacy. Only one reporter had been savvy enough to draw the parallel between the Manson family and Miami's newest cult, Survivor2012; between Helter Skelter and the doomsday espoused by their leader, Zipacna, who had named himself after the crocodile demon of the Mayan underworld.

Said clever reporter had turned up right after the vernal equinox, sans head and heart. Next to him had been Leah's thirty-year-old brother, Matt. Unfortunately, the connections between the Calendar Killings and Survivor2012 were strictly circumstantial; there wasn't any evidence the locals or FBI were willing to run with.

"Not yet, anyway," she said softly. Anticipation burned in her veins, making her impatient. "Itchy's late," she said louder, so Nick knew she wasn't talking to herself anymore. They'd been partners nearly six years. He'd gotten used to telling the difference.

"We shouldn't even be here. Not our case anymore." But Nick didn't look bothered by the thought. Long and lean and dark-skinned, he was dancer-graceful, yet sturdy as a hurricane shelter, and wore a plain gold wedding band she hadn't gotten used to yet.

Leah had danced at his and Selina's wedding a month earlier, and toasted them with a big old, "Better you guys than me," though it'd stuck a little. She and Nick had been there and done that and managed to stay partners in the aftermath, so she had absolutely nothing against the nurse he'd married. Besides, her relationships seemed to have a three-month expiration date, which tended to defeat the whole "till death do us part" thing.

Didn't mean she loved being alone, though. Heck, even her subconscious was telling her it was time to start dating again, sending her some seriously hot dreams that had her waking up wanting and lonely, and thinking of a dark-haired man with piercing blue eyes, some righteous ink, and what looked an awful lot like a MAC-10 autopistol on his belt.

Great. Just what she didn't need—a crush on a gangbanger. Although she supposed—hypothetically—that a 'banger would be better than a doomsday nut who believed that when the Maya's backward-counting calendar hit its zero date in a few years, the world was going to end.

News flash: Not even the modern Maya believed that shit anymore. Most of 'em, anyway.

In the Crown Vic's passenger seat, Nick rolled his shoulders, trying to work out the kinks. "Long day." He was wearing yesterday's khakis and shirt, but somehow managed to make the wrinkles look like a fashion statement.

Leah, on the other hand, was way more wrinkle than fashion in navy pants and a fitted blue button-down that'd done the sexy curve-clinging thing twenty hours earlier, but now chafed beneath the Kevlar vest she'd pulled on for the meet. Her white-blond hair was pulled up in a ponytail and stuffed under an MDPD ball cap, and all vestiges of makeup had *hasta-la-vista*'ed it hours ago.

Long day, indeed.

They should've been off shift at nine. Technically, they *were* off shift, but the snitch's call had been too good to pass up . . . and too tempting to pass along. "Itchy won't talk to anyone but me," she said, faintly defensive because they both knew she should've taken it to the task force handling the Calendar Killings, which had ceased including her the moment she'd ID'd her brother's body.

"So where is he?"

"Damned if I know." She tried Itchy's cell again, but it bounced straight to voice mail.

"Wait." Nick pointed as a figure emerged from behind an overflowing Dumpster at the far end of the alley. "Over there."

Leah's heart did a bumpity-bump as she identified her informant by the faint hitch in his get-along, courtesy of a drive-by a few years back. "That's him." She checked the clip on her .22 and reached for the door handle. "Stay here. You know how twitchy he gets around you."

"Dude was born twitchy." But Nick hit the headlights. "Keep in sight."

Anticipation flared through Leah, alongside something that hummed in her veins and stomach and made her feel like this was it; this was the moment she'd been waiting for—a chance to pin something real on Zipacna and his freakazoid followers.

Taking a deep breath, she climbed out of the car, leaving the door open in case she needed quick cover. She held the .22 at the ready. "Hey, Itchy."

The banger was in his late teens, wearing a pair of low-slung jeans and a T-shirt featuring a cartoon penis and a caption she had no desire to read. His head was shaved bald, and a hollow plug stretched his earlobe around empty space the size of a quarter, making him look lopsided.

He grinned, baring a shiny set of caps with both front teeth filed to points. "Hey, beautiful. Got a present for you."

"Zipacna." It was no secret she thought the head of Survivor2012 was the Calendar Killer, but three warrants had failed to find any evidence in the mansion he'd retrofitted for the bloodletting rituals he conducted, claiming to be descended from King Somebody-or-other. Freak.

Unfortunately, he was a smart freak. She hadn't even been able to pin him with a parking ticket. Until tonight.

Lowering the .22, she patted her pocket beneath the Kevlar. "I've got the cash, and the solstice hits in twelve hours. Time for a couple more bodies. You going to tell me where he kills them?"

Itchy grinned. "I'm gonna do better than tell you, baby." His eyes flicked to a point over her shoulder in a blatant signal.

Shit! Survival instincts going into overdrive, Leah spun and lifted her weapon just as a dark figure stepped from the shadows and lifted a rocket launcher to shoulder height, aiming it at the Crown Vic. Panic spurted and she snapped off three quick shots, screaming, "Nick, *run!*"

But her shots missed and her words were lost beneath the rocket thump. Seconds later, the car exploded and a red-orange fireball howled outward, flattening everything in its path.

The shock wave slammed into Leah, flinging her through the air. She hit a Dumpster with battering force and crashed into a pile of spilled refuse.

"*Nick!*" Head ringing, pulse hammering, she scrambled to her hands and knees in the garbage. *He got out,* she told herself. *He can't be dead.*

Except deep down inside, she knew he was.

"She's over here," Itchy's voice called, and footsteps rattled as a half dozen of Itchy's compadres converged around the Dumpster, warning that she could mourn Nick later. She had her own ass to worry about right now.

Breath sobbing in her lungs, she scrabbled around, found the .22 half-buried beneath a pile of garbage, grabbed the gun, and came up firing.

Her first shot caught a shirtless teen in the chest, punching a hole just above the tattoo of a flying crocodile on his left pec. The guy fell back, but that left Itchy plus four others. She got off another shot before she felt a sting of impact, though no major pain. She looked down and saw the double barb of a high-powered Taser hooked onto her pants. Before she could yank it out, Itchy hit the button and nailed her with fifty thousand volts.

Leah's jaw locked tight, holding the scream inside as everything went numb and she flopped to the pavement, twitching hard.

Then they were pawing at her, groping her as they hauled her up and dragged her out of the alley. She couldn't move, could barely breathe, could do little more than scream inside her own skull as they gagged her, zip-tied her hands and feet, and tossed her in the back of a van. Moments later, she felt a sharp prick in her left butt cheek, and as the doors slammed and the van drove off into the night, everything started to go gray. Then black.

Then nothing.

*   *   *

The blonde leaning over the garden center's display table of annual flats was wearing a tight pink tank top and no bra.

Not that Strike was looking or anything.

"I just love impatiens, don't you?" She bent over further to select just the right six-pack of flowers, giving him an eyeful.

Hello. He dialed down the water wand he'd been using to fertilize the hanging begonias, and moved around the table. "Impatiens are pretty enough," he said, pretending to look at the flowers. "But I prefer the full-sun varieties, myself. No tan lines."

She shot him a *gotcha* look before nodding at his right arm. "Nice ink. Aztec, right?"

He normally wore long-sleeved shirts to avoid just this sort of conversation, especially from people who noticed that his business partners, Jox and Red-Boar, wore similar glyphs. Today was scorching hot, though, and he'd gone with cutoffs and a black T-shirt that bared his marks: the jaguar that symbolized his bloodline and the *ju* that marked him as royalty.

"They're Mayan." He could've told her that the Maya had been the only society in the New World to develop a fully functional writing system, or that it was because they, like the Egyptians two millennia earlier, had been taught by a warrior culture that went back twenty thousand years or so to Atlantis.

He didn't tell her that because, one, she'd think he was whacked; two, lectures weren't sexy; and three, the details, like the forearm marks, weren't relevant anymore. The barrier was sealed, the Nightkeepers unnecessary. In four-plus years, the Great Conjunction would come and go with nothing more than a Michael Bay disaster movie and some empty hype.

Hopefully.

"Very nice," she said again, and it was clear she wasn't just talking about the marks.

"Thanks." Strike was bigger than average—most Nightkeepers were, or had been—and he kept himself fighting fit. Add that to deep blue eyes, shoulder-length black hair worn in a ponytail regardless of trends, and a close-clipped jawline beard, and he had a look that either fascinated women or scared them off, depending.

The blonde didn't seem scared as she took a long look around the garden center.

The sturdy barn-red store was flanked with plastic-covered greenhouses, with the one- and five-gallon shrubs grouped out front like leafy islands sprouting from an ocean of parking lot. The balled and burlapped trees were set around the perimeter, and tables of flowers and veg flats were strategically placed so shoppers couldn't miss them on the way in. "This place is cute," she said finally. "Yours?"

In other words, was he an owner, a contract landscaper working out of the nursery, or a schlub who, at thirty-three, watered plants for a living at seven bucks an hour?

"Mine and my partners'," he said, wondering how she'd react if he told her it was a little bit of all of those things.

He was part owner, along with Jox and Red-Boar, because all three of their names were on the Nightkeeper Fund started by his umpteenth-great-grandfather after he'd sold off most of the old artifacts. Strike also did some landscaping now and then, when he got the itch. And yeah, he was thirty-three, and although he had an MBA from Harvard Biz and used it to manage the fund, at the moment his career pretty much consisted of watering plants and discussing the intricacies of dried versus composted cow manure.

That, and studying spells that hadn't worked in twenty-four years.

"Want to give me a behind-the-scenes tour?" The blonde shot him a look of pure invitation that normally would've had his glands sitting up and taking notice.

Now, though, his libido sort of shrugged and yawned, which gave him serious pause. *Oh, come on.* How could he not be interested in getting some of that?

He ought to be . . . hell, he was *trying* to be, but he was doing the autoflirt thing—and had been for the past few weeks—all because of some seriously funky, sexed-up dreams that had him waking up horny as hell. He could clearly picture the woman in those dreams: her high-cheekboned face and pale blue eyes, a set of full lips that seemed made to wrap around a guy and hang on for the ride, and white-blond hair that sifted through his fingers like spun platinum.

He looked at Pink Top again to make sure. Nope, wrong blonde. Assuming, of course, there was a "right" blonde . . . which was a serious stretch, because even if the barrier were active, which it wasn't, and he'd gone through the talent ceremony at puberty to get his full powers, which he hadn't, Nightkeeper males weren't supposed to be precogs. Which meant the dreams were just dreams, and he should be good to go.

Only he wasn't.

"There's really not much to see out back." He smiled in an effort to soften the brush-off. "Besides, I've got to keep working. My boss is a real ballbuster." There was even a bit of truth to that—Jox might be the royal *winikin* and thus technically Strike's servant, but the garden center was his baby, and woe to he who skimped on watering duty.

Surprise flicked across the blonde's face, along with a hint of temper he figured she was entitled to. "Really? Wow. Guess I called that wrong."

"My bad, not yours." He cranked the water wand and hit a hanging pot of salmon-colored begonias. "Enjoy the impatiens."

As she huffed off and the begonia pot overflowed, a voice from behind Strike said, "What are you, fucking stupid?"

Exhaling and counting to ten backward, Strike dealt with the water first, shutting it off and dropping the hose. Then he turned and held out a hand. "That'll be five bucks, Rabbit."

Wearing low-slung jeans, heavy work boots, and a black hooded track jacket even though it was in the high eighties and rising, with the hood pulled up over his shaved head and his iPod buds stuck firmly in his ears, Red-Boar's seventeen-year-old son was dressed to depress, and wore the 'tude to match.

Smirking, the kid dug in his pocket, pulled out a ten, and slapped it in Strike's palm to pay the "no saying 'fuck' on the job" fine they'd been forced to institute when Rabbit graduated high school a full year ahead of schedule, blew off his SATs to joyride down the coast in Jox's truck, and then e-mailed all his completed college applications to the U.S. Embassy in Honduras while swearing to Jox and Strike that he'd submitted the apps on time.

He'd probably figured—hoped—that his father would cut ties after those stunts, leaving him free to do whatever the hell he wanted. Instead, Red-Boar—aka the only adult Nightkeeper who'd survived the Solstice Massacre—had surprised all of them by rousing his PTSD-zonked self long enough to ground Rabbit's ass, cancel his AmEx, julienne his license, and order the kid to work at the garden center all summer, where he'd promptly started cussing out the customers.

Thus, the "fuck" fine.

Strike pocketed the ten. "You want change?"

"Put it on account." The kid's eyes, so light blue they were almost gray, followed the blonde into the store. "But seriously. How can you not want a piece of that?"

"I take it you're done pruning out back?"

Jox and Strike did their best to keep Rabbit away from the front of the store as much as possible, because they never knew what he'd get into next. Sometimes his ideas were brilliant, sometimes terrifying, quite often both. But Rabbit was Red-Boar's son, which meant he was one of them. It also meant that he was at a serious disadvantage, because his father was a head case, and nobody knew a damn thing about his mother except Red-Boar, who wasn't talking. So Strike tried to cut the kid some slack. In the end, the four of them were a family, albeit a seriously dysfunctional one.

Rabbit lifted a shoulder, still focused on the front of the store even though the blonde was long gone. "Why don't you check on the pruning for yourself, Strike-out?"

"In other words, no." Strike rubbed absently at his wrist, which had started aching early that morning, along with most of the rest of his body. He was tired, and vaguely pissed off for no good reason. There was nothing wrong, but there was nothing particularly right, either.

He was used to living with Jox, Red-Boar, and Rabbit in a strange bacheloresque symbiosis that was part necessity, part history, but it wasn't the life he would've picked. *Four and a half more years until the world doesn't end,* he reminded himself. *You've just got to hang on until then.*

"Delivery's here," Rabbit said, shifting his attention as an eighteen-wheeler turned up the driveway. "I'll sign for it."

"No way." Strike grabbed Rabbit by the back of his hood, knowing the kid was just as likely to blow straight past the truck and down the street to the liquor store, bucking for another shoplifting conviction. He headed the teen toward the greenhouse with a shove. "Prune. Now."

"Fuck you."

Strike patted his pocket, where he'd stuck the ten. "We're even."

He signed for the delivery—more cow shit—and headed into the store, which was functional and homey without being unrelentingly cute.

The walls were lined with shelves and bins holding everything from fifty-cent peat cakes to three-hundred-dollar customized bird feeders, complete with advanced squirrel deterrent systems that made no sense to Strike. Rows of freestanding shelves held the seeds and chemicals, and twenty-pounders of fertilizer, crabgrass killer, and slug repellent were stacked neatly in a row headed for the checkout area, where books and magazines competed for space with other point-of-purchase doodads. The counter was paneled in rustic wood like the rest of the shop, and the high-tech cash register was disguised to look like something out of the forties.

Behind the counter, Jox was perched on a bar stool chatting with the blonde, whom he'd apparently talked into a pink ceramic pot for her impatiens, along with a bonsai money tree.

The *winikin* was wearing khakis and a green long-sleeved jersey that covered the two jaguar glyphs on his arm—one for Strike, the other for his sister. Anna might've renounced her magic and taken off, but the bloodline connection remained unbroken. Jox's dark skin was relatively unlined for his fifty-seven years, his close-cropped hair shot through with silver. He looked relaxed enough, but his expression was edged with the same tension Strike felt in his own gut, the same sense of dread mingled with anticipation.

The thirteenth prophecy spoke of the final five years before the Great Conjunction, when a terrible sacrifice would be required to keep the *Banol Kax* from coming to earth and precipitating the big game-over. Thing was, King Scarred-Jaguar's attack on the intersection twenty-four years ago had sealed the barrier, preventing the few surviving Nightkeepers—i.e., Strike, Red-Boar, and Anna—from using their powers. The seal also prevented the *Banol Kax*—and the gods, for that matter—from even communicating with the earthly plane, never mind reaching through the barrier to possess a willing, or un-willing, host. In all those things, Scarred-Jaguar's vision had proven true, though it had cost him the Night-keepers.

Had it been worth it? Strike didn't know, and a whole hell of a lot of the answer depended on whether the barrier stayed sealed through the final five-year count-down.

With her purchase concluded, the blonde wiggled out, winking at Strike. "Your loss."

"No doubt." He watched her go, thinking that Rabbit was right. He was an idiot.

Scratching a red patch on his inner wrist—he must've gotten nailed by a spider or something—he told Jox, "Your shit's here."

"Thanks." The *winikin* skirted the counter and headed for the back, where a set of swinging doors led to the warehouse and loading dock. "Watch the register for a few minutes. I want to make sure they didn't send me broken bags again."

"Ah, yes. A smell to remember." Strike took Jox's

customary place on the bar stool behind the counter, swallowing hard against an unexpected surge of nausea.

A glance around the storefront showed a few browsers, but nobody who looked like they needed immediate attention. Which was a good thing, because all of a sudden he wasn't feeling so hot. His wrist was burning like a son of a bitch, and when he looked down he saw three right hands where there should've been one. A quick grab told him he hadn't sprouted extra limbs; he was seeing triple. He was also sweating like a pig, and the idea of sticking his head in the john so he could barf in peace was sounding real good.

Narrowing his eyes to cut the spin, he groped for the phone to buzz Jox out back, and came up with a utility knife instead. *This'll do,* he thought out of nowhere.

Moving without conscious volition, he flipped the knife open and sliced the blade across his right palm.

Blood spilled over, tracking down his wrist and across his glyph marks. Then the pain hit, first from the cut, and again when he slithered off the bar stool and landed hard on his knees. His head spun and the nausea increased, but it was more like a pressure in his throat, a burning compulsion to say . . . what?

Jesus, what the fuck's going on? he thought, but the acid burning at the back of his throat told his head what his heart already knew. It was the summer solstice, one of the four days each year that the barrier used to be at its thinnest, when a Nightkeeper's powers had been strongest.

The barrier—and his power—was coming back online after all these years.

Panic mingled with excitement as blood dripped onto the floor, pooling near his right knee. The warm smell touched his nostrils, tangy and sweet and calling to something inside him, something that ripped at his chest like fear. Like heartache.

"Pasaj," he whispered. The word was the basic command for a Nightkeeper to open a connection to the barrier, to his ancestors, and it hadn't worked since the massacre.

Gray-green mist filled his brain, and the world started to slide sideways beneath him.

"Pasaj!" he said again, louder. "Are you out there? Talk to me, damn it!"

He heard distant voices, a woman's cry of alarm. "He's bleeding! Someone help!"

Inside his head, though, there was nothing beyond the spin and the terrible, awful pressure in his throat. Then he saw something in the grayness behind his eyelids. A single slender thread of yellow in the fog. *Holy crap.* Acting on instinct, he reached out with his mind and touched the thread, grabbed onto it, and whispered the second word of the barrier spell. *"Och."* Enter.

And the world around him vanished.

Jox was counting bags of cow shit when he heard raised voices from out front, and what sounded like a woman's scream. Seconds later, Rabbit burst through the warehouse doors, his eyes wild, his hood thrown back, and one earpiece dangling. "Jox, come quick!"

Jox's heart shimmied in his chest. *Oh, hell.* "What's wrong?"

"Hurry!" The kid disappeared back through the doors and Jox bolted after him, spurred by a quick jolt of adrenaline, because anything that rattled Rabbit had to be bad.

Shit, he thought. *The pipes.* The plumbing running the length of the store had needed replacing when they bought the property five years earlier, but there was always something that needed fixing more urgently, so the pipes had waited. Maybe too long.

But when he got out to the front, he didn't see a flood, didn't hear the telltale hiss of a broken pipe. A few customers were gathered around the counter waving their hands and talking loud and excitedly, but the source of the drama wasn't immediately obvious. Pausing, Jox looked around for Strike, who no doubt already had things under control. Then he froze.

He. Didn't. See. Strike.

Brain instantly upshifting from store owner to *winikin*

mode, Jox shoved between two customers to where Rabbit was hunched behind the counter. He grabbed the teen by the sweatshirt. "Where is he?"

Rabbit's face had gone chalky. "He was here a second ago, I swear."

"He disappeared," said a thirty-something woman, voice cracking with excitement. "His hand was bleeding—there, you can see the blood. Then he said something, and—poof! Gone."

Jox stared at the blood pool and the stained utility knife lying nearby. A litany of denial rattled through his brain. *Oh, shit. Oh, no. Oh, shit, no. No. Please, no.*

"The barrier," Rabbit said, his voice climbing. "The solstice is today. He must've—"

"Zip it!" Jox shook him harder than necessary, because he needed Rabbit to stop talking, and also because the kid was right, damn it.

"Poof! Then he was gone," the woman said again, and two other customers behind her nodded, like they'd seen it, too. There were four of them, eyes bright and excited, and a fifth was edging in with his camera phone aimed at the blood pool.

"Excuse me; I need to borrow that." Jox snagged the phone and stuck it in his pocket before the guy could even yelp.

His brain raced. They needed damage control and a search party, pronto. If it'd been three decades earlier he would've had his choice of magi. As it was, he had no choice at all.

"Go get—" Jox started to say to Rabbit, then broke off. "Never mind, I'll get him." He leaned close to the teen and hissed, "Make sure nobody else comes in, and nobody gets out."

Rabbit looked startled. "How am I supposed to do that?"

"Get creative."

As Jox headed up to the apartment above the shop, he knew he was asking for trouble, giving the kid free rein. But Red-Boar was a mind-bender. He could wipe Strike's disappearing act from the customers' brains . . . and he could go deeper if Rabbit went too far.

That was assuming, of course, that the barrier was all the way active. Jox *had* to assume that, because if it wasn't and Red-Boar couldn't go into the barrier and drag Strike's ass out, then they were seriously screwed. The possibility made the *winikin*'s breath whistle in his lungs as he pounded up the stairs and skidded through the main door of the apartment. Going on instinct, he headed for the back, to a door that was almost always kept locked.

The padlock hung open.

Taking a deep breath, Jox pushed open the door and stepped through into Red-Boar's ritual chamber.

They'd had the windows drywalled over, the recessed lights removed, and the walls covered with a fake stone facade. Lit braziers hung at the four world corners, and a small *chac-mool* altar stood against the far wall. Shaped like a man sitting in a sort of zigzag shape, with his feet, ass, and elbows on the ground, and his knees and upper body raised, balancing a flat slab on his kneecaps and collarbones, with his head turned ninety degrees, the *chac-mool*, represented the sacred rain god. It served as altar and throne, and as a place for sacrifice.

Red-Boar sat cross-legged in front of the *chac-mool*, with his eyes closed and his hands lying on his knees, palms up. His right palm was slashed and bloodstained, though already partway healed. Another sign that the magic was working.

"I need you," Jox said quietly, hating to disturb him but having no choice.

Red-Boar's dusky face, with its slashing, hooked nose and wide, high cheekbones, didn't change. He didn't even twitch.

He was wearing his ceremonial robes, which were long and black, with stingray spines forming intricate glyph patterns at the cuffs and collar. The hood was thrown back, revealing his dark, close-clipped hair and the gray streaks at the temples that made him look older than his forty-five years, though his body was big and strong beneath the robes.

His right sleeve was pushed up to reveal the *chitam* glyph that tagged him as a member of the boar bloodline, along with the mind-bender's talent glyph and the mark of an elite warrior-priest. Between those marks, though, was a bare patch where he'd once worn the *jun tan* "beloved" glyph for his wife, along with two smaller *chitams* representing his twin sons, all three of whom had died during the Solstice Massacre.

"Red-Boar." Jox reached out and gripped the other man's shoulder. "We have—"

At the touch, the Nightkeeper exploded off the floor and grabbed Jox by the throat. Pain seared at the point of contact, and a terrible scream erupted in Jox's head as the Nightkeeper slammed him against the wall and held him there.

Red-Boar's eyes seared into him, gleaming with power, with hatred.

Jox flailed, trying to shout at Red-Boar, to tell him to snap out of it, but all he could manage was a panicked gurgle. His vision went gray at the edges, telescoping down to the blackness of the Nightkeeper's eyes.

Then the other man blinked. And let go.

Jox landed in a heap, gasping for breath.

Red-Boar crouched down beside him, not to aid or comfort, but to hiss, "What the *fuck* do you think you're doing, *winikin*?" In his rasping voice, the title was a slur. "You know better than to interrupt magic."

"And you should've known better than to jack in the moment you felt the barrier come back online," Jox got out between gasps. "You should've damn well checked on Strike first."

"You forget your place, *winikin*. I—"

"He's gone," Jox interrupted, and had the satisfaction of seeing the other man go pale.

"He jacked in without an escort?"

"He vanished in front of five witnesses." Jox mimicked the woman downstairs: "*Poof.*"

Red-Boar's breath hissed out as he made the connection. "Shit. Teleport."

Strike's father hadn't had an innate talent beyond the warrior's mark—only about one in three Nightkeepers did—but *his* father had been a teleport, as had a couple of other jaguars in the generation prior. So, yeah, that made sense. But it wasn't good news by any stretch. Teleporting was a tricky talent—the user had to link to a person or place first, then initiate the 'port. Jumping blind was . . . well, it wasn't good.

"Can you track him?" Jox demanded, almost afraid of the answer.

"I can damn well try," Red-Boar said, yanking open the door and heading for the stairs.

But his voice made it sound like "probably not."

CHAPTER TWO

Leah woke in pitch darkness, bound and gagged and draped over a man's shoulder. There was no moment of confusion, no gap between unconsciousness and memory. She came around sick with rage over Nick's death, and with fear at knowing she'd walked into Zipacna's trap and given him exactly what he'd wanted.

We'll see about that, she thought, fanning the anger because she knew she couldn't afford the fear. She had to be strong—for herself. For Matty and Nick. For her parents, who shouldn't have had to bury one of their children, never mind both.

Forcing herself to focus, she examined the situation, using her other senses when the darkness left her blind. Her captor's footsteps crunched on gravel, maybe coarse sand, and there was a faint rasp, as though he was trailing his hand against the irregular wall she sensed right beside them. Other footsteps grated ahead and behind, suggesting a single-file line of five, maybe six people. Vibrations echoed from a wall and ceiling very close by, and that, along with the darkness, said they were in a tunnel of some sort. But water dripped into water on the other side—an underground river with a path beside it, maybe?

The thought brought a jolt of fear, of memory, but she shoved it aside. *No freaking way,* she told herself. *Impossible.*

She wasn't in Miami anymore—she was sure of that much, though she couldn't have said why. She was also pretty sure it was nighttime, meaning that she'd been out of it all day. Long enough to travel.

Focus, she told herself. *Be a cop.* Wherever they were, it smelled old. Worse, the vibe reminded her of the grimmest crime scenes she'd ever worked, ones where the body counts had reached into the dozens and they'd had to use DNA to figure out which parts belonged in what pile. People had died down here—lots of them, though not recently.

The shuffling line—creepy in its lack of chatter—turned a corner and the air changed, becoming drier as they moved away from the underground river. Then the faintest hint of a new smell prickled Leah's sinuses, some sort of incense, and they turned another corner and firelight warmed the tunnel walls, barely detectable at first but growing stronger as they moved on.

In the yellow-orange glow, she saw strangely fluid symbols and pictures carved into the walls—men and women with flattened foreheads and exaggerated noses, fierce animals with long fangs and claws.

Her gut fisted and cold sweat prickled her skin. She wanted to tell herself it was a bunch of props, an elaborate set Zipacna had designed to put the fear of his gods into his disciples. Hell, rumor had it he'd built himself a fake temple in the swampside compound he and his fellow freaks called home. But the air was wrong, the sense of being far underground too strong.

She was pretty sure this was the real deal. He'd kidnapped her and brought her to Mexico, to a goddamn Mayan ruin.

Then the guy carrying her turned the final corner, and the firelight resolved itself to a series of burning torches set around the perimeter of a circular stone room.

In the center stood a dark-haired man, heavily muscled, barefoot and bare chested, wearing loose black pants fastened at the ankles with intricate twists of red twine. His eyes were green, one darker than the other, and he had a flying crocodile inked across his right pec.

Zipacna, she thought with a jolt of fear, of hatred.

His origins were a mystery aside from the claim of royal blood. He'd appeared in Miami eighteen months earlier, bought up a chunk of swamp, and set out to create a social movement. None of her background checks had turned up much more than the obvious: Money wasn't an issue, but sanity was, and he had some serious charisma going for him.

She tasted bile and told herself it was fury, but knew it was terror, a terror that only increased when she looked around and saw crude stone braziers hung from the wall leaking curls of reddish smoke. In between them, human skulls were carved into the stone, their mouths open in silent screams.

Zipacna pointed toward the altar. "Strap her in and scram," he said, his voice sounding jarringly normal. "Stand guard up at the tunnel mouth. Nobody gets in or out until I say otherwise. Understand?"

A howl bubbled up in Leah's throat as her captor carried her across the room, trailed by four other guys with cold, mocking expressions and winged croc tats slapped atop older ink.

She tried to block out the sights and the fear, concentrating on what seemed like her only chance for escape: the moment they'd have to undo the zip ties to get her hands and feet into the shackles. Her heart drummed in her ears as the guy carried her across the room and dumped her unceremoniously on the altar. She hit hard, landing on her tailbone with bruising force and cracking her head against the stone. Pain lanced and she cried out behind the gag, squeezing her eyes shut as she saw stars, along with a light so bright it hurt.

"Careful," Zipacna snapped. "Her blood is even more valuable than her brother's."

There it was, Leah thought on a howl of rage. Confirmation. Practically a confession. And it wouldn't do her a damn bit of good, because it was the solstice. Two more bodies were due, maybe more because he'd brought them south, to the home of his ancient gods.

Clammy hands pawed at her, and a knife touched her belly as her shirt and bra were cut away. She squeezed her eyes shut, partly to preserve the illusion that she was stunned, and partly because, deep down inside, she didn't want to watch.

Then, finally, she felt hands on her ankles, felt a tug and release as the zip tie was cut away. Adrenaline revved her senses. Terror. Rage. *Come on, you bastards,* she urged silently. *Do the wrists, too. Can't you see I'm not going anywhere?*

Instead, they shoved her farther onto the altar and pulled her legs apart. The moment she felt the touch of a shackle, Leah erupted. Screaming behind the gag, she opened her eyes, twisted, and dove for the floor.

Surprise gave her a momentary advantage and she actually managed to break free. She hit hard, scrambled to her feet, and slammed her bound hands into the nearest guy's gut. When he stumbled back, she bolted for the door, heart hammering.

"Damn it, get her!" Zipacna shouted, and footsteps closed in behind her, moving fast.

Sobbing, Leah flung herself through the arched doorway as Zipacna yelled something in a language she didn't recognize, and the stones trembled beneath her feet. Fighting to keep her balance, she skidded around a corner and slammed into someone coming the other way.

For a split second, she thought she was saved. Then she saw the glint of filed-sharp teeth, and knew she was dead, after all.

"Sorry, baby," Itchy said. "Wrong way." He punched her in the temple and caught her when she fell. Over the roaring in her ears, she heard him shout, "Chill. I've got her."

Moments later, she was back in the chamber. Seconds after that, the shackles clicked into place around her ankles, then her wrists. They took the gag off, but she didn't bother screaming, because she knew damn well there was nobody around to hear, nobody to care.

Backup—and home—was far away.

Tears stung her eyelids and spilled free, tracking down her cheeks, and she whimpered when Zipacna leaned over her. She expected him to gloat, to taunt her.

Instead he touched her right wrist, where her sleeve was pulled down over a faded scar. "The gods marked you as their own long ago. Your brother's blood began the process. Yours will complete it." He lifted a black stone blade, turned it so it glinted in the torchlight. "I'm offering you power. Immortality. A place in what the world will become beyond the zero date."

She was trapped in his mismatched eyes, frozen in their magnetic pull, unable to look away. A warm pressure kindled at the base of her skull, urging her to accept whatever it was he was offering. *Yes,* a voice seemed to whisper. *Join us. Help us.*

He leaned closer, so her entire world became his lopsided pupils, the crackle of the torches, and the heavy smell of incense. "Just relax," he said, voice dropping to a hypnotic whisper. "Don't fight it."

"Fight what?" she managed to ask, nearly beyond herself with the fear and the spinning pressure inside her head, the drumming urges that seemed to come from outside her, telling her to do things she didn't want to do, like give in to him, join with him. *He's the enemy!* she screamed inside her own skull. *He killed Nick. He killed Matty.* How could she know that, yet feel the power, the fascination?

"You can be more than you are, more than you ever thought you'd be. But you have to accept the power. Will you take a master inside you?" Without waiting for her answer, he lifted the knife and plunged it into her arm.

Leah shrieked when pain flared white-hot. She thrashed, trying to twist away as he stabbed her a second time, then a third, creating three parallel gashes on her right arm between her shoulder and elbow. Blood spilled from her wounds and onto the stone altar as she kept screaming, unable to stop even though she knew it wouldn't do a damn bit of good.

The blood ran down a carved track, pulled along by the slight tilt of the altar until it pooled in a shallow stone depression between her legs.

Placing the bloody knife beside her head, he pulled a length of parchment from his loose black pants, and used the folded square to mop up the blood. The air thickened around them, going purple-black with incense and smoke. The humming whine grew louder, not just in her head now, but filling the chamber and sounding like a distant swarm of bees.

"Stop," she cried, sobbing now with the fear and the pain, and an increasing pressure that built inside her skull. "Stop it!"

He shouted strange words, and the sound echoed in the chamber until it seemed to be coming from the skeletal mouths that screamed from high up in the walls. Then he spun and flung the blood-soaked parchment into one of the torches. The moment the paper caught fire, a detonation rocked the room, blasting outward from the flames.

The shock wave battered Leah and drove Zipacna back several paces as the purple smoke went black, and the air in the chamber snapped so cold that Leah's breath fogged on her next shallow exhalation.

Expression beatific, Zipacna stared into the smoke, which thickened and twined, reaching tendrils toward him as he threw back his head and shouted, "I invite the masters into the woman. Into me. *Och Banol Kax!*"

Leah arched her back, straining away from the altar, and screamed, *"No!"*

Without warning, the entire chamber shuddered and dropped downward like some sort of ancient elevator gone wrong, falling a few feet and then stopping with a jolt and a loud bang. Moments later, a rushing noise gathered, then grew louder. Then water blasted inward, geysering from the screaming skull mouths and crashing down to the chamber floor.

Leah moaned, beyond herself from terror and the splitting pressure inside her brain. Zipacna leaned over her, running the flat of the knife softly across her belly before he lifted the blade and slashed it across his tongue. Blood welled up and spilled over as he shouted the same words as before. *"Och Banol Kax!"*

The torches flared higher around the edge of the chamber, above the rising water. A tentacle of black smoke reached for Leah, caressing her cheek, then dropping down to stroke her ribs and belly, blatantly sexual.

Please let this all be a bad dream, she prayed, and felt a mocking chuckle rise up from deep inside her.

Zipacna grinned a gory, horrible smile. Blood dripped from his mouth and spattered on her stomach. Around them, the water pooled and collected, climbing to his ankles, then his knees. He pressed the knife just beneath her breastbone and spoke a string of words in that strange language, only now it somehow translated itself inside her head in a mix of purple and bright gold. *As the masters have commanded, I have opened the intersection. With blood I offer myself, offer the gods' keeper, to become* makol, *to become a tool for your—*

Leah could barely hear him anymore over the howling scream that filled her head, where darkness and light spun together, fighting for dominance.

She heard words in that strange language, though she didn't know what they meant, knew only that they were there, and the warm golden light urged her to use them. Filling her lungs, she arched her head back and screamed as loud as she could, *"Och jun tan!"*

At the words, a tornado blasted through the room.

One second Strike was hanging motionless, suspended in the barrier—a murky gray-green mist that had no beginning or end, no point of reference, no way out except a magic that he didn't know how to manage. Then words echoed—a spell he didn't recognize, spoken in a woman's voice that sent shivers down the back of his neck.

And the bottom dropped out of his world. A hole appeared in the fog and he plummeted through, straight back to earth. He knew it was earth the same way he knew it was hours later, nearly the solstice, because the magic of it, the power of it hummed in his bones. Then the world came clear around him, and he realized three things at once.

One, he was in the sacred chamber beneath Chichén Itzá, where his parents and the others had died.

Two, the blonde—the one he'd dreamed of—was there.

And three, she was in deep shit.

A guy appeared in midair at the edge of the circular chamber and hovered for a split second. He was a big man, wearing a tight black T-shirt over whipcord muscles, with ragged cutoffs below. His high cheekbones and piercing eyes were those of a warrior, and Leah knew them instantly from her dreams, just as she recognized his dark ponytail and jawline beard, and the ink on his inner forearm, two marks next to each other with a third above. In that instant of hovering, he looked at her, recognized her, and seemed more surprised to see her than he did to have materialized inside a Mayan temple.

Then gravity took over and he fell with a shout, slamming into Zipacna. The men went down together in the deepening water, which churned with their struggles. Leah screamed as they shot to their feet, streaming water and grappling for the knife.

She strained toward the newcomer, screaming, *"Help me!"*

Zipacna twisted away and slashed a wide arc with the stone knife, forcing his opponent to dodge. The stranger moved like a fighter, but had no weapons. Zipacna slashed again, then spun and crossed to the altar.

Blood poured from his mouth, painting his front a gory red, and purple-black smoke twined around him like an unholy halo. Water licked over the top of the altar as he lifted the knife and said, "The heart of the gods' keeper gives me life beyond the barrier, the power to become power itself."

The stranger lunged across the chamber, shouting, *"Torotobik!"*

The cuffs at Leah's wrists and ankles exploded, the shrapnel driving Zipacna back a pace without touching her skin.

She wasted half a second gaping before she flung herself off the altar, straight at Zipacna. She lacked leverage, but had the advantage of surprise as she got a fistful of his hair in one hand and drove her opposite elbow into his gut. The knife went flying and the stranger dove for it.

Zipacna bellowed and went down, nearly submerging them both in the cold water, which had started glowing a strange greenish white.

A rising howl echoed in the chamber, nearly drowning

out the stranger's voice when he shouted, "Get away from her, you bastard!"

Zipacna thrashed and twisted, reversing their positions so she was the one neck-deep in the water. His eyes took on a strange greenish glow as he wrapped his fingers around her throat and squeezed.

His voice was gravelly and barely human when he said, "You're too late, Nightkeeper. I am *ajaw-makol*, and she belongs to me." He bore down, choking her. Leah's vision went dim, then dark, and a rushing noise filled her head.

Over it all, she heard the stranger say, "Wrong. She's *mine*." He hurled himself forward and plunged the stone knife into Zipacna's back.

Zipacna jerked and arched, screaming in pain. He staggered away from her, convulsing as he grabbed for a deep stab wound beneath his shoulder blade. Slamming against the wall near the doorway, he listed to one side, drawing a red smear on the wall.

But incredibly, horribly, he grinned, his mismatched eyes glowing pure emerald green. "Too late, Nightkeeper."

He slapped his palm against the wall, spoke a low word, and lurched through the doorway. The stranger roared and lunged for the door, but a stone panel slid across the opening, sealing them in.

"Oh, God!" Heart pounding, Leah splashed toward the door. She was halfway there when the chamber dropped a few more feet and the incoming water doubled, blasting from the screaming skulls with pounding force. Moments later, the torches snuffed out, leaving the room lit by the unearthly radiance of the water, which quickly climbed to her throat, then buoyed her off the floor until she was treading to keep her head above the surface.

Heart racing, she turned to the stranger. Remembering the grenade thing he'd done with her cuffs, she said, "Can you open the door?"

He shook his head. "No, but I can try something else. Come here." Swimming now, he gathered her close and fitted her body against his as the cool, white-green water edged up past her ears and touched her cheeks. "Hang on."

Leah grabbed onto him as her head bumped the ceiling. "Hurry!"

His arms tightened around her and she felt that click of connection, the twist in her belly that said, *There you are*. He held her close, said a few words in that strange language. . . .

And nothing happened.

Come on. Heart hammering, Strike tried again, bearing down and thinking of the garden center. *For fuck's sake, teleport!*

He was wearing a new mark on his forearm, the talent glyph of a teleporter. But no matter how hard he concentrated on the garden center, giving himself a destination this time, the yellow travel thread refused to appear in his mind.

Focus, he thought as the water closed over them. *Clear your head*.

Still nothing.

The blonde bowed against him, convulsing. *Gods,* he prayed, *help me get us out of here. Please*.

But there was no answer as her heartbeat slowed and his own lungful of air grew stale.

Pulse racing, he tried again, this time picturing the studio apartment the Nightkeepers—or rather Jox—maintained near Chichén Itzá as a bolt-hole. Maybe the garden center was too far away. Maybe he could manage something local.

Or not.

Darkness closed in. Despair. How was it possible that he'd survived the massacre only to die like this, in the moment it seemed like the world might actually need him after all?

Gods, he thought, though he'd never been a big one for praying, *help me out here*.

And, incredibly, there was an answer. Golden light flared, the power of the sky and sun, the color of the gods. Strike's heart stuttered in his chest as he heard a rattle of scales, a whisper of feathers. And what could only be the voice of a god, pure and clarion.

Accept my power, child of man, the entity said, and it wasn't talking to him. It was talking to the woman he held cradled against his chest. The one he'd dreamed of.

The *makol* had called her the gods' keeper. Yet the writs said that only a female Nightkeeper could become such a thing, and she wore no Nightkeeper's mark.

Accept the magic and the light, the voice urged again, and there was a tinge of desperation in the words.

The Godkeepers were a myth, Strike thought, a dream. Prophesied to arise at the end of the age, destined to fight the *Banol Kax* for possession of the earth during the Great Conjunction with their warrior mates at their sides, they were part of the stories he'd been tempted to stop believing as he'd grown to adulthood and the magic had started to seem like a childhood fantasy. But he now had proof-positive the magic was real. What if the Godkeepers were, too? What if the dreams had been telling him that this woman—this human woman—was somehow destined to become his mate, his Godkeeper?

Come on, Blondie, he urged inwardly. *Come on.* Not because he was in any position to take a mate, but because the gods came first, and if the cosmic shit was really about to hit the fan, the Nightkeepers—or what was left of them—were going to need all the help they could get.

She writhed in his arms, fighting the invading presence even as her heart faltered. Slowed. Stopped.

Come on! Strike shouted inwardly as his oxygen ran out and the universe coalesced to a pinprick of darkness. Terror howled through him, fear for himself, for the woman.

The god's golden voice came again, aimed at him this time, the mental touch growing fainter by the second as the solstice passed. *Save her, Nightkeeper.*

"I don't know how," Strike said aloud, the words emerging as precious bubbles carrying the very last of his air. But then he realized he did. For a god to pass through the portal and link with a Nightkeeper female, she had to be near death. That was the only way to touch the other side of the barrier, except for . . .

Sex.

He acted fast, cursing himself for having not thought of it sooner, for being hindered by modern ethics in a situation ruled by ancient law. He palmed the *ajaw-makol*'s knife from his belt, drew the blade in a quick slash across his tongue, and then opened her mouth to draw a matching scratch on hers.

Then, as he had done in his dreams, he held her close and kissed her.

A loud crack split the room, and the water rushed out, dumping them both on the floor, but he kept kissing her, willing her to respond. To live. To become what she seemed destined to be.

But she didn't move, didn't breathe.

She was dying.

In the space between the purple-black funnel that'd sucked her down and a vortex of golden light that called her onward, Leah found a world of gray-green mist that smelled of her brother's cologne. The familiar scent beckoned her inside and cocooned her in warmth. "Matty?" she called, suddenly certain he was nearby, though that didn't make any sense unless she was dead.

So what if she was? she thought on a sad, soft burst of acceptance. Would it really be so bad to turn her back on that life and—

Blondie.

She frowned at the word whispered on the mist. "Don't call me that." It had been one of her brother's favorite torments, one he'd never outgrown. That and the inevitable blonde jokes. "Where are you?"

Come on, baby. Don't let me down.

The whisper didn't sound like her brother now. It sounded more like . . . She thought for a moment, but couldn't place a name, didn't quite have the face, remembered only a pair of piercing cobalt eyes above a warrior's cheekbones. The image came with a wash of heat and the phantom press of lips.

That's it, Blondie. Breathe.

She felt the lips again, followed by the touch of a tongue, and other sensations began to intrude. The good, solid weight of a man's body pressed against hers, kindling heat where there'd been nothing. She sucked in a breath when the sensation spiraled higher, hotter, catching her unawares and vulnerable.

"I've got you. You're okay." She could hear him for real now, and she could feel a cool, wet stone surface pressing against her hips and spine. She opened her eyes and found herself still in the circular chamber with the carved walls and screaming skulls. The torches were lit again, not burning purple now, but rather a warm amber that softened the sharp planes of the warrior's face. He was lying full-length atop her, pressing against her through their sodden clothing. He stared at her as though he knew her already, and said· something in that same strange language Zipacna had used.

It was probably Mayan, given the circumstances, which should've freaked her shit right out. But somehow the language and the strange goings-on didn't seem nearly as important as the weight of his body and the hard press of his erection at the juncture of her thighs. Wild heat flared, running through her veins like power. Like fury. Like sex.

Sex. The need for it thrilled within her. She was incomplete, unfinished. Suddenly, joining with this man, this stranger, was the most important thing in the world.

What are you doing? a small voice asked. *This isn't you. This is crazy!*

Perhaps, but she didn't care about crazy. A beehive buzz hummed in her bones, gaining in pitch as though something was coming, something was waiting for them at the end of ecstasy. She wanted the craziness, craved the madness.

And though it should have seemed entirely wrong, it was perfectly right when she reached up and touched her lips to his.

She was connected to the gods, yet not. Strike could sense the sky in her, could taste the golden power in her kiss and on her breath, and he could feel it when she slid her hands up his chest, into his hair, and locked on. She was human, yet she was somehow magic as well. The ritual her attacker had used to transform himself from a human into an emissary of the *Banol Kax* had started the process. Now it was up to him to finish it.

They kissed fiercely, passionately. Power spiked amber and crimson, blurring the line between dream and reality. Part of him knew she was driven by something she didn't have the tools to understand, and that brought a pinch of guilt.

Then the torches flared higher, burning around him, within him, calling to him, telling him it was now or never, and never wasn't an option if he wanted to honor the sacrifice of those who had gone before him. Knowing it'd been too late the moment he'd dreamed of her, he whispered, "Gods."

And returned her kiss.

She sensed the change in him, felt power in the moment his hands fisted in her shirt and he kissed her hard and hot and fast, and in the buzz of flame and excitement that followed. Connection arced, binding them together at a level deeper than she'd expected, deeper than she'd wanted. That small, panicked voice inside demanded that she slow down, think about what she was doing, *think!*

Instead, she leaned into him, opened herself up to him, and flowed into the moment as one kiss became many, deep and searching and almost painfully raw. He swept aside her ruined shirt and bra and peeled her out of her damp pants, leaving her clad in only her panties.

His nostrils flared on a sharply indrawn breath. He eased back, and she thought his hands trembled slightly when they went to the hem of his black T-shirt.

"Wait," she said. "Let me." But instead of undressing him, she slipped off her panties, leaving her naked while he remained fully clothed.

Excitement spike, spearing outward from her center until she felt as though she were lit from within, pulsing gold and crimson with femininity.

"Blondie," he said, voice rasping on the word. "Gods." Then he broke, moving fast as he swept her up in his arms and carried her to the stone altar.

In some dim recess of her mind, she thought the candles flared and the smoke went from gold to red, but those details were lost in a tidal rush of sensation and need. *Hurry,* a voice chanted inside her as he fastened his lips on her throat and cupped a hand around her breast, bringing a lightning bolt of heat from her core.

She tugged at his shirt, rushing now, needing to touch him as he was touching her. He rolled her nipple between his finger and thumb, wringing a cry from her, one that echoed strangely inside her skull, as though two voices had shouted, maybe more. She got his shirt off and gloried at the play of his hard muscles beneath the taut masculine skin. Touching her lips to the hollow beside his collarbone, then lower, she went to work on his cutoffs, where the material strained tight across a massive erection. He groaned when her fingertips brushed against his hard flesh, and he thrust against her hand, silently urging her onward.

She freed the buttons and zipper, and then his hands were there, helping strip off his shorts and sandals, until he was as naked as she and they were pressed together, hard against soft, need against need.

The air thickened around them, humming with waiting, with wanting. Then she was finished with waiting. She arched up and kissed him, claiming his mouth with hers and leaving no doubt as to her demand. She tasted his urgency and felt it in the bone-breakingly taut lines of his body, but his hands were gentle when he touched her, when he brushed the soft skin inside her knees, then higher, drawing his fingertips across the acutely sensitized skin of her inner thighs.

She whimpered when he feathered an intimate brush across her center, then nearly screamed when he repeated the touch more firmly, stroking a long, clean line that ended with his thumb atop the nub of her pleasure. "Come for me," he whispered against her mouth. "Open up to me."

"Let me touch you." She reached for his straining

member, but he angled his body away even as he
kissed her.

He murmured something against her mouth, something that sounded like, "We don't have time." But that
didn't make any sense, she thought. Time for what?
Then she couldn't think at all, because he kissed her
long and deep, and the heat rose up to sweep her away.

The hum in Leah's brain intensified, and her body
shook as a strange fracture split her in two. One fragment of her was aware of the press of the stone altar
against her buttocks and upper thighs, conscious of the
way her legs wrapped around him, pulling him into her,
binding them together. A thought tried to break through—
a warning—but the spinning in her head and the growing
heat beat it back as her body bowed into his touch,
welcoming him, demanding him.

"Come for me," he said again, as though her pleasure
were the most important thing in his universe. He ro-
tated his thumb and kept that pressure on her nub as
he traced two fingers around her opening and then
dipped inside in a smooth, liquid glide.

Suddenly, all the restless, shifting energy Leah had
been carrying since the dreams first began collected itself
at the point of their joining, fisting around his fingers
and vibrating deep inside her at a raw, primal level.
"Please!" she cried, not sure what she was asking for.

But he seemed to understand, because he withdrew
his fingers and moved between her legs, so the blunt tip
of his hard shaft rested at her opening. At the first
nudge, she opened her eyes and found his face just
above hers, his eyes staring into hers. Their cobalt blue
depths were dark and intense, and she felt a momentary
flicker of fear. But then he was sliding home in one long
thrust that had her insides knotting and her eyes closing
on a rush of pleasure. She gasped and gripped his shoulders, anchoring herself amidst a storm of sensation. Inhaling deeply, she filled her lungs with the scent of their
lovemaking, part incense, part musk. Then she parted
her legs wider, accommodating his mass, inviting him
deeper, and deeper still.

He thrust once and again, dropping his forehead to

hers, his breathing synchronized with hers, his very heartbeat seeming to come in time with hers. He thrust a third time as her body coiled tight around his hard flesh and the humming sound transformed to something sweeter, almost a melody.

Leah cried out as the first exhilarating rush of orgasm gripped her, stopping the breath in her lungs. He thrust deeply in a hard, ever-increasing tempo that matched the hammering in her ears, in her chest. Her consciousness expanded outward until she could feel the press of his mind on hers as surely as she could feel the surge of their bodies. Then everything contracted inward, an exquisite moment spent poised on the brink of explosion.

In that moment, in that breathless pause, she felt something shift, tearing deep within her, ripping away from her even as she convulsed in a hard fist of heat that spun out endlessly. His deep, masculine voice echoed her cries, and he thrust hard within her and cut loose, a groan wringing from deep within his chest—her name, perhaps, or a curse. A prayer.

The pressure in her brain disappeared, leaving only pleasure in its wake. Joy and exultation spun within her, spiraling outward in a rush that made her want to run and dance and leap for joy. But when she opened her eyes and smiled up at him, she saw none of that same joy in his face.

Instead, she saw despair.

CHAPTER THREE

Reality returned with a serious buzz kill. Goose bumps broke out everywhere Leah had skin—not just because he had that *oh, shit, big mistake* look on his face, but because that expression doused enough of the afterglow to ass-smack her with what she'd done.

Heart jolting, she scrambled out from underneath the guy—a total *stranger*, for crap's sake—and backed away in a defensive crouch. "What. The. *Fuck*. Just. Happened?"

"Nothing," he rasped. "Everything. I don't know. Shit." He sat up and dragged both hands through his dark hair, which had come free from its ponytail.

With his hair hanging to his shoulders and the close-clipped beard along his jawline, his body stunningly naked and ripped with a fighter's muscles, and firelight flickering on the ancient carvings behind him, the whole scenario could've come from another age, when all this would've made way more sense.

Torchlight played over the long, lean lines of him as he stood and snagged his clothes. Naked, he was a statue. A fantasy. Even though they'd just had at each other and she didn't even know his name, greedy need knotted Leah's belly.

Then he pulled on his cutoffs and T-shirt and toed on his sandals, and he became a man again. One she was going to have to deal with, because, um, hello, they were in Mexico. And something very strange had just happened. Several somethings, in fact, starting with a botched human sacrifice and ending with an orgasm.

Brain churning, she turned away from him and got dressed while she tried to put her thoughts in order. Her pants were soaked but otherwise okay, while her shirt and bra were write-offs. Knotting the material as best she could at her midriff, she turned to face him and stuck out a hand. "Detective Leah Ann Daniels, Miami-Dade Narcotics."

Might as well start with the introductions. Then it'd be time for *What the Christ is going on?*

His wide, mobile lips twisted into something that wasn't quite a smile. "Striking-Jaguar, last male of the Nightkeepers' royal house. You can call me Strike."

And suddenly it made way too much sense. Anger and self-disgust fisted in her gut. "Oh, shit. You're one of *them*." She looked around. "Bastard. Where are the cameras?"

He looked surprised. "Cameras?"

She didn't bother answering, instead making a wide circuit of the room, looking at the braziers, the carved skulls, trying to be a cop when the woman in her wanted to scream and start throwing things. "Of course. No sense in him staging something like this and not filming it for blackmail to get me off his back. Or, hell, he could just YouTube it and crash my career. I can see the title now: 'MDPD detective gets down and dirty during Survivor2012 ritual.' What are you, one of his disciples? Nah," she answered her own question. "None of them look as good as you. So, what . . . out-of-work actor?" Her voice climbed an octave. "Oh, bloody hell. Do *not* tell me I just had unprotected sex with a porn star."

Incipient hysteria heated her blood just as the sex had done minutes before, though with far less pleasure. Her brother's friend Vince, the only one left who believed as she did that Zipacna was behind the serial killings, had warned her the 2012ers would go to any length to protect themselves. Of course they'd set her up. It made rational sense.

More, at least, than any of the other explanations she could come up with.

"Jesus, that's a leap." He held up both hands in a *stop the presses* gesture. "Okay, let's hang on here. Chill. Take a breath. I'm not anyone's disciple, or an actor. I'm definitely not a porn star, and I'm not sure whether to be complimented or insulted by that one."

"Then what are you? And make it good." She looked around again, and panic fluttered, because if this wasn't a setup and there weren't any cameras, then there was a very real possibility she was losing her mind, because so much of what she remembered happening couldn't possibly be real: the purple-black smoke touching her; the stranger—Strike? What kind of a name was that?—appearing in midair; the way he'd busted her cuffs with a word . . . and the voice in her head.

If that wasn't crazy, she didn't know what was.

"I told you," he repeated as though it were all very logical. "I'm a Nightkeeper."

"Which means what, exactly?" *And does it mean I'm not nuts?*

He hesitated, then said, "I'm one of the guys in charge of stopping things like this from happening." His gesture encompassed the chamber, the altar, all of it. "The man—the creature—who had you . . ."

"Zipacna." Even saying the name filled her with hatred, more now than ever because of what he'd done to Nick, what he'd tried to do to her. "He's mine."

"No, he's not." There was no give in the words. "Leave him to us, Detective. He's way out of your jurisdiction."

"He's a murderer."

"He's a *makol*."

Zipacna had used the word, too, during one of his chants. "What does that mean?"

"Roughly, a disciple of the underworld who's offered himself for partial demonic possession in exchange for magic and a role in the coming war leading up to the 2012 end date," he said. "Zipacna, in particular, is now the *ajaw-makol*, the top predator, the head dude. The ritual he just used you in, that means he takes his power directly from the rulers of the underworld, the *Banol Kax*. Over the next three months, he'll make other *makol* from evil-minded humans—the more willing they are to undergo demonic possession, the more of their own human traits and intelligence they'll retain. You can tell them by the glowing green eyes, and they're a bitch to kill." He paused, grimaced. "Or so the stories go. There hasn't been a *makol* on earth in more than a thousand years."

Leah's head spun. She should be so out of there. This was nuts. Insane. Completely unbelievable. But she was a cop, and cops followed the evidence. Right now, the evidence—if she could believe her own senses, anyway—was telling her there was something seriously whacked going on. She'd also done enough reading on the semireligious, semihistorical, semiscientific basis of the Survivor2012 doctrine to know that it was, if not believable, then at least internally consistent.

That didn't mean it was real, though. Hell, logic—and what she knew about how the world worked—said it wasn't real. But if it wasn't real, how did she explain what'd just happened to her?

Her options seemed to be limited to: A) magic existed, and she'd gotten caught up in something way outside her comfort zone; or B) magic didn't exist, and she'd been kidnapped, nearly drowned, and then boffed a total stranger.

"So the thing you did with the cuffs," she said, trying to feel her way in a world that was shifting beneath her feet, "does that mean you've got demonic powers, too?"

He shook his head. "The Nightkeepers are the good guys. We've got the gods on our side." He paused. "Look, the short version is that I'm one of the last three surviving members of an ancient group of magi sworn to protect the earth from the 2012 apocalypse. Several hundred of us—including my parents—died in the early eighties enacting a spell designed to permanently seal the gateway to the underworld, Xibalba. Now it's looking like someone, probably this Zipacna—not a very cre-

ative name, by the way—managed to reactivate the
gateway, probably through some large-scale blood sacrifices."

Leah jammed her fingertips into her temples when her
spinning head threatened to float off her shoulders.
"Which leaves it up to you to save the world."

"Right," he said again, and looked at her. "You're
not buying it."

"Unfortunately, I think you are." She squeezed her
eyes shut, trying to slow the spins, trying not to freak
right the hell out and start screaming. "And here I was
last night thinking you were a fantasy, and how that was
better than your being a doomsday nut."

"Last night?"

She realized her mistake too late, and backpedaled.
"I meant just now."

"No, you didn't. Which means you dreamed about
me."

Everything inside her went still. "Why do you say
that?"

Heat kindled in his dark blue eyes. "Because I sure
as hell dreamed of you. Which means this isn't a 'wrong
place, wrong time' thing, or an accident. We were meant
to meet. We were meant to be together like we were just
now." He held out a hand. "Give me your right wrist."

Resisting the urge to stick her hands behind her back,
she did as he asked. "No ink."

"What happened here?" His thumb lightly brushed
over a lighter, roughly circular patch on her forearm.

"Old scar." She withdrew her arm. "No biggie. Don't
even remember how I got it." Feeling trapped, she looked
around the room, focusing on the doorway, which was still
tightly shut. "Please tell me you know how to get us out
of here."

He raised one dark eyebrow, but said only, "Will you
do something for me first?"

Keeping her distance, she said, "Depends."

"It's nothing bad. Trust me." He bent and scooped
the black stone knife from the floor. Offered it to her.
"Take this."

She held up both hands. "I'm so not cutting you." And none of this was real. It was all a dream. It had to be.

He flipped the knife one-handed, so he was holding on to the blade, then closed his fingers over the sharp edge, cutting himself.

"Don't!" She lurched forward, only to stop dead when he flipped the knife again and offered it to her haft-first, seeming unconcerned by the blood oozing from between his fingers.

"Your turn."

The walls of unreality closed in on her, and her laugh came out tinged with hysteria. "I'm not cutting myself. No freaking way. Zipacna already . . ." Her words died as she glanced down at her upper arm and saw slices in the fabric of her soggy shirt, but none in the skin beneath. "What the . . . ?" She pawed at the shirt, pulling it down over her shoulder to see the spot where she'd been badly cut no more than an hour ago.

Instead of gashes there were three parallel scars, thin with age.

The blood drained from her head and her gut clenched with fear and denial. Her voice went thin. "There's no such thing as magic."

"Then this won't work." He held out the knife. "Just deep enough to draw blood."

She stared at the knife, hearing Zipacna's voice in her head. *Accept the power; take a master inside you.* But this guy wasn't Zipacna. He claimed he was going to track the bastard down. The enemy of her enemy was her friend, right?

Ignoring the little voice inside her that said, *Not necessarily*, compelled by an urge she didn't recognize, couldn't name, she took the knife and dragged the tip across her palm. It didn't hurt as much as she'd expected, but the chamber took a long, lazy spin around her as blood welled up, the droplets dark red against her skin. "What now?"

"Repeat after me." He slowly recited a string of words, pausing after each one and waiting while she parsed them out syllable by syllable. As she did, the air seemed to thicken around her, and the room spins upped their revs.

When he fell silent, she looked at him. "That's it?"

He shook his head. "Now say, '*Pasaj och.*'"

She took a deep breath, closed her eyes, and steeled herself. *"Pasaj och!"*

Nothing happened.

She waited. Still nothing.

Letting out a long, shuddering breath, she opened her eyes. The room had stopped spinning, and the wary hope that'd briefly gathered on Strike's face had fallen away to a bleakness so terrible she almost wished she'd felt something. But she shook her head. "Sorry . . . does that mean I'm right and there's no such thing as magic?"

"No," he said softly, and crossed to take the knife from her. "It means I failed." He took her hand and pressed their bleeding palms together, bringing a spark of connection and a hint of sadness. "It means this isn't your fight."

"Bull," she said quickly, though the word came out slightly slurred as a gray curtain descended over her. "Zipacna is mine. He killed Matty and Nick. He—"

"Hush," Strike whispered. "Sleep." He said a few more words in that strange language and gray mist surrounded her, cushioned her.

She felt herself falling, felt strong arms catch her.

Then nothing.

"Here." Rabbit shoved a can of Coke across the kitchen table in Jox's direction.

The *winikin* took the can and stared at it, his wits dulled with fatigue and grief, with failure. Strike had been gone for hours. The solstice had passed, and although the barrier remained active, Red-Boar hadn't been able to find him.

Here one second, then poof. Gone while his *winikin* counted pallets of cow shit and bitched about broken bags.

"Drink," Rabbit urged. "You know—sugar? Caffeine? The old man isn't the only one who needs to recharge."

Magic consumed enormous amounts of energy, so while Red-Boar had searched, Jox had done what a *winikin* ought, forcing the mage to eat and drink, mostly foods that were heavy on fat, sugar, and protein. Even with that, the Nightkeeper's strength had given out eventually. He'd staggered off to bed an hour earlier, muttering something about looking in their few remaining spellbooks when he got up.

He hadn't bothered stating the obvious; that they might already be too late. Strike had teleported with no training, no guidance. For all they knew, he'd materialized inside a mountain.

"I could help, you know," Rabbit said out of nowhere.

Jox looked across the table to find the kid fiddling with his own soda can, practically vibrating with suppressed excitement. *Oh, hell.* This was so not what he needed right now. "Listen, Rabbit," Jox said, wishing one of the others could've handled the convo. "You know there are . . . circumstances that're going to make it difficult to induct you into the magic. It could be dangerous. Probably will be."

Rabbit scowled. "I'm a half-blood. Trust me, I got that. But it doesn't mean I can't do magic, just that it might be different magic. And it's not like you've got a bunch of options. What have you got to lose?"

"It's not as easy as that," Jox said, but held up a hand to stem the coming protest. "But I'll talk to your father. That's all I can promise."

Slumping in his chair, the teen shrugged and pretended to be absorbed by reading the side of his Coke can. "Whatever." His tone made it clear he didn't expect squat from Red-Boar, and frankly Jox couldn't blame him.

"Look, Rabbit. I'll—"

The house phone rang, interrupting. Jox stared at the cordless handset as it rang again, and fear gathered in the pit of his stomach. It could be Strike, he thought. Or it could be someone calling to say they'd found Strike. Or—

Nope. It was one or the other. And until he answered,

the scale was evenly balanced between the two, between hope and despair.

It rang again, and Rabbit said, "You want me to get it?"

"No." Jox reached for the phone with shaking hands and hit the speakerphone button on the second try. "Hello?"

"I'm okay." It was Strike's voice, tired-sounding and on a crappy connection, but it was his voice. He was alive, and somewhere on the earth. He wasn't stuck in the barrier, and he hadn't become an insta-fossil.

Jox exhaled on a rush of relief so intense it would've floored him if he hadn't already been sitting down. "Thank the gods." He went dizzy, and pinched the bridge of his nose when his eyes prickled. "Gods damn it, you had us scared."

"Sorry. I called as soon as I got somewhere with a signal."

Jox waved for Rabbit to go get his father, but he needn't have bothered. Red-Boar came stumbling in, bleary eyed. "Where is he?"

"I'm in the apartment down by Chichén Itzá," Strike answered. "It's a long story." He rapped out a quick report about a murderer who'd gone through the *makol* ritual, and the woman he'd planned to sacrifice.

The words sort of blurred together, though, as Jox dropped his head into his hands. *Thank you, gods. Thank you for keeping him safe when his fuckup winikin was asleep at the switch. I'll never ask you for anything ever again. I promise.*

The vow lasted approximately thirty seconds or so, until Strike said something about a vision.

Jox whipped his head up. "Please gods, you did *not* just say what I think you said."

"I used a sleep spell on her," Strike said, ignoring the *winikin*. "She'll be okay until you guys get down here, right?"

"Who cares?" Red-Boar said bluntly. "She's collateral damage. We need to find the *ajaw-makol* before it starts multiplying. One of those green-eyed bastards is bad enough. We sure as hell don't want an army of them."

"We'll find the *ajaw-makol* and take care of him," Strike said, voice going hard. "But Leah is *not* collateral damage."

"You've had a hell of a day," Jox said quickly, before the two exhausted magi could get into it. "Put some protein into your system, and shut it down for a few hours. We can figure out the rest when we get there."

"Don't handle me, Jox," Strike snapped. "I've been having the dreams for weeks. She had them, too. We recognized each other, for crap's sake. And the *ajaw-makol* called her a keeper of the gods."

Shit. Jox and Red-Boar exchanged a look, while Rabbit grinned at the prospect of a fight.

"Forget the dreams." Jox tried not to hear the words echo decades into the past. "Forget the woman. She's not your priority."

"How can you be so sure?" Strike's voice roughened. "I heard it, Jox. I heard the god begging her to let it inside. I tried to help, tried to make the connection, but—" He broke off with a ragged sigh. "I wasn't fast enough, not strong enough. The solstice passed and the voice . . . left. But it was real. She's supposed to be a Godkeeper."

Right. Like that made sense. Mated Nightkeeper-Godkeeper pairs were supposed to be at the apex of the power scale, second only to the Triad, the three legendary magi who could channel all the knowledge and powers of their ancestors. No way the gods had chosen a human to be a Godkeeper.

Then again, it wasn't like they'd had their choice of Nightkeeper females.

Jox pinched the bridge of his nose, trying to stave off the monster headache he could feel brewing. "You need to eat something," he said, feeling for the boy—the man—he'd raised, who was both his son and his boss. Like his father before him, Strike was always reaching for more, never exactly happy with what was in front of him. And far too ready to bend the rules to fit his theories. "Keep the sleep spell going on the woman and get some rest. We'll be there by dawn."

"I'm not going to let this drop."

"Tell me something I don't know. See you soon." Jox punched off the phone.

"Bloody stubborn jaguars." Red-Boar shoved away from the kitchen table and headed for his room, snapping, "Find us a charter. I want to be on the ground in Mexico before he does something else stupid."

Rabbit jumped up from the table and put himself between his father and the door. "I'm coming with you."

"No fucking way."

"But I can help."

Red-Boar snorted. "How?"

The teen flushed. "Jack me in and I'll show you."

"Not happening. Stay here." Red-Boar pushed past his son. "And don't fuck anything up while we're gone."

Rabbit took a step after him, fists clenched.

Jox crossed to the teen. He didn't touch him because he knew the boy didn't like to be touched, but he said, "Stay here and chill. Once we know what's up, I'll talk to him."

"I didn't ask to be a half-blood." Rabbit's voice shook. "That was his call."

"I know." Jox clasped the boy's shoulder. "For what it's worth, I'm sorry."

Rabbit shrugged him off. "Not your fault he's a prick."

Maybe, maybe not. A *winikin* was supposed to guide his Nightkeeper as well as protect him. Red-Boar might not've been Jox's blood-bound charge, but he'd become his responsibility by default. Jox had done his best, but that hadn't been good enough; Red-Boar's scars ran too deep, leaving the *winikin* once again in the position of trying to save the son when the father put himself beyond salvation.

"I'll talk to him," Jox repeated. "If it comes to it, Strike will probably agree to jack you in without his consent."

"But I won't get a bloodline mark if he doesn't accept me as his own." Rabbit's voice went rough—with anger, maybe, or tears. Or both. "No bloodline mark means no talent mark. No magic. What's the point?"

"We'll figure something out." Jox gripped the boy's

shoulder again, and this time didn't let himself be shaken off. "I promise."

"Whatever." Rabbit shrugged and turned away. He headed for his room and slammed the door. Moments later, the rhythmic thump of bass vibrated through the floorboards.

Jox let out a breath, knowing that Rabbit was so not a complication he needed right now. He hated what had just happened, but Strike needed him, and the king's son was his first responsibility.

Grabbing the phone, Jox stabbed a few buttons and hit up the slightly disreputable pilot for hire he'd put on speed dial, just in case. A good *winikin*—or, for that matter, a fuckup *winikin* who occasionally got a few things right—knew to have contingency plans for just about anything.

The line went live and a thick voice growled, "This had better be goddamned good."

"Five grand if you get us to Cancún before dawn," Jox said, skipping the pleasantries.

There was a moment of silence, then, "It'll be an extra ten if you're carrying illegals."

"No illegals, just two passengers, but time is critical. Family emergency."

"My ass." But the pilot didn't press. "How soon can you be at the airport?"

"An hour."

"See you there." The line went dead.

Jox headed for his room to grab the essentials, but he paused at the kitchen doorway and looked back, not just at the kitchen and attached sitting area, but at the big picture window and the warehouse beyond, where towering stacks of pallets held his fertilizers and feed, soil and seed.

Winikin weren't precogs, but something told him he wouldn't be back.

Rabbit watched his old man and Jox leave, waiting until the brake lights on Jox's Jeep flashed at the end of the sloped driveway and the vehicle pulled out into traffic and accelerated away. Then he waited another five minutes to make sure they hadn't forgotten anything worth coming back for.

Then he got on the phone and called a few people, who said they'd call a few more people, and blah, blah. He wasn't sure if that counted as "fucking anything up," and didn't particularly care. Served the others right if they got home and he'd trashed the place. They could've brought him along. Wouldn't have hurt anyone, or screwed with the Nightkeepers' almighty rules.

But the barrier hadn't sucked him in. Hell, he hadn't even known it'd reactivated until he'd heard the screams and saw what Strike-out had done to himself. Then, when the old man had jacked in to look for him, Rabbit hadn't felt shit, which probably meant the old man'd been right all along and he didn't have a lick of power or worth. He wasn't a Nightkeeper, wasn't anything. He was just a half-blood screwup. And what did screwups do when their parents left them home alone?

They threw parties.

After Strike got off the phone with Jox and Red-Boar—and that convo had been a real case of can open, worms everywhere—he checked on Leah.

She lay on the pullout couch of the studio apartment, beneath a brightly colored serape that was one of the few splashes of color in the utilitarian space Jox had maintained over the years, another of his "just in case" contingencies.

This particular contingency plan had come in seriously handy, because there was no way in hell Strike would've had enough strength to teleport him and Leah back to the garden center, even if he'd been sure enough of the magic to try. So instead he'd carried her into town, weaving as he'd walked and singing off-key so the few people who'd seen them assumed they were tourists who'd had too much to drink.

Her chest rose and fell in the slow rhythm of deep sleep. The very fact that he was able to keep her asleep with such a thin spell all but proved she wasn't a Nightkeeper. The lesser spells, like the sleep spell, worked on humans but not magi.

"But you're a hell of a human, Blondie," he murmured, tracing his fingers down her porcelain-pale face and lingering on the faint puffiness of a split lip and the slight irregularity of an old scar at her temple, near her hairline. "A hell of a human."

But where did that leave them? The dreams—and they were visions, whether Jox and Red-Boar wanted to believe it or not—suggested they were to be lovers, but did that mean something long-term, or had the moment already come and gone? And if so, what was the point? The god hadn't made it through the barrier and the *makol* had escaped. What the hell role was she meant to play in the things to come?

"You're not going to figure it out staring at her," he told himself. He needed more information. So, despite Jox's warning, he chanted the simple counterspell to wake her.

Her eyelids flickered and her skin flushed. She murmured something under her breath. Then her eyes popped open, blue and intense, and locked on him immediately.

She didn't scream—that was the cop in her, he supposed, and felt a flash of gratitude because it gave him time to hold up both hands in an *I'm unarmed* gesture, and say, "I'm not going to hurt you. I'm going to feed you."

That had her hesitating long enough for the rest of the memories to hit—he saw it in the way her face flushed even harder, the color riding high in her cheeks as she remembered how they'd gone at each other in the sacrificial chamber.

The blush—and his own memories—had his skin heating and his blood revving, and a whole lot of ideas jamming his skull. He wasn't about to act on any of them, but some of the sizzle must've shown in his eyes, because she sat up abruptly enough that she swayed.

Draping the serape around her shoulders to cover where the ruined shirt left her half-naked, she lifted her chin. "Don't even think it."

"I'm a guy, which means I'm hardwired to think it." He deliberately turned his back on her and headed for the kitchen. "But I'll give you my word I won't act on it tonight."

"Which implies you think there'll be another night." She winced and rubbed at her temples. "What the hell did you drug me with? My head's killing me."

"No drug," he said, which was the truth. "You just sort of passed out on me." Which wasn't exactly a lie. "We weren't safe in the ruins, so I brought you here."

"Where is here?"

"A friend's apartment. He'll be here in the morning, and he'll help us get home." Which was more or less the truth, though it left out the part where Red-Boar would block off her memories first. When he saw her glance at the door, he added, "It locks from the inside, and the key's in my pocket. And the window is four floors up, so please don't try it. You have my word that you'll be home by lunchtime tomorrow."

He came out of the kitchen carrying a couple of spoons and an assortment of tinned meat. Jox had stocked the apartment's small kitchenette with nonperishable proteins of the sort that'd outlive cockroaches on the evolutionary scale, but damned if SPAM, sardines, and Vienna sausages didn't sound like manna from the gods just then.

"Here." He held out a tin and one of the spoons. "You need protein."

She stared at the tin, then up at him, her eyes very blue against her porcelain skin, which had gone pale as she'd processed everything that'd happened to them, and between them. "I don't understand," she said in a small voice, one that had a little tremor in it.

Aw, hell, Strike thought, cursing himself. She had to be terrified, and he was trying to feed her processed meat by-products. Like that was going to make it better.

He sat down beside her on the sofa, put an arm around her, and hugged her in as nonthreatening a way as he could manage. "I'll explain what I can." He could tell her anything he wanted, knowing Red-Boar would block it all anyway. "And in return, I'd like you to answer a few questions for me."

She sniffed and nodded. "If you think it'll help."

"I do." He used his free hand to tip her chin up, so she would see the truth in his eyes. "You're going to be home tomorrow. I promise."

He'd intended nothing more than that safe vow, that small comfort, but the moment their eyes met it was like somebody cranked his libido to "on." Heat roared through him, and he wanted nothing more than to grab the long white silk of her hair and use it to bare her throat, to hold her in place as he kissed his way down, taking the time he hadn't had before.

She sucked in a breath and held it, and damned if that color wasn't riding her cheeks again, telling him he wasn't alone in feeling the need.

"I said I wouldn't touch you tonight," he rasped, throat tight with the horns that rode him, goading him on, urging him to screw his good intentions and take what they both wanted.

"Did you?" she murmured, leaning in. "It seems to have slipped my mind."

On the heels of that permission, that invitation, he slid his hand up into the long fall of her hair, which was still faintly damp. He felt the echo of the solstice power within him, but more than that he felt the pounding lust that had ridden him since he'd first dreamed of her, since he'd first awakened thinking of her eyes, and of the way she'd felt wrapped around him.

She leaned in, so their lips were a breath apart, and whispered, "Go ahead. Kiss me."

A harsh groan rattled in his chest, and he closed the distance between them and touched his lips to hers, softly at first, a faint whisper of sensation. She murmured pleasure and met him for the next, taking it wetter, deeper, opening her mouth beneath his and inviting him in.

He crowded close, aligning their bodies and loosening his grip on her hair, sliding his hand down to cup the back of her neck. She whispered something, but the blood was pounding too hard in his veins, too fast in his ears for him to hear. "What was that?"

She eased away, cupped his jaw in her hands, and stared into his eyes. "I said, 'Thanks for the key.'"

Then she brought up her knee and racked him in the balls.

The attack was off center enough to be kind, but hard enough to drop him. He curled in pain as she shot to her feet and bolted across the room, headed for the door. "Don't!" he shouted, his words garbling on a groan of agony. " 'S not safe."

But she was already gone, pounding along the hall and down the stairs.

"Shit!" Strike got to his hands and knees and breathed through the pain, tried to find the barrier power when he barely knew where to look, never mind how to handle it. But this was an emergency. No way was he admitting he'd lost her.

He found the barrier, chanted the jack-in spell, and thought of Leah. The travel thread popped up in front of him immediately. *Here goes nothing,* he thought, and grabbed onto the thread with a mental touch and yanked.

The world went gray-green and slewed sideways, and he crashed into an alley two streets over from the apartment, smack in front of Leah.

This time she did scream.

He grabbed her, envisioned the apartment, and zapped them back hard and fast. They landed in a tangle of arms and legs, and she immediately started thrashing, screaming at the top of her lungs. Worse, the world was starting to spin and go fuzzy at the edges, warning Strike that he was running out of magic fast.

With his last ounce of power he put the sleep spell back on her, and she went limp against him.

Breathing hard, he lay there for a minute while the world did doughnuts around him, and he thanked the gods that he'd managed to get her back before the locals noticed her half-naked self parading around the not-very-nice neighborhood. Then he thanked them some more that he'd managed to pull off two teleports and a sleep spell, which meant he wouldn't have to admit to Jox that he'd nearly screwed the pooch and lost her.

Then he lay there a minute longer because his balls hurt and he didn't want to move.

Eventually, though, the floor got hard and he forced himself to his feet. He laid Leah back on the couch and covered her up with the serape, and she murmured something in a soft, sweet voice and turned on her side, tucking her hands beneath her cheek. With her face smoothed out in sleep, she looked very young and vulnerable.

"Vulnerable." He snorted. "Not exactly accurate, eh, Blondie?"

He hadn't enjoyed the experience, but he admired her flair. She'd played him hard and he'd fallen easy, and props to her. She might've gotten away, too, if it weren't for the magic.

Damn, he liked what he knew of her. She was tough and resourceful, soft and sexy, and she'd held her own against the *makol*. She was gorgeous and quick-minded and—

And whether he liked her or not, dreamed of her or not, she hadn't retained any magic past the equinox, which meant she wasn't part of what was coming. And really, that was for the best, given the prophecy.

At the thought, he looked at the far wall, where a framed piece of parchment hung on a bent nail. It wasn't a decorative touch. It was a reminder of what was important. Ascribed to the god Kauil, whose origins and allegiances were unknown, the thirteenth prophecy read: *In the final five years / The king stands ready / To make his greatest sacrifice. / If the dark lord comes / The end begins.*

He sighed. Though he wasn't the king yet, he was next in line, and the only jaguar male left. That meant the prophecy drove him, shadowed him. For so long he'd hoped it meant nothing, that the five-year mark would come and go, that 2012 would come and go. But now the barrier had churned back online, right on schedule, and now there was an *ajaw-makol* on the earthly plane, with the power to bring a dark lord through the barrier on the next cardinal day. It wasn't much of a stretch to think the greatest sacrifice would be coming right on its heels.

And didn't that just suck. Cursing, he pushed away from the wall, intending to pace.

He nearly fell on his ass.

All of a sudden, his legs felt like bungees hooked to nothing, limp and elastic. The urge to sleep was almost overwhelming, and the floor was looking soft as a mattress, but he knew he couldn't pass out. Not now. Not here.

No way in hell was he leaving Leah unprotected. Not with a *makol* on the loose. So he headed back into the main room and scrounged the tinned meat he'd pulled out for their interrupted snack. By his fourth can of by-products, the world had stopped spinning. By his sixth—when the SPAM started tasting like SPAM, which wasn't saying much—he was feeling almost normal, except for the part about needing to sleep for a week. Since that wasn't an option, he went for caffeine instead, raiding the coffee supply and drinking the stuff black, because powdered creamer was just wrong.

Fortified with a mug of sludgelike caffeine, he snagged a package of stale cookies from a cabinet, then headed back to Leah. He tucked the serape more tightly around her, set a chair near her head, facing the door, and sat himself down with the cookies and coffee within reach, along with the MAC-10 autopistol he'd pulled out of the gun locker hidden behind a secret panel in the bathroom closet. With the gun on his lap and a spare clip of jade-tipped bullets nearby, he watched the door. And waited.

And waited.

He was still waiting and watching, and was on his third pot of coffee when the dawn broke with quiet ferocity.

In the aftermath of the solstice, the sun rose almost directly behind the great pyramid at Chichén Itzá, a black step-sided silhouette against the fiery red of dawn. The pyramid—dedicated to the creator god Kulkulkan—was a monumental calendar, with ninety-one steps on each of the four sides, plus the top platform, equaling the 365 days of a solar year. Built atop an earlier temple dedicated to the jaguars gods believed to hold up the four corners of the world, the pyramid of Kulkulkan was designed so a serpent shadow descended the stairs at the exact moment of each equinox, in spring and fall. It overlooked the city of Chichén Itzá, which had been the center of religious and military power in the Yucatán from 800–1100 or so, A.D., housing upward of fifty thousand Maya and Nightkeepers at its peak.

Now, as the sun rose over the ancient city, Strike could just see the parking area that would fill with buses and rental cars in the next few hours, as tourists thronged the ruins, oohing and aahing over the ball court, where teams had competed to toss a heavy ball through stone rings set high on the parallel walls of the court. Little would the tourists know that the ball had represented the sun and the ring had symbolized the center of the Milky Way galaxy, which the Maya had believed was the entrance to Xibalba. In that way, they had reenacted the Great Conjunction over and over again, with the game's winners offering blood sacrifices— and sometimes their lives—to the gods in the hopes of preventing the end-time.

The tourists also wouldn't know that the Sacred Cenote, a giant sinkhole opening onto the underground waterways that were the only source of freshwater in the Yucatán, was not only a sacrificial well into which the Maya had thrown thousands of offerings, it was also one of the two entrances to the sacred underground tunnels of the Nightkeepers. Because, hello, nobody even knew the Nightkeepers existed anymore. Thanks to the conquistadors and their missionaries, knowledge of the Great Conjunction had faded to an astronomical oddity, and the Nightkeeper-inspired Mayan pantheon had been lost to monotheism.

Which meant what in practical terms? Nothing, really, Strike admitted to himself as the sun continued to climb the sky above the step-sided pyramid belonging to a god who might've been forgotten, but was far from gone. The Nightkeepers' duties had been set long ago, codified into the thirteen prophecies. The Great Conjunction was coming whether mankind cared or not. The *Banol Kax* would seek to breach the barrier.

And the Nightkeepers—what was left of them, anyway— would stand and fight.

Exhaustion drummed through him. Or maybe that was depression. Grief. It was impossible not to think about the massacre, about what it'd meant. If the barrier was fully back online and the *Banol Kax* had sent their *ajaw-makol* to prepare the stage for a dark lord's arrival, then everything was happening right on schedule despite the ultimate sacrifice represented by the massacre. Which meant his father's dreams had been lies. Or maybe he'd failed to follow the visions to their conclusion? Nobody knew at this point, which was a real bugger, because it didn't give Strike a damn bit of insight into how to deal with his own dreams. Or Leah's.

"We've known each other only a few hours, Blondie, and we're already up against it," he said to the sleeping woman. He ached over the necessity of wiping her memories and sending her back where she belonged, but the alternative was impossible.

Nightkeepers were born, not recruited.

Footsteps sounded in the hallway outside the apartment, jolting Strike from his reverie. He rose to his feet, autopistol at the ready, and relaxed only marginally when he heard the tapping rhythm on the door that signaled friend.

Moments later, a key turned in the lock and the door opened, and he saw the relief in Jox's face, the condemnation in Red-Boar's.

The sight of the two men loosened something inside Strike, making him feel a little less alone in the world. The second the door shut at their backs, the exhaustion he'd been fighting back all night rose up to claim him. "Don't hurt her," he said. "That's an order."

And he pitched to the floor, out cold.

The party at the garden center was in full swing by two a.m. Music pumped from the surround-sound speakers in the apartment, and someone had rigged the intercom to blast the tunes out in the warehouse. It was so loud, nobody cared that it sounded like shit.

The apartment above the store was jammed, and there were probably fifty or so kids packed into the warehouse. They were dancing in the main aisle and climbing on the stacked pallets of seeds and fertilizer, jumping from one leaning tower to the next and making bets on who'd fall first. A stack of 5-10-10 had already bitten the dust, and it looked like the leaning tower of diatomaceous earth was next. The dancers ground the fertilizer granules to dust beneath their feet, making the air sparkle faintly in the red-tinged emergency lights.

Rabbit stood above it all, watching from behind the wide picture window that opened from Jox's office onto the warehouse. He'd declared the room off-limits by slapping a crisscross of yellow-and-black caution tape over the door and locking it behind him, and so far the barricade had held.

The office lights were off, leaving him watching in the darkness as somebody started lobbing five-pounders of birdseed from the top racks of the thirty-foot-high warehouse. The bags exploded when they hit, sending up millet and sunflower shrapnel and making the dancers scream with laughter.

Rabbit knew he should be out there. This was his frigging party, and he was going to catch hell for it when the others got back. But he didn't move, just sat and watched instead, wishing he'd had the guts to go toe-to-toe with the old man when it'd counted. But he hadn't, so here he was, stuck in the middle of nowhere, doing nothing important. As usual.

"Rabbit?" There was a knock on the door. "You in there?"

The voice was female, which pretty much guaranteed he was going to answer. He cracked the door and saw Tracy Lindh, a dark-haired junior cheerleader he knew in passing, who scored about a seven of ten on the do-ability scale, mostly because her breasts balanced out her chunky legs. "Yeah?"

"I, uh, don't want to interrupt or anything."

"I'm alone. Just taking a time-out. You want in?" He let the door swing wide enough that she could get through, but kept it tight so she'd have to slide up past him.

But she stayed put. "No, I, uh . . . You know that

room in the apartment? The one with the padlock? Well, Ben Stanley and a couple of his buddies—"

Rabbit was out the door before she finished.

He should've been cursing whatever asshole'd invited the terrible trio, when pretty much everyone who was anyone knew they'd made Rabbit's life a living hell since junior high. It'd gotten so bad he'd actually studied so he could graduate early and get away from them.

But all he could think as he bolted up the hallway and skidded through the front door of the apartment, heart pounding in his ears, was, *Oh, shit. Oh, no. No, shit, please, no*—

He broke off when he saw that the door to the ritual room was splintered wide-open, with the padlock still attached to its hasp. Raucous male laughter sounded from within.

Lunging for the door, hoping like hell he wasn't too late, he shouted, "Hey, get out of—"

He stopped dead, heart slamming in his chest at the sight of three guys standing over the *chac-mool* altar, drinking beer from the ritual bowls.

Ben Stanley—a big, arrogant blond jerk who was a second-stringer on the football team and acted like he was captain—stood in the middle. Rabbit didn't recognize the guys on either side of him, because they were wearing the Nightkeepers' sacred robes, one red, one black, with the hoods pulled forward to shadow their faces. The hems and sleeve points dragged on the floor, which was littered with broken nachos and what looked like a big spooge of string cheese.

"Get. Out." Rabbit tried to keep his voice even, but it shook with rage.

They shouldn't be in the ritual chamber. Hell, *he* shouldn't even be in there. Not if the barrier had reactivated.

He'd never doubted the magic, even when it failed to work year after year. Somehow he'd always known it'd work someday; he just hadn't counted on being left behind. And in response, he was just now realizing, he'd made a big fucking mistake.

Probably the biggest of his life.

"Hey, Bunny-boy," the black-robed guy said. "What the fuck is this? You part of a cult? You and your fucked-up father worship the devil or something?"

Rabbit ID'd the voice as belonging to one of Ben's two usual partners in crime: brown-haired, pockmarked Zits Vicker. That meant Jason Tremblay, skinhead extraordinaire, was wearing the royal red.

"Come on, guys," Tracy said, surprising Rabbit because she'd followed him into the apartment. "Lay off. You've gotta admit this is a pretty cool place. You want to be invited back, right?"

Rabbit turned to her. "Go downstairs, okay? I've got this."

He didn't want her to see him get his shit knocked loose.

"Aw, let her stay," Zits whined. "We're just gonna have a little fun." He shook the black robe, making the stingray spines dance. "Is this your dress, Bunny? Or does your daddy like you in the red one better?"

"Go," Rabbit whispered, his heart bumping unevenly in his chest. "Please."

Tracy finally left, and Ben shut the door after her, giving it a shove so it wedged against the busted part and stuck fast. Then he crossed to the altar and dropped the bowl he'd been drinking from, giving it a spin so beer sloshed over the edges.

Rabbit was tempted to tell them that the last thing to hit those bowls had been human blood. He was going to take a pounding anyway. Why not deserve it?

But where before he'd more or less taken what they'd dished out—because resistance was futile and just earned him more of a beating—now he found himself squaring off opposite Ben as Zits and Jason moved up on either side of their leader.

Outside the sacred chamber, somebody swapped out the music, and a heavy throb of drumbeats sounded, seeming to echo up through the floor.

"Wanna tell us what goes on in here?" Zits asked. He slurped from his bowl, beer sloshing down the front of the sacred black robe.

Rabbit wanted to kill him. Really and truly kill him—

a quick slash across the throat would do it, or even better, he could cut the bastard's heart out of his chest and watch as Zits's blood pressure crashed, his brain cut out, and he dropped dead. Better still, he could burn him, robes and all, and listen to him scream.

For a second the image of it was so vivid in his mind, so perfect, Rabbit thought he'd already crisped the son of a bitch. Then the fantasy winked out and he was stuck back in the reality of high school torment, three months after he'd escaped the halls of hell.

This time, though, he wasn't the skinny kid who'd moved to town halfway through junior high and got caught doodling a black-robed wizard in his algebra notebook. This time he was . . .

Nothing. He was nothing. A half-blood who couldn't even jack in.

"He's not gonna tell us," Ben said. "Guess we'll have to make him." He slapped the ceremonial bowl off the altar, sending it across the room. The thin jade shattered when it hit the wall, and the air hummed off-key.

"Hey! Knock it off." Heart hammering in his chest, feeling faintly sick, Rabbit crouched down and picked up the largest piece of jade, which had broken off in an elongated triangle with knife-sharp edges.

Ben stuck his chin out. "Make me."

The humming got louder, reverberating in Rabbit's ears. "Just go," he whispered, gripping the shard of jade and feeling it cut into his palm. "Please, just go."

Heat surrounded him. Built inside him.

There must've been something in his eyes or voice, or maybe the heat and the humming weren't just his imagination, because Jason started edging toward the door. He pulled off the red robe and dropped it on the floor. "Come on, guys. We don't want to get in trouble with the 'rents. This shit looks expensive."

"There aren't any 'rents," Ben scoffed. "Just his stoner dad. You ever see him wandering around here in his brown bathrobe? What a loser." His eyes flicked to Rabbit's hand. "What're you gonna do, stab me with that?" He spread his hands and stuck out the beginnings of a gut. "Have at it, Bunny. You don't have the stones."

Red washed Rabbit's vision, narrowing it to a pinprick focused on Ben's face. All the jeers and indignities, every kick and punch, came back to him in a flare of humiliation.

"Go," he said again, his voice shaking with fear, not of them, but of what was happening inside him. *Say it*, a voice whispered. *Say the word*.

"His hand's bleeding," Zits said suddenly. "And I think he's gonna puke. Come on; let's blow before he does." He yanked the door and took off with Jason on his heels, tripping on the too-long robe and crushing the stingray spines into a twisted mess. But Rabbit was only peripherally aware of those small details.

His whole focus was on Ben. His enemy.

The humming in his head turned into a scream. The heat flared higher and higher still. Finally, Ben realized he was in trouble. His eyes got big and he started edging away, but it was too late for him to escape, too late to stop the thing that built within Rabbit, taking him over, thrilling him. Terrifying him.

Pressure grew inside Rabbit's skull and his fingertips burned, pain erupting as if the skin were peeling away. He tipped back his head and screamed, not sure whether he was trying to make it stop or urge it to keep going.

Ben made a run for it, bolting for the door. He skidded on the nacho crumbs and string cheese and went down on his hands and knees, but kept going, crawling out of the room as Rabbit screamed.

Finally, a word emerged, one he didn't even know he knew—not even a word, really, more a long syllable. A cry for mercy. For vengeance. *"Kaak!"*

Power blasted from him like an orgasm. Flames rose up around him like lovers, touching him, stroking him, urging him on, and he said the word again, calling the fire to him and sending it higher and higher still.

Dimly, far away, he heard screams and running feet. He felt the terror and pain of the others, and drank it in.

"Kaak!" he said a third time, and clapped his bleeding palms together.

Force and flame exploded outward, away from him, flattening everything in its path and leaving him untouched. Leaving him in control.

Rabbit had a moment of pure, perfect joy as the apartment burned around him. Then he passed the hell out.

CHAPTER FOUR

When Leah awoke, she smelled Betadine and alcohol wipes, and heard the hum of ventilation and the turned-low chatter of daytime TV. *Oh, crap.* She was in a hospital. And she was lying on something soft, which meant she wasn't doing the neck-crick nap-in-a-chair routine while waiting for a patient to wake up for questioning.

She was the patient. Damn it, she hated being the patient. Worse, beside the first quick surge of irritation was another emotion, a hollow, aching sense of loss that made her want to curl into a ball and weep.

She racked her brain, trying to find the source, but found only the sadness.

"What happened?" She pushed the words through a parched-dry throat, and they came out slurred, like she had a serious hit of happy pills in her system, blocking some monster pain. Remembering the feeling from the year before, when she'd taken a bullet in the leg during a bust gone wrong, she said, "Did I get shot again?"

She heard motion nearby, and had the sense of a man leaning over her. She wasn't sure why her eyes hadn't come back online yet, but thanks to the drugs she wasn't too worried about it. Besides, his presence was warm and reassuring, though he didn't touch her.

"What is the last thing you remember?" His voice sent a skitter of warmth through her, a little zip of electricity that had her heart bumping in her chest.

"I don't know." Memory was a thick cloud of gray-green mist. "Not much." Had she hit her head? Did she have amnesia? The idea brought a jolt of fear. "Why can't I see?"

"Give it a minute." He paused. "Can you tell me your name, and your parents' names?"

"I'm Leah Ann Daniels," she said, relieved when the information came quickly. "My parents are Timothy and Ann Daniels, and they live in Boca. I've got a place outside town, and I drive a 'sixty-seven Mustang named Peggy Sue. My brother—"

She broke off, sucking in a breath as a big chunk of it clicked into place. Matty was dead, she remembered with a slice of grief so fresh it was like it'd just happened. Ever since then, she'd been trying to nail Zipacna and his 2012ers for the Calendar Killings.

"We were meeting a snitch," she said, remembering Nick's unhesitating support and wondering why that brought another wash of grief. "Itchy. He showed up and . . ." She frowned, bumping up against that grayness again. "I don't remember anything after that."

She let the silence continue for a minute, sure the doctor—because that was what he had to be, right?—would either fill in the gaps or ask her another question. But he did neither.

"Hello?" she tried, wondering if the silence meant she was missing more than a few hours. "What day is it, anyway?"

"Tuesday," a female voice answered. "Welcome back, Detective."

Leah frowned. "Where's the doctor?"

"I'm Dr. Black."

"What about the guy who was just in here?"

The newcomer ignored the question, instead taking Leah's pulse, then running her through the exact same "who are you and who are your parents" questions she'd just answered for the other guy.

Leah's banged-up brain spun. Who the hell had she just been talking to? The easy answer was that he'd been one of Zipacna's boys, sent to see what she remembered. Which meant there'd been something for her to remem-

ber, damn it. Problem was, she couldn't convince herself
the voice had belonged to a 2012er. First off, they didn't
tend to blend. Someone would've noticed. Second off,
though she told herself she damn well knew better than
to judge on looks—or sound—it didn't feel right. The
owner of that voice wasn't a member of Zipacna's cult;
he was . . .

Nothing, she realized, coming up against that gray wall
again. He was nothing to her. Probably just a dream,
or a fragment of TV dialogue that she'd turned into
something more.

Yet the image of piercing blue eyes stayed with her,
even though she hadn't seen his face.

When the doctor finished her exam, she said, "You're
looking good, considering."

"Considering what?" Concentrating, Leah managed to
open her eyes, wincing at the glare and the rasp of her
eyelids. Her eyeballs felt like they'd been scorched, like
all the tears had been burned away, and once the light
leveled off, the dull pain at the back of her head increased to a steadily drumming headache. Her tongue
was sore, too, and her body ached all over, though in a
not entirely unpleasant way, like she'd had really good
sex or something.

Yeah, right.

The doctor turned out to be a forty-something moth-
erly type wearing round-rimmed glasses and happy-face
scrubs that made Leah wonder if she'd gotten turfed to
pediatrics. The room looked vaguely familiar, as did the
view of Biscayne Bay. "I'm in Mercy?"

The doctor nodded as she scribbled something in
Leah's chart. "Yep. Miami's finest."

"How long am I going to be here?"

"Not long. I'll run a few tests, make sure everything
still checks out okay. You were unconscious for quite a
while, but sometimes the body knows best. You may
have needed to shut it off for a while. Considering what
you went through, you're in very good shape."

That was the second time the doctor had given her
the "considering" line, but since she'd avoided the question the first time Leah didn't bother trying again. "My

head hurts. And if I'm doing so well, what's with the drugs?"

"We haven't given you anything." Concerned, she put down the clipboard and crossed to Leah so she could do the penlight-in-eyes, follow-my-finger routine. "Is your vision blurry?"

"Getting clearer by the second, now that I've got my eyes open," Leah said quickly, knowing she was on the verge of adding an overnight to her hospital sentence.

The doc didn't look convinced. "Do you have some-one who can stay with you for the next forty-eight hours or so?"

Which begged the question of where the "utterly sin-gle with no prospects in sight" check mark went on the admissions form—and who'd filled it in for her.

Nick, probably, she thought. Then she remembered that he'd been with her for the gone-wrong meeting with Itchy. "How's my partner? Nick Ramon. Did he bring me in?"

The doctor headed for the door. "The waiting room is practically overflowing with cops. Captain Mendez, in particular, would like to speak with you."

Another evasion, Leah realized, a chill settling in her gut. "Bring her on."

Connie would tell it like it was.

Dr. Black pushed through the door. Moments later, Connie swung through, her heels tapping on the polished floor, her brown eyes fixed on Leah. She was wearing her usual conservative power suit—this one a member of the olive green family—buttoned tight across her thick fifty-something frame, but her serene *I'm in charge* expression showed cracks of concern.

She stopped beside the bed and stared down. The sight of her normally stoic boss with her mouth working and nothing coming out was enough to send a chill through Leah. It was the glint of tears in Connie's eyes, though, that sealed it.

"Nick's dead, isn't he." It wasn't even a question. Leah already knew. It explained the doctor's reticence and the look in Connie's eyes.

It also explained why, from the moment she'd woken

up all the way from her dream, she'd felt as though her heart were breaking.

Strike dumped the borrowed lab coat on an empty gurney, slipped out of Mercy Hospital, and headed down the block to the Vizcaya Gardens, where Jox and Red-Boar were waiting for him. They had helped him hide Leah's unconscious body near where her partner had died—an image Red-Boar had pulled from her mind. Once she was in place, he'd made an anonymous 911 call and stood watch until the cops arrived, and then he'd shadowed them to the hospital in order to make sure she woke up okay.

Red-Boar had bitched about the time suck, but Strike had been adamant. Bad enough he'd had to wipe her memories, had to leave her. He sure as hell wasn't taking off without making sure she was okay. He'd also slapped a protection spell on her when Red-Boar and Jox weren't looking. The threadlike connection running through the barrier would alert him if she thought she was in mortal danger. In theory, anyway. In practice, who the hell knew?

They'd lost too much of the knowledge and magic their ancestors had once commanded.

Fury and frustration bubbled up in Strike as he walked beneath the screaming Florida sun. He wanted to put his fist through something, wanted to drive too fast, wanted to press a willing woman—okay, Leah—up against the wall and pound himself into her until he forgot that he was a king without a people, a protector without much power, a savior who didn't have the foggiest notion how to go about doing what thirteen hundred generations of his forebears had intended for him to do. The writs said that a Nightkeeper answered to the gods first, and then to his people, but what if he had no people? What if he was on his own?

"Then he's just a guy who can do a few parlor tricks, and the world is pretty much fucked four and a half years from now," he said aloud, the words rasping in his throat.

He needed more power, needed more people, needed . . .

Help. He needed help.

You had help, a voice whispered inside. *You let her go.*

"She's better off without me," he said, and meant it.

Strike paid his admission fee to Vizcaya, which was some sort of mansion–turned–tourist attraction. He did a thanks-but-no-thanks on the guided tour and headed straight through the main house, which was huge and rococo, a sort of ode to Italian Renaissance built in the early nineteen hundreds by some industrialist or another. It wasn't his thing, but Jox had chosen the meeting place, and it hadn't seemed worth arguing.

The gardens beside the mansion were pretty, green and hot, and the sound of fountain-borne water mingled with that of jetliners entering their landing pattern on the way to the airport. Strike followed the brochure map out to the meeting spot. Jox and Red-Boar were waiting for him in something called the Grotto, which proved to be a cavelike structure made of coral and carved stone that'd probably sounded really good when the architect first pitched it, but as far as Strike was concerned just looked lumpy and weird. Statues of the sea god Neptune flanked either side of the arched doorway, and a low bench ran around the interior. The coral walls absorbed the sounds made by the few other tourists meandering around the formal gardens, and that, combined with the rush of a large fountain cascading over and in front of the Grotto, gave the illusion of privacy for their council of war.

Jox stood by the entrance, pensive. Red-Boar sat cross-legged on the floor, doing his Yoda impression of eyes-closed, hands-folded-in-lap meditation.

"It's done," Strike said.

"Good." Jox waved him into the small space, then sat near the door, so he could see both in and out. Guarding them, like generations of *winikin* had guarded their Nightkeepers.

Seeing that, Strike felt a layer of strangeness settle around them. How long had they talked about *what-if*?

What if the barrier came back to life before the end-time? What if the *Banol Kax* found a way to contact evil on earth and set out to fulfill the final prophecy?

They'd never come up with good answers before. Why should it be any different now that *what-if* had become, *Oh, shit*?

"She doesn't remember you?" Red-Boar asked.

"You did a good job," Strike answered, hating that it had been necessary. Why had she been in his dreams if she wasn't going to be in his life? Only half joking, he said, "You want to wipe *my* mind now, and we can pretend none of it happened?"

"Mind-wipe doesn't work on Nightkeepers."

"Right. I knew that." Strike sighed and dropped onto the bench. "What now?"

Jox gestured to the garden. "Did you look around on the way in?"

Strike shrugged. "Yeah. Too fussy for my taste, and the staff salary's got to be a killer, but whatever works for you, I guess."

"It's gorgeous," Jox said, more ignoring him than disagreeing.

Strike said, "And this is relevant why?"

But he stood and joined the *winikin* in the Grotto doorway, so they stood shoulder-to-shoulder looking out at the gardens and the fussy mansion beyond, with its pale stone, ornate ironwork, and yellow and blue–striped awnings. Figures moved on the east terrace, setting out chairs and bunting for some sort of event later in the day.

"What do you see?" Jox said quietly.

The quick answer died on Strike's tongue. After a moment, he said, "Shit. People. Mankind. The things we've built."

It shamed him, which had no doubt been Jox's intention. He'd been so caught up in being pissed off about Leah, the barrier reopening, and the *ajaw-makol* getting away, so worried about the visions and what they might mean, so conflicted about the return of the magic and finally being able to jack in . . . that he'd lost track of what the hell this was all about.

It was about saving the world.

"There's just me and Red-Boar left," Strike said, his heart heavy with the knowledge that they'd failed before they'd even begun. "Anna's gone, and all of the others are dead."

There was a long moment of silence. Then Jox said, "That's not exactly true."

The world went very, very still.

Strike's breath left him in a long, slow hiss. "Meaning what?"

Red-Boar's head came up. His eyes fixed on Jox.

"There are others out there, hidden. Raised in secret." The *winikin* said it fast, not looking at Strike or Red-Boar.

Strike wasn't sure how he was supposed to react, wasn't sure how he felt, wasn't sure he'd even heard it correctly. Somehow the words had gotten stuck between his ears and his brain, jamming him up, making his brain buzz.

Other Nightkeepers. Raised in secret. *Gods.*

After a lifetime of thinking he was the only male full-blood of his generation, the concept just didn't compute.

Red-Boar rose, his face gone gray. "*Winikin,* what have you done?"

"My duty. Always my duty." That was said with a hint of self-directed anger, as Jox pulled a folded sheet of paper out of his pocket and offered it to Strike. "I protected the bloodlines from their enemies." The look he shot at Red-Boar suggested he wasn't just talking about the underworld, either, but Strike let that pass as he took the folded paper and opened it with fingers that trembled faintly.

It was a computer printout of names. Not just any names, though. The words *Owl* and *Iguana* leaped out at him, seeming to burn his eyeballs.

A bolt of something that might've been excitement, might've been dread, hit him square in the midsection and fired through his veins. Behind him, Red-Boar dropped down to one of the benches as though his legs had given out.

"Jesus," Strike said. He looked at Jox. "How?"

"That night . . ." The *winikin* swallowed hard before continuing, as though he, too, still saw the bloody images of the massacre in his sleep. "The *boluntiku* smelled the magic. Any connection to the barrier was a way for them to track the children. But there were a few they couldn't chase down, a few who got away."

"The babies," Red-Boar rasped. "They didn't have their bloodline marks yet. The monsters couldn't see them." He paused, shaking his head. "Gods. How did I not know?"

"The babies," Strike repeated, thinking of the crèche in its soundproof globe. Excitement kindled. "You're fucking kidding me." They'd be what—twenty-five, twenty-six now?

And they'd be full-bloods. Nightkeepers. Magi.

The world took a long, lazy spin around him. This couldn't be happening, couldn't be real. Could it?

"How many?" he whispered, almost afraid to ask, because if they were going to pull this off he was going to need a whole fucking army. The sheet of paper suddenly seemed heavy, like it carried the weight of the world. "How many survived?"

"Ten, along with their *winikin*." Jox paused. "With you two and Rabbit or Anna, that makes thirteen. A powerful number."

Strike drew his finger down the list, pausing where two names sat beside the name of a single *winikin*. "Siblings?"

"Twins," Jox said, and there was a wealth of meaning in the single word. The Hero Twins were the saviors in countless Mayan legends, reflecting the fact that twins were a powerful force in Nightkeeper magic. Siblings could boost each other's magic through the bloodline connection, mates through the emotional link. The twin link was ten times stronger than either.

"Gods." Strike looked at Jox—the man who'd saved him, the man who'd raised him. "They don't know who they are? They don't know the magic?"

"They can learn," Jox said with quiet authority. "Each of them was raised by a *winikin*. They know the stories by heart. They can learn the rest."

In the silence that followed, the *winikin*'s cell phone rang. He pulled it from his back pocket, glanced at the caller ID, and frowned. "Police?"

Everything inside Strike went on red alert in an instant, and he nearly lunged across and grabbed the phone before he stopped himself. The protection spell hadn't given him the slightest quiver, and besides, Leah and Jox hadn't swapped cell numbers. There was no reason she or anyone else at the MDPD would be calling.

"Hello?" Jox answered. "Yes, this is he." He listened, stiffened, and his face went blank, then flushed a dull red. After a moment, he said, "His father is part owner in the business."

Strike winced. *Oh, hell.* What'd Rabbit done this time?

The conversation went on for a few minutes, with Jox giving nothing but an occasional, "Yes, of course," and, "Uh-huh," his voice going thicker each time, his complexion going paler. Finally, he said, "Yes, please put him on."

"What'd he do?" Strike hissed.

The *winikin* held up a *wait a minute* finger and said, "Rabbit? It's Jox. Are you okay?" He listened for a moment, and Strike caught the rise and fall of the teen's voice, sounding younger than usual, and atypically high, like he was on the verge of losing it.

Strike's irritation morphed to worry. Had the kid actually hurt himself this time? Worse, had he hurt someone else?

"It's okay, son. It's okay. We'll get through this, I promise. I need you to listen to me. Rabbit, are you listening? Good. It was an accident. There were candles and alcohol, and that's all the cops need to know."

"Oh, shit," Strike said, putting two and two together and getting zero.

"I'll kill him." Red-Boar held out his hand. "Let me talk to him."

Jox turned his back. "I'll take care of everything. I'll deal with it, I promise. Do you still have your ID and the AmEx I gave you for emergencies?"

"*Winikin.*" Red-Boar's voice turned deadly. "Give. Me. The. Phone."

"Good," Jox said, ignoring him. "I want you to get

your ass to Logan Airport and wait for me to call you with a destination. If the cops give you any grief, tell them it's a family emergency and have them call me. Got it?"

When Red-Boar moved, looking as though he were going to deck Jox and take the phone, Strike stepped between them. "Don't," he said quietly. "He's more than earned our trust."

"Speak for yourself." But Red-Boar stalked away, slammed the heels of his palms against the coral-trimmed doorway, and leaned out, breathing deeply.

"Bye, kid," Jox said, then added, "And hey—congratulations, sort of. Next time wait for an escort, though, okay?"

"Oh, *shit*," Strike said as Jox hung up the phone.

"Yep," Jox said grimly, losing the *everything's okay* facade he'd pulled together for the teen's sake. "You guessed it. The good news is that Rabbit's a pyrokine." He left it hanging, but there was no need to say it aloud.

The bad news is that Rabbit's a pyrokine.

And his magic was shit-strong, or the barrier wouldn't have reached out to him, giving him his talent without the proper ceremonies. Not only that, he was a half-blood, which automatically made his talents volatile, and not necessarily subject to the same rules as Nightkeeper magic.

Red-Boar turned back. "Did he hurt anyone else?"

"No." Jox shook his head. "Thank the gods."

"What about—" Strike broke off, afraid to ask.

The *winikin* shook his head. "It's all gone. The cops are willing to call it an accident, but we'll have to take a flier on the insurance. No way they're paying out on a party gone wrong."

Strike tried to take it in, but on some level he was numb to the tragedy. He'd found his dream woman, only to learn that she wasn't his at all. The barrier was open and there was an *ajaw-makol* on the loose. And there were more Nightkeepers. Ten of them, plus their *winikin*.

After that, losing their business, home, and possessions didn't seem all that major. Then again, the garden center hadn't been his dream. It'd been Jox's.

"Hey. I'm sorry." Strike reached out to the *winikin*, then hesitated. They were close, but not particularly touchy-feely. "I'm really freaking sorry."

Jox backed away, holding up a hand. "Don't." There was something broken in his voice. "Just don't, okay? Give me a minute." He sat. Blew out a breath. "It's stupid, really. We would've had to leave anyway, right? That part of our lives is over."

Strike sat beside him. "Doesn't make it any easier."

"Sacrifice." Jox scrubbed his hands over his face. "It's all about sacrifice."

"We'll have to find someplace to train the newbies," Red-Boar said from the doorway, seemingly ignoring the fact that his kid was an untrained pyro who had torched Jox's pride and joy. "Maybe a farmhouse. Something near some good ley lines, with no close neighbors. Maybe the Midwest. Shit." He scowled. "The robes and bowls are probably trash. Altar might be salvageable if the stone didn't crack in the heat. Spellbooks are gone. So what the fuck am I supposed to use to teach the magic to these hypothetical magi?"

"Having them meet us at the training compound would be a good start," Jox said quietly.

Something in his voice had Strike sitting up. "The training center's long gone." When the *winikin* said nothing, Strike got a weird shimmy in his gut. "Isn't it?"

The morning after the massacre, Jox had left him and Anna down in the bunkerlike safe room beneath the archives while he'd collected the bodies and set the Great Hall ablaze as a massive funeral pyre. Then the *winikin* had gathered the robes and a few sacred objects, and all the spellbooks he could fit in the Jeep he was taking. Finally, he'd invoked the training compound's self-destruct spell. Known only to a select few Nightkeepers and the royal *winikin*, the spell was intended to keep the magic away from human eyes. It—as Jox had explained it, anyway—basically shoved the compound into the barrier, wiping it from the earth forever.

It was the last Nightkeeper magic done before the barrier shut down. Or so Strike had always believed. Now, when the *winikin* stayed silent and Red-Boar glared, Strike said, "Jox?"

"The training center is still there," the *winikin* admitted. "It's just . . . hidden."

Red-Boar's voice shook when he said, "You used a curtain spell?"

Jox nodded. "King Scarred-Jaguar preset a disguise spell for me before he left, sort of a level below the self-destruct. Maybe he knew what was going to happen; I don't know." He paused, glancing at Strike. "You can reverse the spell. The Great Hall is gone, but the rest of the training center stands intact . . . including the archives."

Oh, gods in heaven. "The archives," Strike repeated, his brain buzzing with shock, with possibilities. Though most of the spellbooks had been lost to the missionaries' fires, a handful had survived. That collected wisdom, along with generations of written commentaries from various spell casters and magi, had been located in the three-room archive of the Nightkeepers' training compound.

Apparently, it still was.

"Christ." Strike was having a hard time processing this. He was being offered the ultimate knowledge base, but with a serious caveat—to get it, he'd have to go back to the place that still haunted him.

It'd taken years before he could close his eyes and not see the *boluntiku*, not relive the deaths of his friends and their *winikin*. The nightmares were few and far between these days, but they were hard and dark and crippling when they came.

He looked over at Jox. "What does it . . . look like?"

Last he'd seen it, the place had been in shambles, littered with torn clothing and the debris of violence. Six-clawed marks had marred the buildings, and the wrecked cars had been awash with blood.

"Probably not so good." Jox lifted a shoulder. "The curtain spell protects it from sight, but not from the elements. It's been twenty-four years. Who knows what we'll find when we get there?"

Great, Strike thought. But Jox was right—they had to go. There was no turning down the lure of the archives . . . and Rabbit had fucking burned down the garden center. Hating the necessity, he nodded. "New Mexico it is."

They were silent a moment, each caught in memory. Finally, Strike said, "What I don't get is why you didn't tell us about the others sooner. Why not let us all grow up together?"

"I couldn't risk it," the *winikin* replied. "The younger ones never went through their first binding ceremonies, so the barrier didn't recognize them at all. You and Anna had your first marks, though, and Red-Boar was fully bound."

"So if the *boluntiku* came through the barrier again, they'd come straight for us, and once they found us, they'd be likely to kill the youngsters, too." Strike nodded, his gut knotting at the memories. "But after a few years, once you knew it was safe, you could've said something."

"I couldn't risk it," the *winikin* said in his *end of discussion* voice, warning Strike that it wasn't worth pressing. Not now, anyway.

Besides, he could make an educated guess from the way Jox and Red-Boar were careful not to look at each other. *There's something there,* Strike thought, and he wondered, not for the first time, exactly what had happened between the two men back when Red-Boar had disappeared into the rain forest near the sacred tunnels, and returned several years later with his son in tow.

And why the *winikin* had felt it necessary to protect the young survivors from the sole remaining full-fledged mage.

Twelve hours later, Strike, Jox, Red-Boar, and Rabbit stood shoulder-to-shoulder in the New Mexico badlands, staring at an empty box canyon off the Chaco River cut-through.

Some thirty miles away over rough terrain lay the intricate, soaring ruins of the six-hundred-room Pueblo Bonito, which the early Puebloans—with a little help from traveling Nightkeepers up from the Yucatán—had built as a ceremonial home for the gods around A.D. 1000. The larger-than-life stone-and-mortar ruins formed the center of the Chaco Culture National Historical Park, which saw its share of tourist traffic. Farther north, the Bisti/De-Na-Zin Wilderness offered dinosaur skeletons and funky 'shroom-shaped rock formations.

Here, though, a stiff five-mile drive off a gravel track that optimistically called itself Route 57, there was nothing but canyon walls of sandstone, flatlands dotted with chamisa and saltbush, and the occasional rock formation.

The box canyon was maybe a half mile across, widening out past the mouth to form a flattened arrow shape of open land that dead-ended in a sheer rock face about a mile away. High stacks of cumulus clouds dotted the blue sky, and large bird shadows passed now and then, one of the few signs that they weren't completely alone.

Strike squinted into the sharp-edged sunlight and thought he could just make out the shadows of pueblo ruins high up on the rock face of the box canyon's back wall. The memory of climbing up to those ruins with a group of kids his own age was the only thing that clicked. Nothing else seemed familiar.

"You sure this is the right place?" Red-Boar asked suddenly.

It was a relief to hear him speak after so many hours of silence. As far as Strike was concerned, it was also a relief to know he wasn't the only one with doubts. He'd expected to feel something when he got here. He'd expected to remember more, but the canyon was just a canyon.

"This is the place," Jox said with quiet assurance. He stepped back, gesturing for Rabbit to join him. "Let's let these two work."

"Hey," the teen protested. "I want to—"

"Not now," Red-Boar said sharply. "Go with the *winikin.*"

The kid shot his father a look, and Strike could've sworn that the air crinkled with heat for a second. Then Rabbit slouched over to join Jox, temper etched in every fiber of his sweaty-assed, hoodie-wearing self.

Strike glared at the older Nightkeeper. "Do you think we should—"

"Not now." Red-Boar did the interrupting thing again, then palmed the knife from his belt. It was a Buck knife knockoff they'd bought from a roadside stand, not a purified ceremonial dagger, and they wore combat black-on-black instead of the ceremonial robes, but they'd tied fabric strips around their upper arms—black for Red-Boar, royal crimson for Strike—as a nod to the regalia they'd lost in the fire.

With a smooth motion, the older man flipped open the knife and drew it across his right palm, signifying that his would be the lead power for this spell. He tossed the knife to Strike, who caught it on the fly and scored his left palm for the subordinate role.

The moment the first drop of blood hit the sand, the air hammered with an invisible detonation. The ground trembled, then stilled, but the world around them shimmered gold.

"Pasaj och," the men said in unison, jacking in.

Strike could feel the power within, could feel it straining against the barrier. He saw a yellow thread but didn't dare grab on, because he'd promised Jox he wouldn't 'port again until he'd done some controlled practicing. Catching a flash of motion, he turned his head to follow, but didn't see anything. Was that weird? He didn't know.

"Focus," Red-Boar said quietly, and held out his hand. The blood from his palm looked crimson in the golden air, which shimmered some twenty feet away from them at the mouth of the box canyon, as though some sort of field were repelling the power itself.

Strike pressed his bleeding palm to Red-Boar's, boosting the older Nightkeeper.

"Gods," Red-Boar said, and power sang through their connected hands and exploded in Strike's head. The jolt rocketed through his body and blasted outward in a

shock wave that drove Jox and Rabbit back on their
asses. The golden curtain thickened before them, moving
and roiling as if it were a living thing that fought destruction.

Red-Boar rapped out a string of words so quickly and
so oddly accented that Strike couldn't begin to follow,
finishing with a loud cry of, *"Ye-ye-ye!" Reveal!*

The gold burst like ground-level fireworks, raining
down on them in pellets of power that felt cool to the
touch. Air rushed into the space where the golden light
had been, a howling whip of wind that moved the sand
and plucked an eagle from the sky.

The bird recovered quickly, winging away over the
canyon with a screech of protest, then swerving
sharply to the right when a huge leafy tree materialized in front of it. As the eagle flapped its powerful
wings, seeming eager to get the hell away, four other
buildings shimmered to life, becoming solid and recog-
nizable, and punching Strike with a grief so fresh that
he nearly dropped to his knees. He couldn't, though,
because he was held up by Red-Boar's viselike grip
on his hand.

Through the connection, he saw the image of a
golden-haired woman and two toddlers, identical copies
of each other, and felt a wash of love so acute he wanted
to scream with it.

Realizing he was catching Red-Boar's emotional back-
lash, he tried to pull away, shouting, "Jack out!" When
the mage resisted, Strike got in his face, grabbed him by
the jaw, and forced the older man to look at him. "Listen to me! Let them go; they're not real!"

Red-Boar released his hand and the golden light cut
out. The images dimmed, and Strike sagged, bracing his
hands on his knees to stay upright.

Then Red-Boar punched him in the face and Strike
went down anyway.

"What the *fuck*?" Strike rolled and blocked, in case
there was another coldcock incoming, but it'd been a
one-shot deal.

The older man just stood over him, breathing hard.

"They were real to me," he said, and turned and walked toward the newly materialized buildings.

Red-Boar's step didn't change when Rabbit called after him. He didn't hear the quaver in the boy's voice. Or maybe he didn't care.

"Here. Up you go." Jox hauled Strike to his feet with a strength that seemed disproportionate to his size. "You okay?" At Strike's nod, he turned to Rabbit. "You?"

"Whatever." The kid took a good, long look at what had sprung to life in the box canyon, and his lips twisted. "You guys better be able to magic us up about fifty Ty Penningtons, because this place needs a serious make-over."

Strike followed the direction of his gaze—he'd managed to avoid looking at the compound up to that point—and let out a long, shaky breath. It was the scene of his nightmares. Yet at the same time it wasn't.

Yes, the walls were scored with claw marks, but they were faded and worn from wind, rain, and blowing sand. Yes, wrecked cars dotted the landscape, but they were dated, rusted shells now, looking like a more appropriate setting for a junkyard dog than for fear.

Strike had worried that all he'd see was the past. Instead, he saw possibilities.

The main house was as huge as his nine-year-old self remembered, a three-story mansion of mortar-set sandstone with wings running off on either side, curving around, a swimming pool in the back. The driveway ran around the left side to the huge connected garage, and on the right a covered tunnel led to the Great Hall. At least, it had. Now the spot where the rec building had stood was nothing more than a dark stain on the canyon floor, marking the ashes of the dead children and *winikin*.

In the center of the rectangular impression where the hall had once stood, there was a huge tree that hadn't been there before. Yet, oddly, it looked like it'd been there for hundreds of years, because there was no way it'd gotten that big in a couple of decades. It had to be five or six feet across at the base, probably fifty-plus feet high, with lush green leaves that seemed completely out of place amidst the arid dryness of the New Mexican landscape.

"What the hell?" Rabbit said.

"It's a ceiba tree," Strike answered, though he'd been thinking pretty much the same thing. Their ancestors had planted the sacred "world trees" in the center of their villages and plazas. They'd believed the ceiba's roots ran to the underworld, and its branches held up the heavens. He turned to Jox. "Did you plant it?"

The *winikin* shook his head, seeming stunned. "No. It makes a hell of a memorial, though. Wish I'd thought of it."

"Someone did," Strike said, though he couldn't bring himself to say what he knew they were both thinking. It was one thing to jack in to a concentration of psi energy that existed at the barrier between the planes. It was another to suggest that an actual god had planted a tree in their backyard. A tree that grew exclusively in rain forests. One that shouldn't have had leaves during the dry season, and looked like it'd been there far longer than was actually possible.

He stood there for a moment, wondering if this was the point where he woke up from the dream. Instead, he stayed exactly where he was.

After a moment, Jox looped an arm across his shoulders and hugged him close, as he had done when Strike was a boy. "Come on, kid. It's time to call your people home."

But as Strike followed his *winikin* through the main entrance of the training compound built by his ancestors, he wasn't thinking of the massacre and times past, or the renovations they'd need to do to get the place livable, or even of the strangers he was supposed to turn into a tiny army. He was thinking about Leah, and how she'd stood up to him, chin jutting like she was leading for a punch; how he'd watched her sleep, her face going soft and vulnerable; and how she'd looked at him after they'd been together, how she'd seen him as a man rather than something so much more complicated.

And as he stepped through the doorway into the entryway of the king's mansion, where the past and future ran together and made his heart hurt, he wished like hell that he could've been just a man, could've been *her* man. But he wasn't and couldn't be.

He was a Nightkeeper.

PART II

✳

APHELION

*The point in the earth's orbit when it is
farthest from the sun.*

CHAPTER FIVE

June 23

Alexis Gray strode toward the Fish Shack, fuming. Her long legs ate up the distance across the pier to the restaurant, which was far more elegant than the name implied, and her waist-length hair, which was streaky blond this week, crackled with static electricity. That, along with a low mutter of thunder in the distance, warned that a squall was coming in over Newport Harbor.

If I'm lucky, the storm'll sink his damn yacht with his lying dick caught in the tiller.

Alexis glanced down the marina, where her suckfest newly ex-boyfriend, Aaron Worth—aka the Worthless Prick who'd screwed his way through the Riviera—had tethered his pride and joy front and center for everyone to admire. The yacht, that was, not his dick, though it turned out both pieces of equipment had been around the world a few more times than she'd thought. Meanwhile, she'd been holed up in her beachside office, managing the scum-sucking cheater's portfolio for him and making him money hand over frigging fist.

Which, it turned out, had just given him less of a reason to come clean with her.

Or maybe he was right; maybe he'd tried to tell her it wasn't working and she'd been too stubborn to listen, too determined to keep their sinking relationship afloat.

God knew, Isabella called her mule-stubborn more often than not.

Smiling at the thought of the godmother who'd raised her from the age of two, Alexis shoved aside the thoughts of her "sorry about the triplets in the bedroom; how am I fixed for liquid assets?" jackass ex and opened the door to the Fish Shack.

The smell of garlic and fresh bread greeted her first, followed closely by the maître'd, Tony. "Your usual table, Miss Gray?"

"Not in a million years." That was another of those front-and-center things dictated by Aaron, who liked to sit smack in the middle of the huge window facing the boardwalk. "I'm meeting Izzy today."

Tony's smile broadened, though she wasn't sure if it was because she was guyless for lunch, or because her godmother made pretty much everyone smile. He waved through the dining area to a covered porch that faced the sea. "She's in the bar."

"Perfect." Alexis headed in that direction, thinking that she could always count on Izzy to know what she needed even before she did. Today, that included a drink before noon.

In the bar area, Izzy sat at the farthest table down, close to the water and the incoming storm. When she saw Alexis, her dark eyes lit and she raised an umbrella-topped glass. "Cheers. The wind just changed."

"You have no idea." Alexis hiked herself up onto the stool opposite her and waved to the bartender. "Two of whatever she's having, along with a basket of fries and the catch of the day."

Izzy's lips twitched. "Hungry, dear?"

Dark, petite, and graceful, with a wonderfully calm way of dealing with life, Izzy was the diametric opposite of Alexis in so many ways, both physically and emotionally, that it was a wonder they got along. Then again, maybe it was because of those differences that it worked so well, even though just being near her godmother made Alexis feel huge, ungainly, and loud, like a flatulent elephant in an antiques store. She'd long ago decided she loved Izzy too much to mind, though, even if she still envied her long dark hair and olive-toned skin, and the way she never seemed to age or doubt herself.

"I'm starving." Alexis glanced through the clear plastic sheets the waitstaff had pulled over the screened-in porch, preparing for the squall. "Not much sea for such a heavy sky."

"Give it ten minutes." Izzy paused. "How are things?"

"Complicated," Alexis said, wondering if her godmother had somehow known early that morning, when she'd called with a lunch invite, that her goddaughter's life was going to have taken a big dump in the great cosmic toilet bowl by noon. "Let's just say the weather's not the only thing that's going to be changing around here."

Izzy idly rubbed her inner right forearm in a habitual gesture, pulling the skin tight across a pair of old, faded tattoos. One was of a disembodied hand touching a smiling face; the other was a stylized symbol that might've been a vaguely reptilian head beneath a puff of smoke.

Alexis had expected questions, or sympathy, or something after her dire pronouncement. Instead, Izzy had a seriously weird look on her face.

"Iz?" Alexis asked after a moment. "Are you okay?" Her problems with Aaron took a quick backseat to a spurt of worry. She'd lost both her parents before her second birthday. If she lost Izzy, too . . . Panic backed up quickly, closing her throat and making her force the words. "What's wrong? Are you sick?"

Izzy shook her head but remained silent as the bartender delivered their drinks. When he was gone, she said quietly, "You know all those stories I told you growing up?"

"Of course," Alexis said, puzzled. Granted, the first words out of Izzy's mouth weren't *I went to the doctor,* or *I have cancer,* but she wasn't sure she was relieved yet. Her godmother's expression was too strange. "What about the stories?" she asked, then as a thought occurred: "Are you finally thinking of getting them published?"

Izzy had all these great stories about gods and ancient

magical warriors. More detailed than Tolkien, more mythos-based than *Star Wars* . . . Alexis had always thought the book would sell in a heartbeat. God, she could practically see the cover, with a handsome, dark-haired warrior who wore a hawk's insignia at his throat, and—

She jolted, then coughed and grabbed for her drink to cover the depth of her response to the image. Where the hell had *that* come from? *More important, where can I meet him?*

"Not exactly." Izzy reached over and took her god-daughter's right hand, turning it palm up to show the lighter underside of Alexis's forearm, where she'd neglected her tanning. "What if I told you that all of those stories were true?"

Cara Liu frowned at her father, Carlos. "I'd say, 'Bull-shit,' but you raised me better than that." She pulled off her Stetson and messed with her long, dark hair, feeling the different texture of the white section in front, the one her friends called a skunk stripe. Beneath her, Coyote, the blue roan gelding she'd raised from a foal, shifted his weight and flicked an ear back as though sensing her distress but realizing she wasn't in any immediate danger under the wide-open Montana sky.

The horses stood on a low ridge that sloped down to the farthest fence line of the Findlay Ranch, which Carlos had managed for more than two decades. It was Cara's home. Her sanctuary. She'd come back for the summer intending to take stock of her life. Instead, it looked like she needed to deal with the distinct possibility that her father was losing his mind.

She glanced at him, searching for a sign that this was some sort of elaborate setup, maybe for a welcome-home party. Hell, she'd even settle for one of his famous "I feel like you're going in the wrong direction" talks.

At sixty-three, Carlos sat straight in his saddle, his spine stiff as always, as if he were forever trying to combat his five-foot-nine-inch stature. His dark hair was short and gray-shot, his skin deeply tanned with the color neither of them lost completely even during the long winter months. Now, as she'd seen him do so many times before, he stared off toward the horizon, where blue-gray mountains rose up to touch the low-hanging clouds, and the look in his eye made her think he was seeing something else entirely.

"This is a joke, right?" she said. "I'm being *Punk'd*. Where are the cameras?"

Carlos shook his head. "No cameras, baby, and no joke. Twenty-four years ago King Scarred-Jaguar and the Nightkeepers sacrificed themselves in order to close the intersection, but in the last minutes before the spell took hold, terrible creatures came through and killed all but a few of their children." The faraway look in his eyes darkened. "I was there. I saved and raised the child entrusted to me. Now the king's son has called the survivors home."

"This *is* home," Cara protested automatically.

"Give me your hand."

"Seriously, where are the cameras? Who put you up to this? It was Dino and Treece, wasn't it? They haven't forgiven me yet for that thing with the goat."

"Your hand, Cara Liu." He was deadly serious.

A tremor started deep down inside Cara's stomach and spread outward. She'd known her father had been depressed since her mother's death eighteen months earlier, but she hadn't realized it'd gotten this bad. She should've come home more, should've called more.

What the hell was going on? And what was she supposed to do with a grown man who'd confused fiction with reality but otherwise seemed like his old self?

Using her knees, she cued Coyote to move up alongside her father's sorrel, so the two horses were nose-to-tail and she faced her father squarely. She saw sadness in his eyes, and regrets. She didn't see craziness, but what exactly did crazy look like?

Wishing she'd taken Abnormal Psych last semester instead of Ancient Mythology—most of which she'd already known anyway—she held out her right hand, expecting him to grab it, maybe give her something he thought proved what he was saying.

Instead, he drew the jade-handled knife he'd worn at

his waist for as long as she could remember, and sliced the blade sharply across his palm. Blood welled up as Cara gasped. Before she could recover, he grabbed her hand and cut her as well.

"Daddy!" She tried to jerk away but he held her fast, gripping her wrist tightly as she struggled. "Stop it. Let go!"

Coyote shied sideways, but her father hung on to her wrist, dragging her from the saddle as the blue roan bolted off. She fell in slow motion, her father lowering her to the ground and following her down, still holding her wrist. Once they were both kneeling, he shifted his grip and clasped her bloody hand with his.

She thought he whispered, "I'm sorry." But she couldn't be sure, because there was a sudden roaring noise in her head, and the grass seemed to surge beneath her as he spoke in a language she'd never heard before, but that seemed to call to something deep inside her when he said, *"Aj-winikin."*

No cameras, she thought, gasping for breath as an invisible pressure grabbed onto her, holding her in place. *It's for real. Oh, God. Oh, shit. Oh, shit.*

Terror flared alongside pain.

Carlos lifted his face to the sky and raised their joined hands so their mingled blood ran down the insides of their forearms, where he wore a couple of old tattoos. "Gods!" he shouted now in English, maybe for her benefit, maybe for his own. "Accept this child as your servant!"

Wind erupted from nowhere, lashing the hot summer air against them, around them, forming a swirling vortex with them at its center. Cara's straw Stetson blew off and her hair whipped free, plastering itself to her face and getting in her mouth when she screamed, "Daddy!"

Then, as if that scream were a sign, the wind funnel abruptly reversed itself, sucking upward into the cloudless sky. And disappearing.

In the utter silence that followed, which was undisturbed by even the rustle of branches or the cry of a hawk, Cara scrambled up, eyes bugging. "You're losing it. Or I am. Maybe both of us. Mass hallucination."

"Hallucination?" He took her hand and turned it palm up, then held it beside his. The cuts were gone, leaving only long, thin scars.

Cara gaped. "That's impossible."

"It's magic," he said simply. "Push up your sleeve."

Numbly, dumbly, she did as she was told, unfastening the single button that held the bloodstained cuff of her denim work shirt in place and rolling it up, part of her knowing what she was going to see before she saw it.

Her forearm, which had been bare that morning, was now marked with the perfect outline of a canine head, a tattoo where there hadn't been one before. Its nose was rounded, its tongue and teeth pointed, its mouth slashed in a snarl. Below it was the image of a hand touching a face. Her father made a sound of utter satisfaction and held his own forearm next to hers. There, he had the same two marks, along with a newer mark she didn't remember having seen before, shaped like a bird of some sort. Maybe a hawk.

His voice was gruff with emotion when he said, "Welcome to the family, Cara."

She struggled to breathe normally, struggled to do *anything* normally as her heart pounded in her chest and low-grade nausea twisted in her gut. She looked around and saw that the ridge and fence line looked as they always had; the sky was blue and the sorrel grazed peacefully nearby. Coyote was long gone, but he'd always been spooky like that. Luckily, he also had a good homing instinct. No doubt they'd find him in his pen, chowing down on his evening ration of pellets.

That thought, that normal, everyday thought, lodged a ball of emotion in her throat, part panic, part . . . excitement. She glanced at her father and saw pride in his eyes, as though she'd just done something wonderful, just *become* something wonderful. Which she had, she realized. If her father was telling the truth, she'd woken up half a semester away from a journalism degree she wasn't sure she wanted anymore, and in the space of the past five minutes she'd become Wonder Woman. A magic user. *Holy crap.*

Her lips curved and she touched the marks on her

arm, feeling a faint buzz jangle through her system at the contact. "Does this mean I can do all those things you used to tell me about? It's all real? I'm a . . . a Nightkeeper?"

"Um. Not exactly."

She narrowed her eyes. "What do you mean, 'not exactly'?"

Quick hurt flashed across his face and was just as quickly masked. "You're my true daughter. My heart. My blood." Then he waited, as he'd done ever since she was a little girl when he wanted her to figure out something for herself rather than telling her the answer straightaway.

When it clicked, Cara shot to her feet, elation morphing to betrayal, anger, shame—a sickening mix of emotions that cranked her volume as she shouted, "You're fucking kidding me! I'm a *winikin*?"

He didn't chide her for her language, which just proved she was right.

She wasn't Wonder Woman. She was a sidekick. Even worse, she was a sidekick to—

"Oh, no." She backpedaled, nearly falling when she stumbled on a rock. "Oh, hell, no. You're shitting me. *Sven?*"

But if—even for an instant—she bought into the delusion that the *winikin* were real, then her adopted older brother fit the description of a Nightkeeper all too well. Where she and her father were small and olive-skinned, with dark hair and eyes, Sven was their exact opposite in every way. He was over six-three and as wide as two of her father standing side by side. His skin was fair, his dark blond hair prone to bleaching in the sun, and where she had always been happy with the small pleasures of ranch life, he'd lusted for bigger and better, for the next challenge, the next conquest.

Sven lived life right out loud and loved being the center of attention. He was the true golden boy. At least, he had been. She hadn't seen him in close to five years, and that wasn't nearly long enough for her.

Her father nodded. "Yes. Sven is a Nightkeeper."

"How fitting," Cara said, looking at the mark on her wrist. "He's a dog."

"The Coyote bloodline is old and respected, as are its *winikin*," he said, voice chiding.

"Don't call yourself a servant, and don't call me one, either," Cara snapped. "I'm nobody's slave."

"A *winikin* is no slave," her father said with quiet dignity. "We protect the magic users, and help them stay the moral path."

"News flash. You didn't do so hot on the morality thing." No wonder he'd never wanted to face the truth about Sven. That would've meant accepting that the child—the Nightkeeper child—he'd raised wasn't perfect. Far from it, in fact. Sven had been a spoiled, mean-tempered brat who'd grown into a moody teen, and from there to a young man who'd been far too attractive for his own good, and did his own thing regardless of how it affected others.

"Cara—"

"I don't want this," she said, scrubbing at the mark on her arm. "Take it back."

"I can't . . . I need you. The Nightkeepers need you. The king has recalled the survivors, but one among them has lost his *winikin*. They've asked me to teach him, which means I need you to take my place watching over Sven."

She glared at him, furious that he'd done something like this without asking her. "Fine. I'll slap some makeup on it, or get a coverup tattoo. Maybe scrub it with some bleach first."

"That won't change anything." He didn't even have the grace to look ashamed. He seemed calm now, calmer than he'd been since the funeral, or maybe even before that. It was like he knew where he was going for the first time in a long, long while.

The realization terrified her.

This shit was for real.

"Daddy," she whispered, her heart breaking a little when she realized that nothing would be the same ever again. "I don't want this. I can't . . . work for him, whatever you want to call it. I can't be around him."

He looked sad. "You don't have a choice."

She didn't argue with that, because there was a hum in the back of her brain that hadn't been there before, an impulse that made her want to walk, to pace, to jump on the sorrel and ride hard, covering ground, headed southeast to the Carolina coast, where—the last they'd heard, anyway—Sven was wreck diving for conquistador gold.

"I won't go to him," she whispered. "You can't make me."

Her father stood and strode toward his horse, and for a half second she thought he was going to ride away and leave her there. Instead, he leaned down and retrieved her hat from where it had snagged on a thick stand of heavy grass. He dusted off the straw brim and crossed to her, holding out the Stetson like a peace offering. "Please. He needs you. We all need you. There are so few of us and so little time." He paused. "Remember the stories I told you about the end-time?"

She stiffened, thinking back to the darkest of his dark stories. "The apocalypse?"

He nodded, glancing once again up into the sky. "It's coming, baby. You and me and the others . . . we've got a little over four years to save the world."

Patience White-Eagle lowered the phone and pressed her palms to the kitchen countertop.

Gods, why now? After all those years she'd wished the magic worked, wished she really were the person Hannah claimed, why did everything have to change *now*?

She lifted the phone again. "Are you sure?"

"I wouldn't have made this call otherwise," her godmother replied simply, and with quiet dignity. Hannah was more mother to Patience than godmother, having raised her from infancy. She'd insisted on the distinction of being called "godmother," though, just as she'd insisted on so many things relating to Patience's biological parents. Some days it had seemed stifling and unnecessary. Other times, like when the *winikin* had started teaching Patience about the responsibilities of her blood-line, the rules had made sense.

Now, though, nothing made sense. Or, rather, it did, but Patience didn't like the sense it made. Not one bit, which left her standing in her utterly normal-looking kitchen outside Philadelphia, talking on a disposable cell phone about things that were far from normal.

She'd believed Hannah's stories . . . or at least she'd thought she did. Now, though, she wondered whether on some level she'd seen them as a lovely fantasy, fairy tales that made her feel special without really changing anything. Because if she'd believed in the Nightkeepers and their purpose, really believed it deep down inside, she wouldn't have made some of the choices she'd made, would she?

Maybe, she acknowledged. *Maybe not.*

She glanced at the gleaming toaster she'd bought just the week before, catching her reflection in the chrome and wondering how she could still look like a normal, if overly tall, blonde-and-blue twenty-four year-old, when she was, apparently, also something more.

"Where and when?" she asked finally, because there had never been a question of whether she'd come when her king called—she had a king; how messed up was that?—it was purely a question of how to juggle the other responsibilities Hannah knew nothing about.

"I'm flying out tonight. If you like, we can meet at the airport and drive over together." Hannah always made everything seem so matter-of-fact, regardless of whether she was talking about a quick swing through Jiffy Lube, or the end of the world.

Patience mentally ran through her options, which were pretty limited. "I'll have to check into flights and stuff, and get someone to cover my classes for the foreseeable future." Fortunately, as the owner of White-Eagle Martial Arts, she didn't have to ask for the time off. She could just make it happen. Other things, however, weren't so easy. "How about you e-mail me the directions and I'll meet you there?"

"Sounds like a plan," Hannah said. Patience expected

her to hang up without saying good-bye, which was her way. Instead, the older woman's voice softened. "Are you okay with this?"

Do I have a choice? Patience thought, but she didn't ask the question aloud, because she'd been raised knowing that she wasn't like the other kids—she needed to be better, faster, smarter, a little more of everything. "I'm fine," she said, willing herself to believe it. "I've waited my whole life for this call."

"Good girl," Hannah said. And hung up.

Patience just stood there for a long moment, staring at the toaster.

She was a magic user. A Nightkeeper. Her king was calling her home.

Thing was, she already *was* home.

Keep yourself apart, Hannah had taught her. *Be ready to disappear at a moment's notice. Once the end-time has passed you can live the life you want. Until then you belong to the Nightkeepers. There is no other attachment more important than that.*

She hadn't listened, though. Or, rather, she'd listened, but an impulsive spring-break trip to Cancún and way too much tequila had dictated a change in plans.

As though called by the thought, her husband's footsteps sounded in the hallway. Moments later, he filled the kitchen doorway, all broad shoulders and rippling muscles, graced with thick sable brown hair and a sharply angled, handsome face that should've been in magazines but instead was hers. All hers.

Lips curving, she crossed the kitchen, slipping the cell into the pocket of her jeans as she went and hoping he wouldn't notice it wasn't her usual phone. Heat rose when she bumped her hip against his, then moved in for a kiss.

They'd been together a little more than four years and it was still the same heat, the same addiction. She craved him like a drug, with an aching intensity that seemed, if anything, to grow stronger as time passed.

Just as she was thinking of backing him down the short hallway to the master bedroom of their split-level, he broke the kiss and touched his forehead to hers, leaning down so she saw his gold-flecked brown eyes up close, and saw the shadows deep within them.

She leaned back in his arms and frowned. "What's wrong?"

"I just got off the phone with Taylor. There's been a major cluster fuck with the zoning on the Chicago project. It was supposed to have been handled, but . . ." He lifted one shoulder. "I'll probably be gone through next week, and I hate like hell to dump everything on you."

"I can get Joanie to help me out," Patience said, trying to camouflage the immediate spurt of relief. As a rising star in the world of corporate architecture, he often had to take off on a moment's notice. The emergency call couldn't have come at a better time, as it gave her the weekend to figure things out. She tightened her arms around his waist, loving the good, solid feel of him. "Promise to miss me?"

"I already do." He kissed her quickly, then disengaged. "I've got to pack. My plane leaves in a couple hours."

The next twenty minutes were a whirlwind of getting him out the door. Before he left, though, he took her hand and turned it palm up so he could kiss the tattoos at her wrist, a stylized lizard's head beside a cluster of circles that looked like a Pacman gone wrong. His own tattoos, consisting of a matching Pac-Man beside a tribal-looking eagle's head, were covered by the sleeve of his starched shirt and suit coat, but she knew they were there, knew the symbols bound them together just as surely as their white-gold wedding bands.

The tattoos, like their relationship, had come from a half-remembered night of carousing in the Yucatán. They'd awakened in her hotel room, two strangers who'd obviously made love, with dirty feet and fresh tats that, oddly enough, hadn't hurt. Patience could only assume that she'd chosen the tattoos, placing them where Hannah said the Nightkeepers wore their bloodline glyphs. The lizard was her bloodline signature. The eagle, she guessed, had come from his last name, which was now hers. She didn't know about the Pac-Man.

He smiled as he linked his fingers with hers and leaned in for a last, lingering kiss. "Miss me."

It was a command, not a question, but she didn't argue. Instead, she pressed her cheek to his and hung on a moment longer than usual. "Back atcha."

Then he left, striding down their flagstone walkway with his garment bag and computer case slung over his shoulder. Uncharacteristically, Patience stood at the front door, watching as he backed his Explorer out of the garage and drove off with a beep-beep and a wave.

She couldn't help feeling that she wasn't going to see him again.

When the alarm went off before dawn, Sven grabbed for the clock, intending to chuck it at the nearest wall. He came up with his cell phone instead, and realized that was what'd been ringing.

"Oh, for fuck's sake." He flipped the thing open, squinting into the too-bright light in an effort to make sense of the caller ID, but last night's drunk hadn't yet turned into today's hangover, and he couldn't see the letters.

Didn't matter, though. His so-called partner was the only a-hole likely to be calling at this hour, and if Fontana was calling postparty, he'd be too blitzed to make a lick of sense. He could wait. Besides, it was already too late to answer—the damn call had gone to voice mail while Sven was staring at the display.

Head still drumming with the backbeat from last night's dance music, he dropped the phone on the floor and rolled over, dragging the bedsheet with him. The motion earned a feminine, "Hey!"

Surprised, Sven rolled back and did the squinting thing again, this time making out a pouty brunette. *Huh. Go figure.* He didn't feel lucky, but apparently he'd gotten there sometime last night. *Sweet.*

She crooked a finger and slid him a look as she shimmied her torso in a fake shiver. "Can I have the sheet back? I'm cold."

"Take it." He tossed it in her direction, too out-of-it to decide whether she was actually cold, or sending him a green light. "I gotta pee."

Okay, even woozy he knew that wasn't a great line.

But by the time he'd taken care of business and splashed some cold water in the direction of his face, he'd regrouped and was ready for a second—and hopefully more memorable—assault on Mount Brunette.

"Hey, babe," he said as he strolled into the bedroom. "I was thinking—" He broke off when he saw that the bed was empty.

Bummer.

Figuring on writing it off as her loss and catching another few hours of shut-eye, Sven was headed back to the bed when he heard female voices out in the main room.

Voices, as in more than one female. *Cool.* He was the man.

Suddenly really, really wishing he could remember the night before—and hoping he could talk them into round two—he pulled on a pair of swim trunks and strode through the door into the main room of his beachside apartment.

And stopped dead at the sight of the girl, or rather the woman, standing in the open doorway. Sunlight spilled in behind her, gleaming on her dark, white-streaked hair and outlining her boy-slim, athletic body.

She might have been wearing shorts, a tank, and sandals instead of jeans and a work shirt, but he knew her instantly even through the fog in his brain. The gut-punch was unmistakable.

"Cara?"

She didn't say anything, just let her gaze roam around his apartment, where surfboards and dive gear were piled atop depth charts and the odd artifact, competing for space amid what he liked to call creative clutter but suspected she would see as garbage.

The brunette—who was still wearing his sheet, for chrissake—looked at Sven, brow furrowed. "This your girlfriend or something?"

"No," he said quickly. "She's—" Then he broke off, because he'd never been able to figure out what to call her. She wasn't his sister, not really. She wasn't his friend, either, not now, anyway. She was—

"I'm his little sister," she said, apparently not sharing

an ounce of his dislike for the term. Focusing on him, she said, "Get dressed and pack your things. We're leaving."

Sven's gut iced over. "Is something wrong with Carlos?"

"Yes and no." She paused, and for a second he thought he saw a crack in the disdain she was projecting like plate armor. "Look, please don't ask me to explain. Just pack."

The brunette pouted and turned to him. "Are you going to let her talk to you like that?"

The look in Cara's eyes said, *You owe me.*

And the hell of it was, he did.

Sven nodded slowly. "Yeah. I am." He glanced at the brunette. "Get dressed and get out. Apparently I have a plane to catch."

CHAPTER SIX

"Nearly half of them have confirmed." Strike went down the list. "We've got flight info for Alexis Gray, along with Coyote-Seven and Patience Lizbet, and their *winikin*, one of which is a substitute, so we can shift manpower over to Nathan Blackhawk when the time comes."

He and Jox were sitting on lounge chairs out on the pool deck of the mansion, while the cleanup continued around them. They'd been at the training compound in New Mex for a week now, and after few days of DIY had sucked it up and used the Nightkeeper Fund to hire a couple of local crews to strip the junk and update the facilities. Granted, it would've been better to keep the place out of the public eye, but that just hadn't been feasible. Besides, with the traffic they were expecting starting in the next few days, it would've been pretty tough to keep the place a secret for long.

So far, none of the workers had mentioned the little detail that there hadn't been any buildings in the out-of-the-way box canyon up until a week ago, yet the place clearly dated back to the turn of the twentieth century and showed a couple decades' worth of neglect. Either the locals didn't know about the compound's appear-disappear-reappear routine, or they'd decided the generous pay made up for the freak factor.

"Carlos is a good man," Jox said. "A good *winikin*. He'll help Blackhawk adjust."

That had been the first bit of bad news after the initial buzz of learning about the survivors: At least one of their *winikin* hadn't lived long.

Jox's list was twenty-four years old, garnered from notes dropped to a P.O. box in Shiprock, a few hundred miles north of the compound. As per the escape protocol drilled into each *winikin* at maturity, they'd left basic contact information and a confirmation word, and then gone underground and found their way into regular society, focusing on the child—or children—they'd saved. They'd modernized the young Nightkeepers' names to make mainstreaming easier—the smoke, lizard, and harvester bloodlines had become the surnames Gray, Lizbet, and Farmer for the females. Among the males, Coyote-Seven had been shortened to Sven, while Blackhawk, White-Eagle, and Stone had been common enough surnames that they'd stayed as they were.

Through the magic of Google and a private investigator named Carter, a friend of a friend of Jox's who would cheerfully hack into the IRS database for a hefty fee, they'd found current addresses for almost all of the survivors. Unfortunately, they also learned that the *winikin* to the sole survivor of the hawk bloodline had succumbed to his wounds within a few days of escaping from the *boluntiku*. His charge had wound up in the foster system with no clue who—or what—he was. Carter had eventually turned up info indicating that Nathan Blackhawk had bounced around a bit until he wound up in Chicago, where he'd done a few years in juvie, and a few more in Greenville for grand theft auto. Since then, he seemed to have gone straight, moving to Denver and launching a small but successful computer gaming company.

And he'd ducked every one of Strike's calls.

"I'm going to have to go there in person." Strike grimaced and looked around. "There's a shitload left to be done before this place is workable."

They'd made some progress, granted. The kidney-shaped pool had been pumped, scrubbed, resealed, and filled, and the subcontractor had installed a new filter system and creepy-crawly pool cleaner. The pool area, a seventies-era cement deck that was pretty low on the priority list for updating, was surrounded by the mansion on three sides. The fourth side was open, with a view of the traditional ball court the Nightkeepers had used to blow off steam, and occasionally for ceremonial games. The two high parallel stone walls, with a single stone hoop set some twenty feet up on either side, had stood the test of time pretty well, as had the "real" ball courts in the Yucatán and Central America. Pretty much everything else in the training compound was in tough shape, though.

The plumbing, electricals, and carpets in the mansion were being gutted and redone, and they'd made the decision to tear the barn down and start over with a steel-span building, rather than trying to salvage the sagging wreck. They would use the space not for horses and mules for pack trips into the backcountry, as before, but for what Jox was dubbing Magic 101—on the theory that it'd be best to unleash the untrained magi in a fireproof space.

"Go to Denver," Jox said, waving him off. "Admit it—you're dying to get away from this place. Too many memories."

"For all of us." Strike couldn't deny that he was edgy being back in the compound. There were ghosts in every room of every building, and around every corner. In the aftermath of the massacre he'd made it a point not to think about his life before, and over the years those memories had faded. Now, triggered by each sight and smell, they'd returned with a vengeance.

His father had loved baseball. How had he forgotten that? Scarred-Jaguar had taught Strike to switch-hit, and had pounded fungoes for fielding practice. They'd watched the Rangers on TV, and took weekend trips twice a year for back-to-back games at Arlington Stadium.

And his mother . . . his mother had been thin and elegant, with close-cropped dark hair and a core of steel, wearing a warrior's mark in her own right. Yet she'd been the one to kiss his skinned knees and make them better. She'd nearly fainted at the sight of his scalp split open when he'd fallen from the pueblo ruins at the back of the compound, after trying to make it up to the walled-off kiva on a dare. How had he forgotten any of those things?

"It hasn't been fun for any of us," Strike said. "Don't think I haven't seen you turn a funny color now and then, and Red-Boar . . . well, you know."

The older Nightkeeper had withdrawn even more, shutting himself away in the four-room house behind the mansion where he'd lived with his family before the massacre. Rabbit lived in the second bedroom of the small cottage, helping with the demo when he felt like it, and spending the rest of the time sitting high up in the pueblo ruins with his iPod.

The four of them were farther apart than they'd ever been before, which made Strike wonder how great a leader he was going to be if he couldn't even manage the team spirit of one *winikin* along with a zonked-out Nightkeeper and his half-blood son.

"Your father was a good king," Jox said, as if he knew Strike needed the reassurance. "In some ways you're very like him; you walk the same, and the way you fill the room just by being in it, that's the same. That's genetics, and the blood-magic. But in other ways you're not alike at all; you question yourself and others around you far more than he ever did, and you're more a man of today than he was of his time. That's environment, I think. Nature versus nurture. He was raised knowing every single day of his life who he was and where he fit within his people. He was taught to lead, and his warriors were taught to be led."

Strike grimaced. "Not exactly the situation we've got now."

"Blood tells," Jox said. "You're your father's son. You'll find a way."

"I'd better, or none of this is going to matter in a few years. Or, hell, a few months." There was no doubt in his mind that when the fall equinox came in just under eleven weeks, the *ajaw-makol* was going to try to bring a *Banol Kax* through the barrier, thus triggering the thirteenth prophecy by bringing a dark lord to earth in the final five years before the zero date.

That was assuming they didn't find a way to neutralize the creature first. Since they didn't have an *itza'at* seer to track the evil, they'd had to improvise. He'd asked the investigator, Carter, to get all the background info possible on the man Leah had known as Zipacna, and his Survivor2012 group. According to the PI, the 2012ers hadn't seen their leader since the solstice, and when Strike had teleported Red-Boar to their group's headquarters, neither of them had detected *makol* magic from within, suggesting that the bastard was in the wind.

Carter was watching for Zipacna to reappear, and the PI was tracking bulk purchases of several rare ingredients necessary to the magic of the *Banol Kax*. Hopefully, one of those lines of investigation would lead them to the *ajaw-makol*.

In the meantime, Strike had a fighting force to assemble.

He said, "We don't have arrival info for the eagle, stone, or harvester bloodlines, but I spoke with their *winikin*, who've promised to get their Nightkeepers here by the first of next month at the absolute latest . . . which is cutting it close."

Although the barrier was most active during each solstice and equinox, other conjunctions could be used for ceremonies if necessary. The next one on the calendar was the aphelion, which fell, ironically, on the Fourth of July. Strike and Red-Boar were planning to use that day to jack in the new trainees and get them their bloodline marks, and their first taste of power. That'd give them a little over two months to cram in an entire childhood of magic theory before the next ceremonial day, the Venus conjunction, when they'd perform the talent ceremony that would give the newbies their talent marks and increase the Nightkeepers' ranks from two to lucky thirteen.

After the Venus conjunction, they would have a scant nine days until the fall equinox, when the *ajaw-makol* was most likely to make his move, and when the skyroad connecting the heavens and earth would once again open up, providing the Nightkeepers an opportunity to bring a god to earth and create a Godkeeper.

Again, in theory.

"The trainees will be here in time," Jox said. "Their *winikin* won't let you down." His tone indicated that they'd better damn well not. He held out a hand. "Give me the list. I'll make a few more calls and see about tracking down the stragglers."

They hadn't been able to contact the last two *winikin*. The star twins' *winikin* wasn't returning calls, and the serpent boy's *winikin* was nowhere to be found.

"Sounds like a plan." Strike rose. "And do me a favor? See if you can get Rabbit interested in the construction projects. I don't like how much time he's spending by himself."

"Like father, like son." But Jox nodded. "I'll see what I can do."

"Thanks." Strike paused. "I guess I've got a date in Denver, then." Not like he was going to make an appointment. Nathan Blackhawk was in for a surprise.

"Make sure that's where you go." Jox fixed him with a look. "No detours."

"Shit." Strike scowled at his *winikin*. "You sure you're not an *itza'at*?"

"Doesn't take a seer to know you've got a woman on your mind, and it doesn't take a genius to figure out which one. Remember, 'The king's duty is to the gods above all others, then to his people; all else comes after,' " the *winikin* said, quoting from the writs. He paused, then said, "Red-Boar and I talked about this some. His theory is that the dreams came from the barrier as it was reactivating. In the last few months before a mage hits puberty, the hormones go totally wonky. Since you didn't get your talent mark back when you were a teenager, there's a good chance all those hormones got packed into a few weeks once Zipacna's sacrifices thinned the barrier enough that the magic started to leak through."

"I've heard Red-Boar's wet-dream theory," Strike muttered. "That's not what it was."

"You've always had a thing for blue-eyed blondes

with a bit of an edge to them. Is there any wonder that's what your subconscious fixed on?"

"I didn't see just any blue-eyed blonde. I saw Leah."

"The mind can play tricks." The *winikin* laid a hand on his shoulder, a fatherly gesture that irked the shit right out of him. "Five of the survivors are female, including the twins."

Strike gritted his teeth. "Matchmaking, Jox?"

The *winikin* didn't bother looking ashamed. "Mate-bonded Nightkeepers are stronger together than they are apart. You'd serve your people better to choose one of your own kind."

Thoroughly annoyed, and halfway wishing his father had been a dogcatcher or something, Strike pushed himself to his feet. "I'll call you from Denver."

Nathan Blackhawk scowled as he scanned his laptop screen. Handheld computer sales were up, indicating that the gamers had latched on to the upgraded pod, which gave players near VR quality control over their characters. Problem was, the games themselves weren't showing the same spike, whereas his competitors' products were flying off the shelves.

"Goddamn violent-ass kids," he muttered under his breath, spinning in his chair and glaring at his office walls, which were painted the same glossy black as his furniture. "They'd rather blow shit up than use their brains."

It didn't escape him that he'd been exactly that sort of kid until a stint in juvie and a social worker who hadn't taken "fuck off and die" as an answer had set him more or less straight. But it probably served him right for thinking he could change the thought process of an entire generation with the physics of extreme sports and a handful of quest sagas that contained far more actual history than your average LOTR rip-off.

It'd taken balls—and admittedly a bit of bloodless disregard—to leave the software company that'd given him his start, promoting him to developer despite his lack of a formal degree. It'd taken even more testicular fortitude to hire a bunch of nobodies like himself and call the whole mess a software gaming company, but he'd made it work; for the first three years Hawk Enterprises had made obscene amounts of money selling the same sort of bloodthirsty pap the rest of the industry spewed out. When Nathan had started tweaking things a year ago, though, sales hadn't kept up, and now the frigging profit-and-loss charts were looking grim.

"Hey, boss?" A quick knock on the door frame followed Denjie's hail. Before Nathan could answer—or not—the sandy-haired programmer, rotund and wearing tight black jeans, an obscene concert T-shirt, and electric blue–framed glasses, stuck his head through the door.

Nate held up a hand before Den could start. "I know, I know. I'll have a decision for you on the new blood-'n'-guts slasherfest by this afternoon."

The programmer drew himself up to his full five-seven. "If you're referring to *EmoPunk III*, then I'm not sure why there's any question in your puny excuse for a brain. *EP3* is going to be a freakin' best seller."

"It's also freakin' nasty, and guaranteed to curdle the gray matter of anyone stupid enough to play it."

"Which is why it's going to outsell the shit out of your pathetic *Viking Warrior* franchise, and do double the numbers of all the celebrity skateboarder VRs combined. But that's not why I'm in here." Den hooked a thumb over his shoulder. "Guy's here to see you."

Nate frowned. "What guy?"

"Dunno. Dark hair, cool tats. He buzzed from downstairs, said he had an appointment. I put him in the conference room."

"I don't have any—" Nate broke off as Den ducked out again, clearly not giving a shit whether or not the guy's story was true. "Damn it."

Nate knew he really ought to get a receptionist, someone who'd help him organize things and run interference. But he'd never bothered, mostly because their games were sold under the aegis of a bigger company, which meant that Hawk Enterprises flew pretty far under the radars of most gaming crazies, leaving them relatively unmolested.

That, and the fact that he liked to do things his way, all the way.

The bad news was that the lack of a receptionist meant he was sometimes ambushed by ambitious low-level developers, along with the occasional wacko who wanted to meet Hera, the stacked blond heroine from the *Viking Warrior* games. Not to mention that he got to personally field the weird-ass phone calls, like the one he'd gotten the week before from some guy who claimed to have information about Nate's parents. Yeah, like he'd never heard that one before.

The good news about having no receptionist, though, was that it left him free to ignore people until they went away. He seriously considered doing exactly that with the guy in the conference room, but since his other options seemed limited to P&L statements or going over the *EP3* projections again, he climbed to his feet and headed for the conference room.

The offices of Hawk Enterprises took up the front quarter of a warehouse, with the rest of the building left open for real-time modeling of X-stunts using VR suits and the semipermanent half-pipes and ramps they'd built with some of the early money. At the moment, most of the pending projects were either in the conception phase or final testing, so the stunt area was deserted. That was a relief, because it could get damn loud back there when the adrenaline junkies got the music blasting and started trying to outdo one another.

Bypassing the break room—no way he was offering his uninvited guest coffee until he knew what the guy wanted—Nate headed down a short corridor to the conference room.

Whereas the developers had each done up their own offices—ranging from Nate's all-black to Glitch's ode to *Battlestar Galactica*—the conference room looked pretty normal. The same could not be said for the man who stood staring through the floor-length windows overlooking the half-pipe in the warehouse beyond. He was six-five if he was an inch, with long black hair dropping to his massive shoulders and features that looked like they

belonged in *Viking Warrior 5: Odin's Return*. He was
wearing black cargo pants, scarred lace-up boots, and a
wide webbed utility belt, with a white button-down shirt
that saved the look from being straight out of military-
surplus-goes-Goth. Barely.

The stranger turned and took a long look that made
Nate feel as though he were being judged, or maybe
weighed. "You're Nathan Blackhawk," the guy said. It
wasn't a question.

"And you're trespassing," Nate replied, more or less
pleasantly. "Lucky for you I'm in a good mood. You've
got five minutes."

"That'll do." The stranger shot his cuffs, unbuttoned
one, and bared his right forearm to reveal four black-
ink tattoos: a stylized leopard's head of some sort, along
with three unfamiliar symbols that stirred something
deep inside Nate.

"Nice ink," he said casually, wondering if he should
call Denjie in, or maybe the cops. This guy was registering pretty high on the freak-o-meter.

"Ever seen anything like it?"

"Should I have?"

"Where'd you get the chain?" the stranger asked, jerking his chin at Nate's chest. "The hawk medallion."

"None of your goddamn business," Nate said, trying
to keep it on the level, though the pucker factor was
rising quickly. "You're down to four minutes and you're
bugging me. I'd suggest you state your business or go
away."

"I need to talk to you about your parents."

The single sentence, the dream of so many kids in the
foster system, shot through him on a sizzle of anger. He
pointed to the door. "Get. Out."

"Or not." The stranger moved suddenly, grabbing
Nate's wrist.

The battle rage of Nate's youth rose fast and hard,
and he twisted away and swung a punch. The stranger
dodged, got his wrist again, and barked out a word.

And everything went gray-green.

Nate howled and flailed, and suddenly they were outside on the warehouse roof. Scratch that; they were five

feet *above* the warehouse roof for a second before they fell, slamming down in a heap. The stranger recovered first, mostly because Nate felt like he was about to barf up a lung. The guy dragged Nate up, got him halfway over the edge of the roof, and held him there by the front of his shirt. "Are you ready to listen to me yet?"

Nate didn't answer. He gaped. "How . . . what . . . ?"

The stranger nodded, cobalt blue eyes gleaming with satisfaction and something else, something that glittered gold for a moment, then was gone. He reached into the breast pocket of his button-down shirt, withdrew a card, and tucked it into Nate's shirt pocket. "Call this number when you're ready to hear what I have to say. Better yet, just show up at that address. We'll explain, and we'll show you how to use the power that's in your blood." He shook his head. "Bad luck, you losing your protector so young. We've got someone lined up for you, a man named Carlos. He'll get you up to speed."

"Screw you," Nate snapped. "I have a business to run."

Okay, so maybe that was just about the dumbest possible response to being teleported and hung halfway off the side of his own roof, but he was pretty rattled.

"Your games won't matter worth shit four years from now unless you help us out." The stranger cocked his head. "You want to save the world? You're not going to do it with history lectures disguised as video games."

"And I suppose you're going to tell me how I am?"

"You bet your ass." The stranger tapped the card. "Call me." Then he pulled Nate in, away from the edge, and sent him stumbling across the roof.

When Nate turned back, the other man was gone.

Exhausted and nursing the beginnings of a hell of a postmagic hangover—though the shock value had been way worth it—Strike headed for the parking lot outside Blackhawk's converted warehouse, where he'd parked the lame-ass minivan he'd rented rather than risking a series of teleports he was nowhere near ready to navigate.

He was getting better at 'porting, which required him

to picture either a person or a place as a destination. If he thought of a person, the travel thread would appear and take him to their location. If he thought of a place, the thread took him there. He could zap someplace he'd never been based on a photo, but had to be careful about being seen. More, he had to be absolutely certain that he pictured his destination accurately, or he could get his ass stuck halfway between, or worse. Ergo, he was being stingy with his teleports . . . except that the stunt he'd just pulled with Blackhawk, thinking "roof" and getting there, suggested the power stretched farther than any of them suspected.

He wasn't ready to see how far he could push it, though. Thus, the minivan. Once he was in the car, he phoned home.

Jox picked up the call on the fourth ring, and after they'd done the *hey, how are you* thing, asked, "How'd it go with Blackhawk?"

"We'll see. He's going to be tough. Wanted nothing to do with me at first." Strike popped on his cell phone's headset, cranked the engine, and headed for his next appointment, which was in a seriously seedy part of the city.

Carter had finally tracked down the last *winikin*, servant to the serpent bloodline . . . in a mental institution. Through him, the investigator had managed to find the grown Nightkeeper child, also in Denver. The coincidence of two survivors both winding up in the same city had given Strike a bad vibe, as had Snake Mendez himself when he'd gotten the guy on the phone.

Seriously bad vibes. Like *pack a MAC and some jade-tips* bad. Which might've had something to do with Carter's mentioning an outstanding arrest warrant for assault and battery.

"You change his mind?" Jox asked about Blackhawk.

"Either that or I scared the ever-living shit out of him," Strike admitted. "I sort of zapped him onto the roof and dangled him over the side."

"Don't worry, he'll show. The hawk bloodline has too much magic and ego for him to blow it off." The doorbell chimed in the background, and Jox said, "Hang on;

someone's here. Let me just—" He broke off, and then said, *"Hannah."*

And the line went dead.

Jox saw her through the wiggly glass panel beside the front door—just a glimpse, then gone as she reached for the doorbell and rang it a second time. It might've been anyone—anyone female, at least—but he knew it was her. Maybe it was the way she moved, maybe the bright colors she was wearing—strong purples and reds and greens. Or maybe it was just wishful thinking. But there wasn't an iota of doubt in his brain. Hannah had come.

So why, exactly, was he still standing there like he'd grown roots?

"No real reason," he muttered, and forced his feet to unstick. He crossed the foyer and opened the door as she was aiming for doorbell ring number three. "Why are you ringing?" Jox said. "This is your home as much as—"

He broke off as she turned to him, and he saw that the jade green scarf she wore tied around her head was more necessity than fashion statement, dipping across her forehead at an angle and covering her left eye and ear. From beneath the lower edge of the scarf, parallel scars trailed across her cheek and the side of her neck. Six of them.

"Hullo, Jox," she said.

"Hannah." Those damn roots were at it again; he couldn't move. He told himself to just step up, and hug her, for gods' sake. They'd been friends. Hell, he'd kissed her. Twenty-four years ago, but it still counted, right?

Only that'd been before. *After*, they'd said that night, and dared to make plans. Except now it was after, and nothing had gone as they'd hoped. He wanted to say he was sorry, wanted to tell her he still sometimes dreamed about that night, when he'd heard her scream and ran the other way. He wanted to let her know that he'd cried when he'd realized she'd made it out with the baby. He wanted to tell her that he'd carried her address with him for nearly a decade before finally acknowledging that he was never going to call. But the roots had spread up to his tongue, and he couldn't get the words out. Just stood there staring like a moron.

Her good eye, which had been soft and hopeful when he'd opened the door, slowly darkened with disappointment. Her lips turned down, farther on one side than the other because of the scars. She glanced back toward the parking area, like she might head back to her car and take off, but then she squared her shoulders beneath her brightly printed floral shirt and stared him down. "Awful, isn't it?"

"No," he said, but it came out too weak. "Hannah, no. Never." He moved toward her, but it was too late.

She stepped back on the pretext of bending to pick up her duffel—it was black with turquoise and pink flowers—and slung the strap over her shoulder. "Where to?"

"You're the first to arrive," he said, finally getting his tongue unglued from the roof of his mouth. "Where's . . . I guess calling her 'the baby' doesn't work anymore."

That got a smile out of her. "She'd kick your butt for trying. My Patience teaches martial arts. She's a real warrior."

"Now that's good news. Where is she?"

"She'll be here." Hannah sagged a little under the weight of the duffel, but when he moved to take it she shook her head. "I'm fine. Just point me to a bedroom and I'll unload."

He waved to the mansion at large. "Take your pick. We stripped the rooms and redid the walls and floors, so you've got your choice between drywall and carpet or drywall and hardwood, but you can tap the fund for paint and whatever. Just grab a room and have at it."

"Are you in your father's quarters?"

"Yeah, I . . . yeah." It'd been beyond difficult to move into the three-room apartment, but it made the most sense, given its proximity to the royal suite. Of course, that was before Strike moved into the pool house, unable to stay in his parents' quarters—or anywhere else in the mansion, for that matter. Which had made Jox's room choice sort of pointless.

Hannah gave an *of course you did* nod. "Then I'll take one of the singles in the *winikin*'s wing."

"You don't have to," he protested. "There's room for all of us in the main building."

"It wouldn't feel right. You, of all people, should know that."

"What's that supposed to mean?"

"Nothing bad." She closed the distance between them and lifted a hand to cup his cheek. She smiled at him, and the expression was a touch sad, but it stripped away the years and the scars, and he could see the girl he'd known. "Only that your sense of propriety was too bone-deep to have changed, even after all this time." Without waiting for an answer, she brushed past him and headed for the hall leading to the *winikin*'s wing.

Jox cursed under his breath. That had so not gone the way he'd planned. He should follow her. He should ask for a do-over, ask if he could give her a hug, a kiss— hell, a kidney. He was halfway across the sunken great room, headed to do just that, when the phone rang.

He hesitated. Told himself to ignore it, to do what he wanted for a change rather than what he was supposed to do. He made it two more steps. . . .

Then he cursed, detoured to the kitchen, and grabbed the ringing phone. "Jox here."

"It's Carver," the PI said. "I found the last two."

Jox closed his eyes. He'd found the twins. *Thank the gods.* "Where are they?"

"Dead."

CHAPTER SEVEN

Strike navigated the minivan through a twisty series of increasingly narrow streets made narrower by strategic piles of trash. The slow summer dusk had caught up with him, and he flicked on the rental's headlights. The yellow beams picked out the last landmark he'd been given—the freshly burned-out shell of an apartment building, with the busted-out windows and debris that went with such an event.

According to Carter, the fire had broken out the night of the solstice. Strike hoped to hell that was a coincidence.

The buildings on either side didn't look much better than the torched wreck. Their windows were blank, broken, or boarded up—sometimes a mix of all three—indicating that they were empty . . . or at least not occupied by tenants of the paying variety.

Strike parked nose-out in case he had to make a quick exit, and made sure the night dwellers got a look at the autopistol when he climbed out of the mom-mobile. He set the alarm, and the minivan gave an ineffective-sounding *beep-beep* and blinked its lights twice, like an obedient poodle sit-staying in the middle of a minefield. The lights did that delayed-off thing, lighting Strike's way to what used to be the front door of the burned-out wreck.

When he heard the slide of footsteps and the clink of

metal-on-metal behind him, he said, "You don't want to mess with me. It's been a long damn day and I just want to do my business and get out of here."

He didn't expect a response, so it was a surprise when a shadow detached itself from a doorway and sauntered toward him. It was even more of a surprise to see that it was a woman, and a hell of a sexy one at that.

She was long and lean, her face sharp enough to be interesting instead of pretty. Her hair was blue-black and slicked away from her face, and she wore a white halter top along with tight black leather pants and tall boots, an outfit that would've gotten her in trouble in this sort of neighborhood if she hadn't accessorized it with a Beretta nine-millimeter on one side and a cute little .22 chick gun on the other.

By the time she reached him the minivan headlights had clicked off. In the reflected moonlight, he saw her tilt her head and give him an up-and-down. "What sort of business?"

"My own."

"Try again."

"Don't have to."

He thought she'd insist. Instead, she curved her lips in a sweet smile and melted back into the darkness, until all that was left of her was a faint, mocking chuckle. "Well, then, Strike. Have at it."

Which meant either she worked for Snake Mendez, or she was prescient. With the general dearth of actual magic among humankind, Strike was betting on the former as he headed into the damaged building, kicking in the door when the knob jammed.

It wasn't like he was going for stealth. He just wanted the meeting over with.

Cinders crunched underfoot when he strode into the building, damning himself for a fool for not having brought the basics, like night-vision goggles or—duh—a flashlight.

"Sloppy," he said to himself, and halfway thought of trying a quick light spell. But although teleporting came naturally, he'd been struggling with some of the other basics and didn't want to risk a misfire. So he worked by moonlight, moving farther into the building, trying to make out the shapes of what had once been walls and doorways.

"You Strike?" a deep voice said without warning, seeming to come from all around him.

Strike raised the MAC, though there was nothing to shoot at but dark and more dark. "You're a hard guy to track down, Mendez."

"A smart man would've taken the hint."

A roadside flare hissed to cherry red life, sputtering as it was tossed in a spinning arc. It landed on a pile of fire debris off to Strike's right, bathing the scene in an eerie red glow. In the blood-colored illumination, a tall figure materialized out of the shadows, staying close to what looked like a door, or maybe a busted-out window. An escape route. Which made sense, given that Mendez had a warrant outstanding on him.

"I need you to come back to New Mexico with me," Strike said. He lowered the pistol. "I can tell you about your family."

"I know everything I need to know." But Mendez moved forward into the light. The flare showed a big, towering man with a shaved-bald head, sharp features, and pale, intelligent eyes. None of that was a surprise— all of the Nightkeepers were larger than average and practically oozed charisma. The other man's loose gray long-sleeved T-shirt, jeans, and skids weren't surprising, either, though they were tamer than Strike would've expected, given the setting. What was surprising were the tattoos, both because the narrow cuffs of arcane symbols at his wrists were vaguely familiar, and because it was one of the rules the *winikin* had been charged with upholding: The young Nightkeepers weren't supposed to mark their skin. The skin was sacred to the gods, as was blood.

The big man followed Strike's gaze. His eyes flashed as he lifted his hands, crossing his wrists so the tattooed cuffs formed a world cross, the ancestor's icon for the ceiba tree. "You don't approve, *Nochem*?"

The word for "leader" or "king" in the old tongue rocked Strike back. "You know?"

"What do you think?" Mendez uncrossed his wrists, shoved up a sleeve, and offered his forearm, holding it near the light so Strike could see the serpent bloodline glyph, along with the warrior and another, unfamiliar mark. "Kinda cool how it's working now, after all these years."

Shock jolted through Strike. "How did—"

"The gods showed me the way." Mendez snapped his fingers, and a green glow ignited from the tip of his index finger, curled up into the darkness, then guttered and winked out.

In its wake, magic rippled on the air. Power.

Impossible, Strike thought. The *winikin* were sworn not to teach the magic outside the training compound. Yet Mendez knew the old language and the glyphs. If his *winikin* had broken those dicta, what others might he have ignored?

"Let's just say Louis pointed me in the right direction," Mendez said, as though Strike had spoken his thoughts. He shot his sleeves, so the marks were once again covered. "And don't bother hauling him up on charges or anything. His sanity checked out a few years ago." He circled a finger at his temple. "Last I knew, he was in the Parker House of Nuts." He paused. "Dude was bonkers. Kept babbling on about the end of the world."

"He was right," Strike said.

"I know." Mendez grinned with zero humor. "Thing is, I don't figure I owe humanity much of anything, and I sure as hell don't owe you. Unless, of course, you're offering something in return for my services." Another snap, another flame, and though Strike could manage something similar, the color worried him.

Nightkeeper flame was yellow or red. Green and purple were the colors of the *Banol Kax* and the *makol,* but he didn't get that sense off Mendez, either; it was as though he had dark tendencies, but hadn't yet chosen a side.

Strike had a feeling that when he did, it was going to mean trouble. He didn't really want this guy in the compound, but he didn't want to fight him, either. And thirteen was their magic number. There had to be a way to make it fly, because he couldn't walk away from one of the surviving Nightkeepers. "Come with me," he said finally. "We'll work something out."

Mendez snorted. "Here's how it's going to work. You take care of the cops and the ass-pain bounty hunter bitch they've got tracking me, and I'll take a look at your setup. If I like what I see, I'll stay and let you convince me to fight on your team. If not, I'll give you a chance to buy the spellbook off me."

A nasty feeling twisted down Strike's spine alongside a jolt of adrenaline. Did Mendez somehow have one of the lost spellbooks? How? That should've been impossible. "Where's the book now?" he asked, as if he'd known about it all along.

"Safe," Mendez replied. "So why don't you—"

"Sorry to interrupt," a new, female voice said unexpectedly. "But I'm interrupting." There was a *zap-hiss*, and an arc of blue light flared behind Mendez. The big man bowed, going rigid on a silent scream, and then collapsed.

"Freeze!" Strike shouted, levering the MAC as a smaller figure crouched over Mendez's prostrate form. When the figure shifted, he saw black leather and high boots, and recognized the hottie from the alley. "Back off before I put a round in you," he said.

Dual clicks sounded next to his head, one in each ear, as two huge dudes came up behind him on damn silent feet with damn big guns. "Don't be stupid," Leftmost Dude said. "She doesn't want to hurt you. Said you're too pretty to mess up, and the car is a hoot."

Gods, Strike thought on a groan. *Saved by a minivan.* "Okay." He held up the MAC and opened his fingers in the universal gesture of *no harm, no foul.* "Maybe we can make a deal."

"I'm the bounty hunter the cops have tracking Snake here," the hottie said without looking up. "Trust me, with what they're offering, you can't afford me."

Mendez groaned and sucked in a harsh, rattling breath. "Bitch."

"Back atcha," she said, and hit the button on her

Taser, sending another fifty thousand volts or so shooting through his system.

When he was finished twitching, she gestured to her men. "Let's get this meat loaded on the wagon and get the hell out of here." She crossed to Strike, stopping just shy of him. "Can I give you a word of advice? Whatever you're looking for, find an alternative. Snake here is . . ." She trailed off, as if searching for exactly the right word. "Let's just say that of all the seriously screwed-up people I deal with on a daily basis, he is by far the most damaged. He's like a rottweiler that had a really bad puppyhood . . . you can gentle it all you want, but when it comes down to it, the thing's going to be just as likely to bite your arm off as wag its tail."

Strike looked down at the unconscious man. "Shit."

"Couldn't have said it better myself." She turned away. "Stay cool, minivan man."

"Wait!"

She turned back. "What? You want to kiss him goodbye or something?"

Despite everything, Strike found himself grinning, enjoying her. "No. Your name. For reasons I can't even begin to decipher, I'd like to know your name."

She sketched a bow. "Reece Montana at your service. Now, bugger off."

And just like that, the bounty hunter—and the thirteenth Nightkeeper—were gone.

"Well, shit," Strike said, and headed back for the minivan. It was sitting right where he'd left it, and still had all four tires in good working order. He'd be paying to have the thing repainted to cover up a particularly creative suggestion spray-painted across the back door, but what the hell. It could've been worse, given the neighborhood.

He checked his voice mail once he was on the road, and found one from Jox. The message was a simple, "Call me," but the *winikin*'s tone was off.

A bad feeling tightened Strike's gut as he phoned home and punched it to speaker. "What's wrong?" he said the moment Jox picked up.

"Carter found the twins," the *winikin* reported, his voice flat with grief. "They're dead."

Strike yanked the wheel and sent the soccer-mobile screeching across the highway, ignoring the blare of horns behind him. When he was stopped at an angle across the breakdown lane, he slapped the minivan into park. Sat and breathed. "Gods *damn* it."

"They were in New Jersey, headed along Skyline Drive the night of the solstice," Jox said. "They went off the road near midnight."

Which probably meant the barrier had reached out to them just like it'd grabbed him, Strike thought. The twin link would've made them more susceptible to the lure, and more powerful once they were jacked in. But fucking bad luck—destiny, whatever—had put one of them behind the wheel next to a sheer drop at exactly the wrong moment. And now the Nightkeepers were down to eleven. Ten, if he counted out Mendez.

Heart heavy, Strike said something reassuring to Jox, who sounded like he was taking it way hard, and rang off. Cranking the minivan into drive, he pulled back into traffic and headed for the car rental place. Once he'd dropped off the keys, he found a secluded spot for the 'port magic. He didn't particularly want to go back to the training compound, but he had a duty, damn it. It was like the king's writ said: His first duty was to the gods and his people, then to mankind and his family. His own needs barely made the list.

Closing his eyes, he touched the barrier for a boost of power and imagined his mental turbines coming to life. Once he had enough magic to work with, he thought of home, and a yellow travel thread shimmered into existence in front of him. He reached out and touched it, felt the power sing through him. When it peaked, he sent himself into the thread, into the barrier.

There was a blur of gray-green, a gut wrench of sideways motion, then the jarring halt he didn't think he'd ever get used to. Displaced air slammed away from him as he materialized a few inches off the ground, and he stumbled upon landing, windmilling his arms to keep his balance when he tripped over a hump of grass.

Except there shouldn't have been any grass. For that matter, it was dark out, when New Mex would've still had light, and the air was moist and verdant rather than desert dry.

Ergo, he wasn't in New Mex.

Heart hammering, Strike looked around. He'd zapped in at the front of a three-story house that towered over its ground-level neighbors on either side, which were nearly hidden behind tall, leafy hedges, as though the owner of the three-story liked privacy. The street out front was lined with palm trees, and the car parked by the front door had a sleek and somewhat dated silhouette.

He'd bet his next meal she was a '67 Mustang named Peggy Sue. He'd thought of home and his powers had brought him, not to a place, but to a person.

To Leah.

Leah knew she was dreaming, but she couldn't be bothered to wake up when the dream was so much better than reality.

Reality was a roomful of cops looking at her sideways. Reality was Nick's empty desk chair across from hers, and a cardboard box where her partner's things should have been. Reality was the memorial service, and the funeral, and Selina asking her to say something at the service when she couldn't, she just couldn't. And reality was Matty's memory fading bit by bit.

Basically, reality sucked.

The dream, though . . . *Wow, and hello, baby. Where have you been all my life*?

In tonight's installment of her fantasy life, her dream warrior stood in the shadows of the attic eaves, staring at her. He was tall and dark, with high, slashing cheekbones, piercing eyes, and the aristocratic line of a thin beard. He was wearing black combat pants and boots and a white oxford, and held himself like a leader, like he didn't take crap from anyone. She appreciated that in a guy, as long as he didn't take it too far into Neanderthal territory. But this was her dream, wasn't it? Her rules, her desires.

She lay on the futon mattress up in the attic, where she'd slept since Nick's death. In her bedroom she'd felt hemmed in, restless. Up here, she could stretch out beneath the wide skylight and feel the starlight on her skin.

Naked, she turned on her side and let the light sheet fall away, baring herself to her dream lover, needing to let loose of the grim control she kept on herself during the day so her recent frustrations wouldn't have her lashing out at the people around her. But here, with him, those frustrations turned to pure heat. A strange hum built in her bones, in her ears, in the air around her, and a flush climbed her skin, warming her, prickling when her pores opened and her neurons flared to life, as though they'd been dead numb all day and were just now awakening. The moon caught the edge of the skylight, dimming all but the brightest stars, and the tiny points of light called to her, sending heat throbbing beneath her skin.

Daring him, she crooked a finger. "Come here."

He moved out of the shadows into the moonlight, his steps soundless on the wide attic floorboards. Slowly, so slowly, he dropped to his knees beside the mattress and bent over her, but didn't touch.

"Leah," he whispered, his voice rasping across her name like a caress. Like a prayer.

"I don't know your name," she said softly, lifting a hand to touch his jaw, and finding it warm and solid and masculine beneath her dream fingertips.

"You don't need to." Something flickered in his eyes—sorrow, perhaps, or guilt.

She wanted to argue, wanted his name, but that small desire didn't seem as important as the larger roar of lust brought on by the feel of his strong jaw against her palm, and the rasp of his close-clipped beard as he leaned over her, leaned into her. And touched his lips to hers.

The kiss was a whisper at first, though not a question. It was more like a test, though she didn't know if he was challenging himself or her.

Heat came quickly, digging her with sharp claws of need, and she arched up to him, offering. Demanding. And the moment of hesitation was gone.

He came down on her with a muttered oath, and then his hands were everywhere—touching and stroking and shaping her. She arched into him, gasping as pleasure flared, hard and hot. The intensity of his touch and her response would've been too much, too soon if it hadn't been for the edge of tenderness in the way his tongue touched hers when she opened her mouth, strong and sure, but coaxing a response rather than demanding it.

There was no need for either a coax or a demand, though. She was right there with him. Hell, she was powering past him, ahead of him, waiting for him to catch up.

Then again, this was her dream. Why shouldn't she be in charge?

As the kiss spiraled hotter, harder, she plastered herself against him, feeling his strength through his clothing, the nap of the fabric an exquisite torture against her bare, sensitized skin. He stiffened and hissed out a breath as she hooked his shirt from his waistband and slid her hands beneath, walking her fingernails across the hard ridges of his abs and lingering on the trail of rough, masculine hair leading down. But when she made a move for his belt he caught her wrists in one of his hands and broke the kiss to say, "Relax. This is about you, not me."

Of course it is, she thought. *It's my dream.*

Bathed in the warmth of desire, she lay back at his urging and spread her legs, offering herself to the night sky and feeling the weight of his eyes, the pressure of a thousand stars burning down from above.

Heat roared within her when they kissed. Need hammered when he touched her breasts, which were heavy and ached with desire. The world spun when he touched her with his clever fingers, his agile tongue; then she felt the rasp of his beard against the skin of her belly, and lower. Then he was tonguing her, nipping at her sensitized flesh and making her squirm, making the heat spiral harder, making the world contract inward until there was nothing but the two of them and the dream haze.

She turned toward him, lifting and bending one leg to tilt herself more fully open to him, and her breath came in short, staccato bursts as tension coiled within, tighter and tighter still until she couldn't breathe. She buried her fingers in his hair and urged him up her body, so they were pressed chest-to-chest, tangled in each other, wrapped around each other. She tasted herself on his lips, tasted him, his need and frustrated desire, and though he'd said it was about her she wanted it to be about the two of them. Together.

When she opened her eyes to say as much, she found his eyes open as well, found herself caught in their depths. Then he touched her where his mouth had just been, slipped two fingers inside her, and set a hard, fast rhythm that mimicked the beat of her heart, and matched the stroke of his tongue against hers.

Gasping, she strained against him as a rush of sensation built, coalescing around his fingers, around them both. Then the universe exploded. Golden light flared in her mind, in her body, warming her, pleasuring her. She cried out and clung to him as the orgasm gripped her, rolled over her, washed through her.

When it was done, the world spun around her and she clung to him still, his solid body her only anchor in an existence suddenly gone unsteady. She stirred against him, opened her eyes to look at him and found them still in her attic, still in each other's arms.

Suddenly, the fantasy seemed awfully real. The dreams had never taken her this far before, never continued through completion to the aftermath. They'd never left her feeling both satisfied and terribly alone.

"This is real, isn't it?" she whispered, not sure whether the huge emotion that welled up inside her was hope or fear.

His cobalt eyes went sharp with regret, and he shook his head slightly. "No. It's a dream. It's all a dream."

He touched his lips to her forehead and said something, two words in a language she didn't know, but which sounded familiar somehow. But before she could ask how she knew the sounds, gray-green mist crept to the edges of her vision, cocooning her in warm lassitude.

She fought the pull, fought a sudden, overwhelming sleepiness. "Wait! What—"

"Sleep," he said softly. "This is all just a dream."

He cut off her protest with a kiss. And as she slid into

the kiss, she tumbled off the edge to sleep, taking with her the power of his touch and the safety of his arms.

Strike was hard and sore, and his body burned for release, for completion, but he denied both and turned Leah in his arms, fitting her up against him so they were nestled together back-to-front. Then he pulled the light sheet off the floor to cover them both.

The sleep spell wasn't as comprehensive as Red-Boar's mind-wipe, but she'd already thought she was dreaming. She'd wake and think of him as a pleasant fantasy, which would have to be enough.

He knew he should feel guilty, and maybe that would come later. For now, there was only the satisfaction of holding her in his arms. She fit against him perfectly, small enough that he could tuck her head beneath his chin, tough enough that she could hold her own against him, against the *makol*.

Deep down inside him there was a faint warning tug, a twitch of unease that his connection to her was too strong to be anything but meant by the fates, by the gods.

"No," he said aloud. He wanted—needed—to claim something for himself. A moment of private humanity. His feelings for Leah, which he was careful not to examine too closely, weren't part of his being a Nightkeeper or the son of the king. Maybe they had been at first, but not anymore. Now, the attraction was about his being a man and her being a woman.

Jox was right—he'd always had a thing for edgy blondes. More, he respected the loyalty to family and friends that had driven her after Zipacna. Her need to fight for what she believed in. She was a cop, a protector in her own right, one who didn't let herself get pushed around even in situations far beyond her understanding. Yet at the same time, she was all woman in her responses, in her unabashed enjoyment of her own body, and his.

If he'd been nothing more than a man, or if it were five years later, with the zero date come and gone without drama, he would've done whatever it took to make her his own. As it was, that was out of the question, a danger to both of them. So he'd take this one time— and he swore to himself that it would only be once— and let her go, hoping she'd dream of him.

He'd keep the protection spell in place and make sure the *ajaw-makol* didn't try to touch her again. He'd watch over her, just as he was bound to oversee the safety of the human race. But that was it for the two of them together. Hell, he shouldn't have even come into her house tonight, but once he'd realized where he was, he hadn't been able to override the compulsion. Hadn't wanted to.

Tomorrow, he would meet the new Nightkeepers. Tonight, he'd wanted one last thing for himself. But when his cell phone vibrated in his pocket, twice over five minutes, he knew his time was up. Undoubtedly it was Jox wanting to know where the hell he was, and when he'd be back. And though Strike was feeling vaguely out of step with his *winikin* these days, it wasn't fair for him to disappear. There had been too much of that already.

So he gathered himself and slipped out from underneath the sheet, tucking the single layer around Leah as she stirred and murmured something sweet and low. A faint frown touched her lips and crinkled her brow, forming soft lines in the moonlight.

"Sleep," he said in the language of his ancestors, and touched his lips to hers. "Be safe."

Then he closed his eyes and tapped the barrier for power, envisioned the training compound, and teleported away.

CHAPTER EIGHT

Strike woke late the next morning, groggy and disori-
ented, and dreading the day ahead. He used the small
bathroom at the back of the pool house, pulled on a
pair of cutoffs, and stumbled outside. Squinting against
the too-bright summer sun, he headed across the pool
deck and through the sliders into the mansion, making
a beeline for the kitchen, and coffee. He stepped through
the doorway to the great room that formed the center
of the first floor—

And stopped dead as five pairs of eyes snapped to
him and five strangers stopped talking.

Oh, shit, he thought. *They're here.*

It was stupid for him to be surprised. He'd known the
new Nightkeepers had begun arriving the night before,
had even seen some of the luggage when he'd zapped
in, chowed a snack, and gone to bed. But somehow he'd
thought he'd have a chance to confab with Jox and Red-
Boar before meeting the newbies.

Apparently not.

The five gorgeous twenty-somethings were sitting in
the sunken middle of the main room. The long leather
couch held two women, a streaky blonde who was six
feet tall if she was an inch and a smaller brunette with
green eyes, both wearing business casual. Next to them
sat a big sprawl of a blond guy wearing swim trunks and
a shirt advertising a bait store. Two other guys sat in the

flanking chairs, both dark haired and intense-looking. One of them was clean-shaven, short haired, and all business in a navy suit and tie he wore with the ease of familiarity. The other sported a careful layer of stubble on his jaw and long wavy hair, along with a trendy, open-throated shirt that had a pair of shades looped over the first button.

Strike's precoffee brain did the first-impression thing, summing them up as the Valkyrie and the Ingenue, the Surfer Dude, the Business Guy, and the Playboy.

They were also complete and utter strangers. He didn't know why that surprised him, but it did. Maybe deep down inside, he'd figured he'd recognize them because he'd known their parents when he was a kid.

Jox came out of the kitchen on the opposite side. Skirting the upper level of the room, he joined Strike and handed over a mug of coffee, whispering, "If you weren't going to dress for the occasion, you could've at least brushed your hair."

"Shit." Strike looked down at himself, bare chested in a pair of cutoffs and nothing else, and stifled a curse. No need to question where he scored on the first-impression scale: somewhere between Scuzzy Bedhead Guy and Please Don't Tell Me That's Him.

"You'll do fine." Jox clapped him on the shoulder and turned to leave.

"Hey!"

The *winikin* paused. "What, you want a fanfare or something?"

Yeah, actually. Well, maybe not trumpets, but he'd sort of imagined that when it came time to meet the newcomers, Jox would at least introduce him, maybe play up his father or something. But that was the point, wasn't it? He wasn't his father, and this wasn't his father's time anymore. So much had changed, they were going to have to rewrite some of the rules and protocols as they went. Starting now.

So Strike didn't ask for a fanfare, instead saying, "Where are the others?"

Jox jerked a thumb over his shoulder, in the direction he'd been headed. "Their *winikin* are in the kitchen getting reacquainted. I figured we should stagger the intros so your head doesn't blow up." He paused. "Besides, Carlos's daughter is pretty shell-shocked."

"She can join the club."

"No." Jox shook his head. "It's more than that. Carlos didn't give her the option . . ." He trailed off, shook his head. "Not your problem. I'll handle it."

Strike glanced over his shoulder to where the five newbies had returned to their conversations, but were keeping a collective eye on him. "Who are we missing? I know Mendez is in jail, and obviously Blackhawk hasn't seen fit to show yet." And he was going to have to figure out a way to make sure that happened. "But that still leaves us one short."

"Working on it."

"Another holdout?" Strike said, hoping that was all it was.

"She said she was coming, then didn't show. Her *winikin*, Hannah, has gone to pick her up." Jox paused. "I sent Red-Boar along in case there's trouble."

Something in his tone warned Strike not to ask. Hannah was the name Jox had breathed over the phone with such reverence the night before, yet there was none of that in his tone or expression now. There were only fatigue, frustration, and worry.

Or maybe I'm the one who's tired and frustrated, Strike thought. For a brief, crazy second he pictured himself zapping back to Miami—do not pass go, do not collect two hundred dollars. He could get a job and accidentally-on-purpose bump into Leah. They could get to know each other like normal human beings and see if what had started between them was real.

What if it is? said his conscience. *So what? Maybe you get married. Maybe you have kids and the picket fence. You won't make it past your fourth anniversary. Boom. Gone. Game over.*

Damn it.

So he sighed, shoved aside the lovely fantasy of walking away from it all, and held up a *hold on* finger to the newcomers. "Give me five minutes and we'll try this again."

Four minutes later, fortified by caffeine and wearing jeans, a concert T, and rope sandals—on the theory that he shouldn't sell a bill of goods he couldn't deliver—he strode back into the great room and sat on the back of a chair with his feet on the seat cushion, so he was higher up than the rest of them. Then he said, "Okay, take two. As you probably guessed already, I'm Striking-Jaguar. Call me Strike."

They did introductions first. The streaky blond Valkyrie, Alexis Gray of the smoke bloodline, looked him in the eye and had a man-strong handshake. The brunette Ingenue, Jade Farmer of the harvester bloodline, spoke so softly he could barely hear her. Surfer Dude was Coyote-Seven, who went by Sven and didn't look like he was taking much of anything seriously. Business Guy was Brandt White-Eagle, who looked like he wanted to be somewhere else, and Playboy was Michael Stone, whose easy smile and surface charm did little to change Strike's first impression of a player.

Once they'd done the intro thing, Strike tried to think of something grand and wonderful to say. In the end, though, he was neither grand nor wonderful. He was just a basic sort of guy. So he went with the basics. "I'm assuming your *winikin* have explained the situation?"

All five of them nodded. Strike would've bet a hundred bucks that none of them had the slightest clue what they were about to buy into, but it wasn't like he could pull a Monty Python and start shouting, "Run away, run away!" And if he couldn't bail, then they shouldn't get the option, either. They were all in this together, bound by a bloodline responsibility none of them had asked for.

So instead of offering them the illusion of an out, he held out his right arm and flipped his hand palm up. "I know you've seen marks like these on the people who raised you. You're going to get your first ones exactly seven days from now, on the Fourth of July."

"What happens then?" This from Surfer Dude. Sven.

"The aphelion," Strike answered. "It's one of the minor astral events when the barrier increases its activity. We're going to hold the connection ritual, which will bind you to the barrier and give you your bloodline marks, along with your first link to the power." He paused. "That doesn't mean you'll be able to do major magic—that'll come after the talent ceremony, which won't be until mid-September."

There was a moment of silence, and he could almost feel the newcomers trying to figure out which question to ask first.

Finally, Alexis said, "What happens in between?"

"You'll be studying spell theory, working out, training, preparing to fight." Pausing, he scrubbed a hand across the back of his neck, remembering the horns that'd ridden him in the days leading up to the solstice, when the barrier had reactivated. "There's also a good chance that you'll experience some, um, sexual side effects."

Sven crossed his legs. "You mean we're going to go Bob Dole?"

Bob—oh, Viagra. Strike shook his head. "Exactly the opposite. You'll most likely spend those two months horny as hell."

Sven grinned wide and shrugged. "I can handle that. Get it? Handle?"

"What are you, eighteen?" Alexis shot over at him, her eyebrows arched in disgust.

Which made Strike wonder where their resident juvenile delinquent had gone. If Red-Boar was off tracking down their straggler, that left him and Jox on Rabbit duty.

"No, I'm honest." Sven jerked his thumb at the other guys. "And if these two are being honest, they'll back me up."

Michael shot him a *keep dreaming* look, but White-Eagle ignored them both. He leaned forward, bracing his shirtsleeved forearms on his knees. "Is there any other way to get the bloodline mark besides this connection ceremony?"

Strike shook his head. "Not as far as I know." But that made him think about the marks on Snake Mendez's arms, which meant there was probably at least one other way to connect.

"What about before the massacre, when the barrier was still active?"

Strike sent White-Eagle a sharp look. "Maybe. I was nine when it went down. You'll have to ask Jox, or Red-Boar when he gets back. Why?"

White-Eagle lifted a shoulder. "Just trying to figure all this out." He shifted in his chair, glancing over his shoulder. "You mind if I hit the bathroom? Too much coffee."

"Go." Strike waved him off. "We're not going to do hall passes or anything." But as the big man moved off, walking with the same smooth glide Strike remembered from his childhood, when he'd watched the Night-keeper warriors train under his father's guidance, he wondered whether hall passes might not be a good idea, after all.

He had a feeling White-Eagle's disappearing act had nothing to do with coffee.

The minute Brandt hit the john, he closed and locked the door, and whipped out his cell phone. Hitting the number labeled HOME SWEET HOME, he murmured, "Come on, Patience, come on. *Pick up!*"

Finally, she did. "Hey, baby. I was just thinking about you. How's Chicago?"

"I lied," Brandt said succinctly. "I'm not in Chicago. I'm in New Mexico, near Chaco Canyon. Which I'm guessing is where you're supposed to be."

There was absolute silence on the other end of the phone.

Knowing that was all the answer he needed, Brandt closed his eyes for a second, damning himself for never pressing her about her family, for never pushing the conversation they should've had years ago, when they'd woken up with their bloodline marks and hidden the truth from each other. "They're coming for you," he said. "Don't pack, don't ask any questions, just get out of there."

He hung up, trusting that she'd know what to do, and why.

Patience couldn't breathe. She couldn't think. She sure as hell couldn't move.

Brandt was a Nightkeeper, too. *Holy crap.*

It made a crazy sort of sense, really. He was ridiculously big and handsome, and had always seemed larger than life. And when they'd met on spring break, she'd fallen for him instantly, as if they'd had some sort of karmic connection. They'd met at the ruins of Chichén Itzá and gotten drunk together, only neither of them had remembered drinking that much. Apparently the memory lapse hadn't been alcohol. It'd been the spring equinox.

She sank to one of the kitchen chairs, brain spinning as she looked at the marks on her arm. "Oh, boy," she breathed. "That's not a tattoo, is it?"

Get out, Brandt's voice whispered in her head. *They're coming for you.*

Her heart hammered. She'd already decided not to go, decided it wasn't worth giving up her life for a responsibility she'd never asked for, didn't feel prepared for. And besides—

The doorbell rang.

She bolted to her feet with a shriek. Something sizzled through her blood, feeling like anger, only hotter, headier. Her skin felt too tight and her mouth went dry, and her feet barely touched the floor as she ran from the kitchen into the nursery, where Harry and Braden were asleep in their oversize crib, wearing their footie pj's with cars on them.

Or rather, Harry was asleep and Braden was wide-awake, plotting his next mischief. She could tell from the look in his eyes, and the ESP that she'd found had come with motherhood.

She held a finger to her lips. "Ssh. Don't make a sound."

He must've realized she was serious, because he didn't immediately do the opposite of what she asked. Instead, he touched Braden's shoulder, waking his brother. She got them out of the crib, balancing one on each hip even though, at nearly three, they'd grown too heavy for her to comfortably carry them both. But she stalled at the nursery door.

Where was she supposed to go?

The doorbell chimed again, speeding her heart rate even further and making her blood hum in her ears so loud it almost sounded like the wind, only there was no wind inside the house, no wind outside, no wind—

It wasn't wind, she realized with a sudden certainty that came straight from her bones. It was power. Her power.

A flicker of movement caught her peripheral vision. She looked down, and gaped when she saw nothing. Literally nothing. She had disappeared, along with the boys.

I'm invisible, she thought as shock fisted itself around her throat and squeezed until only a thin trickle of air got through. *Impossible.* Except it wasn't impossible. She was a Nightkeeper, wasn't she?

"No. I'm not," she whispered. "I don't want to be."

She had other priorities now. Her sons were more important than her being a Nightkeeper and saving the world. She didn't want the boys used, didn't want them thrown into an impossible war, didn't want them orphaned the way she and Brandt had been. Yes, she'd had Hannah and he'd had his godfather, Woodrow, who must've been a *winikin,* as well. But it wasn't the same, had never been the same as having parents.

"You need to be really, really quiet," she whispered to the invisible boys, and thought she felt the warm bundles in her arms nod acquiescence.

Breathing through her mouth, she tiptoed out of the nursery, listening for any stray sound that could give her away, and hearing nothing. *You can do this,* she told herself. *You can.*

The doorbell was at the front of the house, but there were two other exits—the garage and the back door. She would've gone out through the garage, but starting the car would negate the whole invisibility bonus. That left the back.

A quick glance showed her that the coast was clear. She eased out, juggling the boys and trying not to feel the pull in her right shoulder, which she'd strained during a judo class the week before. She'd head around the side, cut through the Fitches' backyard and across the next street over. Her friend Joanie lived two blocks down from there. She'd help.

And by then, Patience figured she was going to need some help. Already the buzzing had decreased, and a heavy pounding had started up in her skull. She didn't know how much longer she could sustain the *now you see me, now you don't* routine. Steps dragging, she started toward the Fitches' yard, only to backpedal furiously when Hannah appeared from around the front, her brows furrowed.

Patience's heart gave an uneven bump at the sight of her godmother's lovely, scarred face beneath a bright pink scarf. She hated knowing she had to disappoint one of the most important people in her life in order to protect two others. Then again, she hadn't liked keeping her marriage or babies secret from Hannah, either, talking on disposable cells and finding neutral places to meet a couple of times a year. She'd been living a second life, living a lie, and now it was coming back to bite her in the ass.

Get moving, she told herself. *Just go and don't look back.* Instead, she stood for a moment and watched Hannah, wishing impossible things.

The *winikin* moved to the back door and said something unladylike when she found it hanging open. She raised her voice and called, "She's gone!"

"Not exactly," a male voice said from directly behind Patience.

Before she could turn, before she could react, something went *pzzzt* in her brain and everything turned dark. Strong arms caught her as she fell, bearing her weight and grabbing her sons as they started to struggle and squall.

"Easy, boys," the man said, and took them. "Here. Meet your auntie Hannah."

The last thing Patience heard was the man muttering under his breath, something about half-bloods and idiot neophytes who thought their powers worked on mages. *No,* she wanted to say. *I might be an idiot and I'm definitely a neophyte, but my sons aren't half-bloods. Their father is a Nightkeeper, too.*

And that was the whole problem, because they were her babies. They weren't weapons in a war nobody could win.

Nate Blackhawk considered himself a straightforward guy with straightforward goals. He never wanted to spend another night in jail. He wanted to work for himself. And he wanted to make his first million before he turned forty without being ashamed of how he'd done it.

But he'd never really wanted to be a hero, or a magician.

Sure, he'd written games for both. Even Hera, the kick-ass hottie at the heart of his *Viking Warrior* franchise, could see the future sometimes. But he'd never really pictured himself in the role of sorcerer's apprentice . . . until the dark-haired guy with the tats had hung him off the roof and left him with a business card and some bruises.

He'd tried to tell himself it was all part of an elaborate scam, that the guy had somehow found out he was an orphan—not exactly something that was front and center on the Hawk Enterprises home page—and was using that as an in. But that didn't explain the teleporting trick, and it didn't explain why the stranger had asked about Nate's medallion, which was the one thing he possessed that he was pretty sure had come from his parents.

As the SUV limo bounced its way along the optimistically named Route 57, deep in the middle of nowhere New Mexico, Nate pulled the medallion out from beneath his white button-down and rubbed his thumb across the metal disk, feeling the etched marks that looked like a hawk if you turned the piece one way, a man if you turned it the other.

He'd had the thing for as long as he could remember. According to the records, he'd been wearing it when he'd appeared in the waiting room of the University of Chicago's Lying-In Hospital at the age of two. He'd been wearing soiled pj's stained with blood that wasn't his, he'd had the words "My name is Nathan Blackhawk" written on his forehead in ballpoint pen, and he hadn't spoken for nearly fourteen months thereafter. For a while, they'd thought he was mute.

He'd had night terrors regularly until his teens and then sporadically ever since—amorphous dreams of bright red-orange creatures that dripped flame and killed everything around them. The prison therapist had told him the monsters represented his mother, and his anger at her for leaving him alone, but Nate was pretty sure the monsters were just monsters. He didn't hate his parents. He'd never met them, and if they hadn't cared enough to keep him, then he didn't care enough to hate them.

But that didn't stop him from being curious about what the stranger had hinted at.

He'd thought about it for a couple of days, until the bruises had gone from red to purple, and then he'd okayed *EmoPunk III*—God help him—downloaded the storyboard for *Viking Warrior 6: Hera's Mate*—he still wasn't sure about the hero—and hopped a flight to New Mexico.

Odds were he'd be back in Denver tomorrow, feeling like a schmuck.

He hadn't even called ahead, figuring on a surprise attack. Beside, the guy had left his address, sort of. The card said simply: *Rt. 57, Chaco Canyon.*

Now he was thinking the surprise was on him, because 57 was a damn gravel track, and they hadn't passed a house or cross street in a good ten minutes. There was nothing outside the air-conditioned cabin of the stretch pimp-mobile besides sun, scrub brush, and more sun, with the occasional rock for variety.

"Great," he muttered. "This is a total waste of time." He didn't tell the driver to about-face, though. Instead, he palmed his handheld and called up a set of graphics, not of the pasty-faced hero his developers had come up with, but of Hera.

Big, blond, and angular, but with a pixie-delicate face and wide hazel eyes, capable of kicking ass equally well in swordplay and hand-to-hand, she was his queen, the cornerstone of Hawk Enterprises. The guys on his team might tease him about his imaginary girlfriend, but as far as he was concerned she was perfect. She never bitched at him for being a slob, never complained when he slept at his desk. She was always there when he wanted to see her, but disappeared with the touch of a button. Okay, she wasn't real high on the bed-warmer scale, and he was pretty sure he'd torpedoed his last two relationships because the women hadn't measured up to the Hera that lived in his mind, but please. He was twenty-six and in no hurry to settle.

She was out there. He didn't know why or how he knew that, but he was sure of it. He just hadn't met her yet.

"Here's something," the driver said through the buzzed-down privacy window as he let the limo roll to a stop. "Want me to try it?"

Off to one side, a two-lane track had been beaten into the prairie, as though a convoy had been through recently. About a half mile ahead of them, it looked like the dirt road twisted down and disappeared. "Does it head toward the canyon?"

"Seems to."

"Then let's go. What's the worst that could happen?"

"We drive off the road, get stuck, try to walk back, and die miserably of dehydration and sunstroke," the driver offered, but he grinned as he said it, and turned the stretch SUV down the track. "Hang on."

It wasn't bad at first, but as they hit the bend in the road and it did, indeed, drop down into Chaco Canyon, Nate gave up his dignity, strapped on his seat belt, and clung to the armrests as the vehicle bounced and shuddered all the way to the bottom.

When they turned the final corner, the driver let up on the gas. "Well, hell."

Something twisted in Nate's gut at the sight of the buildings scattered in a small box canyon about a quarter of a mile farther up. "I guess this is it."

It looked like a construction site at first, with tri-axle dumps raising big dust clouds and double crews working on high scaffolds, securing the roof of a huge steel-span building off to one side. But as they got closer he realized it was a mix of old and new buildings, some under construction, with a patch of blackened earth the size of a football field and a huge tree that seemed utterly out of place. There were other structures in the rear that he couldn't quite make out, and the whole thing was fronted by a new-looking masonry wall that ran from one side of the box canyon to the other.

The gates were wide-open, though, and the driver rolled him right up to the front door of the main house, which was more mansion than house, three stories of pale pink-and-gray limestone, with trim that practically vibrated shiny white from a new coat of paint.

After they'd sat there for a moment, the driver looked at him. "You getting out?"

Yes. No. He didn't know. *Shit.*

Nate didn't consider himself a weenie, but this so wasn't what he'd been expecting. He wasn't sure what he *had* been expecting, but this wasn't it.

He took a deep breath and reminded himself he'd planted a time-delayed e-mail in the system back at work, ready to drop a mayday in a couple of hours if he didn't delete it. "Yeah, I'm getting out." He left his laptop and bags in the car, though. "Give me fifteen minutes to check out the situation and I'll let you know if I'm staying or not."

Then the front door of the mansion opened and his heart stopped for a second, then started up again, hammering in his ears so loud he could barely think. "Scratch that," he said, fumbling for his bags. "I'm staying."

Hera stood in the doorway.

Alexis held her ground as the newcomer strode toward her, his long legs eating up the distance that separated them, his eyes fixed on her. She recognized the look; ten bucks said he was going to invite her for a ride in his mine's-bigger-than-yours chauffeur-driven dickmobile.

Instead, he climbed the marble steps, stopped a few feet away from her, and didn't say a word. He just looked at her.

A shimmer of awareness worked its way across her

skin, sliding along her nerve endings and whispering something she couldn't hear. She rubbed her arms, which were bare beneath a cap-sleeved T-shirt, brushing away the sensation.

Sure, he was just her type—wealthy and slick in his Armani suit and trendy, heavy-framed glasses, bigger than her by a good four inches in all directions, and no-holds-barred masculine, with his dark hair slicked back and a layer of stubble on his jaw. But that was the problem—he was just her type, and as her recent nonrelationship with Aaron the Worthless Prick proved, the men that were her type tended to be spoiled, arrogant brats who should've been spanked more when they were young.

And no, she wasn't volunteering to fix that now. So she narrowed her eyes into a *don't even think it* glare. "Can I help you?"

He blinked as though that was entirely not what he'd expected her to say. Recovering, he two-fingered a card out of his pocket and held it out. "Guy teleported me onto a roof, hung me over the side, then told me to come here if I wanted to learn more."

"No kidding?" She glanced at the card. "Then you've already seen more of the magic than I have, and I've already been here a few days." She waved him in. "We're in the middle of Magic 101." As an afterthought, she stuck out a hand. "I'm Alexis Gray. Smoke bloodline."

He took her hand. His grip was warm and firm, but he'd started to look a little thin around the edges, like he was going into overload. "Nate Blackhawk. What's a bloodline?"

She cocked her head. "Didn't your *winikin* explain all this shit as you were growing up? The whole Nightkeepers-save-the-world-from-the-2012-apocalypse thing?"

"Winikin?" No doubt about it, he'd gone gray.

"Oh, shit," she said, making the connection to a convo she'd overheard between Izzy and one of the other *winikin*. "You're Carlos's orphan, aren't you?" When his bags hit the deck and his knees started to buckle, she jammed her shoulder into his armpit and shouted, "Need a little help here!"

But she was too late. They were both headed for the floor.

Once they got Blackhawk back on his feet and looking more or less steady, Strike herded the trainees back into the sunken great room at the center of the mansion.

"Okay. Moving on." He glanced at Blackhawk, who was looking seriously shell-shocked. "We went over the writs and the thirteen prophecies yesterday. Maybe Alexis can fill you in on that stuff later." He chose her partly because Izzy had given her a strong foundation in Nightkeeper history and partly because Blackhawk was trying way too hard not to stare at her.

Strike wasn't interested in making a match of his own, but Jox was right—they were going to need the Nightkeepers to pair up.

"We were talking about the barrier," he said to the group. "Think of it as an energy field that you can use in a bunch of different ways. Once you've been through both the binding and talent ceremonies you'll be able to uplink, tapping the barrier for the power to perform spells. You can do that pretty much whenever, as long as you've got enough physical energy to sustain the uplink. During the astral conjunctions—the solstice and equinox and so forth—you'll be able to jack in and send your incorporeal form into the barrier itself. In extreme cases, with the strongest of magic and sacrifice, you may be able to punch all the way through the barrier."

Alexis nodded. "Like for the transition spell."

Sven elbowed her. "Suckup."

"Burnout," she fired back.

"Anyway," Strike said, raising his voice to drown them out. "Alexis is correct—a Nightkeeper can sometimes punch through the barrier using a transition spell—in theory, anyway. Now that we're in the final five years of the countdown to zero date, on rare occasions—like the solstice or equinox—it should be possible for a god to travel the skyroad connecting the heavens and earth, in order to enter a female Nightkeeper. When that happens, she'll becomes what's called a Godkeeper, and she'll be able to wield some—or all—of the god's power with the help of her *jun tan* mate."

"In theory?" Sven pressed.

Strike shook his head. "To the best of our knowledge, the Godkeeper spell was lost in the fifteen hundreds when the conquistadors and their missionaries did their damnedest to wipe out anything that didn't look like Christianity. Which amounted to almost the entirety of pre-Columbian civilization."

"Gods coming to earth," Blackhawk broke in, incredulous. "Magical spells. Are you people listening to yourselves?"

Strike glanced at him. "You forgetting the roof deal?"

Blackhawk subsided, but Strike figured the guy was getting close to critical mass, so he took five and handed the new arrival off to his assigned *winikin*, Carlos.

When class resumed, Strike said, "All of you should be able to perform the traditional spells, the ones involving a small blood sacrifice and tapping the barrier. During the second ceremony, some—if not all—of you will get one or two additional marks, indicating that you have inherent abilities the others don't. The talent marks don't always show up at the time of the ceremony—some do; some come later. It's more that the ceremony prepares you to accept them, and opens you to your full powers."

Sven broke in. "What sort of talent am I going to get?"

Strike shrugged. "It's not a sure thing. Most of you will hopefully get the warrior's mark and the fighting powers that come with it, which include the ability to block with a shield spell and attack with fire. Some of the women may get prescience to one degree or another." He didn't figure they needed to know the considerable downside of the rare full-blown foretelling powers until one of them actually got the *itza'at* seer's mark. "About one in three Nightkeepers on average gets another talent." Ticking them off on his fingers, he said, "Teleporting runs in the jaguar bloodline, as does mimicry. Invisibility and flight tend to pop up in the bird bloodlines. Mental talents like mind-bending and mesmerism are common in—"

He broke off at the sound of the front door opening, then shutting again, followed by the quiet murmur of a woman's voice, followed by Red-Boar's deeper tones.

"Sounds like the last of us is finally here." Strike rose to his feet and called, "We're in here."

Moments later, Red-Boar appeared in the arched doorway near the front entrance, and ushered through a Nightkeeper woman who was tall and gorgeous and blond, and looked younger than the others. She was wearing shorts and long sleeves, which jarred, but that wasn't what had Strike freezing in place.

No, that would be the little boys holding her hands, one on each side.

They were identical.

"Twins," he said, breathing past a spike of adrenaline and a crushing pressure in his chest. "They're twins."

"Yeah." Red-Boar nodded. "How do you like that? They're only half-bloods, but still."

Strike saw the newcomer's eyes flash at the term and couldn't say he cared for it much himself, but he didn't get a chance to respond, because Jox appeared in the foyer, caught sight of the kids, and went white. For a second Strike thought he was going to hit the deck like Blackhawk had done earlier.

A petite woman in a flowing print dress, with a pink scarf tied across one side of her face at an angle, stepped around Red-Boar to touch Jox's arm. "I'm sorry," she said. "I didn't know." She turned to Strike. "My name is Hannah, sire. I'd like to introduce Patience Lizbet, of the iguana bloodline, and her sons, Harry and Braden."

"You can call me Strike," he said, but what he really meant was, *Don't call me "sire."*

"Actually, our name isn't Lizbet," the young woman contradicted, color riding high as she looked past Strike and latched onto something behind him. "It's White-Eagle."

Strike turned in time to see Brandt rise from his place on the couch, his expression a complicated mix of joy and resignation as he bent and opened his arms to the boys. "Hey, guys. I missed you!"

Matching faces lit with identical smiles, and matching mouths cried, "Daddy!"

The kids broke from their mother, charged across the foyer, and flung themselves on their father, while the rest of the world, at least from Strike's perspective, came to a grinding halt at a stunning, blinding revelation.

Those. Weren't. Half-bloods.

Holy. Shit.

Suddenly, Brandt's habit of wearing long sleeves, even outside in the scorching sun, made sense.

Patience and Brandt already had their marks, Strike realized. Somehow they'd punched through and gotten their bloodline marks. And for the first time since he'd left Leah alone in her starlit bed, he felt like things were starting to go a little bit right.

"Gods be praised," Jox whispered, voice shaking, and Strike could only nod agreement.

They had their twins. Gods be praised, indeed.

But as Brandt embraced his wife, and the boys clung to both their legs, and the *winikin* and the trainees clustered around them, all talking at once, Strike found himself edging away, feeling very much alone in the crowd. He wasn't jealous, precisely; he was . . .

Okay, he was jealous. Not because he necessarily wanted the wife-and-kids thing right away, but because he wanted to make that choice for himself.

Which was why, when his cell phone vibrated with an incoming call, he was grateful for the distraction. He flipped the phone, saw the private investigator's number, and answered, "Hey, Carter. Tell me you found Zipacna."

There had been no sign of the *ajaw-makol* since the solstice—at least, not that Carter had been able to unearth—but somebody had started buying up a shitload of stingray spines and *copan* incense, along with jugs of an alcoholic beverage called *pulque*.

All of which were crucial to the spells of both Nightkeepers and *makol*.

The PI said, "Zipacna is back in the compound—

there's some sort of gala being held there tonight. And the detective you asked me to flag?"

Strike's fingers tightened on the handset. "What about her?"

"Her name's on the guest list."

CHAPTER NINE

Leah's new partner, Billy Cole, wasn't a bad kid. Baby-faced and borderline pretty, Billy drove like a stock-car junkie, kept his mouth shut when it mattered, and seemed to do good policework. But he wasn't Nick.

Tired after putting in a full shift, and feeling rubbed raw from the sharp edges of a new partnership and the busywork Connie had been giving them rather than putting her back on the street, Leah sighed as Billy drove them back to the PD to clock out for the night. "Long day."

It was the sort of thing Nick used to say when he was thinking of something else, and the memory punched a fist beneath her heart. She missed him, missed Matty. Without them she felt so damn alone, like nobody around her got her, or cared enough to try.

"And it's going to be a long night, too," Billy said, making it sound like a good thing. At her sidelong look, he elaborated. "A bunch of us are going to hit the clubs." He paused. "You want to tag?"

Dear God, no, Leah thought, but managed to stick some regret in her voice. "Sorry, I can't. I've got plans."

He raised an eyebrow. "A date?"

"You don't have to sound so surprised. And no, it's not really a date. More of a friend thing." *With an agenda,* she thought, but didn't say.

She was going to a party at the Survivor2012 compound with Vince Rincon, a computer programmer a good fifteen years older than she, who'd been a co-worker and friend of her brother's. They'd met at Matty's funeral and bonded over their mutual distrust for the weirdos her brother had started hanging with over the last six months of his life. It'd been Vince who'd urged her to follow up with the warrants and searches, Vince who'd shared her frustration when they'd come up empty, and Vince who, a month earlier, had gotten them both tickets to some fund-raiser-slash-recruitment thing being held at the Survivor2012 compound, on the theory that it couldn't hurt to look around.

At the time it'd seemed like a good idea—or, if not a good one, at least an idea, an opportunity to do something that might jump-start the stalled investigation into Matty's murder. Now she wasn't sure she wanted to go. Nick's death and the forced vacation she'd gotten just after had given her some much-needed perspective on the evidence that'd led her to suspect Zipacna was the Calendar Killer.

In all honesty, there hadn't been any actual evidence, only her gut-level dislike for Matty's involvement in Survivor2012. Yeah, there were similarities between the Calendar Killer's signature—removing the victims' hearts and heads—and the ritual sacrifices of the ancient Maya. And yeah, Zipacna and his people were certified freakazoids. But she'd gone after him because she didn't like him, didn't like what he stood for, not because policework said he was the killer.

"A friend thing. Got it." Billy nodded. "Give me a call if you get done early and want to hook up."

"Thanks," Leah said, and meant it. She doubted she and Billy would ever have the level of partnership she'd shared with Nick, but appreciated the reach-out.

Once she was in Peggy Sue and headed home, though, loneliness seeped in around the edges of her mind.

It would've been nice to call around and hook up for dinner or whatever, but she'd let most of her old friends slip away over the years and hadn't made others, first because she was studying to be a cop, then because she had Nick to hang around with, and Matty. Now they were both gone, leaving her behind.

Which was why, instead of calling and canceling on Vince when she got home, as if she knew she ought to, she headed upstairs to change.

It wasn't a date. But it was something.

Given free choice in the matter, Strike would've gone after the *ajaw-makol* alone. But since this wasn't about just him, he relayed Carter's info to Red-Boar and the others, so they could plan a targeted attack.

That was when the trouble started.

"Absolutely not," Brandt said, jaw tight. He was sitting on the love seat in the center of the great room beside his wife. The other trainees were scattered around the room, and Strike and Red-Boar stood on the raised area near the kitchen entryway. Hannah and Woody, Brandt's *winikin*, had taken the twins, leaving the adults to hash things out. Rabbit sat at the back of the room, though Strike didn't know when he'd come in. With his hoodie pulled low and his ear buds plugged in, the kid looked totally tuned out. But the glitter in his pale eyes beneath the hood suggested he was enjoying the chaos.

"Excuse me?" Patience turned on her husband, eyes narrowing. "Strike didn't ask you to go. He asked me."

Though a flicker of worry revealed that Brandt knew he was treading dangerous ground, he didn't back down. "Think about it, hon. You're not trained. Hell, you just figured out you can make yourself invisible—which, by the way, is *very* cool. But you don't have your talent mark yet. What if the ability comes and goes until you get it? Are you willing to risk that? Think about the—"

"Don't go there," she snapped, cutting him off. "Don't even bring the boys into it. I can make myself invisible, and I can make whoever touches me invisible. If I can help these two"—she gestured to Strike and Red-Boar without looking at them—"take care of this *mako* . . . well, whatever it's called, then I will. Isn't that what we're all here for? To defeat darkness, save the world, all that crap?"

"You're not doing it," Brandt said, his square jaw locked mule-stubborn.

"It's not your choice," Patience fired back.

"Actually," Strike said, raising his voice to carry, "it's mine."

The room went silent.

He bit back a curse. Brandt was right—it was too soon, their talents too unfinished. But if they could kill the *ajaw-makol* before he got too strong they'd buy themselves more time to train.

"Look," Strike said. "I realize you guys don't know me. You didn't know my father, or, hell, even your own parents. You don't remember how it was before, how things worked. So maybe you think there's no real reason for you to buy into the power structure our parents lived by. But I'm what you've got in the way of a leader." He looked from one to the other of them, ending with Brandt. "And you're all I've got, so I won't put any of you in danger unnecessarily. I swear it."

He waited it out, waited to see if any of his new Nightkeepers called him on his father's choices or asked him whether he would've considered the attack on the intersection a necessary danger. Instead they stayed silent, shifting and looking at each other. All but Brandt, who kept staring at Strike as though assessing whether or not to trust him.

Then, finally, the other man looked away. Glancing at his wife, he murmured, "Sorry. Neanderthal moment. It's your call."

Patience didn't even hesitate. She stood and crossed to Strike. "When do we leave?"

"Now."

The Survivor2012 compound was situated on a ten-acre hump of dry land surrounded on all sides by the Everglades. Leah's previous snoops had revealed that the single bridgelike road leading to the so-called retreat was normally guarded by a decent-size security force, along with cameras and heat and motion detectors. To-night, though, the white-painted wrought-iron gates were wide-open, and a stream of limos and sports cars motored in, straight over the bridge and onward to follow a winding drive past artfully lit reproductions of crumbling Mayan temples.

At least, she thought they were repros. For all she knew, the freakazoids had bought—or flat-out stolen—the temples, moved them, and had them reassembled stone by stone. Because rocks could help save the world, you know.

She pulled up to the circular drive and handed off Peggy Sue to a valet, then joined the line of partygoers headed up to the mansion, where she and Vince had arranged to meet.

And it was a hell of a mansion, too. Zipacna and his cronies might be freakazoids, but they were well-funded freakazoids. The main house was set high above the swamp on built-up fill contained within a huge stone retaining wall, meaning that visitors had to climb a long, narrow flight of stone steps to reach the door. Presumably there was an easier way up, but Zipacna no doubt wanted his guests to get the full effect.

That, or he enjoyed watching them struggle with the stairs in their fancy clothes.

Leah knew she was getting the eye from a couple of male guests in their penguin suits as she headed up. She didn't need the double takes to tell her she looked good in one hell of a little black dress, with her hair swept up in a twist, and the wink of small—but real—diamonds at her ears, throat, and wrist.

She didn't need the looks. But they didn't hurt, either.

Feeling her confidence kick on the hit of female power—enough, anyway, to override the small voice in the back of her head that said this was a waste of time and she should've stayed home—she made it to the top and headed toward the house, which was sort of a Robinson Crusoe–meets–Frank Lloyd Wright amalgam of tree house and modern. Dodging knots of people doing the handshake-and-air-kiss thing out front, she headed through the front door.

A tall, half-naked man moved to block her path.

He was wearing sandals and some sort of loincloth contraption, and had a winged croc inked across his smoothly shaved—and extremely well defined—chest. He had a black stone knife stuck through his rope belt— a prop? an artifact? she wasn't sure—and wore a circlet of bluish white stone around his upper arm. His head was shaved bald except for a long topknot that was encircled at his scalp by a graduated stack of wooden rings that maxed him out at a good seven feet tall, and he was, incongruously, wearing a pair of designer sunglasses and an earpiece. Secret service gone pre-Columbian.

Leah stumbled back a pace in surprise, and the incoming partiers backed up behind her in a logjam of black and white.

"Do you think they're real?" she heard someone whisper.

Before Leah could figure out exactly what "they" were, the guy held out a hand. "Ticket."

Well, shit. Laughing inwardly at herself—what else had she expected, a blood sacrifice?—she handed it over and moved past him.

She hadn't been involved in executing either of the search warrants, so this was the first time she'd been inside the house where Matty had spent a good chunk of his last few months on earth. So she gave herself a moment to look around.

The space was wide and open, and the walls were done up with carved plaster—at least, she hoped it was plaster—reliefs that looked like they'd been copied straight off one of the big ruins, scenes of flat-faced men playing a ball game and then being killed, their heads cut from their bodies and gouts of blood coming from the neck stumps and turning to snakes. *Lovely.* The room itself was packed with minor celebs, local politicos, and various members of the rich and aimless, all dressed in versions of black and white, with a daring splash of red here and there. The 2012ers were unmistakable, wearing the same loincloth-and-topknot deal as the guy at the door—in the case of the women, with the addition of a stretchy band covering their nipples.

Very tasteful, Leah thought. *Not.* But at the same time, she couldn't really blame the 2012ers for pandering to the entertainment value. Miami's elite were notoriously easy to bore.

Music played in the background, almost below the level of hearing, a complicated drumbeat that got inside her, echoing in her chest and in the floor beneath her feet. There weren't any of the REPENT NOW! and THE END IS NEAR! posters she'd halfway expected to see based on what she understood of the Survivor2012 doctrine, which appeared to be an amalgam of the militant us-against-the-world propaganda favored by garden-variety anarchists, plus the time-frame incentive provided by their 2012 D-day and the promise that the cult members were going to lead the coming age.

Given all that, she wouldn't have been surprised to find recruiters working the room, and a signup table at the back. Instead, the decor actually came off as sort of restful and interesting—or she thought it would have if it hadn't been for the crowd. Or, rather, her awareness of the men.

She pretended she was scanning the scene, not looking for anyone in particular, but she knew damn well that was a crock. She was looking for *him*, for the warrior she'd dreamed of. The one she told herself couldn't possibly exist.

Yet she looked for him in the crowd.

There were plenty of wannabes in the assembled group, men who caught her scan and tried to intercept. Under normal circumstances, she might've even given one or two of them a chance to impress her. But tonight she glanced past in search of cobalt blue eyes, dark, shoulder-length hair, and a jawline beard, and felt a beat of disappointment when she came up empty. Which was just stupid, because he was a fantasy. But still.

"Focus," she told herself. "Be a cop."

From her new sense of perspective on the whole Survivor2012 thing—i.e., maybe Zipacna wasn't actually the serial killer who'd murdered Matty—she could maybe see what'd attracted her brother to the group. Matty's fiancée had broken their engagement for unknown reasons—at least, Leah didn't know what they were, and hadn't pressed nearly as much as she should have. His programming job had been in jeopardy due to corporate restructuring and hints of trouble at work. It wouldn't have been the first time he'd left a job under suspicion, either. He and Leah had been diametric opposites—she was truth and justice, where he'd liked to cut corners and find the easy money, though he'd stayed out of actual legal trouble. He'd always been a bit of a follower, too, and once Cheryl had left him, he'd been in need of a leader, and some peace. He'd bumped into Zipacna at some club or another, and they'd gotten into a conversation that'd ended with an invite to the very mansion she was standing in now.

A few weeks before Matty's death, he'd said Survivor2012 had made him feel like he was a part of something. At the time, she'd mocked the Zipacna shtick and offered to make her brother a tinfoil hat. After his murder, she'd focused on the group of nutbags he'd joined, needing to blame someone else. Now she wished she could take back the mockery, wished she could go back in time and really listen to her brother. Wished she'd pushed him more, helped him more.

If she had, he wouldn't have needed to turn to a group like this for a sense of family support . . . and he might not've been in the wrong place at the wrong time during the equinox.

"A penny for your thoughts," a man said from directly behind Leah.

She stiffened, then relaxed as she identified the voice. Turning and dredging up a smile, she said, "Hey, Vince. Just getting my bearings."

The programmer was wearing a tux as uninspired as his penny-for-your-thoughts line, and his medium-brown hair was brushed neatly—and uninspiringly—flat in defiance of its usual haphazard nonstyle. His eyes were a bland hazel, his smile unassuming as he said, "I'm glad you came. I wasn't sure you would after the other day."

They'd gotten into it on the phone a few days earlier, when she'd told him her suspicions were moving away from Survivor2012. Vince had been so fervent in his insistance that Zipacna was the Calendar Killer that Leah had started to wonder if he had another agenda altogether, one that she'd gotten caught up in because she'd needed someone other than herself to blame over Matty's loss.

"I'm here," she said noncommittally. "You said you wanted to show me something."

She was already regretting having come. *Should've broken it off the other day,* she thought. Her grief had moved past the point where she needed to lean on Vince as a connection to her brother. But as she'd started to ease away he'd gotten clingy, suggesting he wasn't there yet. So she'd decided to stick it out a few more weeks or months, figuring she owed him a little longer in the lean-on-me department.

Besides, his background check had come back whistle-clean and he didn't register on her cop creep-o-meter. He was just a guy who'd lost a friend, and was looking for someone to blame. Unlike her, though, he didn't seem to be moving past his conviction that Zipacna was the serial killer responsible for Matty's death. Not yet, anyway.

"Matt told me about a special room where they perform their rituals." Vince's throat worked. "I want to check it out."

"It was included in the last warrant," Leah argued. "They didn't find anything."

Actually, that wasn't precisely true. The crime scene folk had said the room was a mosaic of semen stains, vaginal contributions, and blood—but the former weren't illegal, and the latter hadn't been substantial enough to suggest exsanguination, but instead had been consistent with the smaller ritual bloodlettings the members of Survivor2012 readily admitted engaging in.

"Humor me?" Vince's expression went sheepish. "Look, I know you're losing steam on this, and I understand. I really do. It's just . . . I don't know. I'm not ready to let go yet. I need something . . . more."

Because she could relate, and because she figured it'd give their nonrelationship enough closure that she could walk away without feeling too much like a bitch, she nodded. "Okay. Let's go."

Keeping an eye out for security—half-naked or otherwise—they worked their way across the main room to an offshoot hallway, passing a glossy sign that told them they were headed into the Temple of Wisdom. Said temple proved to be a series of small classrooms furnished with tables and chairs, and flat-screen TVs running documentaries. There were a few partygoers in each room, and Leah slowed down enough to catch snippets of the narration as she and Vince passed.

"The Maya used the tall pyramids as landmarks," said the voice-over in the first room, which held five people deep in conversation. The TV showed an aerial image of three piles of rubble—presumably former pyramids—poking up from a sea of green leaves. "They could see them over the rain forest canopy, and navigate from one to the next."

Which was pretty clever, Leah thought as they moved on.

The screen in the next room, which had a few more people in it, most of whom seemed to be paying attention, showed a CGI rendering of the earth, sun and moon, and the narrator intoned, ". . . the Mayan Long Count calendar is based on astronomy and the end date of December 21, 2012, when the next Great Conjunction will occur. Other cultures, completely separate from the Maya, have also fixated on this date as a time of great change."

"Guess we found the propaganda," Vince said. "Come on."

They moved past two more classrooms—another pyramid lecture and more astronomy, or else the same films running on different schedules—and stopped when the corridor teed into another. A table blocking the hallway to the left was hung with a discreet sign that read, NO GUESTS BEYOND THIS POINT, PLEASE.

"Not exactly high-level security," Leah said as they squeezed past the table and moved into the corridor beyond.

"The cops didn't find anything," Vince said, in what sounded a little like a dig. "Zipacna's probably not worried anymore."

Or he didn't have anything to worry about in the first place, Leah thought but didn't say, because she just wanted to get this over with and go home. The weird vibes coming off Vince only strengthened her resolve to end their nonrelationship ASAP. The only thing keeping her going now was the memory of how fondly Matty had spoken of his friend. Vince had been there for him when Cheryl had taken off. Leah, not so much.

For that, she figured she owed the guy.

"Here." Vince stopped in front of a floor-to-ceiling glass-fronted case holding a bunch of worn stone statues, all stylized variations of the crocodile god Zipacna. "It's behind here."

"If you're going to break something, I'm leaving." Hell, she should leave now. But she stayed put as he pressed his palm against the wall and said something under his breath.

The display case swung inward on concealed hinges. The moment the door opened, torches flared to life, one at each corner of the room that was revealed in the firelight, and a trickle of water became audible. The walls were lined with stones—fake or real, she wasn't sure—carved with row after row of glyphs. Unlike the ones out in the main room, these carvings looked more like formal writing, as though the walls could tell a story if she knew how to read the hieroglyphs. Above the writing, about chest-high, a wavy line of brilliant blue was painted all the way around the room. Above that, human skulls were carved into the stone in relief up near the ceiling. Water cascaded from each of their mouths, tumbling down to a shallow trench running the perimeter of the room and no doubt recirculating in the bizarre fountain.

In the center of the space sat a carved stone altar shaped like a man lying on his back, balancing a stone slab.

"The *chac-mool,*" Vince said, indicating the recumbent figure. "Sometimes a throne, sometimes an altar." He paused. "Sometimes a place of sacrifice."

"Shit." Leah stared at it, frozen. This was way freakier than she'd expected, and somehow familiar. She hated that she could picture Matty here, could picture him doing some of the stuff the task force had included in their reports, which ranged from small bloodlettings to full-on orgies, all part of prayers to a pantheon that hadn't mattered since the fifteen hundreds, in an effort to avert a doomsday nobody sane believed in.

"Come on, before someone sees us." Vince pulled her inside before she could think to dig in her heels, and he let the door swing behind them.

"Wait!" Leah spun and made a grab for the edge of the panel, but she was too late. It shut with a click. There was no latch on this side, no knob. No visible way of getting the hell out.

She whirled on Vince, anger firing. "Open it, *right now*!"

"Shh." He put a finger to his lips and whispered, "They'll hear us. And don't worry; there's a pressure pad next to the door, just like on the other side. We can get out whenever we want. I didn't want to leave it standing open in case anyone comes this way."

"This was a bad idea." Leah pressed on the carvings beside the door, searching for the pad. "Let's go."

"But we haven't—"

"I've seen enough. We're leaving." Nerves flared to life in her stomach, knotting against one another. A throbbing beat rose through the floor and shook the air around her, sounding like a human pulse, only too fast. Like fear. "Vince," she snapped, knowing there was no real reason to panic but unable to stem the rising tide of nerves. "Get over here and get this door open. *Now!*"

The throbbing grew louder, making her want to put her hands over her ears to block it out. But at the same time, it called to her, pulled at her. Tempted her. Pressure flared at the base of her brain. It wasn't a headache, though. More like an entreaty.

What the hell was going on?

"Vince?" she said, barely able to hear herself over the pounding rush. She took a couple of steps toward where he stood beside the altar, calm and motionless, like he couldn't hear the drumbeat, couldn't feel the floor heave beneath their feet.

He started toward her. "You don't look so good. Maybe you should sit down."

He helped her across the chamber and propped her up against the altar while her head spun and her stomach heaved. She wanted to lie down, but she'd be damned if she was going to nap on the altar. "Get us out of here," she said, and this time she heard herself, heard how weak her voice sounded. "Please."

"I want to show you what I found first." He produced a black blade, held it out to her. "Looks like it could be the murder weapon."

Everything inside her rebelled. *Put it down,* she wanted to scream as every chain-of-evidence nightmare she'd ever heard of fast-forwarded through her brain in a split second. *Put it right back where you found it!* Not that replacing it would fix things now. She had no warrant, no probable cause, no—

"Here." He handed her the knife. "Take it."

No, she said, only the word didn't come out, and instead of warding him off, she found herself reaching for the blade with unsteady hands that weren't entirely under her control. She touched the knife, grabbed onto it blade-first, and felt the edge bite into her palm. Vince started backing away as blood flowed, and she thought he whispered something in words she didn't comprehend.

A detonation rocked the room, sending them both staggering.

Three other people appeared in the chamber with shocking suddenness, two men and a woman, wearing black-on-black combat gear and armed to the teeth with automatics and grenades. They advanced on Vince with deadly intent, their backs to Leah.

The drumbeats stopped. The world stopped. Her head cleared, rage flared, and she swung into cop mode and launched herself into the fight. She'd lost the knife in the blast, and she didn't know if the newcomers were part of Survivor2012 or something else, but she wasn't waiting to find out.

"Vince, get the door!" she screamed, and lunged for the guy closest to her, aiming for a choke hold and missing because he was way bigger than she'd thought, nearly six-five if he was an inch. Sensation zipped up her arm when she touched him, arcing from his skin to hers like static electricity. She hissed out a breath but hung on and went for the choke a second time.

He countered, spun and grabbed her, flipping her in a practiced move that put her flat on her back and drove the breath from her lungs. She lay there stunned for a second, staring up . . .

. . . into the cobalt-colored eyes of her dream lover.

"You!" she hissed.

Snapshot impressions bombarded her—the angle of his jaw, the piercing dark blue of his eyes, the black-on-black combat clothes that stretched across his muscular body. Reaction sizzled through her, feeling more like desire than fear.

"Don't worry; I've got you," he said, which was ridiculous, because as far as she could tell, she should damn well be afraid *of* him. But somehow she couldn't make herself protest as he helped her up and crowded her with his big body, backing her across the room. His voice was a deep, sexy rasp when he said, "You don't want to watch this."

"Watch—" Her question devolved to a scream when the other guy—older and sharp featured—pulled a MAC-10 and unloaded the clip into Vince's chest, point-blank. The noise was deafening, the blood spray horrific as Vince's body jerked with the rapid-fire impact.

Leah shrieked and flung herself toward her friend, but the blue-eyed guy grabbed her and held her close while she fought and scratched, still screaming. "Easy," he said over her cries. "He's not what you think."

Then brilliant green light flared out of nowhere, and wind whipped through the chamber, though that should've been impossible. Leah stopped screaming, because a buzzing noise had taken up where the chatter of gunfire left off, rising in speed and intensity as Vince's body slid down the wall, leaving a blood trail.

In the center of the room, the altar began to glow green.

"Get over here," Blue Eyes ordered his companions.

He held Leah tightly against his body, and as the others approached, he said quietly in her ear, "I'm sorry you had to see that, and I'm sorry that I can't stay and explain. Trust me when I tell you I'm keeping you safer by staying away." Then the others were there, hanging on to his arms, and he said, "Close your eyes."

A flash of motion caught her attention, and she saw Vince pull himself up the wall and start limping across the chamber. Which was impossible. Had those been blanks? What the *hell* was going on? "Vince," she screamed, heart pounding in her chest, *"help me!"*

Then the buzz racheted up to a scream, and the world exploded.

Everything went gray-green for a second, and there was a sideways lurch. Then the air changed and a shock wave slammed into Leah and the man who held her, sending them flying. She landed first, with him atop her, driving the breath from her lungs.

She heard him curse, heard the crash of debris all around them, and realized he'd used his body to shield her from the blast. Then she heard screams and shouts and the pound of approaching feet, the sounds echoing differently than they'd been moments earlier. The air was different, too.

She felt the press of a kiss on the side of her neck, heard him whisper, "Stay safe." Then his weight was gone.

"How . . . ?" She struggled up on her elbows. "What the . . . ?"

She found herself lying in the hallway, staring at the sign asking people not to venture into the darkened wing. Beyond that was a wall of rubble where the hallway used to be.

The warrior and his companions were gone.

Leah lunged to her feet as a mob of half-naked 2012ers and dressed-up partygoers jammed the hallway, some running toward the explosion, some away, creating a milling, screaming chaos.

With no suspects to chase, the cop inside her gave way to the woman. Grief slashed through confusion, battering her to her knees. *"No!"*

She'd lost first Matty, then Nick. Now Vince. And in a way, she'd lost her dream warrior too, because there was no way she could knowingly lust after a guy who ran with killers, with terrorists who used explosives to . . . what? Make a statement? Kill a man? And what was with the green light and the noises? Special effects, or something more?

For the first time, Leah seriously considered that she might be losing her mind.

Tears welled up and sobs tore at her chest. Giving in, she bowed her head and wept for the dead, and for a reality that seemed to be falling to pieces around her.

Strike took two steps toward her before he forced himself to stop. Or, more accurately, before Red-Boar's grip on his arm made stopping the only option.

He couldn't pull away, because Patience needed a chain of contact in order to keep up their invisibility. But damn, he wanted to go to Leah, wanted to explain that he'd just made her safe. The *makol* Red-Boar had shot—and who'd triggered some sort of timed detonation from the altar—wasn't Zipacna and had been wearing contacts that concealed his green-hued eyes, but magic knew magic. The bastard had lured her to the chamber somehow. But why? Did his master want to complete the blood sacrifice he'd begun at the equinox?

If it weren't for the protection spell, he wouldn't have known to teleport directly to Leah, and might not have gotten there in time. The very thought was beyond chilling.

"We should bring her back with us," he said quietly, low enough that only Patience and Red-Boar could hear, as the mob of partygoers filled the hallway, everyone talking at once.

"Out of the question," Red-Boar hissed. "Get it through your damn head that she's not for you."

Strike gritted his teeth. "She's in danger."

"And she'll be safer with you?" The older Nightkeeper let the question hang for a beat, then said, "I didn't think so. You said it yourself. You're protecting her by staying the hell away."

Was he? Strike wasn't even sure of that anymore. His attempt to protect her by giving her space had wound up with her going one-on-one with a *makol*. He was going to have to do better. He just didn't know how yet, and wasn't about to figure it out with Red-Boar standing right next to him. All three of them might be invisible, but he could still feel the weight of the older man's glare.

"Hey, lady, are you okay?" a stranger crouched down beside Leah as random people milled around, some rubbernecking the debris from the blast, others talking excitedly. "Are you hurt?" another voice asked, and then it all degenerated into a babble of questions without answers.

"Come on." Red-Boar tugged at Strike. "Let's go."

Strike waited a moment longer, until he heard sirens nearby, and the clipped orders of rescue personnel. Then, when he knew Leah was as safe as she could be right now, surrounded by other cops, he closed his eyes, found the travel thread, and took his people home.

CHAPTER TEN

The next few days were a blur of training sessions and preparations for the binding ceremony, which should've left Strike with zero time to worry about Leah. But somehow he managed to do exactly that.

She'd treated the *makol*, Vince, like a friend. He'd presumably been a second-generation critter, one created by the *ajaw-makol* after the solstice. There hadn't been any sense of a second source of evil in the Survivor2012 compound, meaning that Carter's info had been wrong and Zipacna was somewhere else.

But where?

Shit, he didn't know, and he didn't know what else to have Carter be on the lookout for. He needed an *itza'at*, that was what he needed. A good seer—hell, even a half-assed one—could track the *ajaw-makol* by its magic.

If he was seriously lucky, either Alexis or Jade would get the seer's mark during the talent ceremony, and they'd have a prayer of getting some answers.

If not, well, it was time for coloring outside the lines, which was exactly what had him leaving the mansion on the evening before the aphelion, braced for a fight.

When he reached Red-Boar's cottage, he knocked. "It's me."

After a long moment, the door swung open to reveal Rabbit in full-on sulk mode, wearing cutoffs that showed his thin calves to no great effect, and a dark blue hoodie over his T-shirt. "Yeah?"

"I need to talk to your father. Could you give us fifteen minutes alone?"

Rabbit shrugged. "Whatever."

He slouched out and Strike stepped through, straight into the kitchen of the four-room bungalow. Red-Boar was sitting at the kitchen table, wearing the brown robes of a penitent.

Strike hadn't seen him in the robes—which signified a magi atoning for great sin—in a long time. Initially, Jox had asked him to quit wearing the robes around the garden center because they made the customers nervous. After a while, Red-Boar had gotten out of the habit, and it'd been a nice change to see him in normal clothes day in and day out.

Which left Strike wondering what else in the older Nightkeeper's psyche had backslid.

"We need to talk," Strike said, crossing the kitchen to rummage in the fridge. He pulled out a Coke for himself, tossed Red-Boar a bottle of water without asking, and took the chair opposite him, cracking the soda open as he did so. He drained half of it, welcoming the kick of sugar and caffeine, before he said, "We need Rabbit to make thirteen."

"Bad idea," Red-Boar said, his voice nearly inflectionless.

"The way I see it, we're better off having him on the team than not, especially after the stunt he pulled at the garden center," Strike countered. "And it's not fair to keep him out of the classes."

Red-Boar stared into the bottled water. "I won't accept him into the bloodline. I can't."

It was an old argument Strike and Jox had never won. But they had their theories why.

"Does it have something to do with his mother?" Strike asked. Red-Boar had never spoken of her, had never acknowledged her existence, though the proof stood in the form of their son.

"It has *everything* to do with his mother," the older man said suddenly, his voice descending to a hiss.

"Who was she?"

"Better to ask where I met her. And the answer to that would be in the highlands."

Strike's breath whistled between his teeth. "Mexico?"

"Guatemala."

"Shit."

"Precisely."

Before the conquistadors drove the Nightkeepers north to Hopi territory, the magic users had coexisted with the Maya for centuries. The two cultures had lived in parallel, and maybe because of that, or because of their own fascination with the stars, the Maya had developed a magic system of their own. Some said rogue Nightkeepers had shared their magic, others that the Maya had been in contact with the *nahwal*, ghosts of the Nightkeepers' ancestors, or even with the *Banol Kax* themselves. Whatever the source of their power, the Order of Xibalba, an offshoot cult of Mayan shaman-priests, had developed spells unlike anything the Nightkeepers had ever seen. Something they came to fear.

Members of the order had brought the *Banol Kax* to earth in A.D. 869. The demons had destroyed the city of Tikal before the Nightkeepers had managed to drive them back behind the barrier. In the aftermath, the cultural center of the Maya shifted to Chichén Itzá, and the Order of Xibalba had been banned.

Rumors said it had lived on in secret, though.

Strike pinched the bridge of his nose, hoping to ward off the headache he knew was in his future. "Please don't tell me she was a disciple of the order."

Red-Boar said nothing.

"Shit." Needing to move, Strike drained the rest of the Coke, crumpled the can, and got up to toss it in the recycling bin beneath the sink. "I guess that explains a few things."

"Exactly." Red-Boar grimaced. "Order magic and Nightkeeper magic aren't the same; we can't know how they mixed in Rabbit. Which is why I can't claim him into the bloodline, and why I absolutely don't want him jacked in. If he goes through the binding ritual—"

"He's already jacked in once with no help from us," Strike pointed out. "He's a tough kid. He'll make it."

"I'm not worried about whether or not he'll survive," Red-Boar said flatly. "I'm worried about what will come out on the other side. He's already a punk. What do you think he'd be like with even more power?"

Rabbit's problems aren't entirely his fault, Strike wanted to say, but he didn't have time for an argument he knew he wouldn't win, so instead he said, "I'm sorry, but I'm going to have to take that risk. I want him to go through the ceremony tomorrow." He had to believe it would work. If not, they were stuck at twelve, and that was nowhere near a magic number.

Red-Boar's head came up. "Is that an order?"

He hated to do it, but he didn't see another way. "Yes."

"Then have at it. Your call, your responsibility. I wash my hands of the issue."

Having gotten what he'd come for, whether gracefully or not, Strike headed for the door. He paused at the threshold, though, and turned back. "Was that what you said to my father?" It was no secret that Red-Boar had argued against the attack on the intersection. He hadn't been the only one.

The Nightkeeper's grin held zero humor. "No. I told the king he was a damned fool following damn fool dreams."

"Since you didn't say anything like that just now, I'm guessing you think I'm right about binding Rabbit."

"I think he'll find his way to the magic regardless," Red-Boar said. "I also think that even if we can bind— and control—him, there's no guarantee the gods will count him as one of the thirteen, especially when there's one more true Nightkeeper out there."

"Don't go there," Strike warned. "Either Anna comes back of her own free will or she doesn't come at all."

Red-Boar nodded. "And that's where I think you're being a damned fool."

After Strike-out kicked him out of the cottage, Rabbit headed for the pool, planning to swim a few hundred laps to work off the jittery burn in his chest, the one that made him do and say things he sometimes later wished he hadn't. When he got to the pool area, though, he couldn't settle enough to dive in. The air jangled with a strange, pent-up energy that amped him up even more than usual. He felt itchy, like he wanted to peel his skin off, starting with his toes and working his way up.

Restless, he slipped into the mansion through one of the glass sliders leading to the hall just beyond the great room. He stopped on the far side of the arched doorway and leaned against the wall, so he could watch without being seen, and listen without being asked to participate in the whole lame-ass Magic 101 thing.

Who are you kidding? he scoffed inwardly. *Not like they'd ask you anyway.* He wasn't one of them—his father had made that crystal clear over the years. He'd never really said why, but he hadn't needed to; it was all too obvious. Rabbit wasn't the child of his precious wife, Cassie, wasn't one of the sons he'd lost in the battle. He might be blood kin, but he wasn't family. Wasn't a Nightkeeper.

For whatever the hell that was worth.

Hearing the murmur of voices, Rabbit shuffle-stepped a little closer to peek around the arch. Jox was in the middle of saying something about fractal waves and computer programs—Rabbit had no clue what the hell that had to do with the barrier and magic—when he broke off and turned, his eyes looking on Rabbit. "You want in on this, kid? You could tell these guys what it's like to jack in."

Anger flashing that the *winikin* was making fun of him, teasing him with stuff he wasn't going to be taught to do properly, Rabbit sneered. "Yeah, right. Screw you." He flipped the bird, spun on his heel, and headed back down the hall, moving fast.

And ran smack into Strike-out.

Strike gave him The Look, which was one of the few royal things he did really well. "Apologize."

A hundred or so smart-ass responses popped into Rabbit's head, but for a change he managed to control his mouth. He turned, shuffled back to the arched doorway leading into the great room, and mumbled, "Sorry, Jox."

Strike's heavy hand landed on his shoulder. "Now do what he asked you to do. Describe what it's like to jack in."

Rabbit lifted a shoulder. "You can't describe it; you've just got to do it." Besides, he wasn't sure he could put the terror—and the elation—into words. So instead he said, "After you get your second mark, if you're lucky you'll be able to do stuff like this." He snapped, and an amber flame sprang from his fingertips.

He knew he was pushing it, doing things he wasn't supposed to be able to do. Instead of barking at him, though, Strike said, "Not bad. But with a little teamwork, you can do this." He held his larger hands on either side of the small flame and boosted the power.

The flame turned royal red and erupted to a fireball the size of Rabbit's head.

The teen reeled back, banging into the big man behind him. Power danced across his skin and burned in his blood, making him want to throw his head back and scream with the mad glory of it.

Then it was gone.

For a few seconds, there was utter silence in the great room. The newbies' eyes were big and it didn't look like they were breathing.

Strike lowered his hands, letting them drop to Rabbit's shoulders. "You shouldn't be able to call fire without training," he said quietly.

"So sue me," Rabbit said, equally quiet, totally buzzing with the aftermath of the boosted power.

Strike pushed him forward. "Go on; get in there. You may think you know everything already, but trust me, you don't."

Unprepared for the shove, Rabbit stumbled forward a few steps, then spun. "What are you saying?" He couldn't quite keep the pitiful hope out of his voice.

Strike nodded yes to the question he hadn't asked. "You'll be part of the ceremony tomorrow."

Shock hammered through the teen. "No way the old man is going to let that happen."

"I've taken care of that," Strike said, then paused. "I

think you should move into the main house. It'll make the training easier if everyone's in one place."

Rabbit's mouth went dry. "He kicked me out of the cottage?"

"No." Strike shook his head. "No, never think that. He's just trying—has always tried—to do right by you. Believe that, even if it doesn't always make sense. But things have changed, and they're going to keep changing, and I want you to be a part of it."

A quick suspicion nagged at Rabbit, itching across his skin, but he ignored it because he was finally—finally!— being offered a chance at some real, honest-to-gods, sink-your-teeth-into-it training. Strike was offering to bind him, to—

He gulped as a thought occurred. "What . . . what will my mark be?"

Red-Boar had never accepted him as his son. Would the barrier see him as a member of the peccary blood-line, or as something else?

Worse, what if the barrier didn't recognize him at all?

"I'll see you through it," Strike said, which wasn't an answer, but was kind of reassuring, regardless.

Rabbit's chest felt funny when he nodded. "Yeah . . . okay. Um. Thanks."

Strike's eyes were very serious and a little bit sad. "I should've done something like this a long time ago."

That funny feeling spread up Rabbit's throat and itched at the back of his eyeballs, and to his utter horror he realized he was about to cry. " 'S okay," he mumbled, and reversed course to push past Strike and head for the john.

Halfway there, he turned back and sniffed. "Tell him . . . please tell Jox that I'll be right back. And not to start without me."

Then he locked himself in the bathroom, turned on the water, and bawled like a baby.

For several days after Vince's death and Leah's subse-quent suspension for blatantly disobeying orders to "stay the hell away from the 2012ers," she functioned on auto-pilot.

She grieved, but it was like there'd been so much grief lately that she'd worn out those neurons, making her numb and angry rather than sad. So she ate too little, slept too much, and spent the rest of the time sitting at her kitchen table, surfing the Internet, and trying to make some sense of it all.

On the morning of the Fourth of July, she dragged her ass out of bed midmorning, stumbled down from the attic, where she still slept beneath the stars. When she hit the button on her Mr. Coffee, a fat yellow spark jumped from her fingertip to the machine, and electricity arced with a sizzle and a yellow flash.

Leah shrieked and leaped back, her arm vibrating with the shock and her heart giving a funny bumpity-bump in her chest, as if whatever'd just happened had kicked it off rhythm.

Hello, static electricity, she thought, though the air was humid and her floors weren't carpeted. But what other explanation was there?

Mr. Coffee didn't so much as gurgle when she hit the ON button, suggesting that she'd fried something vital, so she went with tea for her morning caffeine hit as she powered up her laptop and glanced at her notes from the day before.

The Calendar Killer had taken twelve victims that they knew of, two at each equinox and solstice over the past eighteen months, with the exception of the previous month, when the summer solstice had passed without new victims.

Granted, Nick had died that day, but the signature was completely different; the only connection was the ritualistic nature of the Calendar murders, which might or might not point to the 2012ers, and the fact that she and Nick had been waiting for info on the leader of Survivor2012.

Chicken and egg or coincidence? Damned if she knew.

Then there was Vince's death. Guilt twisted tight when she pushed herself to remember exactly what'd happened. She should've insisted that he leave the investigation to the task force. Hell, *she* should've left the

investigation to the task force. If she had, Vince would
still be alive.

Then again, if they'd left it alone, the task force
wouldn't be taking another look at Survivor2012.

The explosion seemed to have been aimed at the heart
of the group, their ceremonies. The Calendar Killings
could—although this might be stretching it a little—have
been intended to throw suspicion on the group. Which
might mean the killer wasn't necessarily a member of
Survivor2012. He could be its enemy.

The thought brought a flash of piercing blue eyes, the
image of a big man who had moved like a fighter and
bombed a charity gala, yet had somehow gotten her out
of a locked chamber before it blew.

Logic said she'd gotten blown clear by the shock wave.
But the door had been shut, and even if it'd been open,
the shock wave would've splatted her on the opposite
wall rather than taking a right-hand turn and dumping
her in the main hallway.

Logic also said that the dreams were nothing more
than a pastiche of her experiences over the past few
months, a way for her subconscious to deal with the
pain. But the skulls in the older dreams had screamed a
blast of water rather than a trickle, and the blue-eyed
warrior had worn cutoffs rather than combat fatigues.
And rather than a murderer, he'd been her lover.

It didn't make sense. None of it did.

But she sure as hell intended to figure it out. For
Matty. For Nick. For Vince.

For her own sanity.

Ignoring the tea that cooled at her elbow, she got to
work. She wasn't looking for the names and faces of
people who might want Survivor2012 gone for good—
the task force was already on that, and with a ton more
computer power than she had at her disposal. No, she
was coming at it from another angle.

She was trying to figure out what made the doomsday-
ers tick. Maybe it was partly because, if she accepted
the 2012ers as the victims rather than the perps, that
meant Matty hadn't been stupid for joining them, meant

she hadn't been irresponsible for letting her brother run with the crowd that'd killed him. Maybe it was because the snippets she'd caught from the 2012ers' educational programs had been oddly compelling. And maybe it was an effort to understand her own response to the dark-haired stranger.

Whatever the source of the compulsion—obsession?—she worked through the day, bent over her computer until her eyes burned and her joints ached and her head buzzed with strange words that made more sense to her than they ought.

She didn't get dressed until midafternoon, didn't have lunch until four. And when darkness fell, she kept working.

As the stars prickled to life overhead, she discovered an author named Ambrose Ledbetter who seemed to know more than all the rest, or maybe he just put it in words that a nonexpert could understand. Either way, his articles seemed to synthesize all the information, ask all the right questions. Ledbetter had written in an article published just before the Calendar Killings began:

> *Thompson's elucidation of the Long Count calendar of the classical Maya gives an end date when the backward-counting calendar will reach zero. McKenna identified complementary patterns buried in the Chinese I Ching also pointing to a paradigm shift on the same day. He called this shift "Timewave Zero."*
>
> *Although the end-time prophecy may seem like the realm of historians (or perhaps only pseudoscientists), recent discoveries suggest otherwise. For one, quantum physicists have identified a degenerating mathematical fractal pattern that will reach its endpoint on the exact date cited in the ancient texts. Perhaps more persuasive is the supported astronomical fact that on that same day, the sun, moon, and earth will precisely align at the center of the Milky Way in a Great Conjunction the likes of which occurs only once every twenty-six thousand years.*
>
> *This alignment is predicted to trigger devastating*

sunspots, shifts of the magnetic poles, and changes in the orbit of the Earth itself, all of which will have heightened effects due to mankind's progressive destruction of the ozone layer. In sum, therefore, both ancient prophecies and modern science combine to predict that the total and catastrophic destruction of our world will occur on December 21, 2012. Legend holds, however, that this destruction may be averted by—

A knock at the door had Leah jolting. She'd been so into the research that she hadn't heard the sound of a car, or footsteps coming up the drive. But the interruption was probably a good thing, she realized as she stood and the room took a long, lazy spin around her. She needed to move around, get her blood pressure above "hibernate."

When the knock came again, she called, "Be right there."

The floor seemed to move beneath her feet, swaying, and the air hummed faintly off-key. She had a hell of a headache—when had that started? She didn't remember. The pressure began at the base of her skull and radiated upward, somehow seeming more like desire for something forbidden than actual pain. It also felt familiar, though she couldn't have said why.

When she reached the door, she left the security system armed and checked the peephole. She saw Connie standing there, looking sleek and stylish even after a full day of work, and faintly irritated by the wait.

"One sec," Leah called. "Let me kill the alarm."

She also took a detour through the kitchen and shoved her computer and the messy pile of printouts into a cabinet. No reason to let Connie know she was working on her own—that would only slow her return to active duty.

An obsessed cop was a cop without perspective.

Which was true, Leah acknowledged as she headed back to the door and disarmed the security system. But an obsessed cop also sometimes saw stuff the others missed.

Giving her appearance a once-over in the hallway mirror, Leah pulled open the door. "Hey, Connie. I was just—"

The world went luminous green. Then black.

Something was wrong. Strike didn't know how he knew it, or what exactly "it" was, but the wrongness hummed over his skin alongside the aphelion's power as he and Jox finished prepping the ceremonial chamber for the binding ritual.

The room was located on the top floor of the mansion, roughly in the center of the sprawling footprint of the big house. It was one of the few spaces they'd left alone during the renovations, mainly because the altar itself was set in a cement pad containing the ashes of nearly seven generations of Nightkeepers. There was serious magic in the room, serious power.

And seriously weird vibes, Strike thought, frowning as he counted the tapers—lucky thirteen—and assured himself that the stingray spines, knives, parchments, and bowls were all set out and ready to roll. "Why do I feel like we're forgetting something?"

Jox glanced over, raising an eyebrow. "Like you've done this before?"

"That's the point—I haven't. So why the willies?" Strike rubbed his chest, where a strange pressure burned. "Maybe I just need some Pepto." *Or a beer.*

Jox crossed in front of the large *chac-mool* altar to grip his shoulder. "You'll do fine."

"Thanks." Strike glanced up through the transparent glass roof of the sacred chamber. The reflected firelight from the tapers meant he couldn't see the stars winking into existence high above, but he could feel them, just as he could feel the lines of power shift into place as the aphelion drew near. "I feel . . . jumpy."

"Hormones," the *winikin* said. "They're going to ramp up during every conjunction for a while, until you're really solid in the magic."

"In any other lifetime, having your father figure tell you, 'Don't worry, you're just horny,' would seem weird," Strike said. "But I find myself oddly reassured.

Probably explains why I haven't been able to get Leah out of my head all day."

Jox made a face, but kept working his lint brush over the royal crimson robes Strike would wear for the ceremony. "That Alexis, you know . . . she's a knockout. Blond, edgy . . ."

"Don't start." Strike's jumpiness flickered toward temper.

"Mating with another Nightkeeper will boost your power by double, if not more."

"And who gives a crap if I spend the rest of my life miserable?"

Jox waved him off. "Tell it to Dr. Phil."

Strike gritted his teeth so hard he thought he felt a molar give. "You don't know the first thing about how I feel."

"The hell I don't," Jox snapped, tossing the lint brush and whirling to face him. "Get your head out of your ass and look around."

Strike fought the anger, fought the power as the planets aligned and the barrier thinned, and his gut told him he was missing something major. "Watch your step, *winikin*."

Jox's voice cracked around the edges when he said, "Do you honestly think this is the life I would've picked? I wouldn't have traded raising you and Anna, but *gods*. Don't tell me I don't know what it means to want someone and not be able to go after her, and don't you dare think you're the only one making a sacrifice." He jabbed a finger toward the door. "Never mind me. Including the *winikin*, there are fourteen people out there who dropped their lives to come here because they knew it was the right thing to do. Have you stopped to think for a second what they walked away from? Whether *they* want to be here? No, of course not, because it's their duty to be here; it's in their bloodlines. Well, guess what? Same goes for you, only double because you're Scarred-Jaguar's son. Get used to it."

"Why, because you did?" Anger and worry rode Strike, had him lashing out. "Leah is mine. Just because you didn't go after your woman doesn't mean I can't have mine."

"She's not yours!" the *winikin* shouted. "She's *human*."

"Did you ever wonder why you didn't go after Hannah years ago?" Strike asked, aiming low when he used the story Jox had told him in confidence. "Did you ever stop to think that maybe you liked the idea of her more than the reality? That she was a pretty fantasy, but the reality would've been too messy? That—"

Jox punched him in the mouth, splitting the crap out of his lip.

Strike reeled back, tasting blood as the *winikin* stalked out, slamming the door.

"Damn it!" Strike took a couple of steps after him, then stopped when the door opened once again and he saw the others standing there, wearing blue trainees' robes and looking pretty freaked.

Way to go into the ceremony nice and focused, he thought. *Shit.* And he wasn't even dressed.

"I'll be back in five minutes," he said, grabbing the red robe and bundling it under his arm. "Get comfortable. Or something."

Booking it to the pool house, he stripped out of his jeans, shirt, and briefs, and pulled on the ceremonial regalia Jox had dug out of storage. The floor-length robe had long, pointed sleeves and a draping hood, with the edges encrusted with small, intricately carved shells. The fabric was bloodred. Royal red, for the last of the royal line.

With it went a feathered headdress that fit close to Strike's scalp and hung down in the back, gaudy with feathers and jade. Last but not least, he pulled three jade celts out of the pocket of the robe. Working by feel, he hooked the flat, carved ovals so they hung down in front of his nose and cheeks, distorting his profile and making it—according to legend—look more like that of a god.

Always before when he'd donned the ceremonial regalia, he'd felt thoroughly silly, as if he were getting ready for Halloween. But now, barefoot and commando beneath the heavy red robe, wearing something that looked like a bad roadside souvenir on his head when he glanced in the full-length mirror inside the pool house bathroom, he didn't see an idiot.

He wasn't sure what he saw, exactly. The guy looking back at him seemed like a stranger, like someone out of another time. Then he got it, and a shiver took hold in his gut, making him think the reflection in the mirror might be the source of his unease.

Because, gods help him, all of a sudden he looked like his father.

He felt a twinge when he said, "Let's just hope I got more of the good parts of him than the bad."

He'd loved his father, worshiped him the way only a nine-year-old boy could. But at the same time, the king had singlehandedly wiped out an entire civilization. Not exactly a proud legacy. Then again, Strike wasn't exactly proud of himself at the moment, either. Jox was right: He had a duty. Everything else had to take a backseat for the next four years, even Leah.

Especially Leah. Seeing her the other day—having her recognize him, and then realizing that she'd somehow come back into the *ajaw-makol*'s orbit—had gotten him thinking about fate and the gods again, about destiny and how many times their paths needed to cross before he'd admit they were meant to be together.

Unfortunately, it wasn't about whether they were destined for each other. It was about the prophecy, the future. And in the immediate future, he needed to get his head off the woman and into the ceremony.

Scrubbing a hand across the back of his neck, where the creepy-crawly feeling of not-quite-rightness had settled in, Strike took a deep breath and headed back to the mansion, reminding himself that tonight wasn't about him. It was about the trainees, and their bloodline marks. It was about the continuation, however tenuous, of the Nightkeepers.

In the ritual chamber, the trainees were ranged shoulder-to-shoulder in a loose semicircle facing the altar. Rabbit, smaller and darker than the others, stood on one end, slightly apart from the group. Patience and Brandt were at the other end. Although they already had their bloodline marks, Strike wanted them to have an escort for their first official jack-in. Besides, he might need their power for an uplink if things went wrong. It didn't happen often, but newbies sometimes went missing in the barrier. When that happened, it was up to their escort to go find them. Which begged a question—where the hell was their second escort?

"Where's Red-Boar?" Strike asked as he stepped to his place beside the altar. If the bastard was boycotting because Rabbit was included in the ceremony, he'd—

"I'm here," the older man said, appearing in the doorway wearing his ceremonial robes, which were black and worked with intricate patterns of stingray spines and boar's teeth. "I . . ." He paused, staring at the *chac-mool*. "Never mind."

Strike winced, realizing that while he'd never been part of the chamber rituals as a child, the older Nightkeeper no doubt had plenty of memories in the room. His own talent ceremony. His wedding. The barrier ceremony for his twin sons. *Ouch*. Serious ghosts.

Without another word, Red-Boar took position on the other side of the altar. "Proceed."

Strike nodded, feeling the power hum. "Let's do it." He rolled up the right sleeve of his crimson robe, baring his marks. Red-Boar followed suit, baring his. Then the trainees did the same, showing that they had no marks.

Strike passed the bowls, parchment scraps, and spines and gestured for the trainees to sit. Once they'd all assumed cross-legged positions, he said, "Okay, gang. Follow my lead, and no matter what happens, try not to panic. If we get separated, stay where you are. Red-Boar or I will come find you."

He picked up his bowl and set it in the hollow formed by his crossed legs. It was the king's bowl, made of sand-smoothed jade and carved with glyphs spelling out the king's writ. Touching the bowl, he sent a quick thought toward the heavens. *Gods, please help me not fuck this up*. Not the most eloquent of prayers, maybe, but he'd never pretended to be a poet. He was just a regular guy with a few upgrades.

Laying a square of parchment in the bottom of the

bowl—okay, technically it was high-grade card stock from Staples, but it wasn't the paper so much as the symbol—Strike picked up his stingray spine, braced himself, and drove it into his tongue. Pain slapped at him, then again when he ripped the spine free and blood flowed into his mouth. *Shit, that hurt.*

He opened his mouth, letting the blood fall into the bowl, where it soaked into the paper. Once the others had followed suit, he lit his taper, then touched it to the one held by the trainee beside him, Patience. The flame was passed from one to another, coming full circle until Red-Boar touched his lit candle to Strike's, completing the circle.

Then, moving as one, they set the blood-soaked pages aflame and snuffed their candles as acrid smoke rose. They leaned in. Inhaled the smoke. And said in unison, *"Pasaj och."* The world lurched and went gray-green, then solidified. And they were in. Or, rather, *he* was in.

Strike found himself standing in the middle of nowhere and everywhere at once, on a soft, yielding surface, with nothing but mist around him, eddying in random swirls created by an unseen wind. Either the others hadn't made it into the barrier, or they'd landed somewhere else.

"Hello?" He looked around wildly. "Red-Boar? Patience? Anyone?" His shout fell dead on the mist. There was no echo, no response.

He was alone.

CHAPTER ELEVEN

Leah awoke in her own attic, lying spread-eagled on the futon mattress beneath the skylight. For a second, looking up at the stars and somehow feeling them hum in her bones, she thought everything was okay, that her stomach was in knots because of a strange dream.

Then she tried to move. And couldn't.

Fear jolted as a hazy memory returned: that of seeing Connie on her doorstep but opening her door to someone else, someone she hadn't seen clearly. Then a flash of green, then nothing.

Heart pounding, Leah tugged at her arms and legs and found them held fast in doubled-up zip ties threaded through eyebolts sunk into the sturdy attic floorboards. She had no leverage; the plastic cut into her skin but didn't give. She was alone, but heard the heavy tread of footsteps downstairs. She had to think. *Think!*

She looked around for a weapon, a plan.

The knife, she thought. She'd brought a carving knife up from the kitchen; she didn't know why. And, wonder of wonders, it was still sitting in the bowl where she'd left it, half buried beneath a parchment diary.

But it was a good four feet away from the outstretched fingertips of her left hand. "Damn it," she whispered, frustrated tears pressing in her throat. "Come on; you can do it. Get the knife."

She squirmed and strained, tugging against the zip ties until blood slicked her wrists and ankles. The pain hazed her vision yellow-gold, and her head pounded with what felt like a sinus headache times a million. The room spun and the golden light brightened, though it was night out and the room was lit with the single beeswax candle.

The footsteps sounded again from below, and this time they were headed her way.

Come on, come on. She reached toward the knife, fingers straining, her entire attention focused on the black resin handle.

And the knife moved.

The rational part of Leah gaped, but the rest of her, the part that belonged to the yellow-gold pressure inside her mind, kept straining, kept concentrating, panicking as the ladder leading up to the attic creaked.

Come on! she thought, only the words that formed in her head didn't sound right, didn't sound like English at all.

Half a second later, the knife slid out from underneath the diary and floated across the floorboards as if it were swinging on an invisible string, coming to rest against her bloodstained palm.

Impossible, she thought, even as she grabbed the knife and twisted her hand, jamming the blade beneath the zip ties and sawing frantically. *That didn't just happen.* Yet somehow she had the knife.

Working fast, she cut her left hand free, then her right, and was working on her feet when the trapdoor lifted and swung all the way open, and a slightly built man appeared, wearing jeans and a cartoon-covered T-shirt, walking backward up the ladder because he was carrying something bulky in his arms. A carved wooden chest, to be exact.

The zip ties gave, and she stumbled to her feet, lunging toward the guy as he hit the top of the ladder and turned. Her brain froze at the sight of filed-sharp teeth and a hollow earplug. It looked like her ex-snitch, Itchy Pasquale, except that his eyes were a bright, luminous green. An impossible, glowing green that should've existed only in the movies. But though her brain cramped with horror, her body kept moving. She hit him waist-high, and her unexpected attack drove them both across the attic floor.

Cursing, Itchy dropped the carved chest and grabbed her blood-slicked wrist in a bruising grip. He twisted her arm up and back with one hand and raised his other hand to her head. The press of a gun muzzle had her stilling.

"Don't make me kill you," he said, his voice rasping in her ear. "Don't—"

She screamed and twisted away from the gun, then reversed and slammed her knife into the side of his neck. He howled and ripped the knife free, reeling back and losing his grip on the gun.

She grabbed the weapon—a good-size Glock—and came up straight into Itchy's fist. The punch drove her away from the trapdoor, away from freedom.

Tasting blood, she fell against the wall, dazed. Pain was a dull roar, overtaken by the command of a strange voice inside her, one that shouted, *Get the chest!*

Itchy swiped at the side of his neck, and his hand came away red with blood. His face contorted and he came at her with the knife. "Fucking bitch!"

Shaking, she struggled to her feet and unloaded the Glock into his face at point-blank range. Blood sprayed, bone shattered, and unidentifiable gristle chunks spattered her in the blowback. Someone was screaming, and it took a second to realize it was her, shouting curses and prayers and sobs, all mixed together as she ran through the clip.

Itchy's body—it had to be a body, because there was no way anything could survive with its head hamburgered up like that—hit the back wall and slid down, drawing a gory streak.

Shaking, sobbing, she bolted for the ladder, her only thought to escape, to get free, to get somewhere, anywhere far away. Then her eyes locked on the carved chest, which sat near the trapdoor. *Yes*, the voice inside her said. *Open it.*

"I don't know how," she whispered. There was no latch, padlock, or keyhole, no obvious way to get the thing open.

Yes, you do.

No, she didn't. But somehow she did. She held her torn wrists over the lid and waited for a few drops of blood to fall. When they did, she whispered, *"Pasaj."*

She didn't have a clue what it meant or where it'd come from, but it worked. The trunk opened, not by the boring old lock-and-lid method, but by freaking vaporizing, puffing out of existence as though it'd never been. Inside the box lay a square packet wrapped in oilcloth and tied with a shoelace. It glowed red and resonated a high, sweet note in her soul.

Mine, Leah thought, and reached for it. Her fingers closed over the packet, and cool heat radiated up her arm as she tucked the thing into the back pocket of her jeans. Her headache snapped out of existence, and the pressure disappeared as though it'd never been, leaving a silence inside her head that crackled with electricity, with power. With urgency.

She had to get out of there, had to get away. She hadn't heard any other footsteps down below, but kept the empty Glock at the ready, figuring it'd be good for intimidation if nothing else.

She was halfway down the ladder when a heavy weight slammed into her from behind.

Screaming and fighting for balance, she pitched forward and landed hard, rolling onto her back as she scratched for freedom, trying to struggle out from underneath her attacker.

Itchy's ruined face loomed over her, which was just unbelievable. He shouldn't still be alive. But as she watched, the flesh started knitting back, eyes and tendons re-forming, meat growing out to cover regenerating bone. *Impossible!* she screamed in her head, but knew it wasn't a dream. It was real.

Shrieking, she jerked a knee up between them and tried to break free, but he was too strong. She couldn't get any leverage as his fingers closed over her throat and bore down. Her windpipe folded closed under the pressure, and her consciousness dimmed.

Help, she cried in her skull. *Help me!*

*　　　*　　　*

Damn it! Strike's mind raced as he looked around the featureless mist of the barrier, searching for the others.

What'd gone wrong? What had—*No, never mind that,* he told himself. *Just go back and get them.* If they were already jacked in, he should be able to tap into Red-Boar's connection and follow from there.

Closing his eyes, he envisioned his corporeal body still sitting cross-legged in the ceremonial chamber back at the training center.

Without warning, red-gold light flared behind his eyelids, and power thrummed through him on a high, clarion note of alarm. Everything inside him froze.

The protection spell had activated. Leah was in immediate fear for her life.

"Leah!" he shouted, rage and anger coalescing in his soul. "Hold on!" He closed his eyes, thought of her, grabbed onto the travel thread that appeared in his mind's eye, and—

Logjammed.

His mind raced. Leah needed him, but so did the trainees. Given that he'd gotten knocked off course within the barrier, what was to say Red-Boar hadn't gotten his ass lost, too? The trainees might be alone, stuck somewhere, unable to get back. But Leah was in danger.

Nightkeepers before mankind, the king's writ said. Mankind before family and personal desire. But the gods were before all else, and it couldn't be a coincidence that Leah's trouble had hit during the aphelion, could it? What if she were still connected to the god somehow?

Caught between the two, Strike stripped off the heavy headdress and tipped his head back so he could say to the gray sky, "Gods, I know I haven't been the best about my prayers, but please hear this one. Please help me make the right choice."

"Go to her." The words came from everywhere and nowhere at once, in an amalgam of many different voices, all speaking at once, though at different pitches.

Heart jamming his throat, Strike looked around. "Who said that?"

Nearby, a human-shaped shadow darkened the mist.

It was tall and broad, in the way of all Nightkeepers, but stick-thin, as if the muscle and substance had melted away. It solidified out of the fog, a man yet not a man, with nut-brown skin drawn in tight wrinkles over bones and sinew, and gleaming obsidian orbs instead of eyeballs. On its right inner forearm, it wore the mark of the jaguar bloodline.

"Nahwal," Strike said quietly, heart thudding against his ribs as he tried to figure out whether he should bow or run. The *nahwal* of each bloodline embodied a small piece of all the ancestors from that line—not their personalities, but fragments of their wisdom and sight. The creatures lived—if you could call it that—in the barrier and showed themselves when they chose, provided information when they chose. They weren't supposed to have distinguishing marks, save for their bloodline glyphs. But as this one approached, Strike saw the glint of a blood-red ruby in its left ear.

Chest tightening, he touched his own left ear, where the piercing he'd gotten in his teens had long since grown over. "Father?"

"The others must find their own way," the many-voiced voice said without inflection. "Go now, or the woman dies."

The mists thickened, and it was gone.

"Wait!" Strike took two running steps toward where the image had been, then slammed on the brakes when the surface beneath him shifted. The ground—or whatever the hell it was—under his feet fell away, sliding like quicksand, or soil running into a growing rift, drawing him with it. The mists around him shifted from green to gray, warning that he was far too close to the edge of the barrier.

"Shit!" Backpedaling, he scrambled to solid ground, then stood, chest heaving with exertion, with the desire to shout, *What the hell is going on?*

But he didn't have the time for more questions. Leah didn't have the time. And though he knew the *nahwal* could've been wishful thinking, that he could be following his father's steps into the place where delusion became reality, he couldn't—just couldn't—leave her to die. So he was going to have to screw the writs and go with his gut.

Closing his eyes, he pictured Leah. Grabbed the travel thread.

And made the selfish choice, hoping to hell it was the right one.

Leah wrestled with Itchy's choke hold, growing weak as oxygen dimmed and her consciousness flickered. Panic kicked alongside an overwhelming sense of déjà vu, as though she'd suffocated before, died before. Only she hadn't.

Please help, she screamed in her mind, arching against her attacker in mindless terror, in supplication. *Please!*

There was a sharp crack, and a huge ripping noise filled her upstairs hallway with sound and light and wind. The next thing she knew, the blue-eyed guy was there, wearing a seashell-dotted red robe that should've made him look foolish but instead made him look like a warrior from another time, a modern samurai.

He took one look at the situation, and his face contorted with terrible rage. He grabbed Itchy by his bloodstained shirt and pants, hauled the bastard off her, and slammed him into the wall. There was a sickening crack, and Itchy's ruined head flopped sideways.

The blue-eyed man lowered the body to the floor. Then, incredibly, horribly, he reached for the knife that'd fallen free during the struggle.

"No!" Leah surged forward when she saw his intent. *"Don't!"*

"It'd be better if you don't watch," he said without looking at her. A muscle pulsed at his jaw, and his face was tight with something that might've been remorse, might've been repugnance, but neither of those emotions made sense. It wasn't like anyone was forcing him to . . .

Cut. Itchy's. Heart. Out.

Leah knew she should run, or better yet, slap a set of cuffs on Blue Eyes and call for backup. But she didn't move. Couldn't move.

Once he was finished with the heart, he went to work

on the head, hacking grimly through Itchy's neck and spinal cord with the rapidly dulling knife, gagging once or twice. The earthy, tangy scent of blood hung thick in the air, and the dark wetness soaked his robes and coated his hands to the elbows, and he looked miserable as he stood and looked down at the mutilated body. Then he spoke a word that made no sense and sounded like a cat urping a hairball.

And the body burst into flame—not normal fire, but a greenish purple flame that twisted with black and shed no heat. It looked like sickness. Like evil. And Leah couldn't stop staring at it.

The fire burned for a few seconds, then flashed so high she had to close her eyes and turn away, shielding herself. When the light dimmed she looked back to find that the body was gone, as was the gore that'd splashed the hallway and walls only moments earlier. Blue Eyes was clean of blood. But the deed he'd just done was written on his face, and in his eyes when he turned to her.

When their gazes connected, electricity seared through her as it had that morning when she'd zapped Mr. Coffee, only so much stronger. Something shifted inside her, realigning the universe and leaving everything just a little bit different than it had been before.

"Are you okay?" he asked, his voice a harsh rasp, as though he'd been through seven kinds of hell getting to her. Only that didn't make any sense. He'd been in the house all along, hadn't he? He was one of them, had turned on them for some reason. That was the only way he fit into the "enemy of the 2012ers" theory on the terrorist attack that'd killed Vince.

But she hadn't heard his footsteps, Leah realized, her brain spinning perilously close to panic. He'd appeared out of nowhere, out of thin air. And she'd made a carving knife fly. The body and blood spatter had disappeared.

Even stranger—and more dangerous—golden heat kindled in her core, and a lurching twist of raw lust threatened to overshadow her better judgment. She was dangerously attracted to this man. This murderer who'd butchered her informant in front of her and acted like it'd been the right thing to do. She wanted to be with him, felt like she already had, already knew what it would feel like.

"Wh-what's going on?" Her voice shook on the question, but she didn't care.

He stared at her for a long moment, as though weighing an enormous decision. Then he held out his hand to her. "Come on. I'll show you."

His sleeve fell back to reveal four symbols tattooed in stark relief on his forearm, symbols that should've meant nothing to her but seemed familiar, as though forgotten memories were struggling to break through some invisible barrier. She stared at the marks, then at him, then asked in a whisper, "Did you kill my brother?"

He shook his head slowly. "I had nothing to do with Matty's death."

She froze, gut twisting. "How did you know his name?"

"A private investigator told me." He kept his hand outstretched. "I'll explain everything. I promise."

And though she knew she absolutely, positively shouldn't trust him, shouldn't go anywhere with him, what was her other option? There were things going on here that made no sense, that weren't going to lend themselves to Internet searches and policework. She owed it to the dead to follow through. And damn, she wanted to go with him, wanted *him*, though that made the least sense of all.

Knowing it was probably a very bad decision, she nodded. "Okay, start talking. If I like what I'm hearing, I'll let you show me whatever you want to show me."

"It doesn't work that way." He crossed the distance between them and took her arm. "I'm sorry."

She pulled back instinctively. "Sorry for— Aaah!" The question devolved to a scream as the world disappeared and they lunged upward, catapulting through a thick gray mist as though they were at the end of a yo-yo that'd just reversed course. She was still screaming as they jolted sideways, then down, and the mist blinked out of existence, leaving them suspended in a glass-ceilinged, circular room that bore way too much of a resemblance to the ritual chamber in the Survivor2012 compound.

Leah's brain took a snapshot in the second they hovered. Eight blue-robed figures were seated in a loose circle below them, with wooden bowls perched in their laps. She recognized one of the women and the black-robed man who knelt before the carved stone altar. They had accompanied Blue Eyes to the 2012ers' compound; Black Robe was the one who'd shot Vince.

A smaller, older guy in jeans and a T-shirt stood near an open door. He was the first one to notice them, his attention jerking to the ceiling and his mouth going round in shock. Then the yo-yo string snapped, and Leah and Blue Eyes fell right in the middle of the circle.

He landed first and then Leah hit, driving the breath from both of them. They just lay there for a few heartbeats, staring at each other. Then reality returned— unreality returned?—and she scrambled off him, her heart jackrabbiting and her breath whistling in her lungs as she tried to suck in enough oxygen to get her brain back online.

"Holy shit," she whispered, looking around the glassed-in room to the night beyond, where high rock walls and a faint glow of dusk suggested she'd skipped a couple of time zones in the blink of an eye. Or traveled through time. Or both.

She felt Blue Eyes move up behind her, and knew it was him without turning to look because of the fine warmth that vibrated across her skin. "Easy, Blondie," he murmured next to her ear. "Don't freak-out on me."

"Cops don't freak." But she was damn close to it as she looked at the blue robes and realized not one of them had moved. Black Robe hadn't twitched either. In fact, none of them had responded to her and Blue Eyes's arrival except the older guy near the door, who was doing a good impression of a guppy.

The expression quickly morphed to that of a pissed-off guppy when the guy closed his mouth, glared at her rescuer, and snapped, "We discussed this."

Blue Eyes set his jaw and got big. "The choice is made, *winikin*. Deal with it."

"Wait a minute!" Leah turned on him, heart pounding, feeling like she'd stepped out of her own life and into someone else's. "What discussion? What choice?"

Before Blue Eyes could respond—if he was even intending to—the other nine people, the ones sitting on the floor like they'd been frozen there, snapped out of it, all simultaneously drawing convulsive breaths and coming back to life as though someone had thrown a switch.

The ones in the blue robes looked dazed as shit, shaking their heads and staring around as if they'd been someplace else and were happy to be back. In contrast, Black Robe, older and tougher and seeming just as pissed off as the guppy, shot to his feet, glanced at Leah, and immediately looked like he wanted to kill someone. Again.

He was maybe a few years younger than Jox, and had a *Last of the Mohicans* thing going on, with a skull trim, hawk nose, and eyes that would've done any predator proud. He looked scary as hell, in a don't-want-to-meet-him-in-a-dark-alley-without-backup way. But when he crossed the room and got in Blue Eyes's face, the two men seemed evenly matched in brawn and charisma. And pissed-offedness.

"What the *hell* were you thinking?" Black Robe spat. "Two escorts means two escorts. As it was, I got kicked off course and had to come back here and follow them. If I hadn't, they would've died in there. All of them. How *dare* you leave them like that to go chase tail? What the fuck kind of kingship is that?"

Leah's chest tightened, not at being called a piece of tail—hell, she'd been called worse—but at the reference to royalty, which underscored that she'd somehow wound up exactly where she'd vowed not to go—deep inside Cultsville. If this wasn't an offshoot of Survivor2012, then it was something similar, and at least two of its members were killers.

Yet she wasn't nearly as afraid as she ought to have been, as though the fear and unreality were blunted somehow by the golden warmth that fuzzed her brain.

She glanced up at her dream warrior, who had taken

a protective stance a little in front of her, as though he thought Black Robe might hurt her. "King?" she asked in a voice that sounded smaller then she'd intended.

"Call me Strike," he said without looking at her.

The name struck a chord, as though she'd heard it before, but the memory was gone before she could grab onto it.

"I saw my father," Strike said to Black Robe. "He told me to go to her. That you and the others would be okay, but she'd die if I didn't go."

Black Robe's breath hissed out. "You'd risk your people for another vision?"

"Don't start. Besides, you got them back."

"Barely." Black Robe's eyes flicked over to the blue robes. "There were . . . complications."

Some of the blue robes were still blinking stupidly, while others were shoving up their sleeves and staring at black tats on their forearms. The youngest of them, a pale teenager, sat apart, both forearms bare.

"Speaking of complications," Leah interrupted, putting herself between the two men so she could get in Strike's face. "You promised me an explanation. You can start with where we are and what the hell is going on."

"What is that?" The sharp question came from Black Robe.

Leah turned. "What?"

At first she thought he was staring at her ass. Then she realized he was locked onto the oilskin packet jammed in her back pocket.

She pulled it free, feeling a little queasy when the red glow spread from the packet to her arm. "I got it from the guy Strike here killed and then vaporized. It was in a trunk of some sort. Trunk didn't glow red like this thing, though." She looked from Strike to Black Robe and back. "You guys want it? Start talking."

"You can see the red?" Strike asked, his expression going intent.

"That's what I said, isn't it?"

Strike looked at Black Robe. "Lose the blocks."

The older man shook his head. "Bad idea."

"Lose. The. Blocks."

Black Robe scowled and looked at the smaller man, the one Strike had called *winikin*. "What do you think?" he asked, as though *winikin* meant "arbiter of common sense" in whatever fucked-up universe she'd stumbled into. At the other man's slight nod, Black Robe crossed to her and touched her forehead, then spoke a few words.

Something clicked in Leah's brain. A rushing noise filled her ears.

And she remembered everything: Nick's death, Zipacna holding her prisoner in the Mayan temple, Strike rescuing her, the water filling the chamber, her nearly drowning. His kissing her awake.

She stood there, frozen in place, staring at Strike, and all she could think was, *Holy shit.* Because he wasn't just a whacked-out doomsday freak with above-average sex appeal and some tricks she hadn't even begun to process.

He was also her lover.

Strike saw it in her eyes, the moment he went from "weird guy wearing nothing but a red bathrobe" to the guy she'd had raunchy, no-holds-barred sex with approximately five minutes after the first time she'd laid eyes on him. Which would have been right after the *ajaw-makol* had tried to cut her heart out of her chest with a stone knife and she'd subsequently drowned and been reborn.

Not to mention the part where she'd dreamed of him coming to her in her attic bedroom, only it hadn't been a dream.

When the color drained from her face and she swayed, he stepped forward to catch her if she went down. "Easy there. Lots to take in."

But she didn't go down. She pulled back, swung from the shoulder, and punched him square in the mouth.

Strike reeled back, cursing and clapping a hand to the lip Jox had split an hour earlier. Not that he could blame her—he figured he'd earned that and more.

"How *dare* you?" she hissed, then winced and dug her

fingers into her scalp, massaging beneath the white-blond hair he'd dreamed of. "Ow, damn it."

He crossed to her and caught her arm when she sagged. "Postmagic hangover. You need to eat something and get some sleep. Then we'll talk."

Even though her eyes were practically crossed with the pain-fatigue of the hangover, she glared up at him. "Take me home."

He knew he should do it, wipe her one more time and take her home. But that just wasn't possible. "I can't," he said. "You're not safe in Miami anymore." They had come after her again, and not just because she was in the wrong place at the wrong time. He wasn't letting her out of his sight until he figured out why.

"And I'm supposed to take your word that I'm safe here?"

"I'm guessing a promise wouldn't get me very far," he said drily.

"I'll take it anyway." She paused. "Along with the MAC-10 you were packing the other night. With one of those under my pillow I'll sleep fine."

And she'd put some serious holes in anyone who disturbed her, Strike warranted. He wasn't too keen on having an autopistol loose in the mansion, and knew that Jox would tear a strip out of him if he agreed, but he couldn't blame her for wanting the protection.

Besides, she'd be unconscious for the next half day or so, whether she liked it or not.

He raised a hand as if he were pledging allegiance. "I swear that you'll be safe here tonight." He didn't dare promise beyond that, and saw her register the qualifier. "As for the autopistol"—he nodded to his *winikin*— "Jox will take care of that."

The *winikin* glared at him. "What does she mean, 'the other night?'"

"Later," Strike grated out. "Christ." His head was starting to pound, too, and the room had a pretty good spin going on. "We all need to eat and have some—" He broke off. He'd been about to say, "have some sex."

Maybe it was the aphelion, maybe having Leah nearby, all blond hair and edgy attitude, standing up for herself even though she was so far out of her depth she could barely see the surface. But suddenly, he wanted nothing more than to take her somewhere private, where none of the others would matter, where nothing would matter but the two of them and the heat they created together.

Hello, pretalent hornies.

Trying to banish the sex buzz he was getting off the blue robes, Strike grated, "Jox? Please show Leah where she'll be staying."

"And that would be . . . ?" the *winikin* asked coolly.

The pool house, Strike almost said, because he wanted her in his space, wanted her within reach. But he didn't dare keep her so close, not with the hormones in the air. "Put her in the royal quarters."

Jox's jaw was locked tight, though Strike didn't know if it was solely because he was pissed, or if he was also picking up on the do-me vibes that were flying around the room, thicker with every passing minute.

Sweat popped out on Strike's brow, and he was careful not to touch Leah when he waved for her to follow the *winikin*. "Go ahead. Jox will take care of everything, including the MAC. Get some food in you, get some rest, and I'll scrounge some clothes for you. When you're feeling steadier, we'll talk."

"Okay." Leah nodded. Her eyes were starting to glaze a little, though he wasn't sure if it was the shock and postmagic hangover, or if she was picking up on the vibes. She shouldn't be able to, because she wasn't a Nightkeeper. But then again, she shouldn't have been able to tell that there was anything special about the oilskin packet she clutched in one hand as she followed Jox from the room.

Strike hoped like hell that the packet contained a fragment from one of the old spellbooks. There was no other explanation for why it glowed red—royal red. He'd wanted to ask her for it, wanted to commandeer it, but she needed to keep it for now, needed to trust that he wouldn't take it by force. Besides, assuming it was one of the lost spells, they couldn't do anything with it right now. Not without a translator.

For the moment, its greatest strength would be helping him convince Red-Boar and the others that the gods well and truly meant for Leah to be involved with the coming battle. Then it'd be up to him to figure out how to manage that without endangering her further.

Step one, he thought as he watched her leave, *keep your hands off her.* Which was going to be far easier said than done. He'd already touched her, already tasted her. He'd heard the sexy catch of her breath against his skin, and knew what it felt like to come inside her.

And it couldn't happen again, or she was dead.

PART III

✳

THE VENUS
CONJUNCTION

*Alignment of the Sun, Earth, and the planet
Venus, which was the morning star used by the Maya
to predict the equinoxes and solstices.*

CHAPTER TWELVE

July 5

Deep in the bowels of the art history building at UT Austin, Lucius Hunt was hunched over his desk, hard at work. Okay, technically he was in his first-floor office, but it was nearly three a.m. and pitch dark outside, so it was feeling bowelish. Or maybe that was his total, utter lack of success at deciphering the line of Mayan text that sat on his computer screen, mocking him.

"I can't tell if the damn skull is grinning or screaming." He hunkered down in his desk chair until he was eye level with his laptop screen, but all that did was give him a crick in his neck. Sometimes being tall sucked.

Thanks to fifteen hundred years' worth of tropical weather at the ruins of Chichén Itzá, the Mayan glyphwork was badly eroded. If he adjusted the contrast, he could distinguish what looked like a skull carved inside the outline of a jellyfish, but that could make it any one of twenty-plus glyphs he'd accumulated for his thesis on the end-time prophecy, depending on what the damned skull was doing. Digital comparison to other symbols in the text had allowed him to narrow his options down to grinning or screaming. If the skull was grinning, he'd found himself an ode to Jaguar-Paw Skull, the fourteenth ruler of the ancient Mayan city. *Boo-ring*.

But if it was screaming . . . if it was screaming, he was

looking at something seriously important, a discovery that could blow the lid off the prevailing theories on the end-time. If the skull was screaming, then the zero date on the Mayan Long Count calendar wasn't a metaphor for social change at all. It was a prophecy, just like the doomsday nuts kept saying. A warning.

Game over.

His boss, top Mayanist Anna Catori, didn't believe the world would end on the day the backward-counting calendar zeroed out. She and the rest of the naysayers chose to ignore the modern astronomers who'd discovered that the zero date on the Long Count calendar was the same exact day the earth would pass through the precise center of the Milky Way galaxy while in conjunction with the sun and moon.

Half the astrophysicists Lucius had interviewed said there was a good chance that the earth's magnetic poles would flip abruptly on that day, making north become south and south, north. The other half said that was bullshit. There seemed to be a general consensus, though, that the sun-moon-earth conjunction in the galactic center was likely to spark the sort of sunspot activity that hadn't been seen in twenty-six thousand or so years, since the last time there was a meta-conjunction like this one.

Oh, and by the way, twenty-six thousand years ago, the magnetic poles *had* flipped, and the earth had actually owned an ozone layer capable of protecting it from the sunspots.

The question was, how much of this had the ancient Maya known, and—and here was where Anna kept accusing Lucius of straying over into the tinfoil-hat zone—what was with the handful of inscriptions he'd found that mentioned the Nightkeepers, a secret sect of warrior-priests supposedly sworn to protect the earth when the zero date came?

Ergo, the screaming skulls.

Excitement buzzed through his veins, alongside the caffeine from the six-pack of Mountain Dew he'd downed since midnight. With T minus six weeks and counting to his thesis defense, he needed one more find, one last bit of oomph to put him over the top and counteract his less than stellar disciplinary record at UT. This could be it.

"Come on, baby. Scream for me." He clicked a few keys on his laptop and swapped the colors over to a deep, vibrant purple, which he'd found sometimes popped details the other views washed out.

The result was a purple jellyfish containing a lavender skull that looked like it was snickering at him.

"Son of a bitch." He pushed away from the desk and scrubbed his hands over his eyes, which burned with fatigue and too many hours at the computer. When he blinked against the sting, he saw his favorite skeptic standing in the doorway to his tiny office.

Anna was a dark-haired beauty in her late thirties, lovely and sad-looking, with the most gorgeous blue eyes he'd ever seen in his life. She was wearing jeans and a clingy blue shirt a shade darker than her eyes, with the sleeves rolled up over the forearm tattoos she didn't like to talk about. One was a perfect representation of the Mayan *balam* glyph, representing the sacred jaguar, the other the *ju* glyph of royalty. Together, they were dead sexy, at least as far as Lucius was concerned.

When she didn't move from the doorway, didn't say anything, he started to think he was having a waking fantasy, the kind where she'd glide across the room, haul him down to the desk, and make love to him amidst his thesis notes.

Then she scowled. "Don't you ever sleep?"

Not a dream, then. *Bummer.*

Lucius glanced at his watch. Three fifteen. Over the past few months he'd been sleeping less and less, kept awake by dark dreams and a strange, growing restlessness. "What makes you think I'm not just getting a really early start on tomorrow?"

She pointed to the line of empties on his desk. "I count six dead soldiers, and you're wearing yesterday's clothes." She paused, her expression softening. "Go home and sleep, Lucius. I don't want to see you back here before noon. You're no good to me if you burn out before the ink dries on your doctorate."

"But I found—"

"Go." She crossed the room, pulled him out of his chair, and shoved him toward the door. "It'll still be here in a few hours. One nice thing about the study of an ancient civilization is that life-threatening emergencies are rare."

The sentiment was so un-Anna-like that he paused. "Is everything okay?"

She avoided his eyes. "Everything's fine. I want to get a jump on things before the grant vultures descend this afternoon."

"Don't bullshit a bullshitter, Anna." *Talk to me,* he wanted to say. *Tell me what's wrong. I'll listen; I want to help*. But he didn't go there, because she'd already let him know in so many little ways that she was flattered, but not interested in a student nearly ten years her junior. Rumor said her marriage to Dick Catori of the economics department was on shaky ground, but she left that at the door. At least, she usually did. Tonight, she seemed to waver, seemed to lean toward him for half a second.

Then she straightened and shook her head. "It's nothing you can help me with."

"Try me."

Her eyes softened to the *you're so cute* look he hated like poison, and she nudged him toward the door. "It's not your fight. Go home."

Lucius didn't like the thought of her sleeping at the lab because things had gotten bad with the Dick, but he'd just look like an idiot if he invited her to his place, a shared apartment furnished in Early Roach, so he said, "Call me if you change your mind."

"I will," she said, but they both knew she wouldn't.

"See you in a few hours."

"Not before noon, or I'm docking your stipend."

He shot her a grin. "Can't threaten me. Half of nothing's still nothing." But the moment the door swung shut at his back, his smile faded.

What was going on? She'd been distracted lately, worried by more than just the grant committee. A bubble of anger worked its way through his normal calm. If the Dick was giving her grief, he'd . . .

You'll do what, he thought bitterly, *tell on him?*

Lucius was two inches taller and a good fifty pounds lighter than his younger brothers and his father, who were all cut in the Hunt mold of dark, handsome, and built. Lucius looked more like his mother and sister, and while light and willowy was gorgeous on them, he looked more wussy than willowy, and doubted Anna's ex-linebacker husband would be impressed.

He'd have to try another angle, then. *So, think*, he told himself as he crossed the narrow bridge at the front of the art history building. *What does Anna need?*

The question bumped against the twitchiness deep inside him, and he glanced up at the waning moon overhead. He could swear he felt the night in his bones, a subsonic itch that added to the restlessness.

His mother used to say he should've been born in another time, when he could've lived the quests he read about and played on VR games. But neither books nor games were enough, had never been enough. He wanted to do something, *be* something more than a scrawny glyph geek who was constantly getting himself in trouble more through accident than design.

Going on instinct, he doubled back, circling the outer edge of the dark, seventies-style building until he reached the window of Anna's first-floor office. The window was closed but the room was fully lit. Trusting that the darkness at his back would shield him from view, he squelched the guilt and peeked in.

He saw his laptop open on the desk, with the monitor switched to a deep crimson that really popped the line of glyphwork he'd been working on. The red showed the skull screaming, clear as day. But that wasn't what had Lucius freezing in place.

It was the sight of Anna, slumped in her desk chair with her eyes closed and blood trickling from the corner of her mouth.

Leah awoke midafternoon, with a serious crick in her neck from having slept on a MAC-10 autopistol and a profound wish that she'd open her eyes and find that the last few weeks—hell, the last year and a half—had been a really twisted dream.

But when she did the eyes-open thing and found herself in a sumptuous bedroom with tall ceilings, thick carpets and drapes, and a faintly impersonal Native American–themed decor that practically screamed "high-end hotel," she had a strong feeling the weirdness was just beginning.

As the events of the night before came clearer in her mind, she was sure of only one thing: She was way out of her jurisdiction.

The red-rock canyon walls visible beyond the wide bedroom windows suggested the Southwest, and what she now remembered of the explanation Strike had given her in the Mayan temple—after they'd had total-stranger sex—suggested she'd stumbled into a cosmic-level battle that went well beyond the MDPD.

It should've been utterly ridiculous even to consider that any of what she'd seen—or thought she'd seen—was real. But what was the alternative? Hallucination? Insanity? It felt way too real, and her online searches on the Survivor2012 doctrine had made it sound like an awful lot of experts—including real scientists, not just doomsday nuts—agreed that something wonky was going to happen at the end of 2012. And if she believed the Maya had predicted the zero date a few thousand years ago, was it such a stretch to believe that there was a religious component to it all?

"But religion isn't the same as actual magic," she said aloud. "An astronomical event isn't the same as gods and demons battling for control of the earth."

In order for her to believe what Strike had told her about the Nightkeepers, she had to accept that the 2012 apocalypse was going to boil down to a battle between good and evil, and while that might make a hell of a movie, it didn't do much for her in terms of common sense. She was a cop. A realist.

"There's no such thing as magic," she said. But she didn't sound convinced, even to her own ears, because if there was no such thing as magic, how did she explain all that she'd seen and done recently?

A tap on the door interrupted her thoughts, which was a relief, because they weren't getting her anywhere.

Scrambling out of the plush, king-size bed, she pulled on her bloodstained clothes and fastened her belt loosely enough that she could jam the MAC beneath it. Exiting the bedroom, she crossed an equally opulent sitting room, taking note of the attached kitchenette and a short hallway beyond, leading to what looked like a solarium and a few other closed doors.

Forget upscale hotel. Apparently she'd rated a small condo.

The main door to the suite was actually a set of double doors, both elaborately carved with the same sort of glyphs Strike wore on his arm. At the thought of the marks—and the man—Leah's skin warmed, anger at his deception tangling with desire. The churned-up heat had her voice sharpening when she opened one of the doors. "Yes?"

Jox stood there, his lived-in face tight with disapproval as he held out a small pile of clothing, with a pair of sneakers on top. "They'll be too big for you."

She bristled to meet his 'tude. "Better than bloodstains." She took the clothes before he could snatch them back. And what the hell was his problem? It wasn't like she'd asked to get herself dragged into this mess. She'd just been doing her job.

More or less.

He bowed stiffly. *"Aj-winikin."* Then he turned on his heel and strode off, somehow making his faded jeans and long-sleeved shirt look like livery.

"Wait," she said quickly. She needed more info, needed to figure out if these people—these Nightkeepers—were the real deal, and if so, whether they were the good guys or the bad. She wanted to believe Strike, wanted to trust him. And that was a serious problem, because her track record really sucked in the picking-trustworthy-men-for-relationships department.

Jox turned back with a scowl. "What?"

"What is that?" Leah asked. *"Aj-winikin.* What does it mean?"

"It means, 'I am your servant,'" Jox replied. "That's what I am, a *winikin.* A servant."

She shook her head, not buying it. "That might be the

translation, but you're nobody's servant. What does it really mean?"

That got her a considering look. "The *winikin* look after . . . people like Strike and the others. When they're children, we help raise them, teach them, guard them. When they're grown we act as . . . I guess you'd say their conscience. We're the little voices that sit on their shoulders and give advice when things are going to hell."

"Like now?"

"You have no idea."

"Dude." She risked a smile. "I blew up my coffeemaker yesterday morning, got kidnapped in my own house, shot the bejesus out of an ex-snitch and couldn't keep him down, and then got my butt teleported from Miami to canyon country. Oh, and I seem to have acquired a one-nighter I forgot about . . . and he's some sort of king." She paused. "I think I've got a pretty good idea."

"You haven't the faintest clue," he said, but there was more pity than snark in his voice.

"They're the Nightkeepers," she said. "They're supposed to save the world."

His eyebrows lowered. "He told you?"

"Yes and no. He told me, but then he made me forget it. Other things back home made me wonder about the 2012 date, though." Like a cult that didn't act like a cult, and a friend of her brother's who'd insisted she keep digging. Shoving aside the guilt and grief—for the moment, at least—she pantomimed typing. "I'm hell on wheels with Google. I started pulling up papers by an Anna Catori out at UT Austin, talking about how the end of the Mayan Long Count calendar doesn't symbolize the end of the world; it's just a metaphor for cyclical social change, sort of a cosmic reset button. But then there's this guy Ledbetter, who seems to think that it predicts full-on armageddon. And I got to thinking . . . what if he's the one who's got it right?"

"Anna is Strike's sister."

Hello, non sequitur. Whatever Leah might've expected Jox to say, that wasn't it. But it was information. "And she doesn't believe in any of . . . this?" She waved a hand around them both. "That doesn't make sense."

The *winikin* shifted from one foot to the other, as though he needed to be somewhere else, or really wished he did. "It's a long story."

"Summarize."

He sighed. "Twenty-four years ago, Strike and Anna's father had a vision that said he could prevent the end-time by bringing together all of the Nightkeepers for an attack on their enemies, the *Banol Kax*."

When he paused, she said, "They all died." At his sharp look, she lifted a shoulder. "He mentioned it. Besides, it's a hell of a big house for, what, a dozen people, most of whom are under the age of twenty-five? And it's been gutted recently. Doesn't take a cop to do the math and figure out that something big and bad— Oh." She broke off, wincing when her mental connect-the-dots reached the center of the spiral. "His parents."

"All of their parents, and the rest of the children, gone." He snapped his fingers, though his expression robbed the gesture of any play. "Just like that. We are all that remains."

And the *winikin* had saved Strike and raised him, Leah realized. That was the dynamic. They might be master and servant on the one hand, but they were parent and grown child on the other. Complicated, like everything else she'd suddenly dropped ass-first into.

"You want more, you'll have to ask him yourself," Jox said, turning away, and this time she knew he wouldn't come back if she called his name.

So instead she said softly, "Why does he live in the pool house?"

He paused and half turned, so he was in profile to her. "When Scarred-Jaguar led his attack on the inter-section, we thought we were safe here, the *winikin* and the children." He paused, and there was exquisite pain etched in the lines of his face when he said, "We were wrong. I got Strike and Anna to the royal family's safe room and we waited it out." He lifted a shoulder.

"Strike recovered okay, more or less, but Anna . . . didn't. She left for college and never looked back."

Leah didn't know what to say. She looked around the suite, which was pleasant, but sterile. Impersonal. "This was where his parents lived." It wasn't a question.

"Their things are in storage. I'm hoping—" Jox broke off. "Never mind."

Tell me, she wanted to say. *I want to know everything. I need to figure out what's real and what isn't, and how I fit into this. You're worried about him; I can tell. But why? Is it just me or is there something else?* But she didn't have the right to ask, because this wasn't her world. Despite what had happened between her and Strike, he wasn't hers. Not really.

So she didn't ask. Instead, she reached into her back pocket and withdrew the oilskin packet. It still glowed red, though the luminescence was muted, as though the power had dimmed. She held it out. "Here. He should have this."

Jox looked at her for a long moment, measuring her. Then he nodded. "Thank you." Taking the packet, he tipped his head in an almost-bow.

Before he could leave, she said, "Wait, please. Last question, I promise." Even though there seemed to be no end to the questions.

"What," he said, tone resigned.

"What are they?" she said. "What does Nightkeeper mean?" It wasn't the most important question, but suddenly it was critical for her to know the answer.

"The Mayan shaman-priests who oversaw the calendars were called the Daykeepers, because they protected the smaller prophecies and kept the calendars moving from one day to the next. Strike's ancestors watched over the nights and kept the *Banol Kax* from coming through the barrier between the planes. That was their job, *is* their job," he corrected himself, then said, "Strike and the others are the last of the Nightkeepers." He paused. "Do yourself a favor and remember that you're not one of them."

*   *   *

Strike woke late afternoon, groggy as hell. But once he was oriented, he couldn't keep down the buzz of knowing Leah was nearby. He shouldn't want her, couldn't have her, but his body didn't seem to give a crap about any of that.

Changing into jeans and a ratty Metallica T-shirt, he made tracks for the kitchen and did a postmagic calorie replacement by chugging a half gallon of OJ straight from the jug—with a quick look to make sure Jox couldn't see him and bitch about backwash—and chowing a package of provolone that was probably intended for dinner.

Once the first pangs had passed and he could focus better, he noticed the oilskin packet propped up against the saltshaker. Which meant he wasn't going directly to Leah. He had another stop to make first.

He slid the packet across the marble countertop so it rested directly in front of him. Then, slowly, half-afraid of what he might—or might not—see, he untied the string and pried up a corner of the oilskin. The first layer gave way to a second, then a third before he uncovered the *makol*'s treasure.

And a treasure it was. "Holy shit." He'd had a hunch based on the glow, but seeing it for real . . . that was different.

The piece of fig bark was the size of two hands held side by side, and was covered with the smallest, most intricate glyphwork he'd ever seen. He didn't have a clue what it said, but he could feel the latent power humming through his fingertips, and it was the red of the royal Nightkeepers, not the purple-green of the *makol*.

"Thank you, Father," he whispered. Then, refolding the protective covering, he tucked the packet inside his T-shirt, next to his skin, and went in search of Red-Boar.

He found the older Nightkeeper in his cottage, sitting at the kitchen table in his brown penitent's robes with a Coke in one hand and a hunk of cheddar in the other.

The moment Strike's foot hit the kitchen tile, Red-Boar scowled and snapped, "Why did you do it? Why did you abandon your people and go after the woman? What the hell were you thinking?"

Snagging a Coke for himself—like the OJ hadn't spiked enough sugar into his system—Strike dragged out a chair and sat. "I told you. I saw my father."

"Like you saw the woman in your dreams." It wasn't a question.

"Yes. No." Strike popped the top of the soda and took a drag. "I saw him in the barrier. Technically, I saw a *nahwal* wearing his earring. It told me to go to her, and I saw her thread. When I grabbed it, *wham*, I was there. She and a *makol* were fighting—she'd done a damn good job on him, but not enough."

Red-Boar's eyes went sharp at the mention of a *makol*. "It survived the explosion?"

Strike shook his head. "Different one." Which meant the *ajaw-makol* had made more of itself. Question was, how many more? Had the two they killed been the sum total, or were there others out there? Knowing they were going to need all the power they could get to deal with the issue, he pulled out the packet and set it on the table in front of the older Nightkeeper. "Open it."

Red-Boar unfolded the oilskin. The moment he saw the codex fragment, his expression went dark. "Shit. We need a translator."

"I know." Strike grimaced. "I hate asking her for this."

"Anna's going to like it even less."

Strike let the silence linger for a moment before he said, "I want you to take it to her. She'll listen to you."

That earned him a baleful look. "You just want me out of the way so you can—"

"Don't," Strike said sharply, interrupting. Then, more softly, "Don't. I'm doing the best I can, and I need you to back me on it."

"Or what?"

"Let's not go there. I need you. The newbies need you." Strike chugged the rest of his Coke, tossed it toward the recycle bin, and missed.

"You need me when it's convenient to have someone backing you up," Red-Boar said evenly, "but not when I disagree with you, or remind you you're not the only one of your bloodline to make bad decisions based on a dream." When Strike would've said something, he held up a hand. "Let me finish. It was your choice to put Rabbit through the ritual, and I think we both know his magic is probably what pulled us away from the trainees and nearly got them lost for good. His power isn't the same as ours, never will be. Trying to make him into a Nightkeeper is only going to end badly."

"So we should ignore him?" Strike snapped. "Do you hate him that much?"

The corners of Red-Boar's mouth tipped up, though there was no amusement in his expression. "Trying to derail the argument by striking your opponent's weak spot? That's not like you. More like my style."

"*Is* he your weak spot?" Strike countered. "I couldn't tell from the way you've raised him. Gods, you didn't even give the kid a real name!"

Something flickered in the older Nightkeeper's eyes. "I've done what I've done for a reason. Never doubt that."

"Whatever." Strike pushed away from the table and stood, annoyed that he was so close to losing his temper, irritated that they hadn't really settled anything, frustrated that—

That was it, he realized. He was frustrated, and it had far less to do with Red-Boar than with the knowledge that Leah was nearby. He might've already had his talent ceremony, might've passed beyond the binding-hormone madness, but that didn't mean he was oblivious to the vibes in the air. *Shit.* It was going to be a long couple of months.

"Go see Anna," he said to Red-Boar.

The older Nightkeeper sighed and touched the codex fragment, and for a moment he looked almost . . . sad. "As you wish."

"Give her this." Strike reached into his pocket and withdrew a long, thin chain. At the end dangled a yellow quartz effigy carved in the shape of a skull, its eyes and teeth worn smooth from the touch of generations of *itza'at* seers.

Anna had left the effigy behind the day she took off, making them promise not to come after her, to leave her alone so she could live a normal life.

Red-Boar's eyes fixed on the pendant, but he shook his head. "Keep it. I can't be the one to give it back to her."

Strike let the skull hang for a moment, then nodded and tucked it in his pocket. "I'll see you when you get back. We'll talk then."

"Sure," Red-Boar said, but his body language all but shouted, *You're an idiot.*

Strike let the cottage door slam at his back, not because he was mad about any one thing, but because he was mad about *everything.* He was stirred up, juiced up. He wanted to run, wanted to howl at the moon like he hadn't since he was a teenager.

And then he saw her, sitting on a plastic deck chair beside the pool.

Leah. Waiting for him.

She rose to her feet when she saw him. Her borrowed jeans were belted on and cuffed at the bottom, and she was wearing a crimson scoop-necked T-shirt that was baggy in front—Alexis's clothes, probably. Her long white-blond hair was slicked back in a no-nonsense ponytail, and there was a dark shadow along her jaw where a bruise was starting to come through. Her expression was guarded and wary, her eyes cool. Cop's eyes.

He had quite literally never seen anything so beautiful in his entire life—and he was pretty sure that was the man talking, not the magic or the gods.

He approached, stopping a few feet away from her. "Hey."

"Hey, yourself," she said back, and they stared at each other for a long time. They'd been lovers but they didn't know each other. Didn't know how to talk to each other.

"Well," he said finally. "This is weird."

Her voice held a bite of temper when she said, "Which part of it, the part where your people killed Vince, the part where we've had two separate sexual encounters and only one semicoherent conversation? Or . . ." Her voice went unsteady. "The part where I dreamed about you before I met you, made a carving knife fly, and freaking *teleported* from Miami to the middle of the desert?" Whispering now, eyes dark with confusion, she said, "That's not possible. None of it is." But it was more of a plea than a statement of fact.

Strike had gone still. "Tell me about the knife."

She gave him a long look, but said, "Last night Itchy had me strapped down pretty good when I came to. There was a knife a few feet away, and I . . . I thought at it, really hard, and it came to me. Floated. Right into my hand."

Which just added more weight to his growing conviction—concern?—that the gods had plans for her. What was he supposed to do with that? "Have you ever done anything like that before?"

She shook her head, then lifted one shoulder in a sort of no-yes-maybe answer. "Yesterday morning I went to turn my coffeemaker on and fried its circuits instead, but that was probably just a coincidence."

Or not, he thought. If she'd retained some sort of magic from her experience at the intersection, it would stand to reason that she'd be more likely to be able to tap the power during a conjunction. Which meant . . .

Hell, he didn't know what it meant.

Waving to a couple of poolside chairs, he said, "We should sit. This could take a while."

"Apparently I've got time," she muttered as she sat. "I called in this morning to put in for leave, and Connie—my boss—said I should take as long as I needed."

"Ouch."

"Yeah. I can't blame her, really. I've been skirting the line ever since Matty was murdered." Her eyes went hard. "I'm not staying away, though. Not if I can help get the bastard who did it. Which brings us back to you. Start talking. Who are the 2012ers, how does the Calendar Killer fit into this, and why . . . why did you guys kill Vince? He was a friend."

"He was a *makol.*"

"He was a computer programmer."

"The two are not mutually exclusive. Look . . ." Strike spun his chair so he was facing her, their knees almost bumping, and when her eyes went wide and she started looking for the nearest exit, he took her hands, telling himself it was only for reassurance, only an effort to keep her in place long enough to get the full story. "It's an understatement to say this is complicated. I'm going to have to ask you to believe that I'm one of the good guys. I know you have absolutely no reason to trust me—hell, you've got every reason *not* to—but I'm asking you to give me a chance. Please."

"I shouldn't," she said softly. But she didn't pull her hands away. "I should've left last night, should've run screaming, but there are things going on that I can't explain. Things that don't fall under the heading of 'standard police procedure.'"

"Yes." He resisted the urge to hold her hands tighter, to move closer. Her skin was soft and smooth beneath his fingers, with the hardness of bone and strength beneath. "I'll explain what I can." Which they both knew wasn't the same as explaining everything.

"You made me think I dreamed you." Her accusation went so much deeper than just the forgetting spell. "If that's not a lie of omission, I don't know what is. And what's worse, there's a big part of me that *wants* to trust you."

"Then do it," he urged.

"I'm not sure I can." Her tone lost some of its edge, making her sound unutterably weary. "You made me forget us making love. I'm not going to play the forced-seduction card, because I know damn well I was a willing participant, and I appreciate the whole saving-my-life thing, but it doesn't seem like you want to be with me. More like you're trying to get the hell away." She paused. "What exactly do you want from me?"

Nothing, he wanted to say. *Everything. Damn it.* "I don't know," he said finally, which was also the truth. "What do you want from me?"

"An explanation," she said softly. "I want to know who killed Matty, and why."

Which put them right back at odds, making him think she had her own reasons for not wanting to pick up where they'd left off the other night. He should've been relieved that she hadn't forced him to talk about what was—and wasn't—between them. Instead, he was irritated.

Which just proved how screwed-up he was these days.

"I'll give you as much as I can," he said. "But I need some context. Tell me about these Calendar murders." When she scowled, looking ready to refuse, he squeezed her hands. "Trust me."

Suddenly, it was very important that she do just that.

"Okay," she finally said, but he wasn't sure whether she was agreeing to trust him, or only to describe the murders. Then she started talking about a serial killer who preyed at the solstice and equinox, and within a few sentences he knew they were onto something. She must've seen it on his face, because she broke off. "The killer's signature means something to you."

Choosing his words carefully, he said, "The equinox and solstice are the times of highest magical activity, the times the barrier between worlds is thinnest. If I were trying to use human sacrifice to jump-start the barrier back into action, those are the days I'd pick for the bloodletting."

"Did you?" Her eyes held his, unwavering.

"No." He projected everything he could into the word, wanting—needing—her to believe him. To believe *in* him. "Our magic is mostly autosacrifice. Self-bloodletting. It's very rare for one Nightkeeper to blood another." He leaned in so their faces were very close together when he said, "We're the good guys, Leah. My father sacrificed almost our entire race to close the barrier. We were waiting for the end date to pass so we could finally live our lives. No way any of us did what you're describing."

"Then who did?"

"Zipacna," Strike said, and there was no doubt in his mind. "Either the barrier thinned enough that one of the *Banol Kax* reached through to him, or he found one of the lost spells and made contact from this side."

"You said Vince was a *makol*, too," Leah said, "but he hated Survivor2012. He was convinced they killed Matty—heck, it was his idea to crash that party. And you said before that the *makol* ritual only works on evil-minded people, or someone who accepts evil in exchange for power. So how could he be—'' She broke off. Then she scrubbed both hands across her face and halfway screamed, "Aah!"

"What?"

She dropped her hands and looked at him, shaking her head, eyes bleak. "This is . . . ridiculous. I can't even believe I'm treating this discussion like it's real. Do you ever listen to yourself and think that what you're saying sounds completely insane? Like you should be waiting for the mother ship?"

"This is religion, not an alien abduction."

"Depending on who you talk to, there's not much difference."

"Then why are you still here?"

"Because of the dreams," she said, avoiding his eyes a little, her color riding high, making him very aware of the curve of her jaw, the long line of her neck. "And because Matty . . ." She faltered. "I need to know why he picked Matty."

But the *ajaw-makol* hadn't just picked her brother, Strike realized suddenly. Zipacna had brought her to the sacred chamber at the solstice. Vince had drawn her back into the Survivor2012 compound when Red-Boar's mind-bending had told her to leave it alone. Itchy had held her prisoner in her own house, no doubt under his master's orders.

When he put those things together, it started to look like her brother hadn't been the main target of any of this. She was.

But why?

As Strike had done the first time they met, he took her right hand and turned it palm up. He traced his thumb across a small square of puckered, roughened skin on her inner forearm. "Tell me about this scar."

She looked away. "It's nothing. I don't even remember getting it."

"Leah," he said quietly.

That brought her eyes back to him, but she shook her head. "Please. Tell me about Zipacna."

He knew he should push. Instead, he said, "In the

Nightkeepers' pantheon, he's a vicious, vindictive piece of work with a taste for blood and the ability to appear as a winged crocodile. His father is one of the rulers of Xibalba, which gives him a power boost."

"I meant the guy in Miami."

"I know." Carter's report on the leader of Survivor2012 had included a few grainy, overenlarged photos and a sketchy history that went a whopping six years back. "You probably know way more about him than I do."

"In other words, almost nothing," Leah said grimly. "What I want to know is whether he killed my brother and Nick. Whether Vince died because of what Zipacna made him."

Strike nodded slowly. "My gut says yes to all three."

"I hear a 'but' in your voice."

"That would be the part where I say, 'but I can't let you go after him.'"

She pulled her hands away, eyes going hard. "Sorry, Ace. You have no right to tell me what I can and can't do."

Yeah, but I have a couple of overflow storage lockers in the basement that'd keep you out of trouble, he thought. He didn't say that, though, because for one, he didn't want to turn this into a battle . . . and for another, he figured he should probably hold the lockup idea in reserve, just in case. So instead he said, "This is bigger than both of us, and I think you know it, or at least suspect that it might be."

"You really, truly think the world is going to end," she said softly. It wasn't a question.

"I believe that the next few months are going to determine exactly that," he said, going with a half-truth. Then he added, "The Nightkeepers believe the world exists in a series of repeating cycles, both spiritual and cosmic, all of which are going to intersect on the end date. The Great Conjunction is coming no matter what we do— that's an astrological fact. It's up to us to block the spiritual side of things. It's what our ancestors lived for. What our parents died for." He took a deep breath. Let it out. "I'm the king's son, which means I have a responsibility to my people and what we're bound to do over the next four-plus years. If I were just a man . . ."

He leaned in and brushed the backs of his fingers across her cheek, and his blood heated when she trembled at his touch.

"Yeah, well . . ." She pulled away from him and stood, moving away a few feet so she could stare out across the compound, past the cottages and ball court to the pueblo-dotted canyon walls beyond, all of which were going purple-red with the approach of dusk. "Don't think I'm staying away from Zipacna just because you're hot."

His lips twitched. "Not even if I offer to be your sex slave?"

"*Are* you offering?"

Shaking his head—and regretting the hell out of the necessity—he said, "I can't."

"Because I'm not a Nightkeeper."

"Because we don't know what you are yet." Another half-truth. "I'm going to have to do some reading, see what I can figure out about your flying-knife trick, and why Zipacna seems to have targeted you specifically." He rose and joined her, so they stood shoulder-to-shoulder, looking out at the dark shadows of the pueblo ruins—the remains of another people who had tracked time by the sun and stars, and believed in magic and the apocalypse.

"What am I supposed to do now?" Her voice came out weary, wary, as though she acknowledged the need for protection but didn't like it. "House arrest isn't really my style."

"Be a cop," he said. "Find Zipacna. Make some calls, pull in some favors, do whatever it takes. You can lean on Carter for the legwork."

"You're not going to let me leave."

"I think it's safer if you stay," he said, hoping she didn't push him to lock her down.

"And you think you're not letting me near Zipacna."

"Again, safer that way. I don't want to see you get hurt." Which was approximately the understatement of the decade. Having her this near had his blood humming in his veins, and having her bent on going after the *ajaw-makol* chilled him to the bone.

She glanced up at him, eyes shadowed. "This was a hell of a lot easier in the dreams."

"Yeah." He nodded, in that moment feeling as close to his father as he ever had. "Somehow it always is."

CHAPTER THIRTEEN

Jox had forgotten what it felt like to be around magi on the prowl. The house practically vibrated with the need for sex. Worse, it wasn't the unfocused horniness of a bunch of teenaged kids—the newbies were in their twenties, and he'd eat his arm if there was a virgin among them. They knew what it felt like, knew what they wanted and where they wanted to get it.

And damned if the *winikin* couldn't relate. Strike was wrong about a bunch of things—with the blond cop topping the list—but he might've been right in some of the things he'd said about Hannah.

Shit or get off the pot, Jox thought to himself as he walked down the long marble hallway to the *winikin*'s wing around midnight. If the war was coming—hell, if the end of the world was coming—better to face it with a partner than not.

Right?

He fought the urge to tug at his jeans and T—or worse, beat a quick retreat to his quarters and change into a better shirt, maybe a nicer belt, and boots instead of sandals. But that would be stalling, and he was no wimp. "Besides," he said under his breath as he reached her door, "it's Hannah. You've known her forever." Okay, so there was that twenty-four-year gap in the middle and all, but still.

Telling himself it'd be okay, he knocked on her door.

She answered immediately, as though she'd been waiting for him. She was wearing flowing drawstring pants of royal blue and a patterned teal-colored top, and had a scarf of the same material tied around her head, pirate-style. When she saw who it was, though, surprise flashed across her face. "Jox!"

"Expecting someone else?" He heard the faint bite in his tone and winced. "Sorry. Not my business."

"No, it's not. Can I help you with something?"

"I wanted . . ." *you,* he should've said, but he was still fighting a losing battle against logic, against the part of him that said he needed to focus on his duties, now more than ever, since Strike seemed to be wobbling off course.

"You wanted . . . ?" She wasn't helping him out, and seemed faintly irritated that he was there at all, as though two weeks after their reunion was far too late for him to come knocking.

And maybe it was. Maybe Strike had been right that he'd cared more for the idea of her than the reality. The thought was a cold wash that had him retreating a step and dropping back to *winikin* mode. "I came to make sure things were under control over here."

"We're good," she said, seemingly willing to pretend that was what he'd come to ask. "Carlos is going to keep Cara close for the next few days while we see how things shake out."

"In other words, while the newbies figure out who belongs in which bed between now and the talent ceremony."

Her lips twitched, despite the tension between them. "What's the current score?"

"Well, Patience and Brandt are a given."

"One should hope. They're married."

"And stupid in love," Jox agreed with what might've been a twinge of jealousy. He ticked off the others on his fingers. "Michael and Jade headed off together—they're either a couple or will be soon. Rabbit didn't get his mark, so he probably won't get the binding hornies— and besides, he's too young for anyone here, so he's on his own. That leaves Alexis, Blackhawk, and Sven, which means either there'll be an odd man out, or some three-way kink."

"Have you seen the way Nate looks at her?" Hannah shook her head. "Sven's out of luck."

"Strike and Alexis would make a hell of a couple," Jox said, still not ready to give up on the idea.

"They would." Hannah nodded. "She's the strongest of the women, she's smart as hell, and she has a knack for strategy. She'd make a superlative queen. But it's not going to happen."

"It might."

Her face softened. "Poor Jox. Still trying to save the jaguar kings from themselves."

Before he could respond to that—if he could even figure out how—there was a clatter of footsteps and Brandt's *winikin*, Woodrow, swung around the corner. He was wearing jeans and a button-down Hawaiian shirt, and his long, graying hair was caught back in a ponytail that made him look like he'd gone native. He was barefoot, whistling, and carrying a bottle of wine in one hand, a couple of glasses in the other.

He hesitated midstride when he saw Jox and Hannah standing close together in her doorway. "Wow. I know I'm late, but you didn't need to call the boss on me." It was said with all of Wood's typical laid-back good humor, but there was a glint of challenge beneath the words.

Oh, Jox thought. So that was how it was.

Disappointed, but also relieved because the decision had already been made for him, he stepped away from Hannah. "You're lucky you got here when you did," he said, forcing humor. "We were talking about organizing a search."

"Doubt you'd have much luck," Wood said, moving to Hannah's side so they formed a unit, blocking the doorway and putting Jox on the outside. "Most everyone in this place is otherwise occupied, one way or the other."

He handed the wineglasses to Hannah, pulled a corkscrew from his pocket, and looked at Jox. Lifted a shoulder. "Sorry, dude. Only two glasses."

"No problem," Jox said, and almost meant it. "Actually, I wanted to talk to both of you real quick; then I'll get out of your way." He thought he saw a flicker of surprised hurt in Hannah's eye, but couldn't be sure. And even if he had, what of it? She had the right to make time with whomever she wanted. They'd never promised each other anything.

Wood gestured with the corkscrew. "Go on."

"Can you be in charge of both Patience and Brandt for a couple of days, so Hannah can spend some time with Leah?"

When Wood nodded, Hannah said, "How much do you want her to know?"

"Everything." He gritted his teeth, totally disagreeing with Strike's plan. "She's going to be sitting in on Magic 101 starting tomorrow. He's convinced himself that even though Red-Boar couldn't detect any connection to the barrier or the gods, she gained power of some sort during the *ajaw-makol* ritual."

She tipped her head and hummed a flat note. "But you don't think so."

"He's not thinking with his head." Not the right one, anyway.

"Because he believes this human may have power."

"Because he saw her even before he met her." He paused. "In a dream."

Wood lost his grin. "He's been having visions?"

"Hannah can fill you in." Jox took a step back. "I'll leave you two to your . . . whatever." He strode off, not wanting to watch the door close behind him.

"Jox," Hannah called softly.

He stopped, cursed himself, and turned. "Yeah?"

She stood alone, having apparently sent Wood inside. Soft light spilled from behind her, picking out the silvery waves of her hair, softening the lines of her face, and buffing away the lower edge of the scars, making her look very young, younger even than she'd been the night of the massacre.

She was silent so long he thought she wasn't going to say anything, that she'd meant only to call his name. Then she said, very quietly, "It's not your fault. You didn't do anything to cause this—not now, and not back then."

He almost resented that she saw it so easily. "I keep hoping it'll be different this time."

"Maybe it will be." But there was little hope in her voice, which told him she feared it, too.

It was like the writs said: What had happened before would happen again.

Hearing footsteps coming up the hall toward him, Sven ducked through the nearest doorway and closed the door to a crack. Not because he was doing anything wrong, but because he didn't want to have to talk to one of the other *winikin*—not about the ceremony, not about the coyote's-head mark on his forearm, which tingled faintly as though the ink—or whatever the hell it was—had rerouted the blood vessels beneath his skin, and certainly not about what he was doing outside the *winikin*'s wing at oh-dark-thirty in the a.m.

He was busy not sleeping, that was what he was doing. Busy *not* thinking about sex. He and the rest of the newbies—except for Patience and Brandt, no doubt, because they had sanctioned shagging privileges and had gotten their marks years ago. And potentially Michael and Jade, who he was pretty sure had hooked up a couple of days ago. The rest of them . . . well, it was either make friends real quick, or hello, self-service.

The footsteps passed and he got a good rear view of Jox, who was moving fast, like he had places to go. Well, good for him. So did Sven. Sort of.

Once the *winikin* had turned the corner and his footsteps faded, Sven slipped from concealment and headed for the third door on the right, where he knocked and waited. Knocked again.

Finally, when it was getting borderline ridiculous, Carlos opened the door. He was wearing Wranglers belted below his slight paunch, with a snap-studded shirt of faded blue, and save for a little gray around the edges he looked exactly the same as he had for . . . well, forever, Sven realized on a sudden slap of nostalgia. He had to swallow hard before he said, "Hey, Pops. Look." He flipped his arm, showed off the coyote. "Remember how I used to bug you about getting a tattoo just like yours?"

"You did it," the older man said softly, turning his own right hand palm up for a forearm comparison. "Congratulations, kid."

"Mine's bigger."

That got a snort. "Don't forget who used to change your Pampers, boyo."

"True, but I've heard stuff shrinks once you're on the downhill side of middle age."

"Bite me."

They grinned at each other, and Sven felt a loosening of something inside him he hadn't even known was tight. He exhaled. "I missed you, Pops." He paused, realizing that although they'd been in the same house for a couple of weeks now, they hadn't really talked. Partly because he'd been sorta freaked by the whole *winikin*-Nightkeeper revelation—okay, really freaked, but fascinated in a *by the way, you're a superhero* sort of way—and partly because the timing hadn't been right. Now, in the wake of a ceremony that'd left him feeling a step closer to the parents he'd never known, he was ready to deal with the parent he had known, and hadn't always done right by. "I'm sorry I didn't come home for the funeral."

Carlos shook his head. "Australia was too far to fly to for just a few days. I understood. Sometimes the needs of the living outweigh those of the dead."

The last part sounded like a quote, underscoring that the *winikin* had a whole other life and culture aside from managing a ranch and raising two kids who couldn't have been more different if they'd tried.

Sven shoved his hands in the pockets of his hip-hanger shorts. "Still, I should've been there." He didn't say that he'd had the offer of a spare seat on an investor's charter plane but hadn't taken it because things had been too damn complicated back then. Still were.

His eyes must've wandered to the door to Cara's room, because Carlos shook his head. "She's asleep."

The lights were up in the suite and the TV was on, though, and Cara was a light sleeper of epic proportions.

Sven nodded, accepting the lie. "Okay. No problem. I just . . ." *wanted to see her, wanted us to maybe go for a walk like we used to.* He'd wanted to inject a bit of normalcy into the craziness, to get her take on things that were moving too far, too fast for his hang-loose brain to keep up with.

"I know." Carlos nodded as though Sven had said all that aloud. "But things are different now." He paused. "She's not your sister anymore, kid. She's your servant. If you want me to wake her, I will."

She's not my servant any more than she's my sister, Sven wanted to argue, but didn't, because there were some things better left alone. So he shook his head. "No, let her sleep. Besides, this should probably come from you anyway. I think . . ." He paused, weighing his loyalties. "I think you should tell her to leave."

The older man's eyes widened fractionally. "Why?"

Sven shifted, faking a shrug. "She's a semester away from her degree. Seems silly to keep her here when I barely even see her as it is."

"And?" Carlos said with no shift in his expression.

She doesn't want to be here, Sven wanted to say. *Can't you see that?* But he didn't say it, because he could also see how much it meant to Carlos to have sired the only second-generation *winikin* in the group, how much he was enjoying having Cara around. So instead he said, "What we're going to be doing here is dangerous." He looked at the coyote mark again, because the binding ceremony had made the whole end-of-the-world-as-we-know-it thing seem a whole lot more real than it had when they'd just been sitting around talking about it. "I don't want her to get hurt."

"Neither do I, but I don't think that's what this is really about." Carlos waited, but Sven didn't say anything else, couldn't explain it to the man who'd raised him when he could barely understand it himself. After a long moment, the *winikin* sighed. "Do you command this?"

Sven nodded, feeling like a total poser. "I do. She's my *winikin*."

"And for that I'm sorry." Carlos shook his head. "I should be the one serving you."

"Nobody's serving anybody here. We're all in this together—I'm just trying to figure out how to minimize the danger."

"It's not a Nightkeeper's job to protect his *winikin*." Carlos paused. "But I'll do as you ask. She'll be gone before the end of the week; I'll take care of it. You just concentrate on learning how to control your powers . . . and yourself."

Which answered one question, Sven acknowledged with a dull thud of pain. Carlos definitely knew about what'd happened between him and Cara, knew why he'd taken off and why he hadn't been back since. He'd always figured Carlos didn't know, for the simple reason that their relationship had stayed close despite the physical distance. Now, he realized it'd been more a case of the *winikin*'s imperative to keep tabs on his charge outweighing the other stuff.

The thought was humbling. And damned awkward.

That wasn't how it was, he wanted to say. *I can control myself.* But that begged the question of why he'd come knocking on her door too late at night, with his blood humming and his senses on high alert.

So instead, he said, "Thanks. I owe you one."

Carlos nodded, but he didn't speak, and he hadn't moved from the doorway, hadn't invited Sven inside.

That rejection, that split in their onetime family unit, had Sven backing away and searching for a grin as he waved, making sure his mark showed. "Mine's still bigger."

The older man's smile didn't touch his eyes. "Size doesn't matter until you know how to use it, kid."

After chowing down enough leftover mac 'n' cheese to feed a boatload of Vikings, and washing it down with a bottle of lemon Perrier, Nate tried to go to back to bed and sleep off the rest of the postmagic hangover. And failed miserably.

Score: Boner 1, Blackhawk 0.

After an hour he finally gave up and headed for the gym on the lower level of the main house, figuring that if he racked enough iron, he should be able to exhaust his dick into submission.

The gym stretched along the short side of the mansion. It was below ground level, so there were no windows, but when he hit the light switch just inside the double door, the fluorescents were bright enough to sear his eyeballs. Like most of the compound, the room wore a fresh coat of stark white paint, new flooring, and had zero in the way of character. But that was okay with him; he was looking to sweat, not have a spa experience, and there were enough top-end machines to promise he'd get a good stink on, along with an equally high-end sound system to crank some tunes.

Hoping the room was soundproofed—or far enough away from the sleeping quarters for it not to matter— he tuned the satellite radio to something heavy on the bass and dance rhythms, gave a couple of halfhearted stretches, and headed straight for the free weights, figuring he'd go old school for the evening's antistiffy program.

Ever since that *hey, here you go, have an instatattoo* ceremony, he'd been a walking hard-on. He felt like a teenager, or like he belonged in one of those Cialis commercials where the voice-over guy warns about the dangers of priapism. *If your erection lasts for more than four hours, seek medical help. Or a woman. Whichever comes first.*

And that was the problem. There was a woman . . . and yet there wasn't.

Alexis wasn't Hera—he knew that. Hera was straight out of his imagination, an amalgam of tits and ass that made her a gamer's wet dream, along with the sharp, strategic intelligence required by any self-respecting warrior-goddess.

However, Alexis was the spitting image of Hera, and

that just freaked his shit right out, because between the lectures and the binding ceremony, he was having trouble believing it was just one of those things. The Nightkeepers didn't seem to go in for coincidence.

Which meant what? That she was his match? His mate?

As he started lifting, he tried to figure out why the thought made him want a one-way ticket to hell and gone. Maybe it was meeting her when everything he thought he knew about himself—and about reality—was taking a serious beating; maybe it was his inner rebel hating the whole your-life-is-ruled-by-destiny thing. Who knew?

He thought about it as he lifted; thought about her.

Sweat started beading on his body despite the central AC, and his muscles had a good burn going after a half hour or so, but a dick check revealed he was still sporting serious wood. If anything, it'd gotten worse rather than better, tenting the front of his gym shorts as he lay back on the weight bench.

Current score: Boner 2, Blackhawk 0.

Glaring at it, he warned, "All right, that's it. Two more sets and I'm bringing out the duct tape."

"Excuse me?"

For half a sweaty second, he thought the damn thing was talking back—and wouldn't *that* be a trip?—and was doing so in Alexis's voice. Then what was left of his brain fired up, and he shot a startled glance at the doorway and saw her standing there, watching him talk to his johnson.

Losing his count and his concentration, he forgot to lock his elbows and his arms folded under the weights. The barbell *whumped* onto his upper chest, just below his throat.

"Shit!" he said, only it came out as a gurgle as he fought to dead-lift the thing from zero leverage.

"Oh!" Alexis sprinted across the room and helped him wrestle the bar off his Adam's apple and onto the overhead stand. "Sorry. I didn't mean to startle you. Are you okay?"

"Fine," he said shortly, sitting up so fast his head

swam. He snagged his shirt so he could pretend to scrub the sweat off his face and chest, and then casually dumped the T-shirt in his lap.

Current score: Boner 3, Blackhawk 0.

From the flush that rode high on her slashing cheekbones and the way she was careful to look him in the eye rather than lower down, he had a feeling she knew exactly what was going on. Either that, or she was dealing with some horns of her own. He should be so lucky.

Then again, maybe he *was* that lucky, he thought when he saw that she'd changed into formfitting workout pants and a soft shirt that hung off one shoulder to play peekaboo with a bra strap, but wasn't wearing sneakers or carrying a towel.

Despite not really being on board with the predestiny thing, he figured he'd be an idiot not to engage in some scratch-the-itch for the next two months if she made the offer.

"You looking for me?" he asked after a moment. *Please say yes.*

"Yeah." She cleared her throat. "Um, well, you see . . ." The flush rode higher on her cheeks, creating two spots of color. "I thought we could . . . Oh, screw it." She held out her hand to him. "Come on."

Nate might not've been raised by his *winikin*, but he was no dummy. He didn't argue. He simply put his hand in hers and let her lead the way.

Score.

Rabbit observed the mansion from the perch he'd found high up in the ceiba tree, where he could watch without being watched in return. He saw most of the newbies pairing up and disappearing into darkened rooms, saw Woody hand Jox his hat. More interesting was the scene between Strike and the blonde out by the pool. He hadn't been able to hear what they were saying, but the end result was obvious: Strike struck out, and the blonde headed back to her room alone.

Rabbit watched her go.

So that was the girlfriend, huh? She was pretty enough, he supposed. Okay, she was damn near a knockout, with long blond hair, slim hips, and legs that kept on giving inside a pair of loose jeans that hung practically off her ass.

Rabbit had heard the old man and Strike arguing about her earlier, had heard the old man muttering long after—he'd caught a few words, like "blasphemy" and "rewriting history" . . . which had entertained Rabbit to no end, and took his mind off what'd happened at the ceremony.

Or rather, what *hadn't* happened.

The old man had tried to tell him it was for the best that he hadn't gotten his mark, but of course he'd say that. Really, the ceremony had just proved what Rabbit had known all along—if he wanted to learn the magic he was going to have to figure it out on his own. He'd never been, and would never be, a priority for his father and the others. So he'd hit the books, do some experimenting. He wanted to know what he could do besides torch stuff. Pyrokinesis was cool as far as it went, but had its limitations, because he didn't just want to destroy stuff . . . he wanted to create stuff. He wanted to control, to rule.

He wanted to be someone.

"Rabbit."

The old man's voice was an unpleasant jolt, as was the sight of him at the bottom of the tree, scowling straight up into the branches, making it clear he knew exactly where his son was hiding. He'd traded his robe for fatigues and boots, but his belt bore no weapons.

For about three seconds, Rabbit was tempted to light the seat of Red-Boar's pants, or maybe give him a hot-foot. Then sanity returned. "Yeah?"

"I'm leaving."

The two words hit Rabbit harder than he would've expected, punching him in the gut and making his breath whoosh out. "For good?" His voice squeaked.

Red-Boar scowled. "No, you idiot. I'll be back the day after tomorrow."

"Oh." And suddenly he could breathe again. Not like he wanted the old man to know that, though. "So?"

"I didn't want you to wonder. And I thought you might want to use the cottage while I'm gone."

Rabbit eased down a couple of branches, so he could see the old man's face. "Are you, like, apologizing for kicking me out?"

"Strike offered you a room in the big house and you took it. No kicking involved."

"Whatever." Rabbit headed back up.

"Wait."

He paused. Looked down. "What?"

His old man took a step back, into a stripe of deep shadows, so it was like his voice came from the darkness when he said, "I'm sorry."

Rabbit scowled, though it helped some to hear. "Sorry for which part? Sorry for not accepting me as your son or sorry for not prepping me properly?"

"I'm sorry the circumstances of your birth dictate that you'll never belong." Then, before Rabbit could wheeze past the gut-punch of pain, the old man turned and walked away, leaving what he hadn't quite said to ring in the air between them: *I'm sorry you were born, period.*

It wasn't a surprise. But it still sucked to hear.

CHAPTER FOURTEEN

Leah slept far better than she would've expected, given her level of sexual frustration—high—and the general weirdness of staying in a suite of rooms that had belonged to her not-quite-lover's parents, the king and queen of what-the-hell-is-going-on-here. Still, she woke tired. She supposed she could blame her fatigue on the postmagic hangover, but that didn't exactly improve the logic of the situation.

Magic. Right.

Pulling on her borrowed clothes, she stumbled into the ornate marble-and-chrome master bathroom and gave herself a once-over in the mirror. The results weren't exactly impressive—the clothes were too big and she had a shiner and no makeup.

"Note to self," she said aloud. "Find a mall. Or an Internet connection to Overstock.com, whichever comes first." Or, hell, she could just have Connie mail her some stuff from home. She'd need clothes and whatnot if she was going to stay.

And yeah, she was going to stay—for the time being, anyway—because she might not appreciate Strike's I'm-calling-the-shots attitude about Zipacna, but he'd been right about a few things. For one, it sure looked like the *ajaw-makol* was jonesing for a do-over of his interrupted human sacrifice, starring her, and for another, this whole mess was going way outside the usual for the MDPD, which meant it was just good policework to cultivate an expert in the field.

And whether or not it ran the logic train right off its rails, she wanted to know more about the magic.

She hadn't been into D&D as a kid, and the whole *Harry Potter* thing had left her cold, but those had been make-believe. The things she'd experienced over the past few weeks were . . . well, whatever they were, she was betting that *if* it turned out she had some sort of power, and *if* she could learn how to use it, then she'd have that much more ammunition against Zipacna. Because whether or not Strike liked it, as soon as she found the bastard, she was going after him personally.

Ignoring the faint twinge of disquiet brought by the thought of going behind Strike's back—and equally ignoring the flare of heat brought by any thought of the dark-haired warrior—she prowled the suite a little, not quite ready to head for the kitchen and face the rest of the Nightkeepers and their *winikin*. She'd seen most of them briefly in passing the day before, and had weathered their *what the hell are you still doing here?* surprise, but she wasn't looking forward to joining their magic lessons later in the morning.

It was all just too freaking weird.

Her prowling brought her to the locked door she'd found the day before when she'd toured the suite, checking all the drawers and closets—because, hey, she was a cop—and finding nothing but bland decor and hotel-neat conveniences. And the locked door just before the solarium.

It was an utterly normal-looking door, save for a pair of glyphs carved into the upper half of the panel, both of which she recognized from Strike's arm: a jaguar's head and a long-nosed, highly stylized human figure holding a staff of some sort.

She didn't need to be able to translate the writing to know what it meant: family only. Which didn't include her, as Jox had so clearly pointed out the day before. But she'd never been able to resist a locked door.

"It's not much of a lock, either," she said aloud, giving the knob a shake. The door rattled in its frame, far looser than it needed to be for the sake of security. Heck, it was more like a suggestion than a real lock.

Her conscience told her they would've left the key if she was supposed to open the door, but that didn't stop her from pushing the panel to the edge of the bolt, twisting the knob, and giving it a hip check.

The lock popped free.

"Oops." Feeling only a little guilty, she stepped through the door into a dark, windowless chamber and fumbled for the lights. There was no switch plate, but the moment her foot hit the floor, torches flared to life at each corner of the square, closet-size space.

She froze, partly because, damn, that was weird, and partly because she couldn't go very far. Right in front of her, a mat lay on the tiled floor. Made of some sort of natural fiber, the neutral beige rug had a green border of strange symbols, and two bright red footprints woven into its center. The footprints faced a waist-high statue that looked like the one in the ritual chamber from the night before, the one Vince had called a *chac-mool*. Behind the statue, a circular plate was set into the wall. Made of highly polished black stone—obsidian, maybe?— it showed her torchlit reflection.

And that of a large man sneaking up behind her.

Leah spun automatically and threw a punch straight from the shoulder.

"Whoa!" Strike feinted and the blow grazed his ear.

"Sorry!" She pulled the follow-up, which put her off balance and sent her stumbling into him. He caught her against his chest, and she felt the vibration of his chuckle.

"Does this mean we can add assault and battery to the B and E charge?" he asked, holding her easily. He was wearing jeans and rope sandals, as he had been the night before, with a worn-soft oxford rolled up to his elbows, showing off the ink. Marks. Whatever. She didn't know what they were exactly, but the sight of the symbols made her hot and cold, thirsty and hungry all at once.

Or maybe it wasn't the marks. Maybe it was him, or the room. Or the both of them together. Whatever the cause, where she'd been able to buffer herself against the attraction—more or less—the day before, now the gut-deep chemistry flared between them, making the air crackle with tension.

Flushing with sudden warmth, she pushed away from him. "Sorry. I was just—" She broke off, then sucked it up and said, "I was just snooping where I had absolutely no business being. I've never been able to resist a locked door."

But it was more than the door, she realized as her eye was drawn back to the statue. It was as though the contents of the room had called to her. Compelled, she stepped onto the mat, fitting her feet to the red shapes on the thatch. The woven footprints were larger than her own, creating a bloodred halo around her feet as she leaned forward and touched the altar.

The stone was cool and slick to the touch, and it felt like, well, stone. Leah frowned slightly. She didn't know what she'd been expecting, but that wasn't it. Then Strike stepped onto the mat, crowding behind her, pressing up against her and covering her hands with his, and suddenly the woven footprints weren't too large at all . . . and the altar didn't feel like stone.

The surface warmed beneath her palms, turning liquid and strange, and an image flashed in her mind, an impression, really—that of her and Strike naked and intertwined in the torchlit darkness, making love atop that very altar, their joined reflection showing in the black mirror.

Need swamped her, making it almost impossible to breathe.

Strike's fingers tightened on hers. Heat poured off his skin, surrounding her, radiating into her where his chest pressed against her back, and where the brush of hard flesh where it hadn't been moments earlier suggested she wasn't the only one having a waking fantasy.

The moment contracted around her, until there was nothing beyond the small sacred chamber and the two of them, and the sexual attraction that bound them together in raw need and magic. It didn't matter that they came from different worlds and had different agendas, didn't matter that he was every tough guy she'd ever dated all rolled up into one *über*-virile package, or that she fully intended to go her own way the moment she had a good handle on Zipacna's whereabouts and how to kill him. What mattered was the man pressed against her, his front to her back, and the searing heat that flowed at the points of contact.

That and the altar. The mirror. The pounding promise of sex.

She slid her hands from beneath his and turned around, and as she did, he moved back a pace but kept his hands on the altar, giving her room but bracketing her with his arms, as though he meant to keep her from escaping. But escape was the last thing on her mind as she hiked herself up onto the altar so they were eye level with each other.

"Leah," he said. Only her name, but with a warning growl in his voice.

She didn't know if he was warning her not to tease, or not to give in when they both knew it wasn't just the two of them in the room. There was power, too, the golden glory of it binding them, bringing them together until their lips hovered just a whisper apart, until she could feel the rasp of his harsh breathing as if it were her own, feel her heart thunder in time with his.

Then the distance was gone and their lips touched. Brushed. Clung.

Held.

His mouth fused to hers. Their tongues touched. And something clicked inside her, a feeling of, *There you are; where have you been?*

It was their first kiss. And yet it wasn't.

She remembered his taste and feel from her dreams and newly regained memories, but all of those encounters seemed like fantasies, cushioned in the gray-green fog of unreality. Now, though, he was here. This was reality. This was real.

He moved into her, stepping between her legs so they aligned center-to-center, hard to soft, and she felt complete, united, whole for the first time since . . . well, since ever. Leaning into him, she slipped her arms around his waist, then higher, so her breasts pressed against his chest. Deep within her, a poignant ache gathered and grew until it became a compulsion, an almost painful need to bind herself to the man she'd dreamed of, the warrior she'd made love to but barely knew.

She wrapped her legs around him, drawing him close, holding him fast as kiss flowed into kiss. She worked her hands under his shirt and higher, desperate to touch him, to bind herself to him. Groaning, he rocked against her, hips pistoning as he got a hand under her shirt and cupped her breast, shaping her, pleasuring her until she bowed against him and shuddered.

Then he broke the kiss and dropped his forehead to her shoulder, pressing his hot cheek to hers. His chest heaved with deep, gulping breaths, moving them both with a rhythmical surge as he withdrew his hand from her shirt and gripped the edge of the altar on either side of her, his muscles so tight they'd gone to cords beneath her fingers. "We have to stop."

It took a second for the words to penetrate, another for Leah to comprehend. "You've got to be kidding me."

"No. I can't do this. *We* can't do this." He pulled away from her and straightened, stepping off the mat and backing to the doorway, so there was a gap separating them.

Irritated—and ridiculously needy, damn him—she dropped down off the altar and stood facing him, hands fisted at her sides. "News flash, Ace. We've already done it at least once. Twice, if unreciprocated oral counts as 'this' in your book."

"Don't," he said softly, his face etched with strain. "Don't make it less than it was."

"Okay, but apparently I made just now into more than it was supposed to be. Want to explain the difference to me?" Her volume was climbing, both with embarrassment that he'd turned her down, and with self-directed anger because she knew better, damn it. Hadn't she warned herself against him only the night before? Hadn't she decided to get her ass out of there as soon as she had a lock on Zipacna and some sense of what she could do to take him down? She was a walking relationship disaster, and as usual had picked the most complicated guy possible to get interested in. Yet she'd done it again, wrapping herself around him, offering herself to him.

And he'd turned her down.

"It's—"

"If the next word out of your mouth is 'complicated,' you'd better be ready to race me to the bedroom for the MAC, because so help me, God, I'll shoot you."

He clamped his mouth shut.

"I thought so. Do better. I think I deserve at least that much." She hated that her voice shook, hated that all this mattered way more than it ought to.

He took a long, deep breath, then said, "There's a prophecy."

"Right. World's going to end. Got that."

But he shook his head, his expression tight. "The end-time prophecy is something every Mayan knew about. I'm talking about a different set of them, called the Nightkeepers' prophecies. There were thirteen of them handed down by the god Kauil; they were a way of tracking the progress of the spiritual end date. We're up to the last one, lucky number thirteen."

Leah took it down a notch, realizing this was something more than, *It's not you, it's me.* "What does it say?"

"To paraphrase, in the last five years before the zero date, the king will have to perform a great sacrifice in order to prevent the *Banol Kax* from coming to earth and starting a series of events that will lead to the apocalypse."

A touch of cool air tickled across the back of Leah's neck, bringing gooseflesh. "What sort of sacrifice? Like human sacrifice? You?"

He nodded. "I think so. My father thought so, too. We all figured he'd still be king when the time came, which is why he . . . did what he did. He believed the 'greatest sacrifice' meant he'd have to put my mother, sister, and me under the knife. He was trying to save us by making an end run around the thirteenth prophecy."

And he led his people into a massacre, Leah thought with a wince. "So you think . . ." She trailed off, making the connection. "You think the dreams mean we're supposed to fall in love, and then you kill me."

"It's more than that. I think you were supposed to become a Godkeeper at the solstice, and then we were supposed to fall in love and become a mated Nightkeeper/Godkeeper pair. That way, when the time comes, I wouldn't just be killing you."

"You'd be killing one of your own gods," Leah said, her lips feeling numb as they shaped the words.

This was crazy talk. It made no sense, didn't align with anything she'd grown up believing about the way religion worked. Yet there was a terrifying sort of internal logic to it, and the things she'd seen had been too damn real for her to dismiss anything at this point.

"That's why I sent you away," Strike said, his voice gone raw. "It's why I made you forget. Red-Boar said you didn't have any connection to the heavens. He said you were clean."

"Zipacna doesn't think so," she said, knowing that was why Itchy had taken her prisoner a second time.

"Neither do I. Not anymore."

"Which leaves us where?" she asked, though she already knew the answer was something along the lines of, "Up Shit Creek."

"I'd send you away if I thought you'd be safe." His expression went hard. "Since I can't do that, I think it'd be best if we don't spend much time alone."

Leah lifted her chin. "You're assuming that if we have sex, we'll fall in love. News flash, Ace. My relationships have an automatic end-time of their own: three months from date one. I've never made it past that, and the hotter the attraction the shorter it lasts. Given the sizzle, I give us three weeks, tops. So why not just do it and get it out of our systems?"

He pushed himself away from the door frame so smoothly he was inside her personal space before she realized he'd moved. He stood too close, making her feel crowded, making her feel wanted. "Because it was more than sex and you know it," he said, his voice a low rasp. "Because I think we'd be good together, and not just in bed. And most of all, because I. Don't. Fizzle."

She knew that shouldn't have felt like the sexiest line any man had ever laid on her. But it did, and that was a problem. "Okay," she whispered, staring up into his eyes. "No sex. Got it." Which should've settled things. But he kept looking at her so intently that she started to wonder if he could read her thoughts . . . and if so, what he was picking up, because she was hell-and-all confused. "What?" she finally said.

"There's more."

She squeezed her eyes shut. "Of course there is."

"The powers you exhibited yesterday must mean you retained some sort of connection to the barrier, one that Red-Boar couldn't trace. If you're still linked to the god in any way, we're going to need to put you into the barrier on the next ceremonial day and figure out how the connection works."

She swallowed, her stomach going hollow at the thought of the limitless gray-green she'd glimpsed during the teleport. "Okay," she whispered. "I'm game." Actually, she was scared spitless, but the idea that she might have power was seriously tempting. With it, maybe she could find Zipacna.

With it, maybe she could kill him.

"There's a risk," Strike said, his eyes never leaving hers. "Rabbit nearly died during the binding ceremony, and he's half Nightkeeper."

"Oh." Leah leaned back against the altar, needing the feel of something solid to hang on to as the world spun around her. "So it's like this. If we become lovers, I could die. If I go into the barrier, I could die. If I go home, I'll probably die. Is there an option that includes me *not* dying?"

"I don't know," he said. "But I promise you one thing: If we can figure out a way, then that's what we'll do."

But there wasn't much of a ring of conviction to his words. And when Leah crossed the small chamber to press her face into his chest, needing something even more solid than the altar to lean on, he didn't push her away, didn't tell her that the no-being-alone-together thing had already started.

Instead, he closed his arms around her, dropped his cheek to the top of her head, and hung on tight, like he was already saying good-bye.

Or Godspeed.

When Anna's husband, Dick, phoned her office just past lunchtime and then spent a good five minutes talking about the weather—hot and sunny wasn't exactly news for Texas in July—she knew he was working up to something she wouldn't like.

That knowledge drummed alongside the headache that'd been a constant low-grade throb since the day before, when she'd been released from Brackenridge Hospital around lunchtime. The docs had diagnosed her crash as "catatonia pursuant to a transiently high fever of unknown origin"—i.e., "Nobody knows what the hell it was, but you seem fine now."

As far as she was concerned, an FUO sounded far saner than, "I read a spell off my grad student's laptop and nearly put myself straight through the barrier."

She'd been so surprised to see familiar words twined into the line of text on Lucius's laptop screen that the words had slipped out before she'd been aware of it, as though something else had reached across and spoken through her. The next thing she knew, *poof.* Instant loss of six hours. And ever since then, she'd had headaches she suspected were the result of her mind fending off the power—and the visions—she didn't want.

She'd known the barrier was reactivating, had felt it at the solstice. She'd just hoped to avoid dealing with it for as long as possible.

Like forever.

"Anna, did you hear me?" On the phone, Dick's voice gained a faint edge.

She shook her head to clear her vision when the walls of her office blurred around her, threatening to become a step-sided pyramid rising up from a sea of foliage. It took several furious blinks before she could focus on the cordless phone in her hand. "Sorry, hon, what was that again?"

"I said I'll be home late tonight, and you shouldn't wait dinner. I'll grab a sandwich or something." He paused, and his tone softened. "I know we were going to go over the bills tonight and figure out how we're going to pay for another round of in vitro, but the dean asked me to meet him at the faculty club. I'll owe you one, okay?"

By Anna's count he owed her several hundred already, and she knew damn well that if she stopped in at the club later, he wouldn't be there.

"No problem." Her lips felt numb, as though they belonged to someone else, another woman entirely, and she wondered fleetingly if that other woman would challenge Dick's glib excuse, or if she, too, would be too much of a wuss to force the answer she didn't want. "I'll wrap a plate for you, in case you're hungry when you get home."

She was dimly aware of a quiet knock at the door. Moments later, the panel swung inward and Lucius stuck his head around the corner. The shaggy-haired grad student winced when he saw she was on the phone. He mouthed, *Sorry,* and motioned that he'd wait outside.

No, she mouthed back, *come in.* She waved him in, knowing her husband all too well.

"Thanks for understanding, hon." Dick's voice gained that false cheer that she'd come to hate over the past few months. "Okay, then, I have to go. I'll try not to wake you when I get home. Love you."

He hung up before she said anything, which was probably just as well, because she didn't know what she would have said in return. She loved him; she really did. And she knew he loved her. But she was tired and discouraged with their marriage, and had a feeling he felt the same way, which left them . . . nowhere, really, and sinking fast. The more months that went by without the pee stick showing positive, the more distant he became. Or maybe that was her drawing away, like he said. Maybe both. But she'd even gotten to the point of wondering why they were going to bother for another try at in vitro when they barely talked to each other anymore beyond vapid pleasantries and scheduling. She'd wanted a baby to add to her and Dick's life together, not as an attempt to fix it.

Feeling hollow and achy, she sat for a moment with the phone pressed against her ear before she sighed and snapped the receiver back in its charger.

Lucius crossed to the side of her desk and folded his long limbs into an easy, graceful crouch, so they were eye-to-eye. "Everything okay?"

Carrying a battered canvas knapsack over his shoulder, wearing worn jeans, a T-shirt, and sandals, with his hazel eyes clear and guileless, his brown hair too long to be stylish, too short to be a fashion statement, he looked so damn young. Too damn young. The eight years separating them could've been twenty, the way she was feeling these days—at least, that was what she told herself, because it was best to think of him as a boy rather than a man, better to ignore the occasional urge to lean on him, especially now, when she was so close to falling apart.

Instead, she forced herself to lean away. "I'm fine."

He tilted his head. "You've been saying that a lot lately," he said. "Why don't I believe you?"

Anna exhaled. "Weren't you headed to the library?"

"I'm on my way."

But he didn't move, just kept looking at her until she was tempted to wipe a palm across her face, thinking she had something on her cheek. A hint of something sparkled in the air between them, an attraction that had no business existing.

"Lucius," she finally whispered, feeling weak and small. "Please go."

"I will. But first, I have something for you." He shifted, dipped into his knapsack, and pulled out a flat, paper-wrapped package. He held it out to her. "A guy came by my office and asked me to get this to you. I'm not sure why he gave it to me and not you, but . . ."

She didn't hear the rest of his sentence, as his voice faded to a buzz—or maybe the buzz was coming off the package, she couldn't tell. She felt the power before she recognized the handwriting, the shock jolting through her like heat. Like temptation.

"I'll take it." She snatched the thing away from Lucius and gritted her teeth when the magic sang up her arm, even through the wrapping.

What the hell was in there?

I don't care, she told herself sternly. *This means nothing to me now. I'm a wife. I'm trying to become a mother. I'm not that person anymore.*

Yet the power called to her, reaching deep down inside and curling around her soul, warming the places that had grown so cold.

"What man?" she asked, more for something to say than because she needed to know. It would've been Strike, her baby brother, coming to bring her back to the fold.

"He didn't give a name, just told me to take the package straight to you, nobody else." Lucius frowned. "Huh . . . that's weird. I can't really picture him. I know there was something seriously cool about him, but . . ." He scrubbed a hand down the back of his neck, and as he did so, she saw that the coarse hairs on his forearm were raised, as if drawn upright by static electricity. His voice went serious. "What's going on, Anna? Things have felt . . . weird around here since the night you conked out, and I'm not the only one who's noticed it. Half the artifacts are suddenly under lock and key, you've got strangers dropping off mysterious packages, the interns are practically living at the library, and I get the feeling you'd be happy if I joined them." He paused. "I'd like to think you know me better than that, so why don't you spare us both the argument and tell me what's up?"

Anna almost told him, but didn't, because he wasn't part of what was going on behind the scenes of everyday life. Hell, *she* wasn't even part of it, not anymore. She was a consultant. A convenience. *I'll give it to Anna,* she could picture Strike saying. *She'll translate it.*

No, she decided, she bloody well wouldn't.

"Trust me, you're better off not knowing," she said, pinching the bridge of her nose. "I'm trying to spare you a headache you can't even begin to understand."

"I'm tougher than I look."

"It's not about being tough; it's about—" She broke off, shaking her head. "Never mind. Everything is fine. *I'm* fine; I promise." She forced a smile. "And if it feels like I keep shuffling you off to the library, it's because I do. Or have you forgotten that you're defending your dissertation in a few weeks?"

Refusing to be distracted, he tapped the package, which she still clutched in both hands. "Are you going to let me see what's in there?"

Not on your life, she thought, but said aloud, "Maybe later."

"Which means no." His voice held faint reproach, but his grin was pure and sweet and held just enough of the devil to have her taking a second look when he said, "You know I'll get a look eventually. I have my ways."

"Keep on believing that." She waved him out. "We all need our little delusions."

But her smile died the moment he was out the door.

She stared down at the flat packet. It seemed like such a small, innocuous thing—an oblong rectangle wrapped in brown paper and secured with packing tape. Inside, though, was something beautiful. Something terrible. She could feel it hum up her arms, begging to be unwrapped. To be seen. To be used.

It was one of the lost spells. It had to be. But where had Strike found it? Where had it been all these years?

Jox had told her the stories, of course. He'd told both her and Strike as part of their training, and then repeated them over again when Red-Boar's young son, Rabbit, had been old enough to understand. The *winikin* had told them how the Maya had welcomed Cortés's ships, ignoring the Nightkeepers who said they should be wary, pointing to the third prophecy: *When the solstice sun rises, a fair-skinned man arrives from the east, bringing destruction.*

The Mayan hosts, believing the lies of the demon-worshiping Order of Xibalba, had welcomed the conquistador's ships as heralding the return of the winged serpent god, Kulkulkan. Instead, the galleons had brought utter destruction. *What happened before will happen again,* said the writs, referring back to the massacre that had driven the Nightkeepers out of Egypt when Akhenaten decreed there was only one true God. And history had indeed repeated itself, with the conquistadors slaughtering all but a handful of the magic users and burning their books, forcing the Maya to convert to Christianity. The accumulated wisdom of thousands of lifetimes had perished in the second massacre, with only scraps surfacing from time to time. What were the chances of one surfacing now, as the portal was wakening, as power was building and the end-time approached?

There are no coincidences, Jox had always said, his voice suddenly fresh in Anna's mind even after all these years. *There is only destiny.* It was that destiny that had driven her away. Now it was looking to suck her back in, looking to make her into something she didn't want to be, to take her away from the things she *did* want to be. A wife. A teacher. Hell, a soccer mom.

She ripped the package open more violently than necessary, because it was hard to be a soccer mom without kids.

Beneath the outer layer of packing, there was a layer of acid-free paper, a layer of cardboard, and another of acid-free paper. Inside that was a flat packet of oilcloth, tied shut with a boot lace. Within that was a scrap of power.

The codex fragment bore lines of glyphwork so ornate that it was difficult to make out the symbols themselves. Soon, though, the lines and shapes began to resolve into flattened faces with heavy, hooked noses and elaborate headdresses, stylized caricatures of animals and plants interspersed with the dots and slashes. And the skulls. So many skulls, all tipped back, mouths opened as they screamed agony into the darkness.

Gods, she thought, feeling awe shimmer over her, through her. *It's gorgeous.* Hideous, but gorgeous, and giving off so much power just sitting there that her skin grew warm in the center of her collarbone, where her quartz crystal used to rest. She even reached up to touch her pendant before she remembered it was gone. Then she let her hand fall and shoved the damned packet in a drawer, locking it tight, as though that would make it all go away.

CHAPTER FIFTEEN

In the weeks following Strike's revelation of the thirteenth prophecy, Leah channeled her excess energy into finding the bastard who'd killed her brother and friends . . . and learning how to kill the creature Zipacna had become. Logic—and rationality—said she should go home and work the case from there. But home wasn't safe, and besides, the things she'd seen and done recently had separated her from that life somehow. She didn't feel like that world fit anymore.

Which was unfortunate, because she sure didn't fit into the Nightkeepers' world, either.

As agreed, she and Strike avoided the hell out of each other. It wasn't easy, considering that they crossed paths just often enough to keep the sizzle at a maddening background hum. But because he'd been right, damn it, the sex hadn't been just sex, and because she didn't want to be anybody's sacrifice, she ignored the hum as best she could and threw herself into her work.

Unfortunately, she didn't have much more in the success department there, either.

She was a bust in Magic 101, showing zero power, which was both a relief and a disappointment—a relief because she wasn't sure she wanted to play the magic game when it seemed like a good way of getting dead, but a disappointment because she really, really wanted to fry Zipacna's ass. Then she found out the deal with the MAC-10s: The bullets were tipped with jade, which was apparently anathema to the denizens of the nine-layered hell called Xibalba. They were the Nightkeepers' silver bullets.

And they were a way for her to fight Zipacna.

According to Jox—who had no use for her but proved to be a bit of a weapons junkie—the jade-tips wouldn't kill a *makol* because its human aspect would protect it from the jade while its magic protected it from getting dead right away. But the jade-tips would sure as hell slow it down long enough for her to do the head-and-heart thing and recite a simple banishment spell. Jox said he wasn't sure whether the banishment spell would work for a human—and of course he said the "human" part with a superior lip curl. That meant maybe the *makol* would vaporize . . . and maybe it'd sit its headless ass up and make a grab for her.

She had a feeling the *winikin* was hoping for the latter. But who the hell cared? At least she had a weapon with some hope of success. All she had to do was track down Zipacna, who might or might not be traveling with a hundred or so of his freak-show disciples.

That turned out to be easier said than done.

She leaned on the Nightkeeper's private eye, Carter, and called in all her markers and then some. She tracked the 2012ers from Miami to the Keys and lost them when they hit the water, headed south. A week later, she picked them back up in south Texas, near the border. Once she had the location, she forced Strike and Red-Boar to take her along on the teleport recon by refusing to give up the location—and the relevant photographs—until they agreed.

They got there half a day too late. Zipacna and his freaks were gone.

Then the same thing happened in Fort Worth, and again in Philly, of all places. Then LA. Each time they were a fraction too late, sometimes a day, sometimes just a few hours, as if the bastard had known they were coming.

"He's got a seer," Strike said at one point. "It's the only explanation."

The knowledge hurt him doubly, she knew—once because they couldn't catch the *ajaw-makol*, and a second time because it drove home the continued separation between him and his sister, Anna—a rift Leah had learned of when she'd come across him one day, sitting at the kitchen table with the mail open in front of him and his head in his hands. Eventually he'd revealed that he'd given Anna a text for translation and she'd sent it back, refusing to get involved. Which left them with no seer, and no translator the Nightkeepers could trust.

With so much of their magic lost over the years—to time, to persecution—they couldn't afford to waste any of their assets. But instead of zapping to UT Austin and dragging his sister's butt back to the compound, Strike had withdrawn completely, giving Jox and Red-Boar control of Magic 101 and spending most of his time locked in the archives. When he did come out in public, he was snarly at best, churlish at worst. Even Red-Boar started giving him a wide berth, which was saying something.

As days turned to weeks, Strike's absence meant that Leah didn't have to work so hard at avoiding him, and she could spend as much time as she wanted on the firing range at the back of the compound, perfecting her aim with the jade-tips without his figuring out what she planned to do. But it also meant that the buzz of desire became an ache of loneliness. And she wasn't the only one missing him, either. The trainees, whom she'd gotten to know little by little, were starting to fall apart . . . and she was the only one who seemed to see it.

Granted, on the surface everything looked pretty good. Patience and Brandt were the perfect couple, and their twins didn't seem to miss not having other kids around. The boys played with each other under the watchful eyes of the *winikin*, or tagged after Rabbit, who had the rep of a delinquent but seemed to get a kick out of the twins. Of the others, Alexis and Nate were a couple, though they didn't spend much time together outside of the bedroom, and Michael and Jade's romance had fizzled out around the one-month mark, right about the time he discovered a knack for casting force fields. Sven was . . . well, he was Sven. He hung loose, seeming even more chilled out after his young *winikin* went back to college. Even Red-Boar, whom Leah tagged as living on the manic-depressive side of life, seemed to have settled into the teaching role pretty well.

But beneath the surface, she didn't like how Rabbit spent so much time alone, and how the others treated him differently, not because he was younger, but because he was half-human, and didn't have his mark. She didn't like seeing Patience and Brandt with their heads together, shutting out the rest of the world—and not in a *we're deeply in love* way, but in a *we're making plans that don't include you* way. She didn't like that Nate spent a big chunk of his time on the computer, trading e-mails with his business partners and working on something about a Viking sex goddess, or that Michael got a dozen cell calls a day and always took them behind closed doors.

They trained hard; she'd give them that, though it wasn't like Jox or Red-Boar would've tolerated anything less. In the mornings Jox did a sort of Nightkeepers for Dummies, which was a blinding speed-sampling of their history, starting with Atlantis—and boy, had that made Leah's cop side cringe—and running through to the present, along with a short version of the *Popol Vuh* creation myth and a dizzying number of prophecies, some coming from the earliest Nightkeepers, others supposedly from the gods themselves.

In the afternoons, the trainees met up with Red-Boar in the steel-sided training building, which was almost always either too hot or too cold. There, they worked on basic barrier spells like shielding and wielding fire. Of the trainees, only Rabbit could reliably make fire, and Michael showed a talent for shields. Patience got pretty good at the invisibility thing—which was the freakiest by far, in Leah's opinion—and even figured out that she could occasionally throw her talent to distant objects or people, especially if her husband was boosting her with his power. Which was all well and good, but Leah didn't see how most of the things they were doing—with the exception of Jox's late-afternoon lessons on the firing range—were preparing them to fight.

Worse, she was pretty sure the others felt the same way. They were taking their classes, finishing their homework, and otherwise doing their own things. And that was *not* a good recipe for teamwork.

Maybe she noticed it because she was an outsider, maybe because Connie had exposed the members of the MDPD to a wide range of touchy-feely exercises designed to build their team spirit. Or whatever. But while the cops had universally mocked Connie's team-building crapola, as far as Leah could tell, the MDPD had been one big, happy, tolerant family compared to the Nightkeepers. And that was bad. They—and that would be the whole-wide-world "they"—needed the magi working together, or very bad things were going to happen. Leah believed that, even if she didn't totally understand it.

A week before the Venus conjunction, she decided she'd had enough of the bullshit, enough of Strike locking himself away and pretending Jox and Red-Boar were a fine substitute for leadership.

So she sucked it up and went to find Jox.

The *winikin* was in his quarters near the royal suite, and answered the door barefoot, in jeans and a T-shirt, and carrying a book about miniature roses. His expression went cool when he saw her standing there. "Is there something I can help you with, Detective?"

You can get your thumb out of your ass and take a good look around, she thought, but didn't figure that would get her very far. So instead she said, "Yeah. I need you to help me arrange a party."

Strike's eyes were nearly crossed, and he was pretty sure he'd put a permanent kink in his neck from sitting at the long archive tables in front of a messy stack of books. Unfortunately, the Mac Pluses that'd held the computerized files had shit the bed long ago, leaving him working with some sort of perverse index-card system.

He'd been going through the cards for weeks now, one by one, searching the short annotations and pulling likely-sounding journals, translations, whatever, hoping for a clue, any clue that would help them understand why Leah had shown powers at the solstice and again at the aphelion, but had lost every hint of magic since. He'd also take something about how to track a *makol* when there wasn't an *itza'at* seer handy.

There hadn't been a Zipacna sighting in nearly three weeks. Strike was guessing he'd gone to ground someplace with some serious power lines—one of the old ruins down south, maybe—and used them to construct a ward barrier. Which meant the bastard was functionally untouchable and free to work whatever magic he had at hand until the equinox, when it was a sure bet he'd be at the intersection, looking to bring a dark lord through.

Time was running out too fast. They had three weeks until the equinox, and it seemed highly doubtful the trainees would be ready. According to Jox and Red-Boar, most of the newbies—with the notable exception of Jade—had mastered the basic pretalent spells of jacking in and manipulating the barrier's energy, but only Patience had shown any spark of breakthrough talent. And Rabbit, of course, but that was a whole 'nother can of worms. Which left them exactly where they'd been six weeks ago—with a group of untrained magi and no idea what they'd be able to do.

At least they had some weapons training now, he supposed. Jox had brought the newbies to the range every day and gotten them up to speed on the MACs, along with a few different types of handguns and a sniper rifle or two. Jade-tips wouldn't substitute for hard-core magic, but given that magic was in short supply at the moment, he'd take what he could get.

Which brought him circling back to Leah. Granted, just about every thought train he possessed eventually came back around to her these days. She was under his skin, in his blood. He knew where she was every minute of every day, both from gut-check awareness and from daily reports. Which was how he knew she'd practically been living on the gun range, and had gotten the *makol*-banishment spell from Jox.

It didn't take much of a leap to figure out that she intended to be part of things when he teleported the Nightkeepers—all whopping ten of them—to the sacred chamber to meet the *makol* on the night of the autumnal equinox. What she didn't know was that he had no intention of letting that happen. Unless there was a very good reason to include her in the attack—like she suddenly developed more power than the rest of them put together—she was going to become very good friends with a basement storage locker that night. He couldn't afford the distraction of protecting her while trying to keep the others under control, finding the *makol*, blocking the intersection to keep the *Banol Kax* where they belonged . . .

Gods. It was too much even to think about.

And he'd just read the same page three times and didn't have a frigging clue what it said.

"Shit." He slapped shut a binder-bound translation of a 1550s journal written by a missionary with a seriously antinative streak and shoved it aside. The binder slid into a teetering stack of accordion-folded charcoal rubbings, and before he could react, the whole mess went over the side of the table and hit the floor with a papery crash.

Knowing Jox would kick his ass if he'd buffed details off the rubbings, Strike cursed. Then, also knowing his increasingly unstable temper wouldn't do a damn thing to speed things up or make them better, he leaned back in his chair, closed his eyes, and let out a long sigh. "This sucks."

"So take a break," Leah said from the doorway.

Going very still, Strike opened his eyes and looked over at her. She'd had a bunch of her clothes and stuff shipped from Miami and was wearing hip-hanging cutoffs and a belly-baring tank, and he wanted nothing more than to rub his cheek across the strip of taut, creamy flesh exposed between them.

Horns locked within him, tightening his muscles and sending his pulse up a notch. "You shouldn't be here."

"Don't worry; I'm leaving. But I'm taking you with me." She crossed the distance separating them, skirting the piles of books and notes as she came, and grabbed his hand. Gave it a tug. "Come on. And don't stress; we won't be alone."

He resisted for about a nanosecond, then let her pull him up out of the chair and away from the archives. Once they were in the hallway, he tugged his hand from hers. It was hard enough being near her, feeling her body heat and letting the light, fresh scent of her seep into him—soap and woman, with an undertone of something sharper, gun oil, maybe, or determination.

They walked through the mansion side by side, a little awkward with each other. Trying to ignore the sexual tension that snapped in the air and dug deep within his gut, Strike said, "You've got something on Zipacna?" But he didn't think that was it; her energy was different than that, more relaxed, though maybe a shade wary.

She shook her head. "I'm declaring a moratorium on that stuff for the next few hours, at least until the party is over."

"Party?" he asked, but the moment she got him through the sliders near the pool, his senses perked up at the smell of smoke and sauce. *Hel-lo, barbecue.*

He heard shouts and good-natured catcalls coming from the direction of the big steel building that had replaced the Great Hall.

Leah said, "Your gods—*the* gods, whatever—can't expect us to keep going forever without cutting loose a little, right? Well, consider yourself cut loose for the rest of today. You need a break. We all do. And I think you need to do some reconnecting."

He barely heard her as he pushed ahead, drawn by the sounds and smells.

When they rounded the corner of the mansion, he saw the Nightkeepers and *winikin* all gathered beneath the ceiba tree in front of the big steel building. They'd dragged out folding tables and chairs and fired up a pair of big gas grills Strike didn't recognize. Jox was manning one of the grills, Woody the other, while Hannah and Izzy chopped veggies and readied burgers, wings, and dogs. Red-Boar and the remaining *winikin* sat nearby at one of the picnic tables. Most of the trainees were in the middle of a touch-football game, while off to the side Jade sat apart, watching the twins sneak up on a lizard that was sunning itself on a flat rock.

They were all contained within the ash shadow of where the old Great Hall had been.

Before, when the Nightkeepers and their *winikin* had gathered in the compound for the four cardinal days, the Great Hall had been jammed with tables. Friends and families—and occasionally rivals and enemies—had packed in elbow-to-elbow for the rituals, and the hard partying that followed.

Now the tables formed a tiny cluster at one end of the ash shadow, and the football game ranged the length of the empty space.

"There are so damn few of us," Strike rasped, stopping to stare at the pitiful handful of magi. "We've lost before we even get started."

"That's probably true," Leah said conversationally. "Unless you get your flipping head out of your ass."

It took a second for that to sink in. Another for him to believe she'd said it. His too-ready temper flared, fueled by his frustration with the situation, with her. He raised an eyebrow in warning. "Excuse me?"

They had stopped at the edge of the ash-grayed footprint of the Great Hall, out of earshot of the football game and picnic tables. The others glanced over, then away. All but Jox, who stared down at the grill.

Which meant the *winikin* had been in on whatever was going on, Strike realized. He'd been ambushed. The knowledge didn't do a damn thing to sweeten his mood.

Either unaware of his temper or figuring it was his to deal with—probably the latter—Leah said, "Look, I know I'm not a Nightkeeper—trust me, that's been made crystal clear. But the thing is, I didn't ask to come here; you brought me. Your gods brought me. Whatever. So I'm going to tell it how I see it." She paused, her voice softening a notch. "You and Jox and Red-Boar got tossed headfirst into a hell of a situation; I get that. But I think they're dealing with it by leaning way too hard on traditions that just aren't relevant anymore . . . and you're dealing with it by not dealing."

"I don't think you're in a position to lecture," Strike said through gritted teeth. "As you've pointed out, you're not one of us." Which was mean, but she had him feeling mean. Did she think he liked spending fourteen hours a day locked in the archive? He was doing it for her, damn it. For all of them.

Something flickered in her eyes—hurt, maybe, or an anger that echoed his own—but she kept her tone reasonable when she said, "All the others were raised, to some degree or another, within the Nightkeeper culture. I'm an outsider. I can see stuff you can't. Besides, in case you hadn't noticed, things aren't happening exactly the way the stories say they should. You've got a human who seems to have a god's powers, but only when the barrier is at its thinnest, a half-blood with wild talent but no mark, and a full-blood with a mark but no apparent talent. Not to mention that you're dealing with a bunch of trainees who grew up in the modern world and have opinions of their own." She paused. "Seems to me that it's time to make some changes."

He hated being ambushed, but had to admit she might have a point. Temper leveling slightly, he said, "Like what?"

She waved to the barbecuers. "Did it occur to you to ask why the *winikin* are cooking while the Nightkeepers screw around?"

"Because—" He stopped himself.

"Right. Because they're *winikin*. Am I the only one here who has a problem with that?"

He cut her a frustrated look. "This is a monarchy, not a commune, and the hierarchy exists for a reason. The Nightkeepers need to conserve their energy for the magic. For fighting."

"But there's not much magic going on at the moment, and even less fighting."

"Don't start," he warned. He gestured to the field, where the football game was more a mess of arms and legs than a coordinated strategy. "Do they look like they're ready to fight?"

"And whose fault is that?" she demanded. "If this is a monarchy, then the king's son needs to give some serious thought to stepping up and taking over rather than hiding in the library."

"I—" He broke off, practically choking on a quick flash of rage. He wanted to grab her, shake her, shout at her. Who did she think she was, talking to him like that, making it sound like he was shirking his duty, when all he'd ever *been* was duty? Every decision he'd made since the summer solstice had been for the Nightkeepers, for mankind, though he'd get no thanks from that corner. Humans were—and had always been—narrow and self-absorbed, too caught up in their small little lives to see—

Whoa. Strike reined himself in, fighting back the anger as best he could. His body hummed with rage, with bloodlust and deep disillusionment. He wanted to run and howl, wanted to fly, though that wasn't one of his talents. He wanted to take Leah, to possess her, absorb her very being into himself until he was complete.

And none of those were his emotions, he realized with a start. They were coming from a hard, hot place at the back of his skull, along with a pounding pressure that felt like hate. Like darkness.

Holy shit, what was going on with him?

"In order to fight," Leah continued, unaware of his inner turmoil, "they're going to need to feel like a unified force. And every team needs a leader. Trust me, cops are about as independent a bunch as you'll find, but we need to know there's someone calling the shots. The trainees need that from you. The *winikin* keep telling them that you're in charge, that the king has the final say, but they barely know you. You've left the training to Jox and Red-Boar, and you spend practically all your time in the archive. How can you possibly run this show if you don't know the strengths and weaknesses of your people?"

They were standing outside, yet he felt as though walls were closing in around him, suffocating him until he could barely breathe. The darkness rose up, threatening to swamp him, to take him over and leave nothing but rage and frustration.

Part of him feared it was *makol* magic that had somehow slipped through the wards surrounding the compound. But it didn't feel like evil; it felt like anger, like the need for freedom.

And it was that last piece of the emotions, that need to escape, that made him think it wasn't coming from an outside source at all. It was inside him—his anger, his frustration . . . and his desire to run away.

The question had dogged him for weeks now. What sort of a king could he possibly make when he didn't really want to be king at all?

"Grub's on!" Jox called, his voice tinny with distance, providing a much-needed distraction.

The football game broke up and the trainees headed for the tables, pushing and shoving one another, and cursing good-naturedly about the game as they loaded their plates and grabbed drinks from a couple of coolers nearby. Strike saw a few curious glances shot his way, but nobody shouted for him to hurry his ass up so they could eat.

Instead, they started without him, which proved Leah's point. While he'd been wrestling with his own demons, he'd lost track of what the others needed. Not only was he not their leader, he wasn't even part of their gang.

"Damn," he said, which seemed to sum things up.

She took his hand and tugged him toward the barbecue. "It's fixable."

Is it? he thought, but didn't say. Instead, he allowed himself to be led to the small barbecue, where he made a concerted effort to engage with the other magi, putting faces and impressions to Jox's and Red-Boar's reports, and trying to channel what he remembered of his father's public persona, which was all he knew of how a king should act.

But as the night wore on and beer and wine flowed, and Jox even broke out the potent ceremonial *pulque*—one shot each, no more—and everyone else relaxed, Strike grew increasingly tense while he fought the red haze that threatened to coat his mind with anger, hatred, and vicious sexual frustration. A single thought kept pounding through his skull, chasing itself around in end-less circles.

How in the hell was he supposed to lead the Night-keepers when he couldn't even manage what was inside his own head?

As dinner and dessert wound down, Leah got more and more keyed up.

She'd gone into alligator-infested waters after bodies the gators considered theirs. She'd faced down gang-bangers. She'd been shot in the leg and kept up the foot chase. Hell, she'd escaped being a human sacrifice in an ancient Mayan temple. There was no reason for her to be nervous about what she had planned next.

Or so she kept telling herself. But she was getting a seriously weird vibe off Strike, one that had her thinking she should've waited on the second part of her scheme, the one Jox didn't even know about. Problem was, they didn't have the time to wait. A barbecue would get them only so far. They needed an identity, something to rally behind. Something that was theirs alone to protect.

So she stood up and cleared her throat, and waited until she had everyone's attention. Feeling like a total freak-show fraud to be telling a bunch of magicians how they should run their own universe, she said only, "I'd appreciate it if you'd all come out to the front of the house. I have something for you."

For a few seconds nobody moved. Then Strike nodded and rose. "Lead on."

His words were neutral, even encouraging, but his ex-pression was closed and cool, like he thought she'd al-ready done enough damage for one night. And maybe she had . . . but she'd never known how to quit while she was ahead. Why start now?

So she led the way around the side of the mansion, conscious of Strike's lethal warrior's grace right behind her, the others following behind him, including the *wini-kin*, and even the sleepy-eyed twins, who tagged on either side of Rabbit, babbling in incomprehensible twinspeak.

She stopped by the front door of the mansion, where

she'd hung the polished brass plaque earlier in the day, still covered in brown paper wrapping.

Sucking in a deep breath to settle her nerves—like that was going to happen—Leah said, "Some of you don't think I belong here, that having me here breaks tradition." She looked at Jox and Red-Boar, standing off to one side of the main crowd, and could all but hear them thinking, *Yeah, so?* "And maybe you're right. I don't have the same magic that you do, I wasn't raised in your culture, and I'm not related by blood. But I am a trained cop, and a good one. I can shoot. I can fight. And I know, for better or worse, how to manipulate people." That got her a few shuffles, and even some frowns. She held up a hand. "I'm giving you honesty here. And honestly, what I see is a bunch of strangers with similar goals. You're not a unit yet. You're not the team you're going to need to be in order to fight whatever's coming through at the equinox."

She deliberately used "you" rather than "us" because she wanted them pulling together, and if uniting against her was what brought them into alignment, then so be it.

"What do you suggest?" Strike asked, but she got the idea he was playing along so the others would think she had his support, not because she actually did.

"Team Building 201," Leah answered. "You need a name. Not you as a people, or your bloodlines," she said quickly when the dirty looks started. "For this place." Her gesture encompassed the mansion, the training compound, and the wide box canyon lost in the darkness. "For your home."

"This isn't—" Jox began, then broke off.

"It wasn't your home before," she agreed. "It was a place where you gathered for feasts and training." Personally, she thought it should've had a name back then, regardless. "But wake up. It's a new day, and things are going to need to change. Starting now. So I'm giving this place a name."

Without further ceremony, she ripped the paper free, baring the intricately engraved plaque.

There was a collective indrawn breath, and in the moment of silence that followed, one of the twins laughed, the sound rising into the night high and sweet and pure.

Finally, unable to stand it one second longer, Leah turned to Strike, who'd frozen and gone pale. "What do you think?"

I think you humble me, Strike thought, but he couldn't get the words out. So he took her hand and held it while he stood and stared at the name she'd given the Nightkeepers' home.

SKYWATCH.

It was engraved in big letters above a line drawing of a ceiba tree, with three Mayan words inscribed below, the letters formed from the tree's spreading root system.

Skywatch. It clicked. It was right. The sky was the realm of the gods they served, the gods who'd charged them with watching over the barrier. More, *waatch* was the Mayan word for "soldier," though she might not have known that. Or maybe she did, he thought, looking at the words carved below the tree of life.

She'd not only given them a name; she'd given them a motto. A coat of arms. A battle cry in modern Quiche Mayan. *Waquqik*—to fight. *Cajij*—to protect. And—

He frowned. "What's *kuyubal-mak*?"

"It means 'to forgive,'" Jox said, his voice rough. "But there's nothing to forgive."

"I think there is," Leah countered. "If there weren't, you would've pressured him to take charge long before this. You would've dragged him out of the pool house and locked him in the royal suite, and you sure as hell wouldn't have let him hide out in the library for the past two months. You would've forced him to take the crown— or whatever it is that your king wears. But neither you nor Red-Boar did any of those things. Thus, I have to assume there's a reason." Taking a deep breath, she said, "I'm thinking it's because, deep down inside, you're not sure you want him to be king."

Strike didn't know which was worse—that she'd said it, or that there was dead silence in the aftermath.

Finally, Jox said, "You presume too much, Detective.

You don't know us, and you sure as hell don't know Strike."

"I think I do." Her eyes met Strike's. "And I don't think he wants to be king. If he did, he'd be arguing with me right now." She closed the distance between them, said softly. "I think you're afraid you'll make the same mistakes your father did. And I think you're figuring that if you don't become king you'll nullify the thirteenth prophecy. No king, no greatest sacrifice."

Strike told himself the rage wasn't him, the hatred wasn't him. But that was all he could see or feel, all he could be just then. A scream built in his soul, and he felt the darkness closing in on him. Suffocating him. He tried to find words to tell her—to tell any of them—what was going on, but he was afraid that if he opened his mouth something terrible would come out, something vicious and violent.

So he didn't say anything. He just closed his eyes and imagined being someplace else, someplace alone. He was so revved on anger, on power, that he zapped blind before he'd intended to, the world dissolving around him before he'd envisioned the travel thread or picked a destination.

Then the universe jolted sideways, the floor fell out from beneath him, and he dropped with a yell.

He fell too long, and hit bottom too hard, but the spongy surface yielded beneath him, cushioning the impact. He felt the feathery touch of mist on his face, and knew where he was even before he opened his eyes and saw a world of gray-green.

He'd zapped himself into the frigging barrier. And the anger—oh, the anger rose up, gripping him, tearing into him. He arched and screamed with the rage, with the bloodlust and mad hatred that came from outside him, from within him, until he wasn't sure where he left off and the craziness began.

Gods. His mouth drew back in a rictus, his eyes rolled wildly, and his heart stuttered in his chest. Darkness blurred the edges of his vision, and he was pretty sure he was dying. Panic closed in.

He was barely conscious of the mist swirling nearby,

thickening and taking on the shape of a stick-thin Nightkeeper with obsidian eyes and a ruby stud in one ear. The *nahwal*.

"Father!" he shouted, though he wasn't sure if he said the word aloud or only thought it in the small corner of his mind that was still his to control.

"It is time," the *nahwal* said in its voice-of-manyvoices. It leaned down and gripped Strike's wrist, and its touch burned like flame and acid, the worst pain he'd ever known.

He threw back his head and screamed.

The gray-green mist disappeared.

And he was home, reappearing exactly where he'd left from, standing in front of the main door, staring at the sign that said, SKYWATCH: TO FIGHT, TO PROTECT, TO FORGIVE.

The others were gone. The anger was gone, too, leaving him hollow and drained. He only had the strength left to whisper, "Forgive me, Father."

Then he collapsed on the welcome mat and passed the hell out.

After Strike pulled his disappearing act, leaving Leah standing there looking like a complete idiot, she held it together until she reached her rooms. His rooms. Whatever.

The moment she was through the carved double doors, though, she let go of the control she'd been holding on to by the last thread. She halfway expected tears, though she'd never been a weeper, halfway expected destructive, lamp-throwing anger, which was more typical for her. But either the two canceled each other out or she'd used up all her emotional space and had nothing left.

She sank to the couch in the sitting area, exhausted. Empty. There were no skitters of warmth or electricity. She doubted she could kill a gnat, never mind a coffeemaker. Her supposed powers were long gone, leaving her as nothing more than what she was—a cop with a big mouth and zero subtlety who didn't really belong in Skywatch.

Skywatch. She hoped the name—and the motto—stuck. Her timing and delivery might've sucked, but she was right, damn it. They needed something to rally around, and Red-Boar and the *winikin* needed to accept that the past was gone and it wasn't going to repeat itself, no matter what their writs said about the cyclical nature of time. The trainees weren't going to fight because their *winikin* told them to. They needed to believe in the cause, in themselves, and in one another. And more important, they needed to believe in their leader. She didn't care if he called himself king or Papa Smurf; he needed to step up.

Instead, he'd brushed her off and then freaking zapped himself straight out of the argument, which was against the rules of fighting. And he'd been really pissed, too, like he hated the fact that she was standing up to him.

"Which is way too bad," she said aloud. "If he doesn't like a woman who gets in his face and tells him where to get off occasionally, then he can—" She broke off, because he didn't have to do a flipping thing. The decision was going to have to be hers.

She could stay—if they'd let her—and add whatever weight she might have to the coming battle. Or she could go home, fast-talk her way back onto the job—which would undoubtedly include some serious shrink action—and keep hammering at Survivor2012.

She didn't want to go back . . . but she wasn't sure she could stay, either. Strike was using her as an excuse to avoid the others—which wasn't fair to any of them—and his disappearing act suggested he wasn't looking to change that strategy. Besides, she knew how to kill Zipacna now; she just had to find him, and she could do that as effectively from the outside as she could in the compound. She could defend herself. She didn't need to stay.

More important, she didn't have any reason to. She wasn't Strike's Godkeeper, and she wasn't his mate. Hell, after tonight, she probably didn't even rank as a friend.

"Shit," she said, hearing the single word echo in the too-big suite. Then she started packing.

Twenty minutes later, figuring she'd "borrow" a car and call Jox later to let him know where to pick it up, she slung her duffel over her shoulder and headed out without saying good-bye to anyone, because she didn't particularly want to see the looks of relief when she said she was leaving. Telling herself she wasn't going to cry, she swung open the front door, slamming it into something lying on the welcome mat outside.

It took her a second. Then her heart stopped in her chest. "Strike!"

She dropped down beside him, scrambling for a pulse. She found it—sort of—but it wasn't the thready beat that held her attention as she raised her voice and shouted, "Jox! Need some help here!"

No, what drew her attention was the new mark on his forearm, one that hadn't been there an hour earlier . . . and which looked a hell of a lot like a flying snake.

CHAPTER SIXTEEN

Strike awoke profoundly pissed off, which was unusual for him. Even more unusual was the fact that he was holding a woman's hand.

He cracked an eye and took stock. He was in his bed in the pool house, and it was well past dawn. He was naked save for a pair of cutoff shorts—Jox's idea of sleepwear?—and Leah was sitting in a chair beside his bed, her head pillowed at the edge of his mattress on one folded arm. Her other hand was holding his. The sight of her face smoothed out in repose and their fingers intertwined atop the covers softened the edge of anger that rode him for no good reason.

"Hey," he said quietly, wincing at the crack in his voice, and again he remembered the events of the night before.

She opened her eyes and stared at him for a moment, unblinking. Then she straightened and slid her hand from his, trying to make it seem like no big deal. But the withdrawal was intentional, he knew. And it stung.

Worse, he deserved it.

"You were right," he said before his mood could take over and make him say something stupid. "About me hiding in the archive, about us needing something to rally behind. You were right about all of it. And the name is perfect. The motto's perfect." He levered himself up and swung his legs over the side so they were sitting facing each other, knees bumping. Leaning in, he caught the hand she'd just reclaimed. He raised it to his lips, then pressed it against his cheek even though he was about a day and a half past needing a shave. "Thank you."

Her eyes filled. "You took off. I felt like an idiot."

More than that, he realized, she'd felt rejected. And why wouldn't she? It wasn't as though he'd bothered explaining what had been going on inside him. What still was going on inside him, he knew, feeling the anger roil within. He glanced at his arm, at the mark of the flying serpent, and wished he knew what the hell it all meant. It was probably a reference to the creator god Kulkulkan, but beyond that he was clueless. Worse, he couldn't settle his brain enough to think it through.

How was he supposed to lead the others when he could barely control himself?

"I'm sorry." When she tried to pull away, he pressed his hand over hers on his cheek, which was as much of a hug as he dared give her until he got said what needed to be said. "Over the last few days I've been having . . . moods, I guess you could call them. Anger attacks. Only it's not my anger, not really me, like it's coming from outside me."

Her eyes sharpened. "From the barrier?"

"Or something." He wasn't yet ready to verbalize his deepest fear: that somehow the *Banol Kax* had gotten a foothold inside his head. Looking at his forearm, he said, "And then there's this. The flying serpent."

"Jade couldn't find that specific mark in the archive, and none of the *winikin* remember having seen anything like it before," Leah said before he could ask. "Red-Boar thinks it probably means you're bound to the creator god Kulkulkan through your Godkeeper mate." She paused. Grimaced. "You know, the Godkeeper mate you don't have because one, the god didn't come through the barrier during the solstice because I'm 'only human' "—she emphasized the phrase with finger quotes—"and two, because neither of us is sold on the predestined-mates thing." Her grin went a little crooked and she didn't meet his eyes. "I'm not looking for long-term, and we both know that a couple of dreams and some hot sex does not necessarily a lasting relationship make. And besides—"

He touched a finger to her lips, cutting her off. "Don't," he said, as a whole bunch of messy emotions crowded around inside him. "Don't talk yourself out of believing in what's happened between us."

To his surprise, her eyes filled. "Why not? What good does it do me to keep thinking about something that's going nowhere? You're afraid that if we're lovers then the gods—the prophecies, whatever—are going to demand me as a sacrifice. I get that. I even appreciate it, because I'm nobody's sacrifice. But if that's the case and we can't even talk to each other, never mind sleeping together, what's the point of me being here at all?" Her voice went thin. "It sucks going to bed alone every night, knowing you're right across the pool deck, and knowing that you'll buck tradition by having me here, but you don't want me enough to take it all the way."

"That," he said through gritted teeth, "is bullshit." The anger fought to come, and he fought equally hard to hold it back, though he wasn't sure anymore how much of it was him and how much wasn't.

"Is it?" Color rode high in her cheeks. "Then why—"

He cut her off again, this time with his lips, shifting his grip from her hands to her hips, and bracketing her knees with his, blocking her escape.

There was no finesse to the kiss, no soft question or coaxing. It was all about the anger that had ridden him for days now, and the raw need he'd been holding in check for far longer than that. *Don't tell me I don't want you enough,* the kiss said. *Don't even think it.* It was because he wanted her so much, needed her so much, that he'd stayed away from her for so long. Only now she was right there in front of him, in the place where he slept, and he was near the breaking point.

But when he broke, she was right there with him.

She didn't resist the kiss, didn't shove him off and ask what the hell he thought he was doing, didn't blast him for the mixed messages. No, she met him head-on, leaning in and grabbing on, one hand in his hair at the nape of his neck, the other wrapped around his upper bicep, fingers digging in. She opened her mouth beneath his, a demand rather than an invitation.

Their tongues touched and slid, and the taste of her raced in his veins. He crowded closer, or maybe she did—he wasn't sure who moved first—but they twined together, her hands streaking across his bare shoulders and back, her T-shirt-covered breasts brushing against his naked chest.

He went hard against the fabric of his cutoffs, the material a rough contrast to the silk of her skin when he slid his hands beneath her T-shirt. She made a soft, urgent sound at the back of her throat, one that called to everything primitive and male within him. He wanted to drag her across his body and press her down on the bed, wanted to take her, to possess her, to brand himself across her skin so there would be no question that she belonged to him and he to her, and nothing else in the world mattered.

Which was the problem.

Shuddering with the rampant need that rode him, locking horns with the logic that told him he had to stop now, he forced himself to end the kiss. He couldn't make himself pull away, though. Instead, he pressed his forehead to hers so they were leaning into each other, holding each other up. "It's not that I don't want you enough to risk the prophecy," he said, his voice rasping. "It's that I want you so much, when I'm with you the other stuff fades. You could become so much more important to me than the others." He paused as a tremor within warned that maybe she already had, that their relationship was already clouding his judgment the way his father's love for his family had altered the decisions he'd made as king. "I can't let that happen," he said. "Not if we're going to win this war."

He expected her to argue, almost hoped she would. Instead, she said softly, "Then let me go. I can protect myself now . . . and you'd be a teleport away if I got in trouble. I think it'd be better, easier for both of us."

She wasn't asking for permission, he knew. She was

asking him to end it, to release her from their nonrelationship, or at least give her the distance to regain her footing in the rational world.

But he couldn't. "Stay," he said, a single word that held both command and longing, even to his own ears.

She drew away so they were no longer supporting each other. "You don't need me here, and the others don't want me here. Why should I stay?"

Because you're safer here than on the outside, he wanted to say. *Because my gut tells me the gods aren't finished with you and me, despite what Red-Boar says; and because you were right last night when you said we need an outside perspective, and that I need the occasional kick in the ass.* But while all of that was true, he knew it wasn't what she was asking. So he said, "Because I want you to. Please stay, at least through the conjunction."

Her eyes went dark. "And then?"

"And then we'll see."

He expected her to press. Instead she nodded. "Until the conjunction, then." She touched his arm, tracing each of his marks with a fingertip in a light caress that let him think about nothing but the softness of her skin and the taste of her breath on his lips. "Where did you go?" she asked, tapping the last mark, the one he'd gotten the night before.

It took him a second to refocus, another to answer. "I zapped myself into the barrier." He didn't mention that he'd jumped blind, and that he might've ended up totally in limbo if the *nahwal* hadn't reached through and given his subconscious mind a destination, as Leah herself had done the very first time he'd teleported. "When I got there I saw my father, or the *nahwal* I believe is my father and Red-Boar believes is a figment of my imagination." He paused. "The *nahwal* told me that it's time, but I think he's wrong." He paused, exhaling heavily with a look toward the mansion. "They're not ready for a king."

"Are you ready to be king?" she asked, still touching his arm, her fingers resting above the serpent's wings.

"No," he said, shaking his head. Not with what felt

an awful lot like a demon rocketing around in his skull. Not until he figured out how she fit into everything that was going on around him, inside him, and whether the thirteenth prophecy would require her death if he took up the Manikin scepter, which was the symbol of the Nightkeepers' king. "But I'm ready to be their leader. I'm ready to find out what the flying serpent mark means, and I'm ready for the others to get their talents so we can start functioning as a team. In fact . . ." He glanced at the bedside clock radio and winced when he saw it was past ten a.m. already. "Can you ask Jox to get everyone together for a meeting? You were right last night. It's time for me to get off my ass and do my damn job."

"Not exactly what I said, but close enough for government work." She rose, her expression guarded, as though she'd taken everything that'd just happened, everything they'd just said to each other, and shoved it deep down inside for later consideration. "I'll tell them to meet you in the main room for an organizational sit-down, so you can come up with a plan for the days we've got left before the conjunction. I'll give you fifteen minutes to grab a shower and mainline some coffee."

"Thanks. And, Leah?"

She turned back near the door. "Yeah?"

"I'm glad you're staying. And I'm sorry. For all of it." He was sorry for disappearing on her the night before and leaving her to look foolish in front of the others. More, he was sorry for not being the man who could give her the stars and the moon, and all the love she deserved. And he was sorry that, even knowing he wasn't that man, he couldn't let her go.

"Apology accepted," she said, though he wasn't sure which part she'd agreed to. Sending him a small finger wave and a sad smile, she slipped through the door, out into the sun-bright day.

When she was gone he sat there for a moment, staring after her, feeling shaken and stirred up and far more like a man in the grips of obsession than the levelheaded leader he was supposed to become, or the king his people needed him to be. He wished he knew how to balance the two, how to be a better man. But at the same time, he was realizing that something had changed. He didn't know whether it was because of Leah's lecture the night before, the motto she'd given to Skywatch, or his trip into the barrier, but for the first time he wasn't wishing for an escape or an out.

He was trying to figure out how the hell to get it all done without losing himself in the process.

Leah was feeling shaky and achy as she crossed the pool deck to the mansion, squinting in the too-bright sun.

A few of the twinges were from doing the sleeping-sitting-up thing while waiting for Strike to come around, but the vast majority were from that hell-and-gone kiss he'd laid on her, the one that proved she'd been lying to herself when she'd tried to say that being with him hadn't been as good as she remembered, that she'd fantasized it into something it wasn't.

Nope. It was all that, and then some.

Which was a problem, not only because he was determined not to let it happen again, but also because she couldn't be sure how much of the connection was real and how much was a product of the circumstances.

It was a given that what'd happened in the sacred chamber during the solstice had been courtesy of a god, probably Kulkulkan, trying to gain a foothold on earth by going co-op with her gray matter. And perhaps the sizzle the day after the aphelion had been part magic, too. But since then she hadn't shown a lick of magical talent, and the sizzle was still alive and kicking harder by the day.

Okay, so she was hot for the guy, magic or no magic. But what about him? There was no way she could separate the man from the sorcery or his upbringing, and if he believed the dreams meant the gods intended them to be together, that was the direction his brain was going to go, whether or not they were compatible. And aside from the whole save-the-world thing, she was enough of a girl to want him to want *her*, not just the woman the gods had shoved at him.

Though she'd ended her share of relationships, she'd

heard enough of the old, "it's not you, it's me," to know that it really *was* her most of the time. She was too much work for not enough payoff, too judgmental, too driven by the job and her own concepts of right and wrong.

Was it so much to ask for a guy who wanted those parts of her, too? One who was willing to fight for her, not just against their common enemy, but against the tenets that said they couldn't be together?

And that brought her right back to the thirteenth prophecy and the whole, "I'd love you but then I'd have to kill you" thing, which just sucked beyond sucking.

Trying to banish the faint suspicion that his interpretation of the thirteenth prophecy was a cosmic version of, "it's not you, it's me," Leah pushed through the doors leading from the pool deck to the mansion's great room, intending to hunt up Jox and pass along Strike's message.

The *winikin* was waiting for her just inside the door, wearing jeans, a light-colored long-sleeved shirt, a pair of rope sandals, and an expression that said he wished she'd just go away. Permanently.

"Oh." Leah stopped in her tracks, feeling off balance. "You're here."

"I was headed out to check on Strike." The *winikin* moved to push through the door.

Leah blocked him. "He's fine. Told me to tell you to assemble the trainees for a meeting." Jox just stood and glared and she did the same, and though she hadn't intended the standoff, she figured they'd been headed there all along. "Go around me or go through me," she said evenly. "But I'm not moving."

The *winikin*'s mouth went tight. "The barbecue was a good idea, as was the name." It took her a moment to realize he'd actually said something nice to her, but he blunted the shock by saying, "That doesn't mean I think you're good for him."

That stung—especially given her and Strike's recent conversation—but she didn't let Jox see that he'd scored. Instead, she said, "The trainees, Jox. Now."

He held his glare for a five-count before he said, "They're in the training hall. I'll go tell Strike to meet you there."

Then he brushed past her, and even though he'd been the one to leave, Leah felt thoroughly dismissed.

Tears prickled at the backs of her eyes, but she refused to give him the satisfaction, keeping her head high as she marched through the mansion and out the other side, muttering imprecations under her breath.

Once she was outside and the double doors were shut at her back so he couldn't see, she leaned against them and took a moment. "Damn it."

She'd tried to make friends with the *winikin*, knowing how important he was to Strike and the others. Failing that, she'd tried to negotiate a workable peace, and thought they'd made some progress in that department.

Apparently not, though she wasn't sure what she'd done wrong. Probably something to do with Strike's flying-serpent mark and her being human. And there wasn't much she could do about that, was there?

Shoving away from the doors with a muttered curse, she strode to the steel-span building on the far side of the ceiba tree. Before she'd even entered the training hall, she could hear shouts coming from inside, and as she swung through the door she was figuring on a pickup basketball game. But the trainees weren't playing, she saw the moment she was inside.

They were working.

Rabbit sat off in a corner, frowning as he kindled a red-orange fireball the size of his head and held it suspended between his hands. Brandt stood nearby, holding his palms up and out, as though he'd been frozen midmugging. Then Patience blinked back in, becoming visible standing opposite him with her palms pressed to his. Sven, Alexis, and Nate were war-gaming it in the middle of the football field–size room, spinning and feinting with blunted stone knives, three against one as Michael blocked the attacks with shield magic. The only one missing was Jade.

Holy crap, Leah thought, freezing in place. She'd seen bits and pieces of the magic before. Hell, she'd made a kitchen knife fly. But she'd never seen it all at once like this, couldn't even begin to imagine what it would be when they reached their full powers and learned to link up, never mind what it must've been like before, when there had been hundreds of magi fighting as a unit.

For the first time she thought she really understood what the massacre had meant, not just to the Nightkeepers but to the future of the world. And in understanding it, she thought she understood Jox a little bit better, too.

It wasn't personal for him. It was all about the balance of power, and Strike would be far stronger paired with a true Godkeeper than with her.

"Hey!" Alexis called, catching sight of her. "Leah's here."

Where before her entrance would've earned her a perfunctory wave or two and some sidelong looks, now the others stopped what they were doing and headed in her direction.

Forcing herself not to back away, Leah said, "You're all here. You're practicing." Which was obvious, but this normally would've been their break time, when they would've scattered to do their own things.

"Strike wasn't the only one who got a kick in the ass last night," Nate said. "Jox got the other *winikin* in on it, too, and they let us have it."

"Really?" Leah wouldn't have guessed he'd been that far on board with the idea of rallying the troops. Then again, agreeing with her openly would've meant admitting he'd fallen down on the job.

"They were right," Patience said, her soft voice preceding her appearance as she shimmered back to visibility beside her husband. "Most of us were coming around to the realization that we're running out of time and there's way too much left to learn . . . but we needed the push."

Alexis nodded. "Which means we owe you one."

There was a chorus of agreement and even Michael, who pretty much defined inscrutable, shot her a grin and dipped his head in acknowledgment.

It was the first time Leah had been the focus of all their attention at once, and to her surprise it was a formidable charisma hit, like she'd been noticed by the gods themselves. She also wasn't prepared for the clutch of nerves, the feeling of, *Oh, shit. What did I get my-self into?*

They weren't just looking at her like she'd helped them out by throwing a barbecue. They were looking at her like they expected her to tell them what was going to happen next.

She'd told Strike they needed a leader, but there was no way in hell she'd intended for it to be her.

Taking a big step back, toward the door, she said, "I'm glad I could help. Strike's on his way for a huddle, and—"

"He's already here," his voice said from behind her.

Leah spun, her heart kicking because she hadn't heard him come in, and jolting again at the sight of him, big and male, wearing a set of older, worn combat clothes, the black gone gray at the seams.

Their eyes locked, and her breath went thin on a surge of lust when she saw herself reflected in him, saw the heat of their kiss and the edge of frustration that rode him as much as it did her. In that instant she would've given anything for things to be simple between them.

Because they weren't, she broke eye contact and took a big step away from him, angling around him toward the door. "Ah. Have a good meeting."

She wanted to sit in on the meeting, to be a part of the strategizing. The Nightkeepers needed to think, not just about the talent ceremony a few days away, but about the equinox on September twenty-first, when they'd teleport en masse to the Yucatán, to defend the intersection their parents had died trying to destroy. But at the same time she selfishly didn't want to be there, didn't want to watch Strike settle into a role that took him that much farther out of her reach.

"Stay," he said quietly, as though he knew exactly where her mind had gone. "Sit with me."

"I can't," she said, taking another step away. "I don't belong here."

"You could."

She snorted. "Right."

"Take this." He dipped into his pocket and came up

with a thin chain threaded through a highly polished black figurine the size of her thumb.

Made of a milky green stone, it was intricately knapped in the shape of a man's profile in the Mayan style, with a long, flattened forehead, a prominent nose, and wide lips. Antlers protruded from the man's temples.

"What is it?" she asked without reaching for it, part of her afraid it meant something in terms of their nonrelationship, part of her afraid that it didn't.

"It's called an eccentric, which basically means it's a small ceremonial item." He crossed to her and draped the chain over her head himself, his fingers brushing lightly against the sides of her neck, bringing shivers of too-ready awareness. "It's the deer god. He represents wisdom."

"And?" she pressed, knowing nothing in Skywatch was ever that simple.

"And it's the symbol of . . . of an important adviser."

He'd almost said, "the king's adviser," she knew. A glance at the trainees showed they knew it, too. And for the first time, she saw consideration rather than outright rejection of the concept. Or maybe those considering looks were strictly for her.

She touched the eccentric, feeling nothing more than warm stone and a prickle of disappointment that she didn't feel more. It should've been a powerful charm, she knew. On her, it was nothing more than a pretty necklace. "I shouldn't," she said.

"You're our outside perspective," Strike said. "Stay." It wasn't quite a request, wasn't quite an order, but she felt the power behind the word, and the need.

She nodded before she was really aware of having made the decision. "Okay. I'm in."

And, boy, was Jox going to be pissed. Then again, she thought as light dawned, maybe he already knew. It was a good bet that his attitude earlier had something to do with the eccentric. He must've known what Strike was planning.

"Good," Strike said, and stepped away from her. Turning to the others, he said, "Thanks for being out here practicing. Obviously, we all figured out a few things last night. I'll start by saying I'm sorry for checking out on you over the past bunch of weeks. I thought I was doing the right thing, but Leah convinced me otherwise."

"You weren't the only one half-assing it," Nate admitted, stepping up and taking the spokesman's role. "We talked about it last night. We're ready to buckle down if you are."

It wasn't exactly a promise of undying fealty, Leah knew, but it was a start.

"Deal." Strike stuck out a hand and Nate stepped up to shake on it, and the others formed a rough line behind him.

To Leah's surprise, Nate moved to her next and held out a hand. "Thanks for the wake-up call."

"You're . . . you're welcome." She shook his hand, and he moved off so she could press palms with Alexis next, followed by each of the others in turn. As Leah shook each of their hands, the sense of unreality grew, not because of their acceptance but because the setup was suddenly seeming far too much like a receiving line.

She started edging away from Strike. "I should—"

He caught her arm. "Stay." He looked at the group and frowned. "Where's Jade?"

"I'm here," she called from the open doorway. "Sorry I'm late."

Quiet and studious, with brilliant green eyes and long, dark hair caught up in a messy bun atop her head, carrying an armload of books and wearing jeans and a T-shirt rather than combat clothes, she looked far more like a harried librarian than a mage as she hurried across the cavernous space toward the others.

She stopped in front of Strike, seeming oblivious to having just interrupted a moment. "I think I've got something useful."

Leah tensed on a jolt of hope. Had she found a way to track the *ajaw-makol*?

"Go ahead," Strike said, his voice inflectionless, as if he were afraid to hope.

Jade started to open the top book on her stack, but then the others slid. "Hold these." She shoved the books unceremoniously into Strike's arms and took back the volume she wanted, cracking it to a marked page so she could show him what looked like a woodcutting of a male figure with Nightkeepers' marks on his arm, facing off opposite a naked, human-shaped figure with no nipples or genitalia, and eyes that held no whites or irises, just flat blackness.

"It's a *nahwal*," Strike said as the others clustered around to get a look. "The in-barrier embodiment of each bloodline's accumulated knowledge, without any of the individual personalities of the dead."

"Not exactly," Jade corrected. "It's a special kind of *nahwal*, one that doesn't connect to any specific bloodline, and isn't fixed with past and present knowledge."

Strike fixed her with a look. "It's a precog?"

She lifted a shoulder. "I'm not totally clear on that. But there's a spell called the three-question spell. Once per lifetime, a Nightkeeper can summon this *nahwal* and ask it three questions that it's bound to answer truthfully." She glanced at Leah. "I don't know if it'd work for a human, but it might be worth a try, given that you've shown Nightkeeper-level magic during prior cardinal days."

Leah's breath backed up in her lungs at the thought, at the spear of hope it brought. If they could get some answers about what'd happened to her, and what was supposed to happen next, they'd be able to make a better plan. Hell, they might even be able to lock her into whatever powers she'd somehow acquired during the aphelion.

She wouldn't be a Nightkeeper, but she wouldn't be powerless either. She'd have something to use when she went up against Zipacna, something to bring to war with the others.

Almost afraid to ask for anything more, she glanced over at Strike. Their eyes locked and she felt the punch of heat, of connection. And though she was no mind reader, she sensed the same wish in him, the same seemingly impossible hope.

Maybe, just maybe, they could use the spell to figure out how to circumvent the thirteenth prophecy . . . or use it to their advantage.

CHAPTER SEVENTEEN

Lucius didn't mean to eavesdrop on Anna's conversation . . . it just sort of happened.

The astrology babe on the campus talk-radio station was babbling something about Venus coming into conjunction that night, and he'd just finished up with his office hours for the week. He was packing up to hit the library and pick up an obscure translation of the *Popol Vuh* he'd requested through interlibrary loan, when he heard the raised voices coming from his boss's office two doors down.

"Jesus, Anna! I don't know where you're coming from sometimes. You've been nagging me to set aside time for you, and now that I have, you're too busy to grab a bite? For Christ's sake, I can't seem to win for trying these days." The Dick's voice carried a harsh, dismissive impatience that set Lucius's teeth on edge.

"Based on what? One night out of the past four months? That's fair." Anna was trying to keep her tone reasonable, but he knew her well enough to hear the hurt.

"This isn't about what's fair or not. I'm trying to—" The Dick broke off. "You know what? Forget about it. I'll just eat at the club."

A door slammed and footsteps rang in the hall. Once they'd passed, Lucius stuck his head out his office door and flipped the retreating form of Anna's husband a double-barreled bird.

"God, what a jerk."

For a second, he thought he'd said that, because he was sure as hell thinking it. Then he turned to find the sentiment shared by Neenie Fisher, a second-year grad student who'd only recently joined Anna's team full-time.

She was petite and borderline mousy, with pale eyes and thin lips that didn't exactly command attention. Rumor had it she was dating some sort of local grunge rock star, which suggested she could catch attention when she wanted it.

Not so much in the glyph lab, though.

"Hey, Neenie." Lucius glanced back to the empty hallway where Anna's husband had been moments ago. He wanted to agree with the jerk comment and add a few of his own, but he usually tried not to bad-mouth Dick Catori out loud.

Neenie, however, had no such compunction. "I don't get it. Anna is frickin' gorgeous—why does she put up with that guy? Did you hear him? It's like he doesn't give a crap that she's putting in overtime trying to translate a codex fragment that is, as far as I can tell, completely new to the literature. Doesn't he get how huge that is? I mean, honestly. I'll bet if he had some sort of economics emergency—is there even such a thing?—she'd let him bail on dinner. Heck, she probably has more than once, and I bet I can tell you the name of the emergency. My friend Heather's in his Intro to Econ class, and she said that Desiree—"

"Stop." Lucius capped a hand across Neenie's mouth, having learned that there wasn't much else he could do to shut her up when she got on a roll. "Back up." He took his hand away. "What codex fragment?"

The fact that she didn't immediately launch into an explanation spoke volumes. Instead, her eyes went wide and she slapped her own hand across her mouth. "Oh!"

Aware that they were out in the hallway, two doors down from Anna's office, and she was likely to be in a pretty prickly mood after the spat with her husband, Lucius dragged Neenie into his office and shut the door. "You weren't supposed to mention it to me, were you?"

Eyes still wide, she shook her head, keeping her hand firmly over her mouth. "I promised," she said, words muffled behind her hand.

"So unpromise," he said, as if it were no big deal, which it probably wasn't to someone like her, a conduit through whom gossip flowed at approximately the speed of sound. "Come on . . . you know you want to tell me."

Looking undecided—which as far as he was concerned was a big step up from "Oh, shit, I'm gonna get canned if I tell"—she dropped her hand from her mouth and looked around his office. "Well . . ."

He followed her gaze, saw it lock onto a small, graceful figurine of a jaguar, and winced. "That's real jade. And it's hand-carved."

He'd gotten the effigy at a small open market at the foot of the Guatemalan highlands during one of his early trips out into the field with Anna. The statuette wasn't old, but it hadn't been cheap either.

She looked back at him and raised an eyebrow. "Then I guess a promise is a promise."

He scowled, grabbed the effigy, and held it out to her. "You suck."

"I had brothers. Deal with it." She accepted the jaguar and tucked it into her pocket, then gestured for him to lean closer so she could whisper her secret.

"The door's closed, for chrissakes. Just say it."

"Fine. Go ahead, ruin my dramatic intro." She straightened and made a face at him, but now that she'd given herself permission to give with the goods, she couldn't hold it in a second longer. "The fragment is gorgeous, absolutely gorgeous. Some of the glyphs are degraded, but you can still see an incredible level of detail, and the colors . . ." Her eyes practically glazed over at the memory. "God, the colors are so awesome now, it's hard to imagine what it must've looked like when it was new."

"Hello, Neenie?" Lucius waved a hand in front of her face. "Someone else in the room here, remember? Let's focus. Okay, so Anna showed you a piece of a codex. What did she say, 'Hey, Neenie, come in here and see what I got my hands on'?"

"No." She shook her head. "It was more like, 'Come in and close the door. Now, promise me this is just between us. Okay . . . what does this look like to you?' "

And all of a sudden, he got it. Anna had called Neenie in because she didn't know how to translate the glyphs yet, but she'd shown an almost uncanny knack for being able to identify the pictures themselves.

The writing system of the ancient Maya was seriously complex, the symbols often difficult to interpret, meaning that field epigraphers got real good at pattern recognition real fast, or they moved on, and they often asked one another's opinions and went with the consensus vote, at least until something else in the text proved the interpretation wrong. It also meant that an epigrapher who didn't want anyone else to know what she was working on might use, say, an untrained pattern recognizer to help with the gnarly stuff. Anna must've gotten stumped on something and needed a second set of trained eyes, but hadn't wanted to use someone—namely him—who could translate the glyphs themselves. So she'd taken a chance on Neenie, not realizing that her vault had some serious leaks when it came to keeping secrets.

"What did you tell her you thought it was?" Lucius asked, feeling an itch of excitement. If Anna was working on something huge, it would explain so much of what had gone on lately—from the stress she'd been under, to the weird working hours, to the fact that she'd been kicking him out of the lab as often as possible over the past week.

Yeah, he was cheesed that she hadn't let him in on it, but he'd forgive her if it was the sort of thing that would land her—and, by extension, the senior member of her lab—on the cover of *National Geographic* or *Smithsonian* magazine or something.

Already envisioning the two of them suited up in full kit, posing beside the *chac-mool* throne inside the step-sided Pyramid of Kulkulkan at Chichén Itzá—because that was the sort of thing the big magazines wanted, even if the codex page had come from someplace else entirely and most of their work was done in a lab in Austin—Lucius almost missed Neenie's answer.

Then he got it. And froze.

"What did you just say?"

"I told her I thought it looked like a screaming skull." Neenie gave him a weird look. "Are you okay?"

No, I'm not. I just took a big whack upside the head with the every-glyph-groupie-for-herself stick.

He shook his head, hoping those last few words would rattle loose and turn into something else. But they didn't, leaving him with only one question: Why hadn't Anna shown it to him? She knew damn well he was looking for text with a screaming skull, so he could compare it to the images on his computer, the ones he thought were screaming and she insisted were nothing but more of good old King Jaguar-Paw Skull's laughing skeletons.

If she had one and hadn't showed it to him, it meant . . .

Fuck, he didn't know what it meant.

"What else did you see?" he demanded.

Neenie went a little wild-eyed. "Do you need to sit down or something? You're freaking me out."

"You had brothers. Deal with it."

"Yeah, okay." Still, she edged a little closer to the door before she said, "She kept most of it under that protective paper, so I didn't see all of it. There were a few of those jellyfish blobs with the dots in them."

Which represented numbers, or sometimes dates. "How many dots? Do you remember?"

She shook her head. "That's not how my brain works. I can see the patterns, kind of out-of-focus, but if I concentrate too hard the lines get all jumbled up."

"Great. Well, how about—" Lucius broke off. "Wait. Could you draw it from memory?"

She looked offended. "Of course. I remember this one time my brother Max—"

"Not now. Don't care." He rummaged through his horizontal filing system—aka the pile beside his desk—

and came up with a piece of sketch paper and a pencil with some lead left. "Draw."

She hesitated and looked at him as though considering another negotiation, but whatever she saw in his face must've convinced her otherwise, because she took the pencil and began to sketch.

Lucius watched, his heart actually racing as the images emerged: the curve of a skull with its mouth gaping wide; three blobs stacked one atop the next with dots beside them, spelling out a date; a highly stylized jaguar with its jaws clamped around the neck of a human figure, with spurting blood that formed a waterfall leading to a round circle wreathed in flames.

No, Lucius realized. Not a circle. A planet. Earth. Or, more specifically, the end of planet Earth.

And the transition of a god to the plane of mankind.

"Fuck me," he said, loud enough to make Neenie jump and drop her pencil. "Don't stop now," he said, excitement riding his tone. "Keep going!"

"I can't. That's all I saw." She looked up at him. "What does it say?"

He shook his head. "I don't know."

"You're lying."

"Prove it." He snagged the paper before she could and stuck it in his top desk drawer. "And before you make a stink about it, don't forget you're the one who broke your promise."

She lifted her chin. "I sold out. There's a difference."

Unable to argue that point—and not sure why he'd want to—Lucius crossed the room and opened the door. "Whatever. Go away."

She paused in the doorway and turned back to stare him in the eye, and the semiteasing look fell away from her expression. "You're defending soon. Now is *not* the time to do something stupid."

He dipped his chin. "I know."

But once she was gone, heading down the hall in the same direction the Dick had taken maybe ten minutes earlier, Lucius sucked in a deep breath, told himself there was nothing gained from venturing nothing, and headed for Anna's office.

He knocked and waited for her to call, "Come on in."

Her eyes widened slightly when he entered—not something he would've picked up on if he hadn't been looking, but did because he was. "Expecting someone else?"

"Only because you knocked," she teased, but the humor didn't reach her eyes. She started neatening up her desk, pushing the papers to one side and reshelving a couple of books in the cases to the left of the desk. "What's up? And make it quick, because I was just headed home."

Which meant either she'd decided to give in to her jerk husband, or she was lying. Lucius wasn't sure which option pissed him off more, but he throttled it down. "Never mind, then. I thought you were staying late, so I was checking to see if you wanted anything from Dirty Martin's," he said, knowing she could occasionally be bribed with a Sissy Burger and a chocolate shake.

Her expression eased. "No, thanks. I'm good." She shoved a couple of folders into her soft-sided leather briefcase and stood, slinging the strap over her shoulder. "See you tomorrow, Lucius. And . . . thanks."

"For what?"

She squeezed his hand briefly in passing, then tugged him out into the hallway so she could shut and lock her office door. "For being you."

Which left him completely baffled as she marched off, her heels clicking and her long, red-highlighted dark hair swinging opposite the motion of her walk, which he was pretty sure had an added wiggle in it as she turned the corner.

Damn it, she was going home to make nice with her husband, he realized, which led to a second realization: He really would've preferred if she'd been lying to him. He hated thinking of her with the Dick, hated knowing she was trying to save something that everyone around her could see was fatally flawed.

"Or maybe you're the one who's fatally flawed," he said aloud when he realized he was standing in the middle of the damn hallway, staring after her with his tongue hanging out.

He turned his attention to her office door, and after

a quick check up and down the hallway, gave the knob an experimental rattle.

The lock held, which was no big surprise. It was also a no-brainer that he didn't know how to pick the damn thing. That was the sort of thing the people he read about knew how to do—it wasn't the sort of skill that'd been easy to pick up in the ruthlessly middle-class neighborhood where he'd been raised. However, he and his sisters had been awfully good at sneaking in and out after curfew. And, if he remembered correctly, Anna had been in such a hurry to get home to the Dick that she hadn't latched the window.

"Here goes nothing." He headed outside and around the building, took a quick look around to make sure nobody was watching, slid the casing up, and climbed through.

At least being a skinny, too-tall beanpole was good for something.

He landed hard in a disorganized heap, but there was nobody there to laugh, so he didn't worry about how he looked, only that he didn't knock anything over and break it. Then, after he'd managed to right himself, he got to work, trying to figure out where she would put something she didn't want the casual observer to see.

No doubt she normally carried the codex fragment with her for safekeeping, but he was pretty sure she hadn't grabbed it in the rush of hustling him out of her office. She hadn't dared, because she'd known he would've asked about it.

Therefore, the text was still in the office somewhere. All he had to do was find it.

Anna headed for her car, which was stashed in one of the minuscule lots that peppered the gigantic campus, which had approximately one parking space for every ten students and faculty members. She figured she'd grab a bite to eat and then double back once Lucius left for the night.

She'd hated leaving the codex behind, but hadn't had a choice. It was safely hidden, and if she'd pulled it out in front of Lucius the unshakable, she never would've gotten away. And besides, she could use an hour without feeling the power scrape along her nerve endings, whispering promises, whispering threats.

After Strike had mailed the package back to her with a pleading note—the bastard—she'd ignored the codex fragment for as long as possible. Which had been about a day. She'd deciphered only the first few lines so far, but what she'd gotten both thrilled and profoundly disturbed her.

Why? she wanted to ask her brother. *Why are you trying to pull me back in?* But she didn't, partly because she didn't want to run the risk of falling any farther back into the past, and partly because she already knew the answer: because he needed her. The world was about four years from ending and it was up to him and Red-Boar to fix things, with good old Jox holding their coats.

Anna sighed as she dropped into the driver's seat of her car, a powder gray Lexus with more than fifty thousand on the odometer. Dick had wanted to trade the car in last year, but she'd refused, partly because she didn't see the point in more payments, and partly because there had been something disturbingly symbolic about the argument.

"And here I am," she said aloud over the engine's purr, "trying to decide between a husband who might or might not want to trade me in when I hit fifty thousand miles and a brother who wants me to—" She broke off. Hell, she didn't know what Strike wanted at this point. He hadn't tried to contact her directly. He hadn't even brought the codex fragment in person the first time. He'd sent Red-Boar, one of the few people in the universe she actively disliked.

Telling herself that didn't matter in the grand scheme of things, Anna slapped the transmission into drive and hit the gas far harder than she'd intended. She gasped as the Lexus launched itself out of the parking spot, then shrieked when another car suddenly materialized in front of her. She went for the brake, but missed, stomping down in shock when she recognized Dick's beloved Explorer right in front of her.

The Lexus was accelerating when it hit.

The impact jolted her against her seat belt as a crunching, rending noise surrounded her on all sides. She screamed again, mostly out of surprise and dismay, and then just sat there for a second, staring at the Lexus's popped-up hood, the Explorer's caved-in quarter panel, and the shocked expression on her husband's face.

Oh, shit. She'd T-boned Dick's Explorer.

She hadn't been going fast enough to hurt herself—not even fast enough to detonate the air bags—but she'd sure as hell been going fast enough to do some damage. Hands shaking, she fumbled for her seat belt and shoved open the door. Her legs trembled as she stood and tried to think of something—anything—she could say to undo what she'd just done.

"Are you okay?" He appeared around the back of the Explorer, almost running, his eyes wide and his hands outstretched to her. "Anna, are you hurt?"

She shook her head, feeling the tremors drain away, leaving the beginning of tears in their place. "No, I'm okay. But, Dick, the cars . . ."

"Hush. It's fine." He caught her hands and squeezed; then, as if that weren't enough, he pulled her into his arms and hugged her tightly. "I'm sorry."

"What are you sorry for? I'm the one who didn't look." Her words were muffled against his shirtfront.

"Fuck the cars; I'm talking about us. I was a jerk to you just now, and I'm sorry."

"Oh." She relaxed against him as sneaking warmth unfurled within her chest. She settled against him, feeling safe for a second. Feeling loved. "Me, too."

This was what it was all about, she thought. Forgiveness. Normalcy.

"Where were you going in such a hurry, anyway?"

"I was coming after you," she said without thinking, without having even realized that was what she'd been doing. "I wanted to say I was sorry for being a bitch."

"By wrecking my car." But there was a thread of amusement in his voice, and faint laughter rumbled in his chest beneath her ear.

She grinned up at him. "Got your attention, didn't it?"

"Next time try an e-mail. Or flowers or something."
But his arms tightened around her, and he dropped a
quick kiss on her lips and lowered his voice. "What do
you say we see if these heaps still run, and go find our-
selves a little wine and candlelight, and a table set for
two?"

"You're on," she said, smiling up at him and consciously letting go of the petty resentments and the nagging sense that she should be working on the codex.

This was the life she'd chosen, the life she wanted. It
was up to her to make it work.

It took Lucius twenty minutes and one *duck, here
comes the security guy* before he struck gold, or rather
parchment.

He found the packet wedged between two fat dictionaries of the modern Quiche Mayan language. He worked
the packet free and held it carefully by its edges as he
carried it to Anna's desk and set it down.

Then, very slowly, he opened the brown paper wrapping and the conservatory paper beneath, feeling the tex-
tures change as he worked his way through several layers
of oilcloth. When he'd pulled the last one aside, he
stared at what he'd uncovered.

Dear God, it was beautiful. And horrible. Terrifying
and wonderful. He saw the skull in vivid whites and
blacks, the date, the jaguar . . . the blood soaking the
burning earth. It was all there, and more. It was . . .

It was everything he'd been looking for, everything he
was trying to make the others believe with his theories
and papers, the final proof for a dissertation that had
started losing momentum months ago.

It was perfect. And she'd been keeping it from him.

Anger coiled in his chest, red-black and foreign-
feeling, and when his face felt strange and stretched
tight, he realized he'd bared his teeth.

This should've been my discovery, he thought. *Mine,
not hers.*

He reached out, wanting to touch the colors, wanting
to inhale them, bring them into his body and breathe
them out again as shapes and sounds. The room spun,

contracting his attention into a grayish cone that began and ended with the piece of painted bark.

He'd originally intended—to the extent that he'd had a plan at all—to do a rough translation of the fragment right then, without removing it from her office. He'd planned to use it to springboard additional research, then use his findings to convince her to give him access to the full text. Or so he'd told himself. Now, as he reached out and carefully refolded the packet layer by layer, he knew that he'd never meant to do that at all.

He'd come to steal it.

Mind numb, fingers moving automatically, he slipped the packet beneath his shirt and tucked the tails of the garment into his waistband to hold the bundle in place against his skin. He cinched his belt an extra notch to secure everything, and took a long look around to make sure he'd left no sign of his presence. Then he slipped out the way he'd come in, a thief in the night, prompted by a half-heard whisper in the back of his head, the feeling of stars coming into alignment, and the dark, sensual power humming just beyond his fingertips, whispering to him. Calling to him.

Speaking words only he could understand.

CHAPTER EIGHTEEN

As Leah and the trainees filed into the sacred chamber for the Venus conjunction ceremony, her blue robes swished around her ankles and her stomach clenched with nerves. She didn't think she was the only one fighting to stay calm, either. Sven was a funny gray-green color, his lips almost bloodless and pressed together in a thin line. Jade was sweating lightly, even though the AC was up and she'd be sitting outside the circle while the others underwent the ritual. Michael was his usual inscrutable self, with thick shields hidden behind a sexy smile, but she'd noticed him popping a Pepto tab when he thought nobody was looking. Brandt and Patience were hanging on to each other for dear life. Rabbit had lost some of his normal swagger, his nostrils flaring as he breathed in the *copan* smoke liberally scenting the air, and Alexis and Nate were clinging together in the corner, trying to look like they were fine. Yep, definite barf potential, all of them.

Worse, if one of them went, it'd be a chain reaction.

Hold it together, Leah told herself as the door opened to reveal Red-Boar in his black robes and Strike in royal crimson, both wearing feathered headdresses and celts, and resolute expressions.

There were no nerves there, Leah saw, or if there were, they were well hidden as they all took their positions: the trainees in a circle around the altar with Red-

Boar at the center, Strike on one side of the *chac-mool*, her on the other.

The sight of Strike in full-on *I'm in charge here* mode went a long way to settling her nerves.

Red-Boar flicked his black robes out of the way with a practiced move and sat cross-legged with his back to the altar. Over the top of the *chac-mool*, Strike and Leah faced each other and joined hands. Electricity arced across her skin at his touch, but it served only to bring the nerves right back where they'd been. What if the three-question ritual didn't work?

Worse, what if it did?

She met his eyes, letting his apparent calm steady her fears. Letting the strength of his grip anchor her.

At Red-Boar's gesture, the trainees dropped to sit cross-legged. Then the *winikin* filed in, carrying bowls, parchment, and ceremonial knives that they passed out. When they were gone and the door shut behind them once again, everyone had a bowl and knife except Jade, who sat against the wall, her expression caught somewhere between relief and humiliation.

Without a word, Red-Boar lifted his large, ornately carved stone knife, set it to his palm, and drew the blade sharply across his flesh. Blood welled, then dripped into the bowl, soaking into the layer of paper at the bottom. The others followed suit, then took turns passing a torch and using it to set the parchment aflame.

At Red-Boar's gesture, each of them leaned forward and inhaled the smoke of burning blood, and whispered, *"Pasaj och."*

Seconds later they stilled and their faces went slack, indicating that they'd jacked into the barrier, sending their souls into the gray-green mist but leaving their bodies behind. When they did so, Leah felt . . . nothing. No power surge, no beckoning sense of urgency, no invitation to follow. Nothing except the edge of the altar digging into her ribs and the grip of Strike's fingers on hers.

This isn't going to work, she thought, panic kindling in her stomach. *Whatever the magic was, I lost it.*

"Look at me," Strike ordered. When she locked her eyes with his, he said, "Don't you dare give up."

In the torchlight, his black hair and close-trimmed beard made his dark good looks lean toward dangerous, sending a quiver of awareness through her, a hum of nerves. He looked like he could be a demon, could be a king. He looked like a fighter, a warrior, like the man she'd dreamed of before.

The one she still dreamed of every damn night, and then woke up aching and alone.

"Ready?" he asked, his voice a harsh rasp that licked along her nerve endings like fire.

She took a deep breath and nodded, but didn't trust herself to speak. He wouldn't even be bringing her into the barrier at all, except that the three-question spell was a once-in-a-lifetime deal, three questions per magic user per existence. And while she wasn't a Nightkeeper, they were hoping she had enough of whatever magic she'd once possessed to get her into the barrier and call up the three-question *nahwal* with Strike's help.

Better that, Red-Boar had pointed out with his usual lack of tact, than letting the king's son burn his three questions on his human girlfriend. Jade's research suggested the questions had to be specific to the petitioner, meaning that none of the other Nightkeepers could ask for her. The meant it was Leah or nobody.

"Let's do this." Strike released her hands so he could cut his own right palm, then hers. Instead of letting the blood fall into separate bowls, they locked hands so the red wetness mingled as it dripped into the king's ceremonial bowl, which had a small piece of parchment at the bottom. When the paper was wet with their blood, Strike lit it with one of the tapers, and they both leaned in to inhale the smoke. That put them face-to-face, and Strike shifted and touched his lips to hers. "Trust me."

Then he jacked in. Leah saw the change in his face, saw his eyes go blank and his expression slacken. Failure kicked her hard when she stayed behind, when she didn't feel anything other than the burn in her palm and the tickle of smoke in her sinuses. Damn it, she couldn't follow, didn't have the power, didn't know how to—

Hey, Blondie, his voice whispered in her mind.

Her nerves kicked. "Yeah?"

Close your eyes and grab on.

"To what?" But then she closed her eyes and saw a faint glowing thread that wasn't part of her usual eyes-closed landscape. Excitement kicked her pulse a notch as she reached out with her mind and touched the thread.

There was a soundless explosion, a sense of flying while sitting still. Then her gut wrenched. Power screamed in her ears. And the bottom dropped out of her world.

Leah shrieked as she jolted down, then sideways, and the world went gray-green. She zapped in a few feet off the ground, several yards away from Strike, and fell face-first into a sea of mist, landing on something soft and squishy and vaguely mudlike.

Heart hammering, she rolled onto her back and concentrated on breathing. "Guess we made it." The relief was so sharp it was almost painful.

"This far, at least." Strike grabbed her wrist and pulled her to her feet. Once she was steady, he stripped off the headdress and set it aside, then reached inside his robe and withdrew a pair of stingray spines. "Now for stage two."

She took the spine. Tested the point with her fingertip. "Not very sharp."

"That's what makes it fun. Not." He paused. "You ready?"

She took a breath and nodded. At his signal, she opened her mouth and jammed the spine into her tongue, then yanked it out again. Pain was a quick slap and a longer burn, but she held herself still as blood filled her mouth and then overflowed, spilling down her chin and splashing on the blue robe.

Then, for the first time since the aphelion, she felt something. Sudden power bloomed on her skin, in her core. She smiled through the pain of her torn tongue. "I feel it!"

"Good. Say the words."

She began the chant, words she'd memorized phoneti-cally but hadn't really thought she'd use. Strike took position at her side, holding her right hand in his, joining their blood, boosting her power with his own. At first she was afraid the spell wouldn't work. Then, as the mist thickened nearby and a human figure took shape, she was afraid it *would* work. Somehow, in that moment, getting the answers to the questions that'd dogged her the past few months seemed more frightening than not knowing the answers.

"Steady," Strike murmured at her side. "I'm here."

She leaned into him as the mists parted and the three-question *nahwal* approached, stopping a short distance away. It was a sexless humanoid figure with dead black eyes and no forearm marks or other distinguishing features, no expression on its desiccated face. Its tanned, leathery skin was pulled tight across its bones, and it made no sound when it moved.

"Ask your first question," it said in a toneless voice that seemed to be made of two voices, one high, one low, speaking in synchrony.

Oh, holy freak show, Leah thought, gripping Strike's hand even tighter than before. Drawing strength from that solid contact, she took a deep breath and said, "What is the nature of my magical power?"

Strike, Red-Boar, and Jox had confabbed on the question, going for something broad enough to get more than a yes/no answer, yet specific enough to give them something they could use. In theory, anyway.

The *nahwal* tilted its head and was silent for nearly a minute, unmoving, as though carrying on an inner dialogue. Then it said to Leah, "You are the light half of the god Kulkulkan. Your brother was to be the darkness. Together, you were to be the Godkeeper, able to wield the might to oppose the crocodile lord."

Shock hammered through Leah. Grief. She tightened her fingers on Strike's hand, where their cut palms channeled his power into her. *Kulkulkan is a dual god,* Strike said through the blood link. *Light and dark halves. Since you're human, you can't take all his powers. He must've tried to split himself into two blood-linked humans—you and your brother—figuring to unite you into a single Godkeeper.*

But how is that possible when Matty died long before the barrier reactivated? Leah shot back, head spinning. *And where does that leave me now?*

"Will you ask your second question?" the *nahwal* queried.

Leah thought fast. "How can I bring the darkness into myself and become the Godkeeper alone?"

"You cannot," the creature replied in its two-toned voice.

Shit. Ask where the god is now, Strike prompted.

When Leah parroted the question, the *nahwal* replied, "Kulkulkan's link to you keeps him trapped between heaven and earth, within the skyroad. There, his energy fades."

Which is why my powers are getting weaker over time rather than stronger, she thought. *But that doesn't tell us how to fix it, and I'm out of questions.*

"I'm not," Strike said aloud, dropping her hand and breaking the blood connection before she could protest, before she could remind him that he wasn't supposed to burn his three questions on her.

The *nahwal* turned its attention to him. "Will you ask your first question, son of the jaguar kings?"

"Yes," Strike said. "Why do I wear the flying-serpent glyph?"

"It represents the darkness of Kulkulkan, the war god aspect."

"Then I am to take her brother's place?"

The nahwal shook its head. "No. You are a male Nightkeeper, and carry too much darkness already. If you undergo the transition, you will become a *makol* with the power of a god. Undefeatable evil."

Leah gasped and moved forward, but Strike warned her back with a look.

"Will you ask your final question, son of the jaguar kings?" the *nahwal* inquired in its flat, two-tonal voice.

"How can the god be returned to the sky without harm to Leah?"

"It cannot." For a moment, Leah thought that was all it was going to say, that it would leave them with even more questions than before. But then it continued, "The woman must die before the equinox. If she does, the god's link to earth will be severed and Kulkulkan will return to the sky. If she remains alive at the equinox and the god has not been fully brought to earth, then both the woman and the god will die, and the god's death will destroy the skyroad. There will be no more Godkeepers, no more help from the sky. The enemy will bring the end-time, opposed only by you and your Nightkeepers . . . and you will fail without the power of the gods."

That two-toned pronouncement hung for a moment in terrible silence. Then the *nahwal* took a step back and started going gray-green and thinning to mist. "Your questions are done." Its voice grew fainter. "Gods be with you, son. . . ."

Then silence.

Leah couldn't tell if it'd faded out before saying "of the jaguar kings," or if it'd meant to say "son." A glance up at Strike told her he didn't know, either.

Silence reigned as the mists came together again in the wake of the *nahwal*'s exit.

Then Strike said, "Leah." Just her name, as though there were nothing else to say. And maybe there wasn't. They'd gotten the answers they'd come for.

Unfortunately, the answers they'd gotten sucked.

She nodded, unable to speak past the lump of fear and grief that jammed her throat. She wished she could say she didn't believe a word the *nahwal* had said, that there was no way she was buying into the idea that she had to die in order to prevent one of the Nightkeepers' creator gods from being destroyed. But if the magic was real, how could she say the *nahwal*'s answers were lies?

Strike took her hand again, tugged her closer, and lifted his free hand to touch her, brushing the backs of his fingers across her cheek and down the side of her neck. Despair simmered just beneath the surface of his soul—she could feel it through the link, lending sharpness to the heat that built between them, quick and urgent as he leaned down and touched his lips to hers.

She hesitated a moment, feeling her heart bang against her ribs and thinking of all the reasons this wasn't a good idea—her track record, his priorities, her vow to avenge Matty's death, the whole greatest-sacrifice thing. But all those reasons lost to the one single thing that told her she should take this moment with him, the one thing that had her parting her lips beneath his and lifting her arms to twine them around his neck, holding on when desire built, sweeping her away.

Because as he kissed her, as they leaned into each other, she knew one thing for certain: If he was kissing her, then he thought there was no hope. She was already dead.

She whimpered a little without meaning to, and he drew away, looking fierce and every inch the leader, every bit the protector as he said, "We'll find a way. I promise."

She buried her head in his chest, resting her cheek above his heart. "Take me back to Skywatch."

When Red-Boar triggered the talent ritual, Rabbit was the last to make it through into the barrier, dropping down to land on his ass in the mist, which swirled up around him in greasy puffs of greenish gray. The others had already formed a circle.

As Rabbit scrambled to his feet and limped to join the others—his foot had gone pins and needles for some reason—he saw something flash in his old man's eyes. Most likely regret that he'd made it through. *Well, screw him.* It wasn't like there was any question that he was going to get a talent mark—he already had his talent, didn't he? He'd get the fire symbol. Patience would get air, symbolizing invisibility. And the others? Well, they'd see about that, wouldn't they?

Taking his place between Sven and Michael, Rabbit smirked at the old man. "I'm here. The party can officially begin."

Then he realized it already had. The mists swirled and began to thicken behind each of the trainees. Moments later, the bloodline-bound *nahwal* appeared, one for each of the trainees, except for Rabbit, who would be repped by the old man whether either of them liked it or not.

Only there was one too many *nahwal*, Rabbit saw. Excitement spurted when he thought that maybe another bloodline—his mother's?—was going to claim him.

Then the creature turned to Red-Boar and said in its fluting multitoned voice, "Where is she?"

Rabbit hid the quick flare of disappointment. When the old man looked confused, he snapped, "It means Jade."

The *nahwal* turned toward him. "Why is she not here?"

Rabbit said, "We left her behind. She hasn't got any magic."

"Of course she does." The *nahwal* turned away and blinked its eyes. Moments later, Jade appeared in midair, screaming, and dropped a good six feet to land flat on her face.

There was a moist-sounding thud when she landed, and Rabbit winced in spite of himself. "Ouch. That had to hurt."

"Shut," Red-Boar said tightly, "up."

"What happened?" Jade pushed herself up, eyes wide and frightened. "I didn't . . ." She looked at Red-Boar. "I'm sorry; I didn't mean to—"

"It's okay," he interrupted. "You didn't do anything wrong." He nodded to the *nahwal*. "Your ancestors wanted you here."

She scrambled to her feet. Stared at the *nahwal* as it approached her. "But why?" Her voice squeaked on the question.

"Because they need you," the *nahwal* said. "We all do." The creature gripped her right forearm. Lightning flashed and Jade went stiff, like she'd just been hit with the jolt. Then the *nahwal* faded—like poof, one minute it was there, the next gone—leaving Jade standing in the middle of the circle with a shocked look on her face and a new mark on her arm.

Rabbit couldn't see it clearly, but it looked like a hand holding a pen.

She stared at it. Frowned. "I'm a scribe? Great." She looked at Red-Boar and spread her hands. "Well, that was worth the trip. I can write stuff down."

"Not *stuff*, daughter," the *nahwal*'s voice corrected, coming from nowhere and everywhere at once. "Spells. You, and you alone, can create new spells."

"Oh!" Her face flooded with joy. Then she faded just like the *nahwal* had.

Without further delay, the other trainees turned to face their *nahwal*, who gripped their arms in benediction. Lightning flashed, huge zaps of green-white light that arced across the mist with blinding intensity, with glyph shadows contained within the light. Each of the new Nightkeepers got the warrior's glyph that would confer added fighting power and strength, along with the heightened reflexes necessary for battle. Patience got invisibility, Sven got something Rabbit didn't recognize, and three of the others had dark spots in the mists above them that suggested they might get other talents in the future.

Then thunder grumbled, lightning flashed again, and when Rabbit's vision cleared, the other trainees were all gone. He and Red-Boar were the only ones left.

He closed the distance between them and held out his bare forearm. "What do you say, old man? It looks like put-up-or-shut-up time."

Something moved in his father's eyes, and for a second Rabbit thought he was going to refuse. Then Red-Boar reached out and gripped Rabbit's forearm. But instead of summoning the lightning, he said, "I accept this child as mine, as a son of the boar bloodline."

Shock hammered Rabbit alongside pain. He screamed and sagged in his father's grip as lightning flashed and agony arced through him. Thunder raked the mist, making the moist firmament shudder, and then Rabbit was falling, collapsing.

The last thing he remembered was being caught in strong, black-robed arms as his father swept him up. And brought him home.

Anna writhed beneath her husband, digging her fingers into the thick, strong muscles of his back as he thrust into her and withdrew, thrust and withdrew.

The lights in the bedroom were off, but in the mad dash they'd made from the front door to the bedroom, shedding clothes as they went, they'd left the hall lights on. The illumination spilled in through the doorway,

lighting one side of his face and leaving the other in
shadow as he rose above her, his eyes open and fixed
on hers.

She felt him in every fiber of her being—his thighs
between hers, the faint rasp of masculine hair against
her skin, the slide of his hard flesh within her. The scent
of their lovemaking filled her, excitement riding high on
a sense of, *Christ, where has this been?*

For far too long their lovemaking had been, if not
routine, then certainly nothing special, undertaken as
much on the calendar as anything, days counted forward
from the little "p" she marked on the first day of her
period each month. This was different, though. This reminded her of other times, better times, and as he hard-
ened within her, swelling until she felt the good, tight
stretch within, she saw in his eyes that he felt it, too,
that it mattered to him. That *she* mattered.

Then he thrust deeper, higher, angling his hips so he
pressed just right and sent her tumbling over the edge
before she even knew she'd been close.

Anna gasped and arched against him as her inner muscles fisted, clenching and relaxing, and he cut loose with
a roar. She barely heard him, though, because her orgasm had her in its grip, blinding her, deafening her as
it spiraled higher and higher still, taking her farther and
deeper than it should have.

Oh, crap, she thought as she slid down a slippery slope
of consciousness. *The stars. The barrier.* Orgasm was a
way to touch the heavens and speak to the gods, and as
she crested, she felt the power thrum within her. She
lost herself, lost touch with the here and now and went
someplace else entirely.

She had a flash of the sight she'd long denied, and
stiffened in shock. *"Lucius!"*

"What the *fuck*?" A sudden jolt jerked her back to
reality, but by the time she realized the movement was
her husband yanking away from her, it was too late.

She reached out to him. "Dick—"

"Your fucking grad student?" He pulled away, his
face twisted. "How could you?"

"I didn't," she said. "I wouldn't." But she knew he'd see the long hours and her preoccupation as proof.

"So you're just thinking about him while you're fucking me? That's supposed to make it better? Jesus, Anna."

She wanted to stay and explain, to try to fix what might be unfixable, but she couldn't get that image out of her head. She'd seen Lucius sitting in his apartment, reading the codex fragment aloud. Reading the lost spell she'd only half translated but already knew to be powerful magic.

She had to get over there, had to stop him. Heart pounding, she leaped out of bed and scrabbled for her bra and panties. "I've got to go."

"What?" Dick stared at her, dumbfounded. "You're fucking kidding me!"

She knew there was hurt beneath the bluster. She also knew this was quite possibly the moment that would define the rest of their marriage—or end it. But the text was her responsibility, as was Lucius.

"I'm sorry." She turned away from Dick, though her heart twisted. "I have to go."

He was stone silent, watching as she pulled on jeans and a shirt, shoved her feet into a pair of sneakers, and headed for the bedroom door. She wanted to stay, wanted to explain everything, but he wouldn't believe her. Hell, she'd lived the first nineteen years of her life in the Nightkeepers' world, and she barely believed the things she knew to be true. Dick would never get it.

So she took off, leaving him alone in the bedroom, knowing he probably wouldn't be there when she got back.

Sitting in the kitchen of his apartment, Lucius stared down at his left hand, which clutched a serrated steak knife. He didn't dare look at his other hand, or he might pass out. *Jesus, what have I done?*

Pain radiated up his right arm, stemming from where he'd clenched his fingers around his cut-open palm. Blood leaked from between his knuckles, dripping faster than seemed natural. It wasn't the blood or the pain that had him panicked, though—it was the codex fragment.

He'd bled all over the thing.

Anna was going to kill him.

He didn't remember deciphering any of it, but there were words rocketing around inside his brain, syllables he couldn't quite catch but knew he should understand. The translation eluded him, dancing just beyond the reaches of his spinning mind.

Letting go of the knife, hearing it clatter to the floor, Lucius pressed the fingers of his good hand to his eyes in an effort to stop the pounding pulse behind them.

He sort of remembered deciphering the first couple of glyphs, but then something had happened and things had gone fuzzy for a while until he'd snapped back in and found himself sitting at the kitchen table with a steak knife stuck in his palm and half a pint of A-positive splattered on the stolen text.

Thinking to clean it off or something, he rose from the kitchen table and shambled across the room to the sink. He wadded up a couple of paper towels and pressed them against his cut palm, then wet a couple more of the towels and turned back to the table.

By the time he got there, he wasn't carrying paper towels. Instead, he held one of his roommate's froufrou scented candles and a box of matches.

Don't do it . . . just don't! he shouted inside his own skull as he watched his hands strike a match and light the candle. *Don't, please, no!*

Without volition—his own, at least—Lucius touched the candle to the edge of the blood-soaked codex fragment. The flame licked at the dried bark, turning the edges brown and then black. A chant rose in his mind, overwhelming him, overpowering him until he said the words aloud, giving them shape and substance as the codex burned. He leaned forward and breathed in the smoke of burned blood and paper.

A ripping, tearing noise blotted out everything else, and a void appeared inside him, a sudden emptiness inside his soul, his being.

"Crap!" He reeled and fell to his hands and knees, retching as glowing green foulness oozed from the tear inside him and began to fill the empty spot. Pain sliced

through him, crippling him and driving him to the kitchen floor, where he curled himself into a ball of agony, with his knees pulled up tight beneath his chin. He threw back his head and howled, but he couldn't tell if any noise actually came out, because it was lost amid the screams that seemed to come from his soul, from all around him.

There was a loud boom, a thundering noise he felt as a vibration rather than hearing as a sound, and suddenly he knew he wasn't alone anymore. Something else lived inside him. He turned blind eyes upward, squinting in an effort to see through the darkness.

A dark-haired man stood over him, heavily muscled, barefoot and bare chested, wearing loose black pants fastened at the ankles with intricate twists of red twine. His eyes were a bright, luminous green, one darker than the other, and he had a flying crocodile inked across his right pec. The air around him was shadowed a dark purple-black and radiated with hatred. Malice.

Lucius opened his mouth to beg for help, for mercy, but he wasn't sure he even formed words through the taste of evil and the stink of despair. He was suddenly very afraid he was going to die.

Worse, he was afraid he might not.

Strike dropped back into his earthly body with a flash of pain that he welcomed because it meant he was still alive. He blinked and felt his eyelids grate, shifted and felt his joints pop, and didn't care because the first thing he saw was Leah on the other side of the *chac-mool*, blinking her cornflower blue eyes in confusion, and then, when the memories caught up, making a little, "Oh," of despair.

"We'll figure something out," he said quickly. "I promise."

But they both knew he hadn't promised to keep her safe, or even alive. Things had gotten seriously complicated way fast. The Nightkeepers couldn't lose the sky-road or Kulkulkan. But at the same time, he couldn't lose Leah.

Her expression went wistful. "Yeah," she said, responding to what he hadn't said, rather than what he had. "I know."

He wanted to say something but didn't know what or how, so he stayed silent, and in the next moment Red-Boar exhaled and stirred, and the blue-robed trainees did the same as they all jacked out simultaneously. Strike felt the power surge, felt the echoed satisfaction of a job well-done, and knew that the talent ceremony had gone well.

Thank the gods for small favors.

Letting go of Leah's hands, Strike pushed away from the altar and headed for the door, intending to warn Jox that he was about five minutes away from a kitchen stampede. He was halfway there when a woman's scream echoed in his head. *"Help him!"*

The cry was followed by a mental picture that flashed along the link of a shared bloodline, powered by the magic of an *itza'at* seer. *Anna!* Strike thought on a spike of adrenaline and bloodline power.

The image she sent was that of a young man curled up and clutching his bleeding hand to his chest as his eyes started to glow green. A dark figure stood over him. Zipacna.

Rage flared, and Strike didn't stop to think or ask questions, didn't care that his legs were numb and his head pounding with a postmagic hangover, that he might not have the power to 'port accurately. He grabbed Leah with one hand and Red-Boar with the other. "Hang on!"

He leaned on the older Nightkeeper for a boost, fixing the transmitted image in his mind.

And zapped.

One minute Leah was getting her bearings in the sacred chamber at Skywatch, trying to deal with the *nahwal*'s morbid information dump. Then Strike grabbed her, the world lurched, and the next thing she knew she was in some sort of student apartment, standing in a combined kitchen/living room full of yard-sale furniture and clutter.

And Zipacna was there.

He stood near where the kitchen tile began, his mis-matched eyes glowing pure emerald green as he crouched over a young man who lay in a fetal ball, unmoving. The *ajaw-makol* was wearing loose black pants and held a bloody steak knife in one hand. The creature snapped his head up when the Nightkeepers appeared, and he bared his teeth in a hiss. Then his eyes fixed on Leah and the hiss became a smile.

Rage flared through her, hard and hot and pure, and she lunged at him, screaming an incoherent battle cry. She was dimly aware that Strike shouted for her to stop and Red-Boar cursed and made a grab for her, but nei-ther of them mattered just then. What mattered was the bastard who'd killed her brother, her friends.

Surprise was on her side. She slammed into Zipacna, burying her shoulder in his gut and using the momentum to drive them both away from the young man. They went stumbling into the kitchen and slammed into the stove, which clattered a metallic protest. The *ajaw-makol* roared and pushed away, reversing their momentum and sending Leah flying across the small space to smash into the opposite cabinets.

Without the benefit of jade-tips to slow him down, she went for the kitchen sink, which was full of nasty-ass dirty dishes. Grabbing a knife, she lunged under his swing and stabbed up, going for his heart. The weapon bit through flesh and grated on bone, and blood flowed over her hand, looking darker than it should have.

Zipacna stiffened and roared with pain. "Bitch!"

Quicker than human reactions, he grabbed her and spun her, whipping her arm up behind her back and getting his own knife across her throat, pressing hard enough to have her freezing in place.

"I thought we were friends," he said softly in her ear. Only it wasn't Zipacna's voice anymore.

It was Vince's.

Shock hammered through Leah. Betrayal. "Vince, no!"

Red-Boar's expression went dark, and he hissed, *"Mimic,"* like it was the lowest form of life imaginable.

"No shape-shifting necessary," the *ajaw-makol* said in

Vince's voice. "She was perfectly willing to believe a wig and colored contacts, even when I was only human. Never even thought to check with his coworkers that Vince Rincon was a real person, just glommed on when I said I'd known her brother, and thought the wicked cult members had killed him."

Leah nearly broke at the realization he'd played her all along. She'd been so pitifully willing to go along with the illusion, so grateful for some sort of support that she hadn't looked hard enough at the source. "Why?" she said, her voice a broken whisper. "Why me?"

"Because twenty-four years ago the gods marked you and your brother as their own," he said, leaning so close that his hot breath feathered against her cheek. "Matthew's blood started the process. Yours will finish it."

"No," Leah cried as something broke within her, bleeding rage and pain. *"No!"*

Strike took a step forward, his face tight. "Let. Her. Go."

"Why, so you can kill her and free the serpent to fight another day? I think not. Better she comes with me and joins the other devoted followers I've assembled for my use, for blood or as *makol*." The *ajaw-makol* took a step back, dragging her with him, and power started rattling through him, revving up, feeling black and twisted rather than the gold-red hum of the Nightkeepers.

"No!" Strike shouted, and lunged forward to grab her as purple mist rose up to haze her vision. The moment he touched her, power arced, red against purple-black, teleport against teleport, as Zipacna fought to take her and Strike fought to keep her.

Sobbing, not caring about the blade at her throat, Leah twisted in the *ajaw-makol*'s arms and jammed the heel of her hand into the knife still stuck in his chest, driving it deeper and feeling the spurt of hot blood.

Zipacna shouted in pain. And disappeared.

Leah fell to the ground half cradled in Strike's arms. He caught her against him, breathing hard. "You're okay. I've got you. You're okay."

Except she wasn't sure whether he was trying to reassure himself or her, because if it was the latter, he shouldn't have bothered. It wasn't okay. It probably never would be again.

Feeling numb, like she was already dead, she pulled away from him, lifted her right arm, and stared at the scarred patch. *Twenty-four years ago,* the *ajaw-makol* had said. And yeah, she knew exactly what he was talking about.

"I killed him," she said, her voice a broken whisper. "I killed us both."

As she realized the truth, a roaring whirl of purple-black rose up to claim her mind, and she was almost grateful to let it, to let the world slip away.

Until there was nothing. Until *she* was nothing.

"Leah." Terrified by her sudden immobility and fixed stare, Strike gripped her shoulders and shook her. *"Leah!"* When she didn't respond, he turned to Red-Boar. "I'm taking her back."

"Leave her," the older Nightkeeper snapped. "We deal with this first."

He stood aside to reveal the *ajaw-makol's* victim. He looked to be in his mid-twenties, shaggy-haired, tall and lanky, wearing jeans, a T-shirt, and worn hiking boots. The ruined remains of the codex fragment were crumpled nearby, bloodstained and blackened with flame. A total loss. But Red-Boar was right: They had a more immediate problem in the form of the young man, whose eyes flickered from normal to luminous green and back. If and when they set green, he wouldn't just be a second-generation *makol* created by Zipacna's magic. He'd be a new *ajaw-makol*, created through the parent spell and the magic of the *Banol Kax.*

"We have to kill it." There was far more practicality in Red-Boar's voice than regret. "Give me your knife."

"He's a person," Strike protested. "Not an 'it.'"

"It *was* a person," Red-Boar corrected. "Now it's a liability." He held out his hand. "Give me the damn knife."

"Don't." But it wasn't Strike who said that. It was a woman's voice.

Anna's voice.

Strike turned and saw her in the apartment doorway, and even through his worry for Leah, everything inside him went still. She was older than she had been—they all were—but he saw his sister in the woman who stood before him, saw the same blue eyes that met his in the mirror each day.

"Anna." The word hurt.

"Hey, little brother." But her attention was fixed on Red-Boar. "Don't kill him."

Sudden tension crackled in the air between them. "It is my right and duty," the older Nightkeeper said. "He is *makol*."

"Lucius is my student, my responsibility." She fixed him with a look. "And you gave him the codex."

Strike rounded on Red-Boar. "You *what*?"

Red-Boar dismissed the accusation. "Two months ago, and I told him to give it straight to Anna, who then mailed it back to you. I can only assume you returned it, and this idiot"—he nudged the young man with his toe—"snagged it once he realized what it was."

"He had no idea what it was," she hissed. "Fix him."

"Why should I?" Red-Boar snapped, looking as much at Strike as Anna, as if he were accusing them both of having seriously skewed priorities.

"Because we need Anna, and that's the trade," Strike said. "The student for her power added to ours during the equinox."

She nodded as though she'd known from the start that would be the deal. "I'll come with you, but I'm not promising to stay."

"We'll discuss that later." Strike reached down and gathered Leah's limp form to his chest. He turned to Red-Boar. "Can you save him?"

The mind-bender touched Lucius's shoulder and frowned in concentration. Then he grimaced and nodded. "He didn't finish reciting the spell, so the demon doesn't have a full grasp on him yet. I should be able to push it back beyond the barrier and blank his memories."

Strike nodded. "Do it. I'll be back for you in ten minutes." Then he held out his hand to Anna. "Let's go."

And he brought his sister home.

Anna might've left the Nightkeeper way of life without fanfare, but she returned with a bang when Strike materialized them a few feet above a tiled floor. They hovered for a second, like Road Runner going off a cliff, then dropped in the middle of a group twenty-somethings wearing the blue robes of Nightkeeper trainees.

She hit hard, saw stars, and bit her tongue, and the blood added to the power humming in her veins. When she shifted, she saw a new mark on her arm, the *itza'at* seer's mark. She'd gotten it on the pass through the barrier, whether she wanted it or not. But it wasn't the mark, the pain, the power, or the trainees that grabbed her full attention. It was the nausea of teleport sickness. She'd never been a good traveler.

"Oh, God." She curled up on her side. "I think I'm going to be sick."

"I've got you." One of the blue robes—a strikingly tall blonde with blue eyes and a no-nonsense air—helped Anna up and steered her out the door. "Bathroom's this way," she said. "But you probably know that."

That wasn't nearly enough warning for Anna, because the moment she stepped outside the ceremonial chamber and got a good look at the hallway, she recognized the training compound from her childhood. From her nightmares.

She clapped a hand across her mouth and bolted for the john, where she was miserably, wretchedly ill.

Images pounded at her, some of them from memory, some of them from the sight. All of them bloody and terrible, spewing past the barriers she'd set in her mind long ago, which were breached in an instant by the power of the stars and the horror of being back in a place she'd thought had been destroyed long ago.

When the heaves passed, leaving her dizzy and wrung-out, she stayed hunched over the bowl and pressed her

face to the cool porcelain of the outer rim, not caring
how gross that was. "I'm dreaming," she said weakly.
"I'm going to wake up in Austin, and Dick'll either be
there or he won't, but even if he's not that's okay, because I'm not really here. I'm there, and this is all a
dream."

The blonde crouched down so they were at eye level.
"I tried talking myself out of it, too. Didn't work." She
held out a hand. "You want to get cleaned up?"

Anna stared at the other woman's marked forearm.
"Who are you?"

"Alexis Gray. You're Anna, right?"

"That's me," Anna said faintly.

"You've got his eyes," Alexis said. "Or I suppose
you've both got your father's eyes."

Anna went cold. "I'm *nothing* like him."

"Oo-kay." Alexis held up both hands. "Touched a
nerve. Sorry." She stood. "You want some time alone
to decompress?"

"No, I'm the one who's sorry. I shouldn't have
snapped."

"No harm done." Alexis popped open the mirrored
cabinet above the sink, pulled out a couple of hand towels and a travel-size bottle of Listerine, and offered
them. "If you're done hurling, we should probably get
back out there."

"Yeah. I need to tell Strike to have Red-Boar blank
the codex from my intern, Neenie, too." And how weird
was it to say those names after all this time? Anna
thought. She took the tiny mouthwash, saying, "This has
Jox written all over it. No way Strike or Red-Boar
thought to lay in guest toiletries."

"Good call. Jox and the other *winikin* have the details nailed."

Inhaling sharply, Anna swallowed a mouthful of Listerine and gagged. "What do you mean, 'other *winikin*'?
Jox was the last."

"Long story. How about you get cleaned up and we'll
go find Strike? I'm sure he'll do a better job explaining
than I could."

But Anna thought back to her arrival, and the others

crowding the sacred chamber. They'd been bigger than average, gorgeous and young. As was Alexis. Her heart started hammering in her ears as she reached an impossible conclusion. "You're Nightkeepers."

"Yes."

Her legs went weak, and she whispered, *"How?"*

Alexis pushed open the bathroom door. "Come on. I really don't think I'm the person who should be telling you this."

"Wait." Anna grabbed her arm. "How many are there?"

Sympathy crept into the other woman's eyes. "Counting the toddlers and the convict? You make it lucky thirteen."

And the equinox was nine days away.

PART IV

∗

AUTUMNAL EQUINOX

A day of equally balanced night and day,
containing the moment when the center of the Sun
is directly over the Earth's equator.
The first day of fall.

CHAPTER NINETEEN

September 13

Lucius woke up with a hangover so big, there wasn't a word sufficient to describe it. He rolled over in his bed and groaned, then tried to sit partway up. When that sent a lightning bolt through his skull, he flopped back down. "Ohhhh, crap. What the— Oh, crap."

There was a reason—beyond the whole alcoholic-father-codependent-mother thing—that he rarely drank. He was pretty sure he was allergic. Which begged the question: What the hell had he been thinking? Had he been celebrating something good? Drowning something bad?

Fuck, even thinking hurt. Okay, no more thinking.

Food, he realized when his stomach grumbled. He needed food. Which didn't make much sense if he was hungover, but figuring that out would've required thinking, so he just rolled with it.

"Okay," he mumbled between dry, cracked lips. "Step one. Get vertical." When that more or less worked, he followed up with steps two—cross bedroom—and three—open door. He didn't need to bother with step four—get dressed—because he was still wearing yesterday's clothes. They were streaked with rusty brown, like he'd gone mud wrestling or something, and there was a funky smell coming from somewhere, but his roomies

were both off on field assignments, so he figured he
could eat first, then clean himself up.

Then he shuffled into the kitchen and stopped dead.
There were more of the rust stains splashed everywhere,
like something out of *CSI*.

"Ohhh." He looked down at his clothes as the stains
started making way more sense. Then a fragment of
memory broke through and he looked at his right hand,
where a gaping cut was scabbed over with a big, nasty
clot. "Fuck me."

It didn't start hurting until he looked at it. Then it
hurt like the dickens.

What the hell had gone down last night? He didn't
know, couldn't remember, just stood there staring from
his hand to the kitchen and back, before the downstairs
buzzer sounded, jolting him.

"I'm not here," he said, and headed in the opposite
direction for a first-aid kit.

The buzzer sounded again—three short, angry bursts.

"Still not here." He turned on the faucet and put his
hand under the water. He hissed with pain as old blood
swirled in the sink and ran down the drain, and when
he used paper towels to blot the wound dry, they came
away pinkish brown at first, then red.

*At least whoever it was got the message and stopped
buzzing,* he thought, debating between going for stitches
and using one of those icky wound patches that bubbled
up and looked seriously gross after a few days, but
worked really well.

There was a knock at the apartment door.

Lucius's breath whistled between his teeth and his
head cleared some on a burst of adrenaline. *Ignore it,*
he told himself. *They'll go away.*

"Hunt?" a pissed-off male voice shouted full-volume.
"I know you're in there."

What had he *done* last night?

"I'm not in here," he said under his breath. "Go
away."

But there was another knock. Then the voice again,
quieter this time, and sounding vaguely familiar. "Hunt,
please. I need to talk to her."

Her? Lucius took a quick look around, in case he'd missed there being someone else in the apartment, especially of the female variety. When a really, really bad thought occurred, he peeked in the other bedrooms, and let out a breath when he didn't see anything—or anyone—out of place.

There wasn't another knock, but he could sense the other man leaning against the door. He heard a broken sigh and a whispered name. *Anna*.

Oh, shit, Lucius thought when recognition jolted. It was the Dick. And he was looking for his wife. In a few seconds he was across the room and yanking open the door, his heart hammering far faster than it should've been. "Did something happen?"

First he saw the Dick, followed by the Dick's fist headed toward his face.

Then he saw stars.

The next thing he saw was the cops.

He watched in a numb blur as they confiscated the bloodstained stuff he'd slept in, photographed the shit out of the apartment, and took a couple of his steak knives into evidence, along with the dime bag they'd found in the fridge and a gun he hadn't even known his freak-show roommate owned.

The bad news—like he needed any more of it—was that the Dick knew most of the cops who covered the campus and surrounding area, so Lucius wasn't getting too many favors. The good news was that the one cop Lucius did know happened to be the one in charge of detention and it was a slow day, so he got a cell to himself. Small favors and all that.

He skipped his phone call. There was no way he was calling his parents until he knew the exact situation. And the person he normally would've called to bail him out—Anna—was apparently in the wind. His cautious optimism that she'd left her husband warred with worry. Where the hell was she?

He supposed he could call Neenie, but what was she going to do? In a few hours or whatever, everything should get straightened out. All the blood in the kitchen was his—he was sure of that much, anyway. Even better, when the cops had asked the Dick why he'd been convinced his wife would be at Lucius's apartment, he'd gone red-faced and refused to answer.

Sure enough, a couple of hours after he'd been locked up, a skinny guy in jeans, a polo shirt, and sandals stopped outside Lucius's cell. "Mr. Hunt?"

"You're the public defender?" Lucius asked, looking him up and down and back again. "For real?"

"You want to get out of here, or would you rather wait for somebody in a suit?"

Lucius rose from the cot. "Nothing wrong with Tevas. I take it they figured out all the blood is mine?"

The guy gave him a look. "Please. Evidence only gets processed that quickly on TV. No, Professor Catori's wife called him. She's fine."

"Thank God." Lucius exhaled far too much relief, earning himself a second look. "That she's back, I mean. She's my thesis adviser, and I'm supposed to defend soon, and—" *And I'm babbling. I'll shut up now.*

"I said she called," the PD said, leading him out to a desk and watching while he signed off on his personal effects; such as they were. "I didn't say she was back."

Lucius held out until they got out onto the sidewalk before he said, "Where is she?"

He didn't give a shit whether the PD thought the Dick was right about them having an affair. Something wasn't right. Anna wouldn't just up and disappear. She just wouldn't.

"New Mexico. Something about needing some time away, staying with a friend, et cetera, et cetera." The PD handed Lucius another paper to sign, then stepped back. "You're good. Charges dropped, very sorry, blah, blah."

He turned and walked away, leaving Lucius with the distinct impression that the PD, too, was a friend—or more likely a former student—of the Dick's. Anna and her hubby were both professors, yet the Dick had been "Professor Catori" and Anna had been "she."

"Don't overanalyze it," he told himself aloud. "Just be glad you're out. Go home, clean up, and get back to work." Maybe with an aspirin or five added to the mix.

Heading for the bus stop, he reminded himself that Anna was an adult—a married adult—and she didn't owe him any explanations or schedule updates. But he couldn't shake the sense that something monumental must've happened to send her to New Mex when she'd never mentioned the trip before. Maybe something connected to the Dick's utter conviction that he'd find his wife at Lucius's apartment. Damned if he knew what it might be.

The bus arrived, and he climbed aboard. As he lifted his hand to grab an overhead anchor, he caught a glimpse of the slice on his palm and frowned. "Weird."

The cut was almost completely healed.

Leah woke slowly, her consciousness dragging itself out of a warm cocoon of sleep back to reality, where it way didn't want to be. Her head felt hollow and empty, and her heart hurt with grief, with guilt. For the first few seconds she couldn't remember why.

Then it all came rushing back; she remembered the *nahwal*'s dire predictions, remembered that Vince and Zipacna were one and the same . . . and she remembered what the *ajaw-makol* had said about her being the gods' chosen.

Making a small sound of pain, she rolled onto her side and curled up, pressing her hands to her face in a pointless effort to shut it all out.

But the mattress dipped beside her and gentle hands touched her, rolling her over. Strong arms drew her against a warm, solid chest. "Come here," Strike said, his voice rumbling beneath the softness of his T-shirt. "Hold on to me. You're not alone, Blondie. You're not going through this alone."

Shock rattled her, and she opened her eyes to find herself nestled in the crook of his arm, lying on the mattress she'd schlepped out to the solarium so she could sleep beneath the stars.

He was fully clothed and resting on top of the comforter while she'd slept beneath in a T-shirt and underwear, as though he'd kept watch over her, not wanting her to wake up scared. His eyes were very blue, his face haggard with emotion and exhaustion as he pressed her head back to his shoulder. "Just one more minute. Then we'll talk."

She resisted for a heartbeat, then gave in and clung, because the fact that they were alone together—in her bed, no less—meant she hadn't imagined any of it, that it'd all really happened.

Stifling a sob, she pressed against him full-length and looped an arm around his waist, holding him close, anchoring herself. Heat rose, and she was tempted to kiss him, tempted to lose herself in the madness. But that would've been an evasion, and she knew it. So she shifted to look at the scar she'd gotten as a child, high on her inner right wrist. He'd asked about it twice before, and each time she'd avoided the question. Now she had to wonder—if she'd told him from the very beginning, would anything have happened differently?

"We were on vacation," she began. "In Mexico. The Yucatán."

The time-share had been billed as a "rain forest retreat on the beautiful Yucatán peninsula only minutes away from the Mayan ruins of Chichén Itzá." The house itself had been okay, but it had been the small, unrestored stone ruins tucked into the rain forest nearby that'd grabbed Leah's attention. She'd been eight years old, Matty six, and she'd had no business sneaking out that night, even less business making her younger brother go with her. But even knowing she'd catch hell if her parents found out, she'd snagged a flashlight and headed out into the warm, humid night, far too brave for her own good, but not brave enough to go alone.

"Don't be a baby," she'd said to Matty with all the lofty scorn of a two-year age gap. "I dare you." And he'd gone along with her, not because of the dare, but because even back then he'd been too willing to follow the leader.

"We went inside," she said, remembering the damp chill of the stones, even though so much time had passed. "It wasn't big, just a stone rectangle the size of a school bus or something. We'd checked it out that afternoon, the whole family, so I knew there wasn't anything scary. Except when we got inside, there was a door that hadn't been there before." She paused. "School had just gotten out when we left. I don't remember the date, but it could've been the summer solstice."

Strike nodded, and didn't seem all that surprised. Which she supposed made sense. The phrase "twenty-four years ago at the summer solstice" was burned into the Nightkeepers' collective consciousness as the night their lives had changed irrevocably.

Hers too, apparently. And her brother's.

"Go on."

"The door led to a long tunnel that sloped down. Matty didn't want to go in. I didn't either, really, but there was something calling me. Like a child's voice, only in my head, telling me it was okay, that I needed to go in there. So I did, and I made Matty come with me." He'd been crying, she remembered. And she'd dragged him along anyway.

She continued, "I don't know how far down we were, but there was this explosion, first orange, then yellow. I remember screaming and turning to run, but something hit me on the back of the head. I fell and lost hold of Matty, and then . . ." She trailed off. "My parents found us the next morning outside the little ruin, unconscious, and rushed us to the nearest hospital. When I woke up, my mother was crying. She stopped when Matty woke up, too. We both had burns on our arms, and . . . that was it." She stared at the scar. "We went home the next day, and I spent the entire summer grounded."

"Did you and he ever talk about what happened?" Strike asked, his words rumbling beneath her cheek.

"Not then. But we got into a fight a few months before he died, when I found out how much time he was spending with the 2012ers. He said there was something about Zipacna that called to him, that I ought to understand what he was going through." She broke off, swallowing hard. "He was so angry . . ." She closed her eyes, making a connection she hadn't seen before because she hadn't wanted to look too closely. "He'd always been a little borderline."

It was starting to make an awful sort of sense. The

temple must've been some ancient place of power,
maybe even one of the hidden entrances to the underground river system beneath Chichén Itzá. She'd wandered in there—or been called?—at the same time that
Strike's father and the other Nightkeepers were fighting
to seal the intersection. After the Nightkeepers died the
barrier started to close off, and Kulkulkan must've
reached out to the two nearest—and possibly, because
of their ages, most open-minded—humans: her and
Matty. The dual god had touched them somehow, making
them his. Matty had gotten the darker aspects, leading
to his later troubles—or maybe he'd been predisposed to
trouble, and that had attracted the darker aspects of the
god; who knew? She'd gotten the lighter aspects, which
included justice. Police work. It fit.

Unfortunately, it also fit that the *Banol Kax* had somehow known about the two of them, or sensed their connection to the god and had sent Zipacna after them.

Matty's blood had held enough power to reactivate
the barrier, Zipacna had said. Hers held enough to bring
the *Banol Kax* through.

All because she'd gone exploring as a child.

That was why she hadn't wanted to talk about the scar
before, for fear that it would be something like this.
Even before she'd learned of the Nightkeepers and the
things going on beneath the surface of everyday life,
she'd known Matty's—and her—connection to the
2012ers and their Maya-based mythology wasn't a coincidence.

"He was crying," she said softly, her voice cracking
on guilt and despair. "He didn't want to go into the
tunnel, but I made him." And in doing so, she'd started
the chain of events that would eventually kill him.

"You were eight."

"I knew better."

"You made a mistake."

"Yes." There was silence between them for a moment.
She could hear sounds coming from other parts of the
mansion, and the steady thump of Strike's heart beneath
her cheek. "He kept a journal," she said eventually, feel-

ing as though the words were being pushed out of her by an outside force, a compulsion to purge all the ugly truths she'd been keeping. "I guess he started seeing a therapist after his fiancée left him. I didn't even know. . . ." She trailed off, feeling the weight of guilt. "The Calendar Killer task force kept it as evidence, but Connie had them make me a copy."

"Did he write about that night in Mexico?" Strike asked, seeming to know she needed the prodding or she'd lose her ability to keep going. "Did he say that was why he was attracted to Zipacna and the group?"

"Not in so many words, but now that I look back, yeah." She nodded. "It was in there. He talked about how he felt like he and Zipacna were connected somehow, like they'd known each other in another life." She glanced at Strike. "Past lives weren't Matty's style. He wasn't real artsy or spiritual. He liked things—possessions, money, pleasures—and he liked to get them the easy way. At first I thought that was the attraction of Survivor2012— the nice mansion, the fat bankroll. When I read that diary, though, it freaked me out. It sounded like he was really buying into the religion, which didn't make any sense." Now, though, maybe it was starting to. "Do you think—" She broke off. "Do you think he became who he was because of Kulkulkan's darkness, or did he get the darkness because his personality already skewed that way?"

"I don't know." He shifted so he could look into her eyes. "Which would be easier to hear?"

She exhaled. Nodded. "Yeah. Doesn't really matter, does it? It's just . . . I can't help thinking that if I'd gotten the darkness I could've handled it better. I was older and stronger; I should've—"

"Hush." He pressed his lips to her forehead. "What's done is done. We go on from here."

She said, "I don't suppose any of the trainees got time travel as a talent last night." It was both a wistful thought and an offer to change the subject.

He gave a rumble of sad amusement. "Unfortunately that's not in our skill set. As of last night, I have one fire starter, one invisible, a seer, a spell caster, and seven warriors. Sven got a talent mark nobody's ever seen before, and I'm the local teleport."

"And the guy in the apartment?"

"Red-Boar got him fixed and wiped his memories." He paused. "Anna came back with me. I don't know how long she'll stay, but she's here now."

"I'm happy for you," Leah said, feeling a catch in her throat. "Brothers and sisters should stick together." Then, knowing they couldn't stay curled up in the royal suite forever—tempting though that might be on many levels—she said, "What happens now?"

He was silent for a moment, then said, "I need to talk to Anna, and see where her head is at. She got her mark on the way through the barrier, but an *itza'at*'s sight can be a tricky talent. If she's not committed to the magic, it won't work." He paused. "Then I need to sit down with her, Jox, and Red-Boar and lay out your situation."

"My 'situation,' " she repeated. "Is that what we're calling it?" Acid burned at the back of her throat. "I suppose it does sound better than, 'We've got two options: Option one, I die before the equinox and the god goes free, or option two, the god and I both die during the equinox and take the skyroad with us, meaning that there will be no Godkeepers ever, and pretty much ensuring the end of the world as we know it.' "

He tightened his arms around her. "You're not alone in this, okay? We're going to find a way." He sounded angry, but not with her, she knew. With the situation. The whole miserable, sucky situation they'd found themselves in.

She pushed away and levered herself up on her elbows, so she was braced above him looking down. "And if we can't?"

"We will," he said, and there was such certainty in his voice that she was tempted to believe him.

But saying something didn't make it the truth, even if the guy saying it was magic.

"Your duty is to the gods first," she said, "then your people and mankind. I'm pretty far down on that list."

"Trust me, I know what the king's writ says." He reached up and cupped her jaw in his palm, and she could feel the ridges of the sacrificial scars from the night before, rough against her skin. "But you said it yourself— this is a new day, with modern men and women playing the role of Nightkeeper. Some of the old ways simply don't apply now. Maybe it's time to make up a few new rules."

Tightening his grip, he urged her down, his eyes darkening with sensual intent.

Heat speared through her. Lust and frustration, her constant companions since she'd come to Skywatch, rose to the surface and her skin prickled with awareness, with anticipation.

But she stilled as the reality crashed in on her, chilling her to her soul. "You're in bed with me because you think there's no point in our staying away from each other, that you're going to have to—"

"No," he interrupted, tightening his fingers on her jaw before she could pull away. His eyes went dark, his voice rough. "No, I don't think that. I *won't* think that. But last night when the *ajaw-makol* went after you, I realized that it doesn't matter whether we're lovers or not. You're already too important to me. Losing you wouldn't just be the greatest sacrifice; it's simply not an option."

"Oh," Leah said, the word coming out on a long, shuddering breath. Just "oh," because what else was there to say? Longing coalesced inside her, a bone-deep desire to be the woman who could love him. Scrambling to find distance and reason, she said, "It's the god. Kulkulkan. He's trying to reunite himself on earth by bringing the Godkeeper of his light half together with her Nightkeeper mate."

"Maybe, maybe not. But more than that, this is us." He shifted and sat up so they were eye-to-eye when he said, "It's just you and me right now, Blondie. What do you say?"

There was a ton left to say, she knew, a whole list of reasons why their being together complicated far more things than it simplified.

But in that moment, alone with him in the glassed-in

solarium with the late-summer sun splashing down around them through privacy-tinted panels, it didn't seem to matter that a future looked damn near impossible. What mattered was the two of them together. And the question that hung in the air between them. *What do you say?* he'd asked, and she had no answer for that, because "yes" was too simple a word for what was between them.

So she leaned in. And touched her lips to his.

The kiss detonated something inside her. The first touch of tongues brought heat screaming, and need.

And rationality was lost. There was only desire.

They'd kissed before. She already knew his taste and the feel of him against her. But it was different this time—there was an edge of desperation when he slid his hand up to fist in her hair.

Heat flared, ripe and dangerous, and need was sharpened with the knowledge that their days were numbered.

Suddenly the sun was too bright, the room too open, the sparse furnishings too modern. Leah's heart beat with the rhythm of wooden drums, and that golden place inside her where the dying god lived had her rising to her feet and stretching out a hand to him. "Come with me."

He stood without a word and followed her to the private temple.

The torches flared as they stepped inside, reflecting their images from the black stone mirror—Leah tousled and bed-ready in a T-shirt that hit the tops of her thighs, Strike looking dark and forbidding and dead sexy in all black.

Then she turned and hiked herself up on the altar as she had done before. Only this time when he moved up against her, so her knees bracketed her hips and they were eye-to-eye, there was no thought of holding back or turning back. There was only the heat spiraling up toward madness as they kissed, straining together.

Leah moaned, the small, vulnerable sound escaping before she could call it back.

"That's it," he said thickly, nipping lightly at the side of her neck. "Tell me where and how and I'm there for you, Blondie."

He rocked his hips against her, creating torturous friction. She arched into him, offering herself to him even as she tugged at the hem of his T. "Hope you weren't too fond of this." She grabbed a corner of the fabric between her teeth, bit down, and used her hands to yank the material apart.

The shirt tore neatly up the middle, all the way to the reinforced collar, which she parted with a quick jerk, leaving the fabric hanging off him on either side, baring his heavily muscled torso and the faint line of masculine hair that ran down the center of his ripped abdomen and disappeared beneath the waistband of his jeans.

When their eyes met, she grinned. "Sorry about the shirt."

"Screw the shirt; that was hot." He got a couple of handfuls of her shirt and drew it up and off over her head while she nipped at the strong line of his throat and jaw.

Glorying in the feel of him, the reality of him, she suckled his skin, reveling in the harsh rattle of his breathing and the stroke of his hands as he caressed her hips and sides, then traced inward to touch her aching breasts with a soft skim of pressure, a rough hitch of pleasure. Her nipples tightened harder still beneath his touch and she rocked against him, moaning deep in the back of her throat, though she didn't let the sound free.

"Did you dream of this?" he demanded, rearing up so they were pressed chest-to-chest, staring into each other's eyes. "Did you dream of me?"

"You know I did." She kissed him, wet and hot and openmouthed, stroking the bare skin of his shoulders and back beneath the ruined shirt, which he shrugged off and tossed aside. "I dreamed of us beneath the stars."

"Tell me," he whispered, his breath hot against her throat as he stripped off his jeans, then her underwear.

"I slept in the attic," she said between kisses. "Under a skylight. I touched myself and thought of you."

"Show me." His voice was harsh, his excitement vibrating to her core.

At any other time, with any other man, she would've told him he was dreaming. But because it was here and now, with the man she knew better than anyone, yet not at all, she took his other hand in hers. "Like this."

She guided him to her breasts, showed him whispered touches and long, slow strokes. She was aware of the firelight and magic around them, and the warrior who stood against her, watching with fierce intensity when she spread her legs wider, opening the place where she was already wet and wanting. She guided him there, guided him until he was touching her the way she'd touched herself up in the attic, the way she'd dreamed of him caressing her so many times before.

Soon light and lingering wasn't enough, and she pushed his hand against herself harder, quickening the tempo. Sounds broke free—a gasp, a moan—and needs coiled tighter within, and she whispered, "Condom?" They'd had unprotected sex once before, and their blood had mingled, but there was no sense being stupid about the pregnancy thing, especially under the circumstances.

He grinned. "Great minds and all that." Heat coursed through her as he pinned her with his body, reached across to his discarded pants, and retrieved the flat square of a wrapped condom. When he withdrew it from his pocket, there were multiple crinkles, and three others fell out.

Leah found a grin amid the heat, amid the deadly seriousness of it all. "That's optimistic. I guess you planned ahead."

As he dealt with the protection, he touched his lips to hers and whispered, "I have faith."

Ignoring the faint twinge that statement brought, Leah leaned into his kiss, into the heat, and murmured her pleasure when he shifted against her and poised himself for entrance. Her body ached with need, lending a sharpness to the desire as she looped one leg around his hips, urging him home.

Yet still he paused, holding himself away from her.

Frowning, she opened her eyes and found herself caught in his.

"There," he murmured. "That's better."

The connection stripped her bare. Claustrophobia threatened, fluttering panic at the edges of her consciousness. She scrambled for a joke, for a snippy comment that would reduce the moment to what it should have been—sex between two consenting adults who liked and respected each other, who desired each other, who had common goals.

"Don't." He touched her lips. "Don't try to make this less than it is."

Don't try to make it more, she would have said, but he moved before she could, sliding into her and disrupting all rationality with the feel of him. The reality of him. His hard, thick length filled her, stretched her, set off neural detonations within her that took away speech, took away thought, and tunneled her vision so all she could see was the fierce love in his eyes when he took her. Claimed her. Made her his own.

Her inner muscles clamped onto his invading length, stroking him as he thrust and withdrew, thrust and withdrew, each time seating himself deeper and deeper still until— *Yes, there.*

Her breath whistled through her teeth on a hiss of pleasure, and she changed the angle, drawing him deeper and watching his eyes go hot with the new sensations.

He growled low in his throat and increased the tempo of his thrusts, sliding in and out of her, simultaneously touching her core and her clit with each drive home, coiling the long-denied orgasm so tightly her body became a vibrating knot of tension. The sensation built, then faded into the hot, tingling numbness her body hid behind in the final few seconds before implosion.

Her mind blanked. Her senses spun with the awe of it, with the hugeness of sensation as everything inside her paused for one. Breathless. Moment.

And then it came, she came, the rush of pleasure starting in her fingers and toes and all the places where they touched, where they strained together. The shimmer coalesced inward, rushing to the point inside where she gripped his cock with the first long, drawn-out pulse.

She said something, maybe his name, maybe something more dangerous, but she was beyond knowing, beyond caring, crying out as the inner contractions sped up, playing him, taunting him. He grew impossibly thick, impossibly hard, and his whole body went tight as he bellowed and came with her, within her. His orgasm caught the tail end of hers, kicking it back into the stratosphere, cramping her, wringing her with wave after wave of pleasure that held her paralyzed. Helpless.

Fulfilled.

When it was over, Strike muttered something and dropped his forehead to her shoulder. They leaned into each other as the torches continued to heat the air around them. A high, golden hum touched Leah's soul for a moment, then was gone, leaving her feeling strangely empty and unsettled.

"You're not in this alone, Blondie," he murmured against her neck, stroking a hand along her back in a gesture that was simultaneously reassuring and possessive. "You're mine now."

But instead of making her feel better, his words gave her pause, warning her that none of this was simple. Nerves tightened in her belly, bringing the sense that what they'd just done had gone too far, that it'd shifted something that shouldn't have been moved. "Being your lover doesn't make me a Nightkeeper."

"Maybe not, but being consort to the son of the king has to count for something."

It took a moment for that to sink in. Then, chilled, she leaned away from him, waited until he looked at her. "You made love to me for my own protection?"

Dark anger flashed in his eyes. "I made love to you because I couldn't damn well *not* make love to you anymore. Don't turn it into more than that." He cursed. "That didn't come out right. I meant that you shouldn't read ulterior motives where there aren't any. I wanted you; you wanted me. End of story. What happens next is completely separate from this."

Only it wasn't, and they both damn well knew it. It'd never been that simple between them and wasn't about to start.

She got it now. He thought that if they were lovers, the others might not force him to go through with the sacrifice, knowing that a mated Nightkeeper was stronger with his mate than alone, stronger still with a god-bound mate. But that didn't even begin to address the fact that they apparently had a creator god stuck halfway between the planes, and the thirteenth prophecy loomed large.

Strike, like his father before him, was trying to bend the traditions to save someone he cared for. And if his strategy failed, as it had done for his father before him, the results could be catastrophic.

"Don't go up against Jox and Red-Boar for me," she said quietly. "Not without a backup plan."

"And don't you tell me how to do my job." He turned away and started pulling on his pants with quick, irritated efficiency, and she could feel the darkness simmering very close to the surface. She could sense the anger that rode him, the frustration, and knew that what they'd just done had, if anything, made it worse.

Knowing he needed an assurance that she couldn't give, she dropped down from the altar and pulled her shirt and panties back on. The two of them were close together in the small space, but the gap separating them suddenly seemed wider than ever.

She touched his arm, where his marks stood out in stark relief against his skin in the firelight. "I'm just one person, Strike. Like it or not, you've got a way bigger responsibility than that."

"Tell me something I don't know," he grated out. He sounded angry, but when he spun to face her, she saw grief on his face. "Do you *want* to die?"

"Of course not," she snapped, "but I don't want to live four more years knowing the world is going to end because I'm still in it."

He looked at her long and hard before he said, "You know what? Maybe I do."

Then he strode from the small chamber, bare chested and pissed off. And he didn't look back.

CHAPTER TWENTY

Strike had a good fume on as he headed to his quarters for a new shirt. Gods, it seemed impossible that he could want someone so much, and want to strangle her at the same time.

It flat-out pissed him off that in the aftermath of some pretty fantastic, earth-rocking sex, Leah had dropped into cop mode on him, looking for evidence in a situation that was governed by *religion*, for chrissakes.

His gut told him there had to be a way to break the connection between her and the god—or better yet, to bring Kulkulkan through to earth—without either of them dying. But instead of trusting him, she'd all but accused him of bending the rules to suit his own needs at the expense of the other Nightkeepers, or the end-time war. And if that thought came too close to some of his father's failures, then so be it. He wasn't going to stop thinking for himself and blindly follow some two-thousand-year-old prophecy just because he was afraid of making a mistake.

Even if it could cost the world the rest of the Nightkeepers? a small voice whispered inside him, sounding very like his mother, or what he remembered of her.

"It won't," he said aloud. "I won't let it." But what if the choice wasn't his? What if everything unfolded as had been foretold?

And there, he realized, was the crux of things. He

hated feeling as if he were acting out a script that'd been written long ago, hated the idea that free will was an illusion, that no matter what he did it was going to come down to his taking up the Manikin scepter and sacrificing the thing that mattered most to him.

"Fuck that," he muttered under his breath, determined not to let it go down that way. But he also knew that Jox and Red-Boar would be on the side of tradition—and, damn it, logic—no matter what arguments he made.

So he went in search of his sister.

He found her in the suite they'd shared as children—two bedrooms and a main room they'd divided with a strip of masking tape. She stood in the middle of the bedroom that had once been hers, wearing the same jeans and sneakers as the night before, along with a borrowed shirt of pale blue cotton. Her dark chestnut-highlighted hair fell to her shoulders in soft waves, and her eyes were the same cobalt blue he saw in the mirror every morning.

Strike knocked on the door frame. "It's me." Then he stalled.

There hadn't been time for an emotional reunion in the grad student's apartment, and he hadn't made time for one the night before. Now, in the light of day, it seemed like it was too late, like they'd already settled into the uneasy coexistence that had plagued their growing-up years. He'd been the patrilineal heir to a dead culture; she'd been an *itza'at* seer whose powers had just begun to awaken right before the massacre. And boy had that been shitty timing. While he'd dreamed for years of the *boluntiku* attack and the deaths of all their playmates and *winikin*, she'd been forced to relive the attack at the intersection itself, her seer's powers showing her the deaths of their parents, the slaughter of the other magi.

Among the survivors, only Red-Boar had seen the same things, forming a bond between them. When the older Nightkeeper had disappeared into the Yucatán rain forest a few years after the massacre, he'd left Anna behind, alone with the memories. At first she'd withdrawn into herself. Then, when Jox had enrolled both of the children in public school, she'd flourished into a normal high schooler, turning her back almost gratefully on the world they'd lost.

Strike had understood even back then. But that hadn't made it any easier when she'd left for college and they'd all known she wasn't coming back. Only now she *was* back, and this time it was up to him to make sure she stayed.

She hadn't answered his hail, just stood there in the middle of the room, staring out the double windows that showed the ball court, and far beyond that the canyon wall, with its darkened pueblo shadows. Her blue eyes were dark with memory and sorrow, and Strike wanted to go to her and tell her everything was going to be okay, that he wanted to protect her now the way he hadn't been able to when they'd been younger.

But though he would do his damnedest to protect her—protect all of them—there was no way he could promise anything more. Not with the equinox just over a week away, and so much left to figure out. So instead of making promises he couldn't be sure to keep, he crossed the room and stood next to her to look out the window.

And, because there really wasn't much else to say, he said, "Welcome home, Anna."

A watery laugh burst out of her, and she sucked it back in as a sob. Still not looking at him, she said, "God, I hate this place. Nothing here but bad memories."

"We're making new ones now. We have no choice."

Now she did turn to him, her blue eyes wet with tears and hard with accusation. "There's always a choice. This is America. Land of the free and home of the brave, et cetera."

"You know better than that," he said, hurting for her but at the same time feeling the kick of too-ready anger. "We are, as we have always been, a culture living within another. We live alongside America but we're not part of it." They couldn't follow human laws while doing the things they would need to do over the next few years.

"I'm part of it," she said, but her voice was wistful. "I have a husband, a job I love, friends who care about me. The perfect normal life." There was an edge to her voice that suggested it wasn't as simple as that, but she continued, "I don't want to be here. I can't help you."

"Yes, you can. The question is, will you? Like you said, it's a free country. You know where the garage is. Keys are on the pegboard." The prickles of anger had him aiming low. "I'm sure Jox wouldn't begrudge you his jeep. Gods know you took more than that the last time you ran."

She turned to face him, glaring. "I didn't take a damn thing that wasn't mine to take."

"You took yourself. I didn't have that option." He hadn't meant to say that, hadn't even known he was feeling it, but once the words were out there, they gained weight and truth. He'd wanted to run like she had, wanted to break away from Jox and Red-Boar and the calendar that ruled their lives, the waiting.

"Immaterial now, isn't it?" she said. "We're right back where we started."

He let out a long breath. "Yeah. Sometimes that whole history-repeating-itself thing really blows, doesn't it?"

That startled a laugh out of her, and for some reason, maybe because of the familiar push-pull that hadn't changed since they'd butted heads over the masking-tape line as children, or maybe because the situation with Leah was teaching him that sometimes the circumstances were what complicated the emotions, it was suddenly easy for him to drape an arm over his sister's shoulders and hug her against his side.

She leaned into him, looping an arm around his waist. "I missed you."

"Back atcha."

And for a moment, a few precious heartbeats, it was enough to stand there with his sister and watch a high cloud scud across the blue sky above the canyon wall and feel, if not complete, at least like some small piece of his life had come to rest where it belonged. For now, anyway.

Too soon, though, he had to break the short peace. "I hate to push, but we don't have much time. There's an *ajaw-makol* out there. I need to find him, need to kill him before the equinox." It wouldn't solve the God-keeper problem, but it would be a major step in the right direction.

But Anna was already shaking her head. "I can't control the visions," she said. "Hell, I can barely see anything. A few times, like when I saw Lucius in trouble, it's blasted me out of nowhere. But when I try to see . . . I get nothing." She shrugged, the motion transmitting where they leaned against each other, comfortable together despite so long apart. "I think I'm blocking subconsciously."

Strike was disappointed but not surprised. Gods knew her powers had brought her nothing but pain so far. Why wouldn't she want to stop them?

He shifted to face her, dipping into the pocket of his jeans and withdrawing the yellow quartz effigy carved in the shape of a skull. He held it out to her. "This will probably help."

Something moved in her expression—a complicated mix of pain, regret, and reserve, along with reluctant eagerness. She took the pendant, let the chain trickle through her fingers while the skull rested on her palm. Then she closed her fingers around the effigy and nodded, accepting the responsibility that went with it. "Thank you."

Taking a deep breath, he said, "There's something else. I need your help going up against Jox and Red-Boar, and it's probably going to get ugly."

She nodded. "Of course." There was no question, no discussion, just "of course."

Something loosened a little inside him. "Okay, here's the deal." He gave her the five-minute rundown, starting with the dreams he and Leah had both experienced prior to the summer solstice, and going up through the *nah-wal*'s answers to the three-question ritual. When he got to the part about needing to either free Kulkulkan or bring him through the barrier, he saw something kindle in Anna's expression. He broke off. "What is it?"

"I think I know someone who might be able to help."

* * *

Strike called a council of war that afternoon, beneath the ceiba tree that symbolized life and community. By the time Leah got out there, the others were already seated on either side of the long picnic table, with Strike at its head. He pointed to the empty space on his right and said simply, "Yours."

She was no expert in the hierarchy department, but the dark looks that one word earned her from Red-Boar and Jox suggested it was a position of power, probably the queen's spot. She might've argued, might've sat at the far end of the table in a vain effort to make a point she wasn't even sure of anymore, but the look Strike shot her said, *Don't even think it, Blondie.*

So she sat.

On either side of her ranged the other Nightkeepers, with the *winikin* beyond them. Nate and Alexis were sitting as far away from each other as possible, suggesting that their relationship hadn't survived the talent ceremony and subsequent drop in the mating urge. Sven was staring off into space, Rabbit was hiding beneath a pulled-down hoodie and a sneer, and the other four—Patience, Brandt, Jade, and Michael—looked like they'd shown up ready for anything.

Leah, on the other hand, wasn't sure what she was ready for. The midmorning sex—and subsequent fight—had left her feeling shaky and out of sorts. She didn't really know where things stood with Strike, and when she caught his eye all she got was a hard, no-nonsense look she wasn't at all used to from him.

"Okay," he said when everyone was settled. "Here's the deal." To her surprise, he brought them all up to speed on the "situation," even though he'd indicated earlier that he was limiting the confab to Jox and Red-Boar.

Even more surprising, from the looks on their faces, this was the first the two senior members of the group were hearing about the Kulkulkan connection. While the trainees and other *winikin* were wincing and glancing at Leah with expressions of *Dude, major bad luck,* Jox and Red-Boar just looked pissed.

The elder Nightkeeper's face flushed and his eyes

went steely, but when he would've interrupted, Strike
held up a hand. "Let's wait on the questions—and the
insults—until I'm done. What we're looking for now is
a way to either bring Kulkulkan through the barrier in
one piece or cut him loose so he can return to the sky—
without endangering Leah, the god, or the skyroad."

"Our entire system is based on sacrifice," Red-Boar
snapped. "Yet you want to work perhaps the biggest
spell there is without anybody getting hurt?"

Strike glared at him. "What I want is for us to think
outside the box. Anna knows a guy who might be able
to help." He waved for his sister to take over.

"His name is Ambrose Ledbetter." Anna passed around
a Web site printout that showed an unremarkable-looking
guy with remarkably bad posture and a scowl not unlike
the one Red-Boar was wearing. "He's prickly as hell and
regularly disappears into the rain forest for months at a
time, but he's one of the best Mayanists on the planet."

"I read a few of his articles when I was researching
Survivor2012," Leah said. She glanced at Anna, whom
she'd met briefly in the kitchen earlier in the day. "Read
a few of yours, too. You guys didn't seem to agree on
much of anything."

"True," Anna agreed. "But my theories were based
in part on knowing the barrier was sealed, and believing
it was going to stay that way. His were . . . well, I'm not
sure where he got some of his information, but now it
looks like he was right."

"What makes you think he knows anything relevant
about the human's problem?" Red-Boar asked, still refusing to call Leah by name.

"Every now and then," Anna replied, "he publishes
something on the Web or in one of the smaller journals
that makes me think he knows more about Nightkeeper
magic than he ought to."

Now Red-Boar looked at her. "Meaning?"

"I think he knows the location of at least one of the
lost temples." Seeing a few frowns of confusion from the
trainees, she said, "During Mayan times, the Nightkeepers maintained a separate temple for each of the major
gods. When the conquistadors burned our libraries and

scholars, the temple locations went up in flames with them."

"The Pyramid of Kulkulkan is the focal point of Chichén Itzá," Jade said in her soft, barely-above-a-whisper voice. "Wouldn't that have been the center of his worship?"

"For the Maya, yes," Anna agreed. "But there was another center for the Nightkeepers' worship. If we can find it, maybe the inscriptions will give us a hint how to help Kulkulkan escape from the skyroad."

"And maybe not," Red-Boar said. "Probably not."

"From what Ledbetter's written over the years, I think he has some of the lost spells," Anna countered. "It doesn't matter what you think of Leah, or even what you think of Strike. If we can get our hands on those spells, wouldn't it be worth the trip?"

She held his eyes until he gave a curt, dismissive nod.

"Good," Strike said. "Get your stuff together. I'll zap you and Anna down south as soon as you're ready. Oh, and bring a weapon."

Red-Boar's eyes blanked. "I thought Ledbetter was a professor."

"Apparently he's done one of his solo disappearing acts into the field. The Guatemalan highlands, to be exact." Strike fixed the senior Nightkeeper with a look. "Go pack."

And, to Leah's surprise, Red-Boar did exactly that.

The meeting broke up soon after, once Strike had run through the training schedule for the next few days leading up to the equinox, and Jox had added some housekeeping complaints. When the trainees and *winikin* dispersed to their tasks, it seemed to Leah that they looked more resolute and, in a way, relieved.

It was Strike, she realized, sliding him a look.

He was deep in discussion with Anna, his head cocked at an angle as he considered something she was saying. Even standing at ease with his sister, he projected an aura of command he'd been missing before, a sense that it was his way or get-the-fuck-out.

He'd lost weight, she realized suddenly, as though what little excess he'd had before had been burned away by the events of the past few weeks. His high cheek-bones stood out sharper, and his eyes were a little more sunken beneath his dark brows, a little more intense in their gleam. And beneath yet another black T-shirt, she could practically count his ribs and the ripped six-pack of his abdomen.

Lust kindled in her belly. They'd had each other only hours earlier, but she wanted him again, now, wanted to get her hands on him, and her mouth.

As if she'd said the words aloud, his head came up and his eyes fixed on hers. The desire flared hotter, tempered with an edge of nerves. The man she'd ass-slapped ten days earlier over issues of leadership was gone. In his place was the ruler she'd wanted him to become.

And damned if he wasn't intimidating as hell. In a totally hot, sexy way, yes, but still, Leah found herself backing up a few steps as he crossed to her, staring into her eyes, making her feel stalked. He stopped a few feet away, yet she could feel his body heat on her skin, feel his energy slide against hers, dark against light.

She licked her lips in an effort to wet her suddenly dry mouth. "Nice job. With the meeting, I mean." Inwardly she thought, *Man up and be a cop. You know this guy. You can handle him. Nothing's changed.*

But something had very definitely changed. It was like he'd come to some sort of inner decision, one he hadn't yet shared with her—if he even intended to.

He leaned in and dropped his voice to an intimate rumble, even though there was nobody within earshot. "I had Jox move my things into the royal suite. It's time."

A shimmer of awareness touched her skin, a quiver of nerves. "Am I . . . where am I staying?"

"Your call." He didn't ask her to stay, didn't tell her he'd like it if she did. Just left it up to her. Her choice. Her commitment. *Damn it.*

She should put some distance between them now, before he figured out what she was planning and made it impossible. It was the smart thing to do, the right thing. But she heard herself say, "I'm staying."

He nodded once, then turned and strode back toward

the mansion, looking every inch the king in a black
T-shirt and jeans. And damned if she didn't want to
chase after him.

Instead, she headed in the opposite direction, back out
to the shooting range, where she unloaded clip after clip
of jade-tips into the shredded practice dummies, imagin-
ing that every single one of them was wearing Zipacna's face.

The section of rain forest where Anna, Strike, and
Red-Boar zapped in was moist and fecund and smelled
disconcertingly like antibacterial Febreze. Once Strike
zapped back out, Anna checked her handheld GPS and
set off in the direction Ledbetter's grad student had
indicated.

It couldn't have been someone easy to find, like Harts-
horn or Cortes at the Institute of the Yucatán, or even
Foohey up in Ottawa. They all had home bases and
scheduled lectures, conferences, and tours. No, it had to
be Ledbetter, who had all of those things and blithely
ignored them to disappear into the highlands for months
at a time, but got away with it because he was deranged
enough—and brilliant enough—that everyone called him
eccentric rather than unreliable. That had worked in her
favor, though. She'd been able to bribe his senior grad
student to give her Ledbetter's approximate coordinates
by dangling the promise of a job at UT.

It wasn't so much that the program in Austin was
better, but the head epigrapher at UT—namely Anna—
had less of a rep for flaking out.

Between magic and GPS, she figured they were maybe
two miles from Ledbetter's camp. Within a half hour of
hard hiking, her calves were burning, reminding her that
the stair stepper was her friend, not just a place to hang
dry cleaning. But she didn't complain, because what
would be the point? Red-Boar didn't care if her feet
hurt. He didn't care about anything but the past. Never
had.

But when she sighed, he paused, looked back, and
said, "Need a break?"

"Several, but not of the kind you're thinking," she

said drily, then motioned for him to keep going. "We don't have time for a sit-down. I'm fine." More or less.

He looked at her for a long moment, then turned away without comment.

Anna followed him, her eyes glued to his wide shoulders, trying not to envision the scars she knew crisscrossed his back beneath the long-sleeved shirt he wore tucked into camo pants and hitched with a stocked weapons belt. She wore the same, though her belt wasn't loaded with nearly as much firepower. Her aim was notorious, and not in a good way.

Shrugging beneath her light pack, she tried to resettle the load, which suddenly seemed off-kilter. Faint nausea stirred, though she wasn't sure if it was hunger or teleport sickness. Thinking to drown whatever it was, she reached for her bottle of purified water.

She had the bottle halfway to her lips when she realized it wasn't nerves or hunger. It was power. Not the kind she was used to, but a deeper, darker kind that grabbed her by the gut and squeezed, making her want to run and hide.

Ahead of her, Red-Boar stepped through a curtain of hanging vines into the sunlight.

"Wait!" she cried, but he'd already stopped dead.

He turned back, expression grim. "Stay here."

"What is it?" Ignoring his order, she stepped up beside him.

They stood on the edge of a small clearing. Or not a clearing, she realized. At some time in the past, a sinkhole had broken through, allowing access to one of the subterranean rivers that formed the only source of freshwater in the Yucatán. Over time, the sinkhole—called a cenote—had filled with leaves and organics that eventually became soil, capping off the cenote and creating new ground within a perfectly circular depression.

The Maya had believed the cenotes were entrances to the underworld; they had probably thrown sacred offerings into the sinkhole. The magic of those now-buried sacrifices would have accounted for a normal power surge. But there was nothing normal about the darkness

Anna sensed. Power hummed through her hiking boots, feeling purple and black and discordant. Drawn by the magic, simultaneously fascinated and repelled, she approached the cenote, testing each step before she put her weight down.

"Don't." Red-Boar's single word was less of a command than a plea, as though he already knew what she would find.

Then again, so did she. The air stank of death.

It wasn't until she reached the center of the depression that she sank into the dirt beneath her feet, not because the cap sealing off access to the subterranean river was giving way, but because the ground itself had been disturbed. She didn't need to see the churned-up earth beneath a scattering of leafy camouflage to know that she was standing atop a human grave. She could tell by the smell of death, of violence.

Her heart ached for a man she'd barely known.

"It might not be Ledbetter," she said, knowing it probably was. The *makol* had beaten them there, taking away a valuable resource.

Red-Boar didn't argue, simply made a wide berth around her, knelt, and used the flat of his machete to scrape away the soft covering at one end. He didn't have to go far. Only a few inches down, he uncovered fairly fresh human remains that started at the neck, with dark, raw flesh and a severed vertebral column.

The head was gone, no doubt taken elsewhere to add to the *makol*'s skull pile. His powers weren't at full strength yet, but they were growing fast. She could feel it.

Red-Boar uncovered the torso and abdomen, and she felt an unreasonable wash of relief to find them intact. He hadn't had his heart cut out. Somehow, beheading was so much less gruesome to contemplate than vivisection. And if that didn't prove how screwed-up her priorities were these days, she didn't know what would.

"Wallet." Red-Boar flipped the leather bifold. "Money's here. Cards. License." He cut a glance at Anna. "Ambrose Ledbetter."

"Oh," she said faintly. Just *oh*, as the world took a long, lazy spin around her and she dropped down onto a nearby log. "Damn."

They hadn't exactly been pals—Ledbetter was prickly on a good day, downright bitchy the rest of the time— but they'd known each other in passing. And now he was dead because of what he'd known. Because of what the *ajaw-makol* didn't want them to know.

Red-Boar stared down at the headless corpse but said nothing. Not that she should've expected anything more, but a pithy "Poor bastard" would've been nice.

Then again, the Nightkeeper didn't waste sympathy on the living; why would he give it to the dead?

After a long, shuddering moment, she forced herself to focus on the practicalities rather than the raw stump where Ledbetter's head should've been attached to his shoulders. "We should bury him properly. Animals will dig him up if we leave him like this."

There was no real reason to bring the body back to Skywatch, and she had a feeling he wouldn't mind being planted near a sacred cenote. Gods knew she wouldn't.

And where had *that* thought come from? When had she started thinking like a Nightkeeper rather than a wannabe soccer mom?

Since the barrier woke up and the pee stick started refusing to turn pink month after month, she admitted bitterly, at least to herself. If she couldn't be a mother, and she was a pretty sad excuse for a wife, she might as well be a princess.

There was little joy in the thought.

"He have any family?"

It took her a moment to process Red-Boar's question, another to frown. "Since when did you get sentimental?"

"Just wondering if anyone's going to raise a stink when he doesn't come home."

"The university will notice, and his students. But friends and family? Um . . ." She frowned. "I'm pretty sure he mentioned a woman once in passing."

"Girlfriend?"

She shook her head. "I don't know."

"You think anyone stateside is going to make trouble?"

Anna lifted one shoulder, staring down at the headless torso. "There's always a risk when you come down here for fieldwork. Families get used to it." Or they fell apart, which happened more often than the community liked to admit. "Besides, Ambrose was even more eccentric than the norm, and had the rep of disappearing for months at a time. Most likely this woman, or one of his students, will go to the university when they realize he's overdue. They'll contact the consulate, and either there'll be a quick search or the government will pretend there was, and everyone will wave their hands and have bene-fit dinners. 'Very sorry for your loss, he was a pioneer. Died the way he would've wanted, doing what he loved, blah, blah . . .' " She trailed off, staring at the hacked-through vertebrae and ragged flesh. "We can't bring him back with us. We'll have to rebury him here."

The question was, where?

They couldn't leave him where he was, first because the grave was far too shallow, and second because if another researcher discovered the site in the future, odds were that he—or she—would eventually want to punch through the cenote cap and study the artifacts that'd been tossed into the sacred well. The discovery of a modern burial atop the cenote would trigger way too many questions.

"Let's put him at the edge of the trees." She gestured to a sunny, pleasant-looking spot she thought the dour old researcher might've liked, assuming he got pleasure from anything other than making other researchers look like idiots.

Gods, she was going to miss knowing the old coot was somewhere on the earth plane with her, she thought, then winced again at hearing herself think like a Night-keeper. In that moment, Dick and her real life seemed very far away.

"Grab his shoulders," Red-Boar ordered. "I'll get his feet."

"Can't we—" Anna broke off, realizing that no, they couldn't. There really wasn't a better way to get Ledbet-ter from point A to point B.

Holding her breath, she grabbed Ledbetter's shirt near the collar, and nodded. "I'm ready."

He snorted. "Don't be such a girl. Get him by the pits."

"Fine," she said. "Pits it is." She forced herself to dig under and lift as Red-Boar tugged on the ankles, and the body came up from its thin covering of leaves and soil with a faint resistance and a noise she didn't want to think about. As they carried him across the clearing, she tried not to breathe through her nose. Not that mouth breathing was a big improvement, but she told herself the heavy, oily taste was purely her imagination.

"He's lighter than I expected," she said when they were about halfway across. Alive, Ledbetter had been nearly Red-Boar's size. Now she could handle her half of his weight without too much trouble.

"Ground's dry in the direct sunlight," Red-Boar said. "He's partway to mummy already."

"Any idea how long he's been here?"

Red-Boar pulled a small, collapsible shovel out of his pack, assembled it, and got to work digging a hole at the site she'd chosen. The ground was moist at the edge of the rain forest canopy, and the flimsy shovel cut through the humus with little effort.

Still, Red-Boar was puffing lightly when he answered, "You said he'd left the States a month ago?"

"That's what his assistant said." Anna looked back in the direction of the cenote as faint waves of energy prickled across her skin. "You think he's been dead that long?"

"Probably not. Critters would've gotten to him. I'd say a couple of days, tops."

Meaning they could've saved him if they'd been faster.

Red-Boar glanced over at her and shook his head. "Don't beat yourself up. It doesn't fix anything."

"I knew him," she said.

"Don't get the impression you liked him much."

"Still," she maintained. "Someone should grieve. He wasn't a bad man, just ornery."

He didn't say another word, just bent to his work. Ten minutes later, he had a credible grave dug, deep enough to foil the scavengers, and long enough to take a body that was nearly six feet, even without the head.

Anna frowned, looking at the corpse. How had she not noticed how big Ledbetter was before? He'd slouched, she remembered now, always hunched over some obscure text, ignoring all efforts at conversation. "He was a strange old man," she said thoughtfully.

"Now he's a dead old man. Let's get him planted and search the area. Maybe the *makol* missed his campsite, or the ruin we're looking for is nearby."

Both seemed like pretty thin chances, but that was what they were down to these days.

Steeling herself, Anna grabbed Ledbetter's arms and lifted, helping Red-Boar angle the body toward the hole.

"A little more to your left," he ordered, and she obeyed.

Loose dirt shifted beneath her foot and she wobbled, trying to get her balance, but lost her footing at the edge of the open grave.

And fell with a screech.

Red-Boar let go of the dead man's ankles, lunged forward, and grabbed her around the waist. She knew she should let go but she didn't move fast enough, and Ledbetter's shirt ripped and came away in her hands.

His body tumbled into the grave, leaving her standing in Red-Boar's arms, holding a dead man's shirt. Red-Boar's pulse hammered against her spine as he held her, warm and strong and bare chested, but those sensations were lost as Anna's heart stopped, simply stopped in her chest when she saw what Ledbetter's shirt had hidden.

Old, gnarled scar tissue covered the entirety of his inner right forearm, right where a Nightkeeper wore his marks.

CHAPTER TWENTY-ONE

Shock gripped Anna, disbelief thrumming as she stared down into the grave and came to the only conclusion she could. "Ledbetter was a Nightkeeper."

Despite the slouch, which had probably been designed to camouflage his true size, Ledbetter had been far too big to be a *winikin*, and there was no way the scar pattern was a coincidence.

"Looks that way." Red-Boar's voice was nearly inflectionless.

"He—" Anna broke off when her voice trembled. "Who *was* he?"

"I haven't a clue." He paused, then shrugged. "Doesn't change the fact that we can't take him with us and we can't waste time. Let's get him planted."

He dropped into the grave and quickly searched the body for other marks, other evidence of who Ledbetter had been and how he'd survived the Solstice Massacre. Finding nothing, he arranged the body in a more natural position. And though Red-Boar was trying to pretend it didn't matter, Anna could see that his shoulders were tight and that sadness shimmered in the air around him—a translucent hum of tears tinged red with anger.

He boosted himself out of the grave, then paused and looked down at the dead man. Then he stripped a jade circlet from his upper arm and tossed it in beside the bundle. The carved armband landed on Ledbetter's chest, just above his heart. An offering. A talisman to accompany the dead man through the underground river to Xibalba, and then out the other side to the sky.

"Wasn't that—" Anna broke off at Red-Boar's sharp look.

"It's not a sacrifice if it doesn't hurt."

Anna wished she had something to give for the journey, but she wasn't carrying anything appropriate. She touched the skull effigy, but let her hand drop without offering the precious yellow quartz. There was a line between sacrifice and stupidity. Still, her heart ached as he lifted the first shovelful of dirt and tossed it atop the carved jade.

Oddly, the noise made her think of Dick. What was he doing now? What did he think about the phone message she'd left saying that she wanted to take a break from the mess their marriage had become?

He hadn't called her back, which was probably an answer in itself.

"All the dead were accounted for," Red-Boar said, interrupting her thoughts. "Jox checked. I was the only one who wasn't a corpse." He drove the shovel into the piled earth and heaved it into the hole, where it fell on Ledbetter's body with a hollow, echoing sound.

"Except for the *winikin* and the babies who got away." She paused. "He didn't tell you about them."

"Because he doesn't trust me. Never did." Once a layer of soil covered the body, he used his booted feet to shove the bulk of the dirt back into place. "Don't really blame him, either. Not after I beat the crap out of him and took off."

Anna wanted to ask about those days, and about Rabbit's mother, but she knew those things didn't really matter anymore. What mattered was today. The next four years. So as Red-Boar tamped the last of the dirt into place, she asked, "Do you think Jox knew about Ledbetter?"

"No. If he'd known there was another magic user out there, he would've called him to the compound when the barrier reactivated." Red-Boar paused. "Which, along with the scars and the fact that the *boluntiku* didn't get him during the massacre, begs the question of whether he was a user at all.''

''He must've been,'' she argued. ''Otherwise how did the *ajaw-makol* find him? And why now?''

''Might not've had anything to do with magic. Might've followed the same thought process you did and figured he'd take out our best source of info on Kulkulkan and the Godkeepers before we came looking for him. Question is, what would Ledbetter have told us if we'd found him with his head attached?''

''No,'' Anna said softly. ''The real question is whether there are others like him.''

Red-Boar met her eyes, unblinking. ''Why don't you find out?''

Breath going thin because she didn't want to try and fail, especially not in front of him, she hesitated a moment before she nodded. Kneeling, she pressed her palms into the soil covering Ledbetter's body. Seeking the quartz effigy with her mind, she lightly jacked in, and then dropped her shields, opening herself to the impressions.

She got darkness. Gray static. An indistinct sense of longing.

Shaking her head, she climbed to her feet. ''Nothing.''

''You need to practice more.''

''You need to step off,'' she said with more weariness than heat. ''Don't assume I'm going to fall into line just because Strike did.''

''You have a responsibility to your bloodline.''

''I also have a responsibility to my husband and my students.'' She glanced over at him. ''Maybe that sounds small to you, but some of us are destined to do small things.''

''Not you. You would've made a good king.''

She stiffened at the suggestion—and the sudden spark of intensity behind it—but said only, ''Thank the gods for patrilinear inheritance, then.''

They stared at each other for a moment in silence before Red-Boar turned away. He said a prayer for the dead in the old language, then palmed his ceremonial knife to prick his elbow, which was one of the most honored autoletting sites. He handed over the blade without a word and Anna did the same, and they let their blood drip down onto the fresh grave.

"Safe journey, stranger," she whispered.

When it was done, they smoothed the disturbed earth above the sinkhole, then split up to search for Ledbetter's campsite. They could've searched together, might have been safer that way, but they both needed the distance. Traveling together had been bad enough. Sharing an experience like burying Ledbetter had been far worse.

Moving into the thicker growth beyond the clearing, she touched her effigy and sent out a faint questioning thread, not jacking in fully, but tapping the power and asking it to guide her to where Ledbetter had been. In theory. In practice her subconscious was blocking the hell out of her sight. And who could blame it? The last time she'd had a full-fledged vision, she'd shouted Lucius's name in Dick's ear.

Branches scratched her face and caught at her clothes as she pushed her way deeper into the rain forest, thorny fingers grabbing at her, begging for attention. *Where have you been?* the undergrowth seemed to say. *Where are you going?*

When she heard the words a second time and magic touched her skin, she stopped, wondering if she'd imagined it. "I can hear you," she said softly. "What do you want?"

She never in a million years expected a response.

But she got one.

The figure of a man appeared in front of her, coalescing out of the humid air. He was taller than she, but stick-thin and wrinkled, with obsidian eyes that had no whites.

Anna gasped and backpedaled, snagged her heel on a root, overbalanced, and fell on her ass. She froze there, her heart pounding as she gaped up at the figure, and pain seared the skin between her breasts where the effigy rested.

A *nahwal*. On earth.

Impossible.

But when she blinked and looked again, it was still

there. Then it turned and disappeared into the undergrowth.

"No!" She scrambled to her feet, pulse racing. "Come back!"

There was movement up ahead, a flash of motion that left the foliage undisturbed. Head spinning with power and desperation and a strange sense of shifted reality, Anna followed on shaky legs, running deeper and deeper into the forest along an ancient path.

Where was—*There!* Power rippled along her skin and she saw another flash of motion as the *nahwal* passed into a low cleft in the earth. Anna followed, flying along the path and ducking through the cave without hesitation, only briefly registering the carved lintel and square walls of a temple. Two steps into the cave, she was plunged into darkness.

Four steps in, the world dropped out from beneath her and she fell, screaming. She hit hard and her head banged against rock. Pain flared and pressure snapped tight in her chest, and for a second she thought she was flying. Then she thought she was drowning. Then burning.

Then there was nothing but blackness around her, inside her. The darkness lasted for minutes, maybe hours before she felt a hand grip hers, lending solidity to the world around her, and heard a voice that called her back from the edge.

"Gods help us." His harsh whisper roused her, though she wasn't capable of more than an answering moan. The world spun around her, made of blackness and pain.

"Sleepy," she whispered, the word coming out as little more than a puff of air. Lassitude cocooned her, warming her until even the pain seemed friendly rather than raw.

Red-Boar didn't answer. She heard the click of him flipping open his satellite phone, heard a bitter curse. "No signal." Then he was leaning over her, touching her gently, though she could barely feel it. "Come on. We've got to get you out of here."

He helped her sit up. That was when the nausea hit. Her vision kicked back in as she doubled over, retching. She saw too-bright light filtering in from outside, saw Red-Boar's forearm clamped across her torso, beneath her breasts, holding her upright as she gagged on bile and little else. The world slewed, but when she sagged down again, reaching for the ground and the blessed unconsciousness of sleep, he wrestled her to her feet, holding on to her forearms just beneath her elbows. "Anna," he snapped. "I need you to stay with me."

Closing her eyes against the painful glare from outside, she sucked in a deep breath, trying to settle the heaves. That was when she smelled blood. Lots of it.

Opening her eyes, she blinked to clear the spots that danced before her. Then she realized the spots were real—spatters of blood on the stone floor she'd been lying on, and on the carved walls nearby. Even some on a small pile of camping equipment tucked into a corner, behind a statue she thought she recognized as the goddess Ixchel. They were in a temple of some sort, she realized, though she didn't remember finding a temple. Come to think of it, she didn't remember anything after she'd ducked into a low-hanging cave mouth in pursuit of—

Everything froze within her.

"I saw a *nahwal*," she whispered. "I followed him."

"Hold your arms over your head," Red-Boar ordered, ignoring her. When she did as she was told, he moved away from her and started tearing strips from a man's checkered shirt. It was Ledbetter's, she realized. They were at his campsite. But what—

"Here." Red-Boar took the hands she'd crossed over her head, bringing them down to eye level. "This is going to hurt."

"What?" She didn't get it at first, but the moment she thought about it, really thought about it, she knew what she'd done. "Oh, no. I didn't. Please tell me I didn't."

She yanked her hands away from him and looked at her wrists. Bad idea. Gaping slashes crisscrossed the skin between her hands and her marks, leaking blood. "I didn't," she whispered. But she had.

Wrist cutting was the most extreme form of autosacrifice practiced by the ancient Nightkeepers, one intended to bring a warrior as close to death as possible, in the hopes that he—or she—would return with a message from the gods. That assumed, of course, that he or she didn't die from loss of blood.

Red-Boar took her hands and began to bind her wounds with the makeshift bandages. He didn't say a word. He didn't have to.

"How bad is it?" Anna asked through dry-feeling lips.

"Ugly but surface on the left, deeper on the right. You got a vein on that side." He finished tying off the second set of bandages, then crossed her arms over her chest with her hands just beneath her chin, and used a loop of cloth to form a makeshift sling that went behind her neck and connected one hand to the other, allowing her some freedom of motion while keeping her wrists higher than her heart.

His dark eyes locked on her with unfamiliar intensity. "Call your brother."

Strike could zap to their position and bring them home. They'd planned for him to do just that twelve hours from now.

Which would be too late.

Anna closed her eyes and concentrated, but got nothing. She shook her throbbing head as ravenous hunger surged alongside the nausea. "I'm tapped out." She'd used up her magical energies, but doing what? She'd sacrificed herself for a message; that much was clear. But she didn't remember getting a message, didn't remember anything after she'd run into the cave after the *nahwal*.

"The satellite phone's no good—I'm not sure if it's the signal, the battery, the system, or what." His throat worked when he swallowed. He locked eyes with her. "Can you walk?"

She shook her head. "You go. You'll get to satellite range or another phone faster if I'm not with you."

"No way," he said flatly. "Not after what just happened. The . . . thing you saw, whatever it was, could come back."

She shivered at the thought, and at the strange sense of longing it brought. *Would that be so bad?* something whispered inside her. Gray-green lassitude stole over her, making her want to lie down and nap. Dream.

"Anna!" Red-Boar shook her, snapping her back to painful reality. "Can. You. Walk?"

She whimpered, wanting to sleep, but nodded jerkily. "I'll try."

"Good enough." He combined the contents of both their packs, jettisoning all but the absolute necessities, then shouldered his bag along with Ledbetter's duffel. At her look, he shook his head. "I didn't shake out his underwear, but nothing jumped out at me." He looked around at the temple they were in. "This isn't the temple we're looking for. The information Strike wants may have died with Ledbetter."

Or else it's inside me. Anna frowned, trying to find a message amid the mush her brain had become. She got a faint sense of *copan* and grief, but nothing more. And she was tired. So very tired.

"Anna." Red-Boar shook her awake once again, his touch more gentle this time, his dark eyes worried. "Come on. We need to move."

She nodded numbly and followed him out, followed him along the machete-hacked trail until her entire world was concentrated in the center of his back, where she fixed her eyes and forced herself to put one foot in front of the other. She stumbled and fell, but righted herself and forged on. Stumbled and fell again, and this time couldn't get up.

Sleep, the voices told her. *Stay with us.*

Then strong arms gathered her up, lifting her. And the world slipped away.

Leah was tucked in next to Strike on the sofa in the great room of the mansion, reading another of Ambrose Ledbetter's journal articles on the Pyramid of Kulkulkan at Chichén Itzá, when the landline phone rang.

"Jox?" Strike called in the direction of the kitchen.

"Got it."

Leah glanced over. "There's a phone right beside you, you know. You could've answered."

"Yeah, but that's why I pay him the big bucks."

She snorted. "Please." Jox might not be on her buddy list, but she wasn't backing down on the *winikin*-are-people-too soapbox. Before she could say more, though, Jox stuck his head through the kitchen pass, his face sheet white. "Hit the speaker. We've got a problem."

Strike cursed and twisted, grabbing for the phone. Rabbit, Patience, and Alexis appeared from the billiard room on the opposite side from the kitchen, drawn by the *winikin*'s shout. Strike punched the speakerphone and turned up the volume. "What's wrong?"

There was a hiss of feedback, followed by a harsh breath and Red-Boar's voice. "You've gotta lock on and get us out of here. She's hurt bad."

"On my way," Strike said curtly, and the phone line went dead. His hand went to his hip and came up empty. *"Fuck!"*

"Use mine." Rabbit pulled his knife and tossed it.

Strike caught it on the fly, scored his palm until blood flowed free, closed his eyes . . .

And disappeared.

Strike blinked in a few feet up, moving fast, and smashed into the ground, churning up a good three-foot gouge in the soft loam before he stopped. Struggling to his feet, he fought to reorient. The rain forest was lush and green around him, and the air smelled of plants and warm earth and blood. He followed the latter scent and found Red-Boar crouched over something on the ground.

Anna.

Strike's heart pounded up into his throat as he dropped down beside his sister. She was deathly pale, unmoving, and blood had soaked through a pair of makeshift bandages at her wrists.

"Gods damn it!" Rage spiking through the fear, he spun on Red-Boar. "How could you let— Never mind." He cut himself off. "We'll deal with that later. Right now she needs a hospital."

He closed his eyes and thought of white walls and the smell of disinfectant, and a bathroom, generic and empty, safe for them to zap into. Then he thought of Albuquerque, though he'd been there only once. He hoped like hell the two threads would combine into a single address.

"You can't make the jump blind," Red-Boar said quickly. "Let's take her to the compound. We can—"

"We can what?" Strike interrupted. "Call for an ambulance? Screw that. Even a helicopter would take too long." He held out his hand, which still leaked blood. "Either grab on and boost me, or stay here. Your choice."

Red-Boar cursed, but he grabbed on and sent power to Strike. The boost clarified the yellow travel thread, though it still wasn't as strong as he would've liked. No choice, though. He wasn't even sure she was still breathing.

"Gods help us all," he muttered, grabbed on, and yanked.

Silence echoed deafeningly in the great room at Sky-watch.

Jox glared at Leah as if all this were somehow her fault. Patience held on to Rabbit's hand. Alexis had slipped out soon after Strike disappeared, probably to warn the others what was going down, and Leah stood there, waiting for the puff of displaced air that would signal their return. As she waited, she prayed.

God, she thought, *or gods—whatever—please let them make it back. Please let Anna be okay.* And though she knew it was small and self-serving, *Please let them figure out how to save me.*

"Come on," Jox muttered under his breath. "Come *on!*"

There was no zap of displaced air. But the phone rang.

Jox hesitated, and then hit the speakerphone. "Hello?"

"We're in Albuquerque. At a hospital. I'm not sure which one."

At the sound of Strike's voice, Leah exhaled a long, shuddering breath of relief. They'd made it back to the U.S., at any rate. She didn't want to think about how they'd gotten to the hospital, though, or she knew she'd get the shakes. He'd flipping jumped blind.

"How's Anna?" Jox's voice broke.

"They're working on her now." Strike's voice dropped. "She sliced her wrists, nearly bled out before Red-Boar found her. He says she saw a *nahwal*, followed it into a temple, and cut herself."

Jox's eyes flicked to Leah. "What about Ledbetter?"

"Dead. And apparently a Nightkeeper. I'll explain when I get back."

In the shocked silence that followed, Leah cleared her throat. "Do you want me to drive out?"

"No, stay put. Red-Boar's already going to have to do some serious mind-scrubbing on our way out, and I don't want to add any more brains to his list. Besides, it's probably not a good idea for you to be out in the open right now."

Because it was in the best interests of the *ajaw-makol* and the *Banol Kax* to keep her alive through the equinox, thus destroying both Kulkulkan and the skyroad.

"Of course." She paused, wanting to say something, but not sure what. So in the end, she went with a lame, "Take care."

"You, too." He paused. "Jox?"

"Still here."

"Put Carter on Ambrose Ledbetter. I want to know who he was, where he came from, who he hung with. Everything."

Jox stilled. "You think there are more survivors out there?"

"If we're damn lucky."

In the hospital, Anna survived and stabilized. But she didn't wake up.

Twelve hours passed, twenty-four. Seventy-two. The equinox approached and Strike didn't leave her side. He sat in the private room he'd put on the Nightkeeper Fund's credit card, registering her as Alexis Gray because Alexis didn't have any family to notify and Anna did.

Maybe—probably . . . okay, definitely—it was wrong to keep Anna's husband out of the loop, but he'd be a complication they absolutely couldn't afford. So it was just Strike watching over her, along with Red-Boar, who stayed nearby in case they needed his talent for damage control.

The doctors came and went and shook their heads when all the tox screens came back negative, indicating that she hadn't OD'd in addition to cutting her wrists, but not able to explain why she was still in a coma. They sent Strike sidelong glances and assured him that sometimes suicides fooled even their closest family members, that he shouldn't blame himself. But they didn't know the half of it.

He'd sent her to find Ledbetter, knowing she wasn't fully trained or in control of her own powers. He'd been so damned sure he was making the right call sending Red-Boar as backup, but the bastard had left her unprotected and she'd nearly died. Might still die, if they couldn't figure out how to reach her. Each hour, he could feel her slipping farther into the mist. And each hour, he could feel the stars and planets aligning, moving closer to the equinox.

In less than a day they would meet the *ajaw-makol* at the intersection. Jox assured him that the team would be ready. The question was, would their leader?

Strike knew he had too many priorities, all of them vying for the top spot. Who was he, king or man? Lover or brother? Leader, savior, or just a guy with a business degree and some landscaping experience?

Fuck, he didn't know anymore. And he wasn't figuring it out sitting here.

He stood and crossed the room. Stuck his head out and snapped, "Get in here."

Red-Boar obeyed without a word. His eyes were down, his expression set, and he wore a brown button-down shirt and matching ball cap he'd gotten from somewhere, making a nod at the penitent's robes he'd hidden behind for so long.

Strike was having none of it. Rage spiked through him at the realization that so much of what had gone wrong since the barrier reactivated—from the burning of Jox's garden center to Anna's condition now—were thanks to Red-Boar and his fucking indifference. Anger burned, hot and hard, and for a second, he wanted to grab the bastard, yank him into the barrier, and leave him there. Let the *nahwal* have him.

Deep breath, he counseled himself, fighting the god's anger alongside his own. Unfortunately, barriering Red-Boar wasn't an option. Despite his questionable loyalties, the older Nightkeeper still had the best boosting skills among them.

That didn't mean Strike had to put up with the other shit, though.

So when the door closed behind the older man, he said, low and controlled, "Enough. I've had enough of the martyr shit, enough of the Yoda routine, and especially enough of the 'watch out for Red-Boar, he's got PTSD and doesn't always react normally' crap."

The other man's head came up. His dark eyes locked onto Strike's, and in their depths he saw something he never expected to see. He saw anger. Hatred. Rage. "Watch your step, boy."

Strike almost retreated, but knew he couldn't afford to, knew this had been coming for a long time. He kept his voice level. "I am my father's son."

Red-Boar bared his teeth. "That doesn't make you king."

"What, you think you should be in charge because you've got seniority?" Following Red-Boar's glance, he said, "Or Anna?" He locked eyes with his onetime mentor, still fighting the urge to flatten the bastard, to cow him, to make him admit—

"Admit what?" Red-Boar said, picking up on the thought because they were so close. "That you're the king? Not until you fucking act like it. Not until you accept the Manikin scepter and say the words. Until then, you're just Scarred-Jaguar's son, as far as I'm concerned. A weak, whiny little boy who hid underground with his sister and their babysitter while the rest of us fought."

"I was a child," Strike gritted, chest tightening on a hard, hot ball of grief, of denial.

"You were a prince," Red-Boar countered, as though that made all the difference in the world. "If you want to be king—and I'm thinking that's a big 'if'—then stop screwing around, stop letting other people tell you what to do, and make some godsdamned decisions!"

They were very close together, arguing low-voiced so it wouldn't carry out into the hall. Strike was hyperaware of Anna lying there, motionless save for the regular rise and fall of her chest. The doctors said they couldn't do anything more. Red-Boar said he couldn't do anything, period. Now, Strike wondered if that was the truth.

"Wake her up," he said. "Now."

Something flashed in the other man's eyes—surprise, maybe, or fear. But he shook his head. "I can't."

"Can't or won't?"

"Can't," he insisted. "Not here, anyway. Not even I can fog that many memories."

"Then start fogging the ones you need to, because we're leaving in five minutes."

"But—"

"You want me to start making some fucking decisions?" Strike leaned in, lowering his voice to a hiss. "Consider this one made. You've got five minutes to work your magic, mind-bender. Either the doctors and nurses think she's being discharged and there aren't any problems, or I'm leaving you in the barrier. Got it?"

Red-Boar didn't say a word. But damned if he didn't do exactly as Strike had ordered. He made a circuit of the hospital floor, shaking hands and touching shoulders, spending the most time on Anna's doctors and the nurses running the computers.

When he returned, he nodded. "It's done. Everyone here thinks she was discharged to a rehab facility. Anyone coming on later will get the same info from the computers."

"Good. We're out of here. I called Jox to give him the heads-up." Strike lifted Anna, cradling her against his chest. Then he touched Red-Boar, completing the circuit. He was pissed enough, the route to Skywatch familiar enough, and Leah's pull strong enough that he didn't need a blood sacrifice to power the three-person transport—he was already there. All he had to do was close his eyes, find the thread, and yank.

The great room materialized around them, the floor slapping against the soles of his boots. He staggered and nearly went down, and then Jox was there, shoving a shoulder into his armpit to get him stabilized.

They were all there, Strike saw as his vision cleared. The *winikin*. The Nightkeepers. And Leah. His people. His responsibility.

"I've got her," the *winikin* murmured, taking Anna's limp form with surprising ease, given that she was a full head taller than he and probably close to the same weight. He bent close and murmured, "Poor child." The endearment should've seemed ridiculous given that she was closing in on forty, but somehow it was exactly right.

Strike reached out for Leah, took her hand. At the touch of her skin on his, he felt the zing of connection, the flow of energy that was theirs alone. And as the golden spark of the two of them together crackled in the air, Anna woke up, sucking in a deep breath and opening her eyes.

Only they weren't her eyes, Strike saw with dawning horror. They were flat obsidian black.

"I have a message for you," she said, but it wasn't her speaking. It was the *nahwal*, staring up at nothing and speaking with its emotionless, multitonal voice.

Everything inside Strike went cold and hard in an instant. "Tell me," he grated.

"The creator god dies because you have not acted."

Leah dug her nails into his palm. Strike tightened his grip on her and said, "Tell me how to save them both, the god and the woman." *Please, gods, let there be a way.*

"For the god to live the woman must die. There is no other way."

"There must be," he rasped. He refused to believe the gods had set him up only to fail her, only to force him to make a choice between the life he wanted and the duty he'd been born into. There had to be another way.

"There is not." The *nahwal* locked its flat black eyes on him. "Make your choice, Nightkeeper. Make it well."

With that, the *nahwal*'s time was up. Anna didn't know how she knew that, but she did, just as she knew that she'd be going with the creature when it returned to the mists. They were bound now. Inseparable. She hadn't just come close to dying back at the temple; she *had* died. The *nahwal* had simply kept her alive until the god-bound power of Leah and Strike together had triggered the message.

Now, it was time for her to leave.

The gray-green mist swirled around her, forming a funnel, a vacuum that drew her away from the reality of Skywatch. She felt herself being sucked down, felt herself accelerating without moving.

The outside world dimmed, and her heart cried out for the people she'd loved—for Dick and Lucius, for her brother and the others.

She heard Strike call her name from far away, heard the crash of furniture being overturned, and men shouting. Arguing. Then pain flared in her palm, bright and white amidst the deepening dark gray, and a hand gripped hers.

Power blasted through the connection, jolting through the mist, and suddenly that someone was there, inside her head, shouting at her.

"Gods damn it, this way!" He tugged her away from the funnel, away from the *nahwal*'s might, and she heard the creature roar in denial. Then the vortex collapsed.

And she woke up staring into Red-Boar's eyes.

That night, which was the night before the equinox, Leah eased away from Strike's sleeping form and watched the faint light of the desert starscape play across his strong features.

Something lodged tight in her throat: a wish, maybe, or a prayer.

Don't make him choose, she wanted to ask the gods, but didn't know how. Besides, the *nahwal* had already said the choice was his to make.

Or maybe, in the end, it was hers, too.

She touched his face and the strong line of his shoulder, and saw his fierce expression lighten, as though he'd felt her caress even in sleep. Her emotions shuddered very near the surface, strong and frightening. Technically, they'd known each other for nearly three months, since the summer solstice. If she believed that what had happened before would happen again, then by her relationship clock their time was up. But she didn't want it to be, damn it. She wanted . . .

She wanted the impossible. She wanted him to choose her even though it meant going against logic, against his advisers, hell, against the gods.

Restless, she rose from the mattress, pulled on a pair of loose yoga pants and one of his T-shirts, and padded from the room, headed for the kitchen. The halls were dark, the mansion quiet around her, suggesting that everyone else was asleep, or close to it.

It was a freeing thought. She'd grown used to living with the others and having to create the illusion of privacy. Now, it felt good to be alone in the night.

Until she stepped into the kitchen and saw Jox.

The *winikin* sat at the marble-topped breakfast bar, with his skinny ass perched on a stool and his pointy chin in his hands. His eyes were closed, and a small pipe sat in a saucer nearby, emitting a thin curl of *copan*-scented smoke.

Leah slammed on the brakes and was in the process of doing a one-eighty when he said, "We could both pretend we didn't see each other, but that's not really the point, is it?"

She stopped and stiffened her spine before she turned. "And what *is* the point?"

A piece of her really wished the two of them could find a way to get along. She admired the hell out of the *winikin*'s fierce loyalty to Strike and Anna, and the traditions of their culture. Unfortunately, it was those very traditions that put them at odds. She didn't fit into his worldview. Never would.

He said simply, "Neither of us wants him to have to choose."

She stilled as he echoed the sentiment she'd been thinking only moments earlier. She gave a cautious nod. "Agreed."

"So what are you going to do about it?" The *winikin*'s expression remained impassive, but there was something new in his voice, something that wasn't usually there on the rare occasion he spoke to her. It sounded an awful lot like sympathy, which Leah didn't like one bit.

"Don't go there," she said. *Please don't go there.*

"Do you have an alternative?"

She took a deep breath that did nothing to settle the sudden queasiness in her stomach, and looked away. "No."

After a silent moment, he said, "Self-sacrifice isn't a sin to the Nightkeepers. It's the ultimate way for a magic user to honor the gods."

She wet her lips, forced the words. "And wouldn't that be convenient? It'd get me out of your precious house and leave the field free for one of the others." She paused, hating the hollow ache that took over her chest at the thought. "Who would you hook him up with? Alexis? Jade? Someone else? Wonder if Ledbetter's got a daughter."

"It wouldn't matter if he did," Jox said softly. "It doesn't take an *itza'at* to know that you're it for Strike. If you die, he'll rule alone."

Emotion was a brutal gut-punch that had tears welling. "Yet you'd rather that than have us try again to bring the god through during the equinox."

"My duty is to protect the son of the jaguar king, and the Nightkeepers." He glanced at her. "For what it's worth, I'm very sorry."

"Maybe Jade will find something useful in Ledbetter's journal."

The *winikin* nodded. "Maybe."

But what was the likelihood she'd manage it in the next twenty hours or so?

CHAPTER TWENTY-TWO

Red-Boar stayed with Anna through the night, making sure she didn't succumb again to the *nahwal*'s pull. Problem was, having him in her bedroom seriously freaked her out. The two of them had always rubbed each other wrong, partly because they understood each other too well. Now he was sitting in a chair next to her bed, wearing drawstring pants and a fleece, both in penitent's brown. Like she was really going to fall asleep with him there.

"I'm fine, really," she said. "You can leave anytime."

"And if the *nahwal* comes back, they'd have to come get me to climb inside your head and kick the bastard out again, which would take time you wouldn't have." He folded his arms across his chest, and she worked very hard not to notice the slide of muscle beneath the soft material of his shirt.

Forcing herself to focus on what he'd said rather than how he looked—and since when did *that* matter to her?—she said, "You wouldn't be here unless you wanted to be, so ergo, you want to talk to me about something. So spill it, old man, and get out of my room so I can rest."

He scowled. "I'm only eight years older than you, for gods' sake."

Damned if he wasn't right, she realized as she did the math. He'd been married and a father at the time of the massacre, but he'd started young. "What do you want?" she persisted, knowing there had to be something.

He shoved a glass of juice across the nightstand in her direction, nearly dumping it on her. "Drink your OJ. You'll need the energy."

"For what, exactly?"

"I want you to go back into the barrier."

"Wait." She held up both hands, sloshing the OJ. "Whoa. I thought the point was to keep me *away* from the *nahwal*. Now you want me to go back in?"

"I'll go with you." He paused. "We need more information."

Her skin chilled. "You can't use the three-question spell until the actual equinox."

"I know. That's why I need you. The *nahwal* has marked you. It will come if you call, answer if you ask."

"Maybe." She paused. It didn't take a flying leap of intuition to guess where this was going, what he wanted her to do. "But you need to get something through your thick skull right now. I don't want to lead the Nightkeepers. I don't even want to be here. Maybe instead of charging into the barrier, you should be asking yourself why you're having so much trouble accepting Strike as leader."

"Because he hasn't accepted it himself," said the older Nightkeeper—though he was right, damn it, that he wasn't that much older than her.

Before, she'd been a teenager and he an adult. Now they were both adults, which gave her the guts to say, "You don't have the right to make that call. The kingship passes from father to son unless the line is broken. It hasn't been broken. Strike is our father's son. He is king, whether he likes it or not."

"He doesn't want it."

"Neither do I." She leveled a finger at him. "So why put me in the same position and think anything's going to be different?"

"Because you're different."

"That's right. He stayed in the program. I didn't." Anna gave up all pretense at resting and sat up, pulling the bedclothes up around her in a protective tepee, even though she was wearing light cotton pj's beneath. "Don't depend on me. I'm not the one you want."

When he didn't say a damn thing, she froze. "That's it, isn't it? You want an alliance. Me running the show, with you as my mate. Me for the bloodline, you for the leadership."

Shock and betrayal tangled with something darker, more tempting. It might even work, she had to admit inwardly. Jox and the *winikin* would never support Red-Boar in a bid for power, but they might support her, support the bloodline.

He met her stare for stare. "You had feelings for me once."

She snorted. "I was sixteen. You were the only guy I knew who was taller than me. Besides, you were mourning Cassie and the boys. That made you safe."

Pain flickered across his normally impassive features. After a moment, he said, "Do you know how long it's been since I heard that name? Since anyone mentioned them aloud?"

"This won't bring them back. Going against succession won't fix anything."

"If your father had listened to Gray-Smoke and Two-Hawk . . ." He trailed off after naming the king's closest advisers, who had normally taken opposite sides in any debate, but had been united in begging him to ignore the visions and wait for the end-time before leading the Nightkeepers to battle.

"That doesn't mean Strike is wrong now," she said, but wasn't entirely sure she believed it herself.

His look said he'd caught the hesitation. "Two jaguar rulers. Two sets of visions that go against tradition, against the prophecies and the writs. How can you not see the parallels?"

"I see them." She frowned, wanting to support her brother's born role but not willing to blindly follow tenets she'd learned as a child and walked away from as an adult. "I'm just not convinced history is always destined to repeat itself."

" 'What has happened before will happen again,' " he quoted.

She waved him off. "Too easy. The world isn't built on aphorisms and it doesn't march to the beat of thousand-year-old prophecies. Think about it . . . Godkeeper issue aside, who would you rather have leading the charge, you and me or the rightful king and his mate?"

"His *human* mate, you mean?"

"She's it for him," Anna said softly. "Don't you remember what that felt like?" The words brought a faint pang, because she'd found it with Dick, though she couldn't say for sure they had it anymore.

"Fine. Great." Red-Boar turned his scarred palms to the sky. "Which just puts us in an even crappier position, because when it comes down to it, he's going to choose the woman over the gods. We need to stop him from doing something really stupid."

"Or you could trust him to make the right decision."

"Look where trusting your father got me."

And she really couldn't argue that. He and so many others had trusted Scarred-Jaguar to know what was right, and they'd died for it. Red-Boar might have survived the battle, but everything important that was inside him had been killed that night.

"I won't lead," she said finally. "I'm sorry."

He sat for a moment in silence, then nodded and stood. "I'll let you rest."

She waited until he reached the door before she said softly, "Hey."

"Yeah?" He looked back, his expression inscrutable.

"Don't do anything stupid."

"Define 'stupid.'"

The trace of arrogance in his voice reminded her of the brash young warrior all the girls had sighed over, even after he'd married and become a father. More, she remembered how that had changed him, made him a man, even in her childhood perception. "Before you do anything, ask yourself whether you'll be proud to own your actions in front of Cassie and the boys when you finally reach the sky."

Her only answer was the slam of the door at his back.

* * *

Leah slept poorly and woke the morning of the equinox feeling strung-out and twitchy.

It wasn't just her conversation with Jox that had her on edge, though it hadn't exactly been fun to have her lover's defacto father tell her to do the world a favor and kill herself. There was something in the air, itching beneath her skin and making her jumpy. Restless.

Twelve hours and counting.

She opened her eyes to find Strike awake, propped up on one elbow, staring at her as though he was trying to memorize her and commit every last moment they were together to long-term storage in his brain. Or maybe that was what she was feeling.

"We should talk," she said, her voice raspy with morning huskiness.

"Let's not." He leaned into her and covered her mouth with his, and though she knew it was a stall, she also knew it might be one of the last times they were together.

Opening her mouth to his kiss, she buried her fingers in his thick hair, hooked a leg over his hip, and offered herself to the moment, to the man she wished she could claim as her own. They strained together, touching, tasting, and the heat built as it always did when they were together. Only this time there was an edge of desperation—theirs, the god's, she didn't know. But she knew the end was near; she tasted it in the bold possessiveness of Strike's kiss and felt it in herself—a sense of needing to take a piece of him with her.

Then he shifted against her, poised to enter her, and she saw the question in his eyes. Tears threatened as she nodded and he slid inside without protection, skin on skin, tacit acknowledgment that after tonight it probably wouldn't matter whether she conceived.

It mattered right then, though. It mattered in the feel of him within her, the sense that she was truly taking him inside her and holding a piece of him close to her heart. She pressed her cheek to his as they moved and found their rhythm, drawing out the pleasure, delaying the moment when they'd have to deal with reality.

Soon though, too soon and yet not fast enough, the

heat built; the tempo changed as he thrust and withdrew, thrust and withdrew, pounding into her, racing with her to the peak. They came together with strangled cries and a rush of love so intense Leah almost closed her eyes against it, denying the emotion. But she didn't. She kept her eyes wide-open, looking into his and seeing the love there. Seeing the heat and the mad glory of what they'd become together.

Then it was past and the heat faded. The world came back into focus around them. And there was no excuse not to have the conversation they were both dreading.

Drawing away from him, Leah touched his cheeks, his chin, the strong line of his nose. When he lifted a hand to do the same to her, she saw his forearm marks, stark black against his skin. She caught his hand and pressed her lips to the glyphs, kissed each one, then kissed the raised weal of the sacrificial scar that crossed his palm.

"Leah," he said, curling his fingers around to cup her face.

"We need to talk about it."

"There's nothing to discuss," he said, his voice going autocratic in a way that was necessary in Strike the leader, but set her teeth right the hell on edge in the bedroom.

"Try again," she said, lowering her voice in warning. *Watch your step, Ace.*

His eyes went cool, though she sensed the heat within him, knew it was a calculated move. "I'm going to try to bring the god through into me," he said, like it was no big deal and the obvious choice. "Jade's working on finding the transition spell as we speak."

Leah's skin chilled even as anger flashed hard and hot in her veins. "And you're just now mentioning this? What do the others think of the plan, given that, oh, there's a good chance that you'll turn into a *makol*? That's why Nightkeeper males aren't supposed to enter the Godkeeper ritual, isn't it? Too much aggression in their psyches, running too close to the darkness."

"It's my decision." But he looked away, not meeting her eyes.

"That's bullshit and you know it." She grabbed his

jaw and turned him to face her. "You're not just a guy, Strike. You're the frigging king."

"I'm the king's son," he said, his jaw setting beneath her fingertips. "Until I take the scepter, the greatest sacrifice doesn't apply."

"Which doesn't make it right for you to risk yourself like this." She felt a panicked, trapped fluttering in her chest, a sense that this was history repeating itself all over again. And though she'd wanted him to care enough to buck the prophecy and fight the gods themselves for her, now that he was offering to do just that she saw the desire for what it was: a pretty dream, a selfish wish. It wasn't a real option, wasn't truly what she wanted him to do.

"It's my choice," he maintained stubbornly.

"No. It isn't." She leaned in hoping he'd listen. "Think about it rationally. If I . . ." She stumbled over the word "die," found a neutral euphemism. "If I go before the equinox, Kulkulkan will be freed to return to the sky and you'll have a chance to bring him or another god through to earth. Alexis could handle it, or Patience. Bonus with her, because she's already got a Nightkeeper mate."

His eyes darkened and his voice went rough with the god's anger, with his own. "You want to die?"

"No!" she said quickly, then softer, "No. But I don't want to live knowing everyone else's days are numbered because of me."

"How about having a little faith?"

"This is all about faith," she snapped, hating that they had to fight about this, hating that each of their options was worse than the last. "I'm choosing to believe that the end of the world is coming, and you and the Nightkeepers are our best chance of stopping that from happening. I'm choosing to believe that there's a flying-serpent god stuck somewhere between the earth and sky because I'm alive, and I'm choosing to believe my death will free it and give you the best possible chance of stopping the next stage in the countdown, or at least the best chance to bring other gods through and increase your

powers to the point that you can beat the *Banol Kax*."
She blew out a long breath, trying to ease the pressure
in her chest. Her voice cracked a little when she said,
"If that isn't faith, I don't know what is."

He slid his hand from her cheek to the back of her
head, tangling his fingers in her hair and holding hard,
as though he meant to keep her there and never let her
go. "I'm talking about having faith in me. Trust me; I've
thought this out. Having me cast the transition spell and
bring the darkness through is the best answer. Then you
and I are the Godkeeper together. Hell, I'm pretty sure
I'm halfway there already—what is all this anger I've
been dealing with if it's not the dark side of Kulkulkan?"

It's you, she wanted to say. *It's your anger, your frustration.* But instead she said, "Whether it's Kulkulkan or
not, the anger is a problem. It'll make you skew too
hard toward the darkness."

A muscle ticked at the corner of his jaw. "I'm strong
enough not to turn *makol*."

"You can't know that, even if you had the spell," she
whispered, gripped with fear that his stubbornness and
his ego would take him too far. "It's too much of a risk."

"It's my decision."

"All due respect, no, it's not, no matter how many
times you say it."

"Don't use your cop voice on me," he growled, eyes
flashing.

She pulled away from him and sat up, pulling the
sheet with her. Anger rising to match his, she snapped,
"Then stop acting like a spoiled prince. Stop ducking
the scepter and pretending that's going to solve anything.
You can't have everything you want—life doesn't work
that way, not even yours."

She knew those were fighting words, but part of her
wanted the fight, welcomed it. They needed to burn off
some of the tension and anger, and if they ended up
pissed at each other, it'd be so much easier to do what
needed to be done.

But he didn't fight back. He rose up and gathered her
into his arms, holding her close. "I'm sorry, Leah. I can't

let you do what I know you're planning." He chanted a quick spell before she could react, and sleep rose up to claim her.

As the grayness rose up to claim her, she slurred, "Bastard." Then she collapsed, knowing he'd catch her when she fell.

She was going to be pissed when she woke up, Strike knew, and there was a good chance she'd never forgive him for cheating her out of her revenge on Zipacna. But he'd rather have her alive and hating his guts than dead because she'd gotten caught up in a fight that wasn't even really hers. So he carried her down to the lower level of the mansion, into the storeroom he'd already set up with a bed and chair, makeshift chamber pot, small refrigerator, and a pile of books.

It was the best he could do. And she was going to despise him for it.

"I'm sorry, Blondie." He arranged her on the bed and pulled a blanket over her against the cool of the lower level. "It's better this way." He would present himself at the altar beneath Chichén Itzá and offer himself up to take the whole of Kulkulkan, severing the god's connection to her and bringing all its magic into him. He would be both Godkeeper and Nightkeeper, sacrificing any hope of a future with her for the sake of her safety.

At least, that was the plan. Jade had better hurry up with the spell, though.

Bending, Strike touched his lips to Leah's cheek, telling himself there'd be time later for them to work things out, for her to learn to trust him. But as he straightened and turned away, it sure as hell felt like he was saying good-bye.

Which was bad enough. Worse was stepping out into the hallway to find Jox standing there, arms crossed, expression thunderous.

"Don't start." Strike locked the storeroom door with an old-fashioned padlock and stuck the key in his back pocket. Then he fixed his *winikin* with a look. "I want your word that she stays put."

Jox's face creased. "Think about what you're doing. Please."

"I know exactly what I'm doing. Your word." Strike's chest went tight at the knowledge that this could be the breaking point of his relationship with his *winikin*, too. Dropping his voice, he said, "I wouldn't ask this of you if I didn't believe. Please."

"Your father believed in his course, too."

"Your word. Or I lock you in there with her."

Jox tipped his head in the barest of nods. "You have my word. And my disappointment."

"Noted." Strike turned on his heel and headed for the stairs, feeling as if the whole world were against him, and not entirely sure he gave a shit.

When Leah awoke, for a moment she thought it was a new day, that she'd somehow made it through the equinox. Then she got a good look around and remembered what had happened in the bedroom. From there, she could easily guess where she'd wound up. Locked in the freaking cellar.

"Goddamn it!" She launched herself off the folding cot and hurled herself at the door. "Strike! Don't do this!"

She grabbed the knob, twisted it, and gave the heavy panel a serious hip check.

And went flying out into the hall.

She stopped, stunned, standing in a dimly lit hallway, chest heaving while her brain scrambled to catch up. The door wasn't locked. Yet Strike had clearly set the room up as her cell . . . which meant someone else had let her out. And she could guess who'd done it.

"Thank you, Jox," she said under her breath, though there was a bite of sarcasm to the words, because they both knew he'd done it so she could kill herself.

Fine, she said as she headed up the stairs as quietly as she could, keeping a sharp ear for any movement up ahead. *But I'm not going out alone.* If she had to die, she was damn well taking Zipacna with her.

He was going to be at the sacred chamber that

evening—it was a given. Strike and the others planned to arrive two hours before the equinox, when the secret door leading down to the hidden tunnels opened up.

Well, she was betting on Zipacna being earlier than that. And she was going to be waiting when he did. Carter had it all set for her—her plane tickets were waiting at the airport, and the weapons and jade-tips she'd paid too much to have smuggled across the border were waiting in a storage facility near Chichén Itzá. She just needed a change of clothes and her passport and she was good to go.

That is, until she, snagged her cell phone, and found a text message waiting for her, sent from an unfamiliar number.

Do you understand yet that the Nightkeepers must kill you to set their god free? Meet me in Pueblo Bonito if you want to live. And the bastard had the balls to sign it, *Love, Vince,* though he hadn't used Vince's phone.

Anger flared alongside adrenaline, and Leah bared her teeth in a triumphant smile. Apparently Zipacna was looking for her, too. Good. That'd save her the trip to Mexico.

Now all she had to do was make sure they both got dead before the zero hour.

Strike knelt on the footprint mat in the sacred chamber that'd been his parents', pressed his knife-scored hands to the *chac-mool* where he'd loved Leah the night before, and bowed his head in prayer.

A dull ache thumped at the back of his skull, drumming with his heartbeat. The barrier was thinning—he could feel it in the anger that curled inside him, dark and tempting, and in the heat that flowed in his blood.

"Gods help me make the right choice," he said, hoping like hell they were listening. "Help me to know the difference between what I want to do and what I ought to do." Those were the right words, the proper ones. But they weren't at all what was in his heart, and knowing it, knowing he was in serious trouble, he said, "Kulkulkan. Creator god. There's got to be a way to save you both. Tell me how. I'll do it. I'll do anything."

For a moment there was nothing. Then there was a flicker in his peripheral vision. Another. His attention snapped to the obsidian mirror above the altar, where torchlight reflected in strange patterns. Stranger patterns, he realized, than they'd been making before.

"Please," he whispered, and felt the anger stir within him. The power.

The reflected flames stirred. Intertwined. Formed a shape, then a scene, and all of a sudden he was looking at the grad student's apartment, only not as he'd seen it, but a scene from before his arrival, when the idiot was reading from the codex fragment, his lips moving with the ancient words.

Then the fire picture was gone, and the flames were only flames.

Strike blinked. Blinked again.

And got it. It was the damn transition spell.

"It's the same spell," he said aloud. "The *makol*, the gods. Same transition spell." That was why Leah had wound up hooked to Kulkulkan at the solstice—Zipacna had enacted the transition spell to make himself an *ajaw-makol*, and in doing so had opened not only the passage to Xibalba, but the skyroad as well.

It was the same. Fucking. Spell. What mattered was the orientation of the user, good versus evil. Only they didn't have the spell, he realized. Lucius had burned it.

"Damn it!" He slammed his palms on the altar and pushed away. Then he froze.

Maybe they did have the spell. Red-Boar had wiped the guy's memories, which meant he'd experienced them. He'd heard the spell. Odds were, he'd filed it—the brain of a mind-bender was a strange, convoluted place.

Question was, would he give it up?

"Only one way to find out." Strike strode from the royal suite, combat boots thudding as the thick bedroom carpet gave way to the tiled hallway. He hesitated near the stairs going down to the basement, but knew he should stay the hell away from Leah just now. The Nightkeepers were leaving in an hour; they'd be back after the equinox. That'd be soon enough to let her out and try to make amends.

Gods willing.

His heart ached with what he'd been forced to do to her, and with the fear that there wouldn't be an "after" for them. But he set all that aside—or tried to—burying it deep as he strode out the back to Red-Boar's cottage and slammed through the door without knocking. "I need you to—"

He broke off because Red-Boar wasn't in his usual spot at the kitchen table. Rabbit sat there instead, his hoodie pulled way down, his shoulders hunched.

"Where's your father?"

Rabbit didn't answer immediately. When he did, his voice broke. *"Kuyubal-mak."*

Strike stiffened. "What did you do that needs forgiving?"

"I unlocked the storeroom."

Everything inside Strike went cold, and he slapped at his back pocket reflexively, finding the padlock key still there. "How?"

"He told me not to tell you I can telekine, too." The teen looked up at Strike, his hood falling back to reveal tear-reddened eyes. "He had me text her cell, too, and tell her to meet him up at Bonito. He said he didn't want to do it here, after everything that's already happened."

This time Strike didn't try to fight the rage. "Do what?" he grated out, though he already knew.

Rabbit gulped miserably. "Kill her."

The landscape near Pueblo Bonito was harshly beautiful, and dotted with the remains of soaring stone buildings erected in the first millennium by the Chacoans. Like the Maya, they had been great astronomers and architects. And, like the Maya, theirs had been an incredibly complex civilization that had flourished for hundreds of years—and then vanished within a few decades.

Broken walls made of stone and wood speared up from the ground or crumbled down along cliffsides, and pteroglyphs paid homage to the sun and stars, and as Leah finally pulled up near the Bonito ruins, she felt what she thought was the hum of magic in the air.

She hoped to hell it was because if she had access to

the magic as the equinox approached, her chances of killing the *makol* were that much better.

Although Pueblo Bonito was a national park, and had its own visitors' center up the road, the ruin itself was deserted. Which she figured was a good thing—witnesses would be a problem with what she was going to have to do next.

Trying really hard to think of it as a tactical exercise rather than the suicide mission it needed to be, she loaded her weapons belt from the knapsack, racking the MACs she'd snagged from the armory and making sure her knives were close at hand for the head-and-heart deal. Then she sat for a second, knowing that once she got out of the Jeep there was no turning back.

Closing her eyes, she sought the mental ghosts that were her constant companions. Matty. Nick. The man she'd known as Vince was gone now, dispelled by the knowledge that he'd been part of Zipacna's elaborate setup. But the thought of her parents joined the memories of her brother and partner. Strike was there, too, heat existing alongside grief. She knew he'd never forgive her for what she was about to do, but she couldn't stand by and watch him gamble the world on the slim chance that his crazy plan would work. He risked dooming the world with his stubbornness, and she'd be damned if she let him do it.

"This is the only way," she said, her mouth gone dry with dread.

Then, knowing there was no place for second thoughts where she was going, she focused on the dead, on the ghosts. On the people Zipacna had killed, what he'd done to them. And though she had gotten the lightness of the god, she found her own anger within, and fanned it to a flame. When she was good and pissed, and carrying a cold, murderous rage that she hoped would see her through Zipacna's extermination and then her own, she got out of the Jeep and slammed the door.

The ruins were spread out in front of her, several acres of walls and doorways, of square rooms and sunken circular kivas connected by mazelike passageways. There was no sign of life save for the cry of a hawk high above.

"You want me to come and get you?" she muttered, pulling the MACs so she held one in each hand and felt like a serious badass. "Then you've got it, because ready or not, here I come."

She wasn't wearing body armor and didn't bother to stick to cover because she knew she had one advantage: Zipacna needed her alive through the equinox. She, on the other hand, needed his ass dead. Thinking herself on the better end of the deal—for the moment, anyway—she set out.

She was three steps from the Jeep when the echoing crack of a gunshot rang out. She heard the whine-*thwap* of the bullet hit, felt the slap of impact. Then blood bloomed low on her shoulder, just above her right breast. She screamed and grabbed for the wound as she dove for cover, slamming to the ground behind a low wall.

Then she scrambled up, braced one of her pistols with her uninjured hand, and returned fire, aiming low near a crumbling wall where she saw a flash of motion, a swirl of brown cloth, and a familiar sharp-edged profile.

Not Zipacna, she realized. *Red-Boar.*

Betrayal roared up within her. The bastard had set her up, no doubt guessing what Strike meant to do and deciding it'd be better if she died sooner rather than later. Rage twisted through her—at Red-Boar for trying to kill her, at herself for not thinking clearly and guessing that the text message had been too conveniently timed. The rage bumped up against a building pressure at the back of her skull, and the contact sparked with golden light. With magic.

Her powers were definitely coming back online with the approach of the equinox, but they wouldn't do her a damn bit of good under the circumstances. She couldn't kill Red-Boar. Strike needed the older Nightkeeper, needed his power and his knowledge—probably more than he needed her, when she came down to it.

She had to get out of there, but she needed to leave the brown-robed bastard alive. Screaming a curse, she unloaded a full clip over Red-Boar's head and started running back toward the Jeep. The text message had been a setup, which meant Zipacna wasn't there, wasn't looking for her. He was down south, preparing for the equinox. She needed to get to the airport, needed to—

Thunder boomed, and Zipacna appeared in front of her in a swirl of purple-black mist, flanked on either side by two other *makol*. They slammed to the ground between her and the Jeep. Heart lunging into her throat, Leah skidded to a stop and tried to backpedal. She turned the MACs on them but got only the click of empty chambers. Before she could grab a spare clip, before she could do anything but scream, Zipacna grabbed her. He grinned horribly, his mismatched eyes glowing green. "You shouldn't have gone beyond the Nightkeepers' wards if you didn't want me to find you, baby."

"No!" she screamed, and turned one of the MACs on herself, knowing she couldn't let herself be taken, couldn't let them keep her alive through nightfall.

She pulled the trigger. Got a click. Still empty.

Red-Boar's weapon chattered. Zipacna cursed and turned so the bullets plowed into his flesh rather than hers. He snapped, "Delay the Nightkeeper." His men scattered, taking potshots toward Red-Boar as they ran.

Then Zipacna tightened his grip on Leah. Power surged around them.

And everything went purple-black.

"No!" Strike landed running, heedless of the rattle of automatic weapons, his entire being focused on the sight of Leah covered in blood and struggling in the *ajaw-makol*'s grip as power whipped and the transport magic took hold. "NO!" he shouted, and flung himself toward their disappearing figures . . .

And landed on his face in the sand, his outstretched hands clutching nothing.

Bullets whined and automatic fire barked, the impact marks walking toward him as two lesser *makol* fired on him from the shelter of a small stone-walled room.

"Stay down!" Red-Boar shouted, and lobbed a jade-packed grenade toward the *makol*'s shelter. It detonated seconds later, and the gunfire ceased.

Strike didn't stop to process. He was on his feet and

in the room with the two bleeding, shrapnel-stung *makol*
in an instant. He got one by the throat and the other by
the scruff and smashed their heads together so hard their
glowing green eyes winked out simultaneously. Then he
got his knife off his belt and sank the blade in the first
one's chest, carving deep until he could shove his hand
in there and rip out the fucker's heart.

Glory surged through him. Rage. Red-gold light. And
for a second, as he held the *makol*'s heart aloft, he felt
like a god.

He did the other one's heart, then both heads, and
roared victory when the bastards puffed to nothingness.
Then he sagged and took two shuddering breaths as
Red-Boar's footsteps approached, moving fast.

Leah, he thought, his heart tearing in his chest.
Gods, Leah.

Straightening, he grabbed Red-Boar by the throat,
spun, and slammed the traitor into the nearest stone
wall, hard enough that rocks tumbled and broke free.
"Why?" he grated, fury twisting inside him. Despair.
"Why?"

"Don't play a bigger fool than you already are," the
older man spat, his voice rasping against the choke hold.
"I'm trying to stop you from making the worst mistake
of your life."

"No." Strike tightened his grip as betrayal and killing
rage washing his vision red. "You're punishing me for
my father's choices."

But Red-Boar's breath rattled in his constricted
throat. "At least he *made* his choices. You're acting like
a spoiled brat, sitting around and waiting for a godsdamned miracle."

"I'm—" But Strike broke off when the accusation resonated too close to what Leah had said to him that
morning, when she'd called him an arrogant prince who
wanted everything his way. Was that really what was
going on? No, he thought. That wasn't him, wasn't the
man he wanted to be.

But maybe it was what the darkness inside him had
made him become, he thought, loosening his fingers and
letting Red-Boar slide down the wall.

Kulkulkan's influence had shaded Leah's brother toward easy living and self-justification. Was that so different from what his most trusted advisers were warning him against now? Or was that explanation in itself too easy? Was it more comfortable to blame the darkness on the god than himself?

In the end it didn't matter where it came from, he realized. Because he knew what he had to do about it. He owed it to his people to give them a ruler, owed it to Leah to make choices not just for them in the moment, but for the hope of a future.

It's time, his father's voice whispered in his mind, though he couldn't have said whether it was a message or a memory. But either way, the whisper was right. It was time. Avoiding the scepter hadn't stopped the prophesied events from coming any more than avoiding Leah had stopped him from falling for her. And turning away from his people now would only cause more destruction.

He was his father's son, which meant more than a fondness for dreams. It meant the blood of kings ran through his veins, and the duty, the responsibility wasn't his to set aside.

It was only his to take.

CHAPTER TWENTY-THREE

Leah swam in and out of consciousness, sick and sore and feverish, her brain fuzzed with drugs. She couldn't see more than a few feet in any direction before her vision went red-gold and blurry, but she didn't need to see that far to know where she was. The stone slab beneath her, the echoes, and the hum of power told her everything she needed to know.

She was back where it'd all started—strapped to the *chac-mool* altar in the ritual chamber that guarded the intersection of the earth, sky, and underworld.

Worse, she was alive, and so was Zipacna. And the clock was ticking.

Eventually her fever broke, or the drugs wore off, or both. Her brain cleared and the pain lessened, and she was able to take stock. She was still dressed in her combat clothes, but the weapons belt was gone. That wasn't a surprise, but it was definitely a problem. Without the jade-tips and knives, she'd be powerless against the *ajaw-makol*, even if she did manage to escape. The spell was no good without a knife, and even at that it was going to be a long shot.

Which left her bound to a sacrificial altar with no hope of rescue until too late, because Strike and the other Nightkeepers weren't due at the intersection until the equinox, and she doubted Red-Boar was going to fess up to what he'd done. For all she knew, the bastard had lied and told Strike she'd gone to Zipacna willingly.

Tears filmed her vision, and grief tore at her. Regret. She should've left a note, should've told Strike what she was planning so he'd have a place to start looking at best, a warning at worst. Because the way it was looking now, he was going to zap into battle and find her there.

After everything they'd done to get around it, he was going to have to kill her and fulfill the thirteenth prophecy. If he didn't, he'd be signing a death warrant for all mankind.

When a tear broke free and trickled down her cheek, she swiped her face against her shoulder, brushing it away. And froze.

The place on her right shoulder where she'd been been shot, which had been covered beneath a four-by-four bandage the last time she'd regained consciousness, wasn't bandaged anymore. Instead, her captors had left the wound open. Only it wasn't a wound anymore. It was a scar.

A faint shimmer of excitement worked through her. She seriously doubted the *makol*'s magic ran to healing spells . . . and if she'd healed herself, maybe she could do other tricks as well. Maybe the equinox magic was strong enough to give her a slim chance of escape.

She closed her eyes and focused inward, and thought she detected a trickle of power within. Without conscious decision, she touched the thin stream of magic and thought, *Hello? Strike? Can you hear me?*

Footsteps sounded outside the arched doorway leading from the ritual chamber.

Leah jolted, her heart bumping at the expectation of seeing Zipacna, the faint hope that it might be Strike. But it wasn't either of them.

It was her brother.

"Matty?" Her breath whistled in her lungs as emotions slapped at her: disbelief and excitement, suspicion, and a longing so intense she could barely suck in her next lungful of air.

I'm dreaming, she told herself. *He's dead. This is all in my mind.*

His footsteps sounded real as he stepped inside the chamber, though. He was wearing the same sort of preppy shit she remembered from his college days, and his tousled hair fell over his forehead just so. His eyes seemed real when they locked on her, his smile was the one she remembered, and his voice was the same when he said, "Hey, Blondie."

"You're not really here." She squeezed her eyes shut, struggling for sanity. "It's the drugs. You're a flashback or something."

But he laughed. "I can live with being a flashback. You've called me worse."

He was still there when she cracked her eyes open, standing next to the altar looking down at her, his eyes clear and blue like she remembered.

"Magic," she said before she could stop herself.

He nodded, and held out his hand to show the slash across his palm. "They brought me back for you, Leah. To show you what you can have if you join us."

Horror sang through her, alongside awful temptation. "I won't become a *makol*. It's wrong."

He chuckled, sounding so much like himself that her heart shuddered. "That's my sister," he said with fond tolerance. "Black and white. Right and wrong. But what's right in this case? Is it right that your boyfriend is going to have to kill you to let his precious god go free? What if I tell you there's another way? A way for you to have it all?"

"Impossible," she whispered, telling herself not to listen, that it was the same self-centered rhetoric she'd accused Strike of only that morning. "There's a balance. You've got to give something to get something. You have to sacrifice."

"Don't you think you've already given enough?" Matty said, eyes and voice going sad. He leaned in close and whispered, "Give it a chance, Leah. Give *us* a chance. The Nightkeepers aren't the good guys—they're just going to screw things up and waste energy fighting the inevitable. Zipacna has the power to guide the com-

ing changes and see mankind through 2012 and beyond."
He paused. "Please, Leah? For me? I've missed you so
much."

Tears lumped in her throat and poured down her
cheeks. She wanted to say yes, wanted her brother
back, wanted absolution for not being there when he'd
needed her to help him stay the narrow path of good
decisions. But she shook her head, denying the impossible because magic could do a great many things, but it
couldn't bring back the dead. "You're not my brother.
You're not Matty."

He tipped his head. "Of course I am. Here, I'll prove
it. Remember that time you, me, and Dad went—"

She didn't listen, couldn't listen. She shut her eyes,
found that trickle of golden power, gathered it up, and
threw it at him with a mental heave.

His voice cut off with a hiss, followed by a mocking
chuckle.

When she opened her eyes, she found a stranger
standing there, looking down at her with the bright green
eyes of a *makol*. "Think you're a clever bitch, do you?"

He had a crocodile tat on his upper pec, visible at the
open throat of his preppy getup. She didn't know him,
but she knew what he was. "Get your ass out of my
room, mimic."

He just smiled down at her. "We're offering you a
chance, cop. You come over, we'll give you your brother
back."

"He won't be my brother, not really. And we'll all die
in the end anyway." She shook her head. "I'm not
dealing."

The *makol* shrugged. "No skin off mine. You join us,
we get a *makol* with the power of a god. You refuse us,
we keep you alive and in a couple of hours you'll be
dead, Kulkulkan will be destroyed, and the skyroad will
be kaput." The creature grinned. "Win-win, baby."

She wanted to scream at him, to curse him, to howl
at the moon, but that would've been buying into the
taunts, so she said nothing, watching him impassively as
he slid the door shut.

Then she let the tears come. Gods, she wanted to be

back at Skywatch. She wanted Strike. She wanted a chance to apologize, to make up for going off on her own and fucking it up so badly they'd wound up in exactly the situation they'd been trying to avoid.

Wanted to tell him that she loved him enough to die for him, but she'd far rather live *with* him, for as long as the gods allowed.

Strike was carrying so much pissed-off power that the air slammed away from him and Red-Boar when they arrived back at Skywatch, sending Jox reeling back a few steps. Anna was there, too, her eyes full of worry and sorrow.

"The *ajaw-makol* has Leah," Strike said, his voice rasping on the words, his entire body vibrating with fear, with fury as he turned on Jox. "Do you hear me? The. *Makol*. Have. Her. Because you didn't watch her, and because this one"—he nudged Red-Boar roughly with his toe—"decided to take care of her himself." And, because Strike had let himself stray from what really mattered. Which ended now. "Where are the others?" he demanded.

"In the training hall," Jox said. "What are you—"

"Gather the *winikin* and meet me under the tree," Strike interrupted, and stalked off, headed for the pool house. He got dressed, not in the ceremonial robes tradition called for, but in the combat clothes and weapons he was going to need.

Wearing a black shirt, black cargo pants, and heavy boots, along with a webbed weapons belt that held a pair of MACs, spare clips of jade-tips, and a couple of no-nonsense combat knives, he strode across the rear yard to the ceiba tree his ancestors had worshiped as symbolizing the heart of the community.

He halted opposite his people, who stood beneath the spreading branches.

Called away from their practice, the Nightkeepers were dressed in black-on-black combat clothes and wore their weapons on their belts, save for Red-Boar, who wore penitent's brown, and Anna in street clothes. Beyond the magi, the *winikin* were ranged in a loose semicircle, with the twins playing at Hannah's feet.

There were nineteen of them in total, ten Nightkeepers, seven *winikin*, and the boys. *So few*, Strike thought, but told himself it would be enough. It would have to be, because he had no other choice.

He never had.

Deep down inside, he knew that taking his rightful place meant the death of his dreams, the end of any hope of a life not ruled by tradition and the needs of others. He would cease being Strike and become the Nightkeepers' king, putting them first above all others except the gods.

Putting them above himself. Above Leah.

"Gods," he whispered, clenching his fists at his sides, not sure if it was a curse or a prayer.

As a child he'd hated the *Banol Kax* for their part in the massacre. As an adult, he'd realized his father had played an equal part in the deaths, and hadn't understood how a rational man could've sacrificed an entire culture in an effort to save his own family.

Now, having known Leah and the promise of what they might've had together, Strike finally understood the temptation, the decision. But he couldn't make the same choice.

He wasn't his father.

"Kuyubal-mak," he said, tipping his head back and letting the words carry to the sky. "I forgive you."

A sudden wind blew up, sweeping across the box canyon and kicking up dust devils. The hum of power built to an audible whine, and the sun dimmed in the cloudless sky as though there were an eclipse, though none was scheduled.

Knowing it was time, knowing it was right, Strike drew his father's knife from his belt and scored both of his palms, cutting deep so the blood flowed freely and dripped to the canyon floor at his feet.

Pain washed his vision red, but the smell of blood and its sacrifice to the gods sent the power soaring as he shouted his acceptance of the kingship, his accession to rulership of the Nightkeepers, the words coming from deep within him, some sort of bloodline memory he'd been unaware of until that moment as he roared, *"Chumwan ti ajawlel!"*

A detonation blasted open the firmament in front of him, the plane of mankind splitting to reveal the gray-green barrier behind. Crimson light burst from the tear, silhouetting a figure within.

Strike saw the wink of a bloodred ruby at the *nahwal*'s ear, and recognized it from before. Except its eyes weren't flat black now.

They were cobalt blue, and shone with pride.

"Father," Strike whispered, going to his knees before the jaguar king.

"Son," the *nahwal* replied, not in the many-timbred voice it'd used before, but in the one he remembered from his childhood. His father's voice. The *nahwal* reached down. Gripped his shoulder. "Rise. A king bows only to the gods."

Strike stood, dimly aware that the Nightkeepers and *winikin* stayed kneeling behind him. The crimson light formed a royal red cloak that flared to the *nahwal*'s ankles, stirring in the wind that howled through the box canyon. Then the crimson light parted, revealing a spear of golden power.

The Manikin scepter.

Carved of ceiba wood and polished by the hands of a thousand kings, the scepter was actually a representation of the god Kauil, with his forehead pierced by an ax and one leg turned into a snake, wearing god markings on each of his biceps.

The nature of the god himself had long been lost to time, but the scepter represented divine kingship. The man who wielded the scepter wielded the might of the Nightkeepers.

Fingers trembling not with fear, but with awe, Strike reached out and gripped the polished idol, which remained within the barrier unless called upon for cermemonies of birth or marriage. Or ascension of a new king.

Racial memory told him the words should come in the old tongue, but this wasn't the old days, wasn't his father's time, so he finished the spell in English, saying, "Before the god Kauil I take the scepter, I take the king's duty and sacrifice, and vow to lead in defense against the end-time." He paused, then said the three words that ended his old life and began a new one. "I am king."

Thunder clapped and red lightning split the darkened sky, and the wind whipped into a howl that stirred up the dust and spun the crimson light into a vortex. Within the funnel cloud, the *nahwal* started to lose its shape.

Strike strained toward it. "Father!"

The last to disappear were its cobalt eyes, which shone with love and regret.

As the tear in the barrier snapped shut, the old king's voice whispered, "I pray that you will do what I could not. Lead with your heart, but don't follow it blindly."

Then it was gone. The air was clear, the sun shining down on them as though the freak storm had never been. Even the scepter was gone, sucked back into the barrier where its power resided.

But it had left its mark on Strike; not on his forearm, where the Nightkeepers' glyphs went, but on his bicep, where the gods—and kings—were marked.

He stared at the geometric glyph, and for the first time in a long, long time, his soul was silent. Gone was the confusion, the grief and resentment. In their place was icy determination.

He turned to the *winikin*. "Who am I?"

Jox was the first to move. He stood and crossed to Strike, then pulled a knife from his pocket, flipped the blade open, and drew it sharply across his tongue, cutting deep. Blood flowed, dripped down his chin, and stained his teeth red when he said, "You are my king." He bent his head and spat blood at Strike's feet in the oldest of sacrifices, offering both blood and water. Then he looked up at Strike, uncertain. "If you'll still have me."

Strike nodded. "I am your king. We'll figure out the other shit later."

Jox bowed his head and returned to the other *winikin*, who repeated the process one by one.

Then Strike turned to the Nightkeepers. "If you accept me as your king, we're going after Leah. She's not your fight, she's mine, but I'm asking for your help getting her back."

"All due respect," Sven said, looking eerily mature in combat clothes, with his hair slicked back in a stubby ponytail. "Saving Leah isn't just your fight. She's one of us, bloodline mark or no bloodline mark."

The others nodded, all except for Red-Boar, who growled, "And if you get her back? What then? She lives only to die at the equinox, taking the god with her?"

"I know how to bring the god through," Strike said. "We'll reunite Kulkulkan's power on earth and use it to keep the *Banol Kax* from coming through the barrier." *Gods willing.*

The older man's eyes were dark and wary. "How can you be certain it'll work?"

"I'm certain," Strike said, holding his stare. "Trust me."

And there it was, the leap of faith he needed from them, from Anna and Red-Boar most of all. He needed them to believe.

Softly, he said to the Nightkeepers, "Who am I?"

To his surprise, Rabbit came forward first, knelt, blooded himself, and spat in the dust. "You are my king."

A look of exquisite pain flashed across Red-Boar's face at the obeisance. The older man hung back as the others stepped up, one by one, until he and Anna were the only ones left.

Anna approached but did not kneel and didn't cut her tongue. Instead, she scored her palm and, when blood ran free, took Strike's hand in hers. He felt the jolt of power, the bloodline connection and the love that hadn't wavered despite their time apart. "You are my king," she said, and leaned in and kissed his cheek.

He hugged her and whispered in her ear, "Thank you."

Then he let her go and turned to Red-Boar. "Who am I?"

Red-Boar met Strike's glare. "There can be no love in war. Your father is still an idiot, even in death."

Strike crossed to him. Got in his face. Growled, "Who. Am. I?"

The standoff lasted five seconds, maybe ten. Then Red-Boar broke and looked away. "You are my king." He scored his tongue, spat the offering, and added, "Gods help us all."

"The spell you pulled from the grad student's head," Strike said. "Give it to me."

"I can't," Red-Boar said, holding up a hand as Strike bristled. "Not won't, I can't. He didn't finish translating all of it."

"Damn it!" Strike spun away, fury and futility railing at him. He looked to the others. "Jade?"

She shook her head. "I couldn't find it."

There had to be a way, Strike knew. And not just because he wanted there to be—because it didn't make any sense for the gods to bring him and Leah this far only to have them fail now.

Which meant he had to have faith, he thought, turning to face his people. His Nightkeepers. "Load up on live ammo and get your body armor. We're going to kick some *Banol Kax* ass and get Leah back."

And after that, he was going to fucking wing it.

Five minutes later, the Nightkeepers were assembled, bristling with guns and knives. Red-Boar was blank-visaged and ready to kill. Rabbit stood at his side, vibrating with energy, his eyes alight with excitement. Anna looked ill, as though she'd rather be anywhere else just then, but Strike couldn't leave her behind when their shared ancestry meant she could boost his power. And the trainees . . . *Hell,* he thought with a little kick beneath his heart, *they look like a team.*

Alexis and Nate might have broken up in the wake of the talent ceremony, but they stood shoulder-to-shoulder now, stern-faced, nerves evident only in the tap of his fingers against a gun butt, and her slight shift from one foot to the other. Brandt and Patience were a unit, Michael and Jade looked ready enough, though Jade would serve only to boost her former lover's shield magic, and

Sven was pale but resolute, his hair slicked back, his features sharper than Strike had thought them.

Three months earlier they'd been normal people, CEOs and screwups, therapists and number crunchers. Now they were magi. They were the Nightkeepers.

And, he thought with a sick churning in his gut, they were mortal. Which had been an unacknowledged sticking point for him, one of the reasons he'd held himself away from them for as long as possible. He hadn't just been fighting for his old life, or for the promise of a new one with Leah. He'd been fighting not to care about his teammates, or, failing that, struggling not to have to lead them into battle.

His father had led his family and friends to their deaths. What if he did the same? What if the greatest sacrifice was the remainder of the Nightkeepers? What then?

"Then we go out fighting," he said aloud, and crossed to them, the scepter magic still churning in his blood, keeping the turbines revving high. "Join up and hang on," he ordered, and when they linked hands, the power nearly took off the top of his head.

He leaned on it, pictured the Yucatán rain forest, and the clearing outside the hidden tunnel leading to the sacred chamber, and zapped.

The moment they blinked in, a group of *makol* massed in the tunnel mouth opened fire.

CHAPTER TWENTY-FOUR

Strike ducked and started running for the leafy tree line, bellowing, "Take cover!"

His pulse pounded and adrenaline hammered through his system alongside power and rage as the entrenched *makol* blasted away with a combination of green fireballs and M-16s. The Nightkeepers bolted for cover as Michael threw up a shield spell that blocked the first volley.

Strike dove behind a low, partially crumbled wall carved with what looked like the flying-serpent glyph he wore on his arm. "Over here!"

The others scrambled in behind him and hunched down as a second salvo whistled over their heads and smashed into the rock wall mere feet from their position.

"I'll get their heads down." Red-Boar angled his autopistol up and over the wall and started firing off short bursts designed to keep the *makol* pinned. Grim faced and resolute, he looked every inch the soldier he'd once been.

Risking a look around the wall, Strike took stock. There were probably fifty of them, their green eyes glowing in the fading light. The good news was that they'd be easy to contain in the cave mouth.

The bad news was that he needed to get the hell past them.

"We need to draw them out," he said, hunkering back down behind the wall. "How about this?" He grabbed a stick, swiped a layer of leaves away, and started drawing a rough approximation of their positions in the moist earth of the rain forest floor. "The *makol* are fierce as hell and hard to kill, but they're not that smart. I say four or five of us work our way around to here"—he marked a spot on the east side of the cave mouth—"and make it look like our flank is exposed."

Red-Boar fired and grunted in satisfaction when there was a cry of pain from the other side of the clearing. Then he glanced at the diagram. "Not much of a shot from there, for either side."

"Granted," Strike said, "but I'm counting on that. I need to draw them out, get them away from the tunnel while the rest of us sneak through on the other side and attack from the rear."

"Too simple," Red-Boar said dismissively.

"But it's relatively low-risk, and we don't have time for anything fancy," Strike countered. "I want Patience, Brandt, Sven, and Rabbit on the east side, drawing them out. Brandt, you're in charge. Nate, you take Alexis, Michael, and Jade to the west, and see if you can get in behind them. Red-Boar, Anna, and I will use the distraction to get into that tunnel."

Red-Boar looked back at him. "You want me with you?"

"No, but you're the best power boost I've got." Strike hated splitting his forces, but he didn't have time to waste battling the *makol*, and he couldn't risk them following. He needed a clear shot at the chamber. And Leah.

Even now, he could feel the stars coming into alignment. He needed to save Leah, save the god—the fear and the mad fury of it pounded in his veins, making him feel larger than himself, and powerful with it.

"Any questions?" He got head shakes and resolution all around, and nodded with grim satisfaction. "Good. Once the rest of you have taken care of these bastards, follow us down into the tunnel. We're going to need you."

With that, he pulled his autopistols and the others did

the same, and they split up, moving in opposite directions to flank the *makol*, and hoping to hell the plan worked.

If it didn't, they were screwed.

Leah was running out of time. Through her weak link to the golden light of the god she could feel the alignment coming to bear, feel the power opening up, blooming within her, but she couldn't do a damn thing with it. All the training, all the spells . . . useless.

She wasn't a Nightkeeper. Never would be. And Strike hadn't come for her. Did he think she was dead already? Worse, had something happened to him? Fear crushed down on defeat, adding to the sense of suffocation that was growing ever more intense with each second.

Jox's words spooled through her head in a depressing loop. *Self-sacrifice isn't a sin . . . it's the ultimate way . . . to honor the gods.*

Was that what it was going to come down to? She cast around the chamber for a weapon, but saw only the screaming skulls and dying gods carved on the walls, and braziers that gave off red-hued *copan* smoke. She needed a knife, or preferably a gun. Quicker that way.

The thought twisted her belly with fear and despair. *Strike, where are you?*

A noise from the chamber entrance had her whipping her head from the altar surface, her heart jolting with the crazy thought that he'd locked on and come for her. But no, it was Zipacna who strode through the door, followed by a second green-eyed *makol* she recognized as the mimic in its baseline form. Both were wearing flowing robes the same gray-green color as the barrier mists.

Zipacna palmed a long, wickedly curved black knife from the belt knotted at his waist, and raised an eyebrow. "Last chance. You accept the spell and you'll live beyond tonight."

"As a *makol*? No way."

"Your loss." He flipped the knife, caught it by the blade, and didn't even wince when it cut deep and blood

flowed. Glancing at his watch—a jarringly normal action—
he said, "You've got forty-two minutes left. Any last
words?"

"Yeah. 'Fuck' and 'you.' "

He waved his bleeding hand at her. "Tell it to someone who cares. Like your brother."

"Leave him out of this." Rage guttered low in her
stomach, battling out the fear.

"Why?" He grinned, baiting her while the mimic
leaned against the wall and watched them with an eerie
lack of expression. "What are you going to do about
it, cop?"

The sluggish swirl of power shone hotter, brighter in
her mind's eye, and she felt something stir. A faint tingle
started in her fingertips and ran up the insides of her
arms, tightening the skin across her breasts and pressing
urgently at the center of her chest. But when she tried
to use the magic, nothing happened.

The bastard chuckled, moving closer and leaning over
her, so she could feel the inhuman chill of him, feel the
tickle of his breath on her skin. "See?" he murmured.
"You can't do a damn thing to me. I am *ajaw-makol*.
I'm untouchable."

She whimpered and stretched, trying to get away from
him, but hit the ends of her shackles too quickly.

Clearly enjoying her fear, he chuckled and swiped his
tongue along her cheek to the edge of her ear.

Anger flared. Revulsion. And somehow the two together were enough to put her over. She felt a click, felt
a door open inside her soul. Golden power flared within
her, exploding in a starburst as she touched Kulkulkan's
power. She sensed the god trapped within the skyroad,
felt his power and anger, his blinding wish to be free.

Tapping that power, opening herself to it, she locked
onto the spell Strike had used the first moment she met
him, and shouted, *"Torotobik!"*

Her shackles detonated, freeing her and driving Zipacna back with a shout. Adrenaline flaring hard and
hot, she didn't stop to think or plan. She lunged forward,
grabbed the black knife from his hand, and plunged it
to the hilt in his left eye, until she felt bone grate.

Roaring, Zipacna reeled to the side, pawing at the protruding haft as blood and clear fluid poured down his face. "Get her!"

But shock slowed the mimic's reactions. She charged him, slammed her foot into the side of his knee, and sent him flying. Then she turned back for Zipacna, intending to finish him, finish them both—only to see him puff out in a cloud of purple-black.

The mimic roared and charged her, and she turned and fled. Bolting through the door into the sand-floored tunnel leading to the sunken river, she ran in search of Zipacna. She had less than forty minutes to make sure neither of them lived past the equinox.

Strike peered through a leafy rain forest curtain, his body humming with the need to move, and move fast. "Come on, come on," he chanted under his breath. "What are you waiting for?" Behind him, Red-Boar and Anna crouched in silence. The west-side team of Nate, Alexis, Michael, and Jade were waiting nearer the tunnel entrance, preparing to attack.

Then a single shot rang out from the bushes on the east side of the tunnel mouth. Another. The *makol* started to shuffle and move, shifting to the side of the cave overhang.

Strike tensed. "Get ready."

Suddenly, Sven leaped out of the vegetation, stood at the edge of the clearing, and unloaded most of a MAC clip into the tunnel mouth. The *makol* scattered, then spun and returned fire as Sven bolted for cover. Mindless with the killing rage, and only as smart as the degree to which their human hosts had accepted the evil, the *makol* followed.

"Go!" Strike lunged to his feet and pounded the short distance to the tunnel mouth, with Anna and Red-Boar right behind him.

A *makol* at the back of the pack turned and shouted in alarm, only to be cut down in a hail of jade-tips as Nate burst from the undergrowth nearby, with Alexis and Michael right behind him, Jade bringing up the rear.

"Go!" Nate shouted. "We've got this."

Strike didn't argue; he bolted for the tunnel, gaining the mouth and disappearing down the stone throat, leaving the sounds of battle behind. But as he pounded down the tunnel with Anna and Red-Boar on his heels, he knew they were cutting it way too close.

The equinox hummed in his bones, stronger than the song of the summer solstice had been, stronger than he'd expected, but still he couldn't pinpoint Leah. He kept trying to throw her a travel thread, kept getting bounced by whatever sort of shielding was at work within the tunnels.

They reached the underground river after what felt like an eternity, turned, and booked it toward the chamber. As they passed an intersecting tunnel, Strike caught a hint of motion, a flash of luminous green, and flung himself to the side with a shout of, *"Makol!"*

Anna hit the deck as the creature lunged. Red-Boar roared a battle cry, grabbed the thing by the throat, and brought his pistol to its forehead. Then he froze.

It was Leah.

"No!" Strike shouted, hiis voice cracking on the word. "Don't!"

Red-Boar looked at him. Hesitated.

And Leah drove a black-handled knife into Red-Boar's gut, yanked it out, and slashed his throat on the backhand. Blood spurted, geysering in an obscene arc as the Nightkeeper's knees buckled.

Anna screamed and reached for him, cradling him in her arms as he fell.

Leah—or the thing that had been Leah—turned on Strike. Her eyes glowed scary strange, and her mouth was distorted in a rictus of bloodlust. But when he looked at her he felt nothing but revulsion. There was no connection. No love.

"Gods help us," Strike said as he raised his MAC.

And fired point-blank.

Anna screamed in horror. Leah's head exploded and she went down in a heap. Ribs heaving, heart hammering inside his chest, Strike followed her down, unsheathing his knife. Working fast, telling himself not to look at her face, he cut her heart out, hacked off her head, and recited the banishment spell, sending the *makol* back to hell where it belonged.

When it was gone, Leah's body went limp.

Strike stood, horror taking root when the corpse remained exactly as it was. "Please, gods," he whispered. "Not like this. Please, not like this." He'd been so sure it wasn't her, so sure he was making the right call.

Then, finally, the body shimmered. Shifted. And changed into that of a skinny man wearing a fungus-colored robe and a tattoo of a winged crocodile. Then purple-green light flashed, and the thing was gone.

Strike's bones went to water and he sagged in relief. "Thank you, Jesus. Gods. Whatever." He exhaled, tried to get his breathing under control. "Shit. Oh, boy. Oh, shit. A mimic. It was a mimic."

"How did you know?" Anna asked, her voice shaky.

"I just knew. I had faith. I knew it wasn't her." Except for a few seconds when he'd thought he had it wrong, thought he'd bought into the thirteenth prophecy without even knowing it.

But the attack had not been without a sacrifice, he knew. He turned to see Anna crouched on the ground with Red-Boar sprawled across her lap, both of them covered in the blood that still pumped from the older man's torn throat in slowing spurts driven by a faltering heart.

Sorrow cut through Strike, and he dropped to his knees beside the dying man. "Gods, no."

Red-Boar's eyes flickered open and locked on even as the life faded. "Happy now, boy?"

"Step off, old man." But Strike choked on the words. He touched Red-Boar's forehead, leaking him power, buffering the pain. "Safe journey," he whispered. "Say hello to the king for me."

But Red-Boar shook his head ever so slightly. "You're . . . king now."

"Yeah," Strike said. "I am."

As his life drained, Red-Boar murmured, "Forgive." Then his breath faded and stopped, and his body went limp in Anna's arms as she bent over him and wept, the soft sound lost beneath the burble of the underground river that flowed nearby.

Shit, Strike thought. *Just shit.*

The loss hurt keenly on too many levels to count, but they couldn't stop to mourn. They'd already wasted too much time. The equinox was close now, very close.

"Anna." He touched her arm. "We've got to go."

She nodded miserably, shifted Red-Boar's body to the side, and climbed to her feet, wiping her bloodstained hands on her blood-soaked pants. "We'll come back for him. After."

"Of course. He's one of us." Whatever he'd done, or hadn't done, Red-Boar had been his own version of loyal. All else was washed clean by the sacrifice.

They tugged the corpse into an offshoot tunnel and made a stab at obscuring the tracks and bloodstains. And then they ran for their lives.

Crouching in the underbrush, fighting green fire with red, Rabbit felt as if he were burning up from the inside.

His mouth was parchment dry, and his eyelids rasped across his corneas without the benefit of moisture. His skin crinkled as he labored by rote: lifting his arms, holding his hands a few inches apart, concentrating until flame flared to life between them, and then pivoting and throwing to block the incoming green flame, so the two streams met in a brilliant blast of white.

His right shoulder hurt like hell. He was thirsty, hungry, and exhausted beyond all rationality, and his head felt like it was about to split open and spill his brains onto the rain forest floor. And he couldn't have been happier.

With Patience and Brandt fighting together on his right and Sven on his left as they worked with the other team, squeezing the *makol* forces and picking off the bastards one by one, he was part of something. He belonged. Even better, he was good at something.

"Hold on," Brandt said. "What the hell are they doing?"

It took Rabbit a few seconds to reorient, another to

pop out from behind the crumbling wall he'd been hiding behind, to check out the scene.

Makol parts were strewn across the clearing, most of them still moving, which was just beyond weird. But until the Nightkeepers got in there and did the head-and-heart thing, the creatures weren't actually dead, just dismembered. Which was kind of cool.

What wasn't cool was the way the dark-haired *makol* with the flying-croc tattoo and pointy teeth, who seemed to be in charge, had gathered the remaining dozen *makol* into a knot.

Then, without warning, a huge green fireball the size of a VW Bug erupted and screamed toward where Rabbit and the others were hiding.

"Take cover!" Brandt shoved Rabbit off to one side, grabbed Patience, and dove in the other direction. Groggy from doing too much magic, Rabbit lay dazed.

The fireball hit right where he'd been and detonated, blasting heat and energy in all directions. The world went white and noise roared over him, flattening the rain forest and sending trees flying in a spray of wooden shrapnel.

When the echoes died away, Rabbit lay gasping, trying to figure out why he wasn't mulch.

Then he felt the humming power of a shield spell a few inches away from his face and realized he was lying on someone's foot. Craning his neck, he saw Sven lying nearby, looking dazed, but holding on to the shield spell he'd thrown over both of them.

"Hey," Rabbit said, breathing hard. "Thanks."

Sven nodded. "Yep."

And that was all that needed to be said. They were a team, after all.

They scrambled up, Rabbit and Sven from one side of the fireball crater, Brandt and Patience from the other, just in time to see the *makol* breaking ranks and bolting for the tunnel, charging toward the position held by Nate, Alexis, Michael, and Jade.

"Nate, *incoming*!" Brandt shouted, and started running after the *makol*, with Patience, Rabbit, and Sven on his heels.

But the *makol* charged right past the other Nightkeepers and down the tunnel.

"Get them!" Nate shouted, bursting from cover with his team behind him. "Don't let them reach the chamber! We'll take care of these guys and catch up." He dropped beside one of the downed *makol* and dispatched it in a flash of purple light. "Go!"

Rabbit bolted down the tunnel, skidding on the loose sand beneath his feet, firing jade-tips as he ran. He heard Brandt call his name but didn't stop.

His old man was down there.

Seeing one of the bastards up ahead, he put on the afterburners and hauled ass. He wound up in a wider section of the tunnel, where three others joined in.

There was no sign of the *makol. Shit!*

Brandt, Patience, and Sven burst into the chamber moments later, sliding to a stop when they saw Rabbit. Nate and the others weren't far behind.

"I lost them," Rabbit reported. "We'll have to—" He broke off as sudden sweat popped out all over his body, and he started shivering. The world hazed red and orange with flame, and a rushing noise started low, at the very edge of his hearing.

"What's wrong?" he heard Patience say, but the words sounded like they were coming from far away. He couldn't feel the hand she put on his shoulder, couldn't feel the stone beneath his feet, couldn't feel anything except the heat—the terrible, awful heat that crisped his skin and made him feel flayed alive.

"Something's coming," he whispered, hunching over as the rushing noise rose up through the octaves, higher and higher until he jammed his hands over his ears to stop himself from screaming.

Then he *was* screaming, they all were, because the heat in his body was suddenly everywhere, searing their hands and faces and driving them deeper into the cave. The sandy floor went scorched black, then melted to liquid, and then warmed further to molten orange-red. Then that orange-red liquid lurched up from the floor of the cave, elongating and stretching, taking shape as a faceless scaled creature that was almost entirely made of teeth and claws, and didn't so much as flinch when Michael unloaded an entire clip of jade-tips right into it. Or rather through it.

"*Boluntiku!*" Rabbit screamed, and turned to run.

The thing hesitated at his shout. Locked on.

And followed.

Strike edged around the doorway leading to the sacred chamber and bit back a vicious curse when he saw Leah shackled to the altar, saw Zipacna standing over her, and saw the blood—so much blood, too much blood. She saw him and her eyes filled as she strained toward him. "Strike! Help!"

He didn't think. He reacted.

Roaring, he stepped into the chamber with his finger nailed to the trigger of the autopistol. The MAC-10 chattered, sending a hail of jade-tips into the bastard.

Zipacna straightened, screaming with pain as he staggered away from Leah, his body jerking with the bullet impacts. But Strike didn't care—he kept advancing, kept firing as the rage inside him turned to something else, something hard and hot and possessive. "Get away from her. She's mine!"

The *ajaw-makol* fell against the wall, motionless, though not dead.

"Cover him!" Strike tossed Anna one of his pistols and lunged across the room. When he reached the altar, his heart stopped in his chest and everything inside him went cold.

Leah's wrists bore crisscrossed cuts, and blood flowed into the shallow channels grooved onto the altar, running downward by gravity flow and collecting in the sacred bowl at the altar's front, where a charred twist of parchment burned purple-black, its magic fueled by the power of her blood.

Tears glistened in her eyes. "I'm sorry," she whispered. "I got free, but when I tried to kill him he caught me again. I grabbed his knife, but . . . I'm sorry. So sorry."

"No," he said, leaning in and gathering her against him. He pressed his cheek to hers, and shuddered at the cool feel of her skin, the limpness of her body, which made it seem that she was already gone.

Her breathing was growing more and more shallow. He felt the god's power growing within her, felt the bonds of the skyroad falling away as Leah died and the creator prepared to return to the sky.

When he pulled away, her eyes fixed on him. "Zipacna?"

"He's yours," Strike said, voice rough with emotion. "He always was." He unlocked her bonds with a touch and scooped her up off the altar, leaking her all the power he could spare, trying to heal her, to keep her heart going.

He propped her up near the *makol* and pressed a knife into her hand. "Take him."

Bolstered by his strength, and by the revenge that had carried her so long, she grasped the knife and bent over the *ajaw-makol*, getting his heart out, but faltering over his head.

"I'll help." To Strike's surprise, Anna moved in and finished the job, then linked hands with Leah for the spell. When they reached the end, Zipacna's body disappeared in a flash of purple-green light. The Anna stood, wiping her hands on her bloodstained pants. "I'll watch the tunnel."

She headed out of the chamber, leaving Strike and Leah alone.

Only they weren't alone at all, he realized when a howling wind whipped through the chamber, and the skulls on the walls began to scream fire.

The equinox had come. The intersection was opening. The *Banol Kax* were poised to enter the plane of mankind, their magic fueled by Leah's blood and the sacrifice of their own *ajaw-makol*.

Leah looked at him through eyes drenched with tears, and held out the knife. "Do it. You have no choice."

Either she died, or they all did.

Strike caught her to him, holding her hard, trying to give her all his energy, all his power, trying to beat back the passing time as he finally understood the impossible choice his father had died trying to avoid. He pressed his cheek to hers. "I love you. I fell in love with you when I wasn't looking, when I was doing my damnedest to do anything but fall, just like I became king when I was trying to be anything but."

She touched his arm where he wore the mark of the gods, of the jaguar kings. "You'll be a good king."

"And?"

Her smile went crooked. "And I love you, too. I don't care if what I'm feeling is because of destiny and the gods, or that it's all tangled up with the prophecies and the end of the world. I love you for you. Not because you're king or Nightkeeper, but because you're mine."

They met halfway in a searing kiss that tasted of need and desperation, and the power of the equinox. Strike felt light and dark align, felt the powers within them start to meld. He felt the dark force of the true demon Zipacna poised behind the barrier, ready to spring free at the moment of alignment, when the barrier would thin enough for the creature to burst through. He felt the god Kulkulkan straining at the bonds of the skyroad, longing to be free, longing to fight. The god's darkness battered him, latching on to his soul and dragging him down, away from gray-green neutrality and toward the underworld, which glowed the lumious green of a *makol*'s eyes.

No! he shouted in his soul. He fought the undertow, the temptation of power and madness, focusing on the feel of the woman in his arms. He poured himself into the kiss, willing love to be the thing that mattered most, the sacrifice necessary to bring the god to earth through the two of them, joined as a single keeper.

I love you, he thought, or maybe she thought it in his head somehow; it didn't matter. What mattered was that they were there, together. *Forever.*

At that thought, that single word, he felt a flare of power, a surge of golden light. Then the halves became whole, light blending with darkness, the two together making something so much stronger than either alone.

Deep within him something tore, a curtain ripping in half and letting through a ray of golden illumination. Instead of fighting it, he welcomed it, welcomed the light and the power and the sense of Leah that it brought. *Yes*, he said inside his own skull. *Welcome, my love.*

The kiss turned blatantly carnal, a celebration of both sex and love, and a promise made between them. He felt a cool burn on his arm, and knew from her jolt that Leah felt it, too.

There was no time to look at the new marks, though. They had to bring the god through the barrier. He took her hand and looked into her eyes, and from somewhere deep inside his soul he found the spell they needed. *"Och ta kaan."* Become the sky.

Power detonated inside him, around him, but it was too late. Far overhead the stars aligned and the equinox came to bear without the greatest sacrifice having been made.

The barrier fell, and a demon came to earth.

Thunder blasted in the sacred chamber, driving Strike to his knees as he held Leah tight. Mist roiled within the room, thickening to dire clouds that flickered with unholy luminescence, and the stone surface beneath him began to shudder like a living thing. A roar split the air, driving his heart into his throat. On its heels, a terrible creature emerged from the mist. Its crocodilian head was the size of the room itself, all wickedly sharp teeth and dead dark eyes. Zipacna.

The demon traveled through the intersection as an insubstantial spirit, like its *boluntiku* brethren, filling the chamber and overlapping the stone walls on either side as it passed, first a head and stubby neck, then short, powerful legs with razor-tipped claws the length of Strike's forearm. It moved faster and faster as it came onto the plane of mankind and accelerated toward the surface, giving Strike glimpses of leathery wings and an armored belly, then powerful hind legs and a long, scaly tail with a trio of wickedly pointed barbs at the end.

Then it was gone.

"Oh, father of gods," Strike said, the words coming from deep down in his chest as he realized that he'd failed before he even began. He'd run from the thirteenth prophecy, hadn't made the sacrifice required, and Lord Zipacna had made it through the barrier.

The end-time countdown had begun. There was a demon on earth. He'd failed his bloodline and his people, failed the gods.

"Not yet we haven't," Leah said, reading his thoughts through their bloodied hands. Her voice sounded strange, as though it carried the echo of trumpets. Then she turned to him, and his heart shuddered in his chest.

Her eyes were the molten gold of a Godkeeper.

"Leah," he said, grabbing her by the arms. "Gods, Leah!"

"It's okay." She took his hands, gripped them hard. "Boost me."

Instead of sharing the blood link, he cupped her face in his hands and touched his lips to hers. "I love you." Then he sank deeper into the kiss, dropped the barriers that had once held their souls apart, and gave her everything that he had to give.

And together, they called the feathered serpent god to earth.

CHAPTER TWENTY-FIVE

Rabbit ran for his life, leading the *boluntiku* away from the others, then doubling back through the maze of tunnels, which were lit with bloodred light that came from everywhere and nowhere at once.

He was doing his damnedest to keep the thing away from the sacred chamber, trying to give his old man and Strike a chance to save the world, but he was losing steam. His breath burned in his lungs, and his legs were on fire as he bore down and widened the gap, running with muscle and heart and a touch of magic, a litany of, *Oh, shit, oh, shit, oh, shit,* sounding in his brain.

The *boluntiku* screamed, sounding like a thousand fingernails scratching down a mountain-size blackboard.

"Fuck!" Rabbit accelerated away from the scream, careened around a corner, and nearly slammed into Alexis.

"Go!" She shoved him toward a cross-tunnel. "Shield yourself!" When the *boluntiku* appeared around the corner, she waved her arms. "Hey, over here!"

Realizing she was trying to tag-team the lava creature—and oh, holy hell, hoping it worked—Rabbit stumbled into the cross-tunnel and cast as much of a shield spell as he could muster in the magic-damping confines of the tunnel system.

Behind him, the *boluntiku* screamed, spurring him on, but Rabbit's foot snagged on something and he went sprawling on top of one of the other Nightkeepers, who was lying in the middle of the tunnel. *Shit!* Flipping onto his back, he checked behind him, but the heat was dimming as the *boluntiku* moved off, following Alexis.

Rabbit hissed and turned to see whom he'd stumbled over. "For fuck's sake, what are you—"

He broke off and screamed. It was his old man.

Stone dead.

Throat sliced open.

Rabbit's breath whistled out and he didn't suck another in. *Gods,* he thought. *Gods-gods-gods. Oh, gods. No, gods, please, no.*

"Rabbit!" Alexis's shriek was scant warning as the air crackled with sudden heat and the *boluntiku* morphed up through the floor just beyond his father's body.

It glowed red-orange, painting Red-Boar's slack features in sharp relief and making the jagged cut across his throat gape dark and obscene. The lava-creature hissed and reared back, extending a scaled arm and flaring its six-clawed hand for a swipe.

Rabbit knew he should run, but he couldn't move, couldn't leave the old man. He stared down at the body, tears dripping off his chin. "Dad?" His voice cracked, and he didn't care.

The *boluntiku* attacked, going solid at the last possible second.

Gunfire chattered, and a hail of bullets hit the thing in its scaled chest and gaping maw, driving it back. The creature screamed in pain and puffed to vapor, and the next volley went straight through, cutting off prematurely when Alexis's MAC jammed.

"Damn it!" She worked fast, jettisoning the mag and slapping another home, but it was too late. The *boluntiku* hissed and went for her, going solid before she could rack the first round. It swung for her. . . .

And bounced off a shield when Nate appeared out of nowhere and threw up a block at the last moment. He dropped it almost instantly and put himself between Alexis and the creature. "Rabbit," he snapped, "get behind me!"

But Rabbit still couldn't move. He could only bow his head as the fiery creature rose above him and screamed fingernails-on-blackboard. It slashed at him, popping to solid as it did, and—

Thunder cracked inside the tunnel. Lightning. A terrible wind howled through the narrow confines, driving the *boluntiku* back, sucking it up in a funnel of golden light. The few remaining *makol* were sucked up as well, pulled from the tunnels where they'd hidden while the *boluntiku* did its work. A howling, rushing noise rose to a horrible crescendo, so loud that Rabbit plugged his ears with his fingers and hunched down, waiting for it to pass. Power sang through him, the gold of the gods, and he knew that it was somehow traveling through him, racing through stone to the world beyond the tunnels.

The noise died away a moment later, ending with the high, clear note of a trumpet and the smell of *copan*. A single crimson feather, nearly the length of Rabbit's arm, drifted down to the tunnel floor.

Nate watched it land. "They did it." He shook Alexis, whom he was holding in a loose embrace, though neither of them seemed to have noticed. "They fucking did it!" He turned and started tugging her up the tunnel. "Come on!"

"Wait." She held him back and pointed. "Look."

Nate saw Red-Boar and cursed. He came close, crouched down, and laid a hand on Rabbit's shoulder.

Rabbit ignored him and kept staring at the old man, thinking about all the times he'd said it wouldn't matter if Red-Boar up and died, for all the attention he paid.

He'd been wrong. It did matter. It mattered a shitload.

"We've got to go," Nate said. "Strike and Leah might need us up on the surface."

"I can't—" Rabbit's voice broke, so he coughed and tried again, not caring that there was a sob hitched among the words. "We can't leave him here. Not like this."

"We'll take him with us," Nate said. "But we have to go now. We have a job to do."

Was that how the old man had approached each day? Rabbit wondered. Yeah, that was about it. His existence had been a chore, his son an afterthought, his whole being concentrated on what might've been.

Hell. Rabbit sniffed and swiped at his face. Then he climbed to his feet, scooped up his MAC where it'd fallen when he tripped, and nodded. "Let's go."

They carried the body out so they could bring it back to Skywatch for the proper rituals. But really, none of those things were necessary, were they? Finally, the old man was where he'd wanted to be all along.

He was with his family.

Strike zapped them to the surface as the golden serpent blasted through the tunnels and out into the open sky. Anna staggered and nearly fell from the teleport sickness, and he caught her on the way down. That left Leah on her own for a second, without his power or blood link, but that was okay. She stood apart, her feet braced on the leafy ground and her face turned up to the sky.

Part of her watched the winged serpent gain altitude, sweeping over the pyramid that bore its name. She saw the glitter of golden scales in the moonlight, and the darker hue of brilliant plumage that would be bright red in the daylight, but looked black against the darkness of night. She saw all that, just as she saw Strike settle Anna on a crumbling carved wall nearby, and felt him take her hand, linking his power with hers through the bond of their love.

She saw and felt all that with part of her consciousness. But another part of her soul flew with Kulkulkan.

She felt the joy of flight and freedom, the burning need to drive the demon back to its hell. An exultant cry burst from the god, a clarion call of trumpets that echoed in the night sky above Chichén Itzá. A battle cry. A challenge.

For a moment, there was no response. The sky seemed empty.

Then the winged crocodile appeared from behind a cloud, screeching a banshee wail that spoke of death and the flames of Xibalba. The god Zipacna, son of the underworld's ruler, was full of hate and anger and pride, his sole purpose to kill the feathered serpent and clear the way for the rest of his kind to come to earth.

Screeching again, the winged crocodile twisted in mid-air and dove, with his fearsome claws extended and his giant mouth open in attack.

Leah grabbed onto Strike as the god swerved and spun and slapped at the demon, scoring a deep line in the crocodilian scales and then dropping down and raking razor-sharp talons along Zipacna's back, creating bloody furrows that had the demon arching with a scream of pain as the god beat feathered wings to flit away.

Kulkulkan dodged and slapped again. And again. Blood ran from the winged croc's armored hide, raining down on the forest below and flaming as it hit. But through her connection to the entity Leah could tell that its time was running out. The barrier was thickening as the equinox ebbed, leaving only minutes more to push Zipacna back through the intersection, or risk giving the *Banol Kax* free rein on Earth.

"He needs help," Leah said. "We have to help him!"

"We will," said a new voice. It was Alexis's voice, Leah realized, and suddenly the others were there, all of them cutting their palms and linking up, and offering their joined power to their king. Strike took the link, then turned to Leah and touched his lips to hers.

Heat sparked and power blasted, a door opening in the barrier, channeling through the young magi and into Strike, from him to Leah, and through her to Kulkulkan.

The god screamed exultantly as the golden mists flared sun-bright with the power of the Nightkeepers. The flying serpent snapped its wings taut and thundered up into the sky, trumpeting the attack as it slammed into Zipacna, raking and clawing at the croc's softer underbelly. God and demon beat their wings together, fighting the air to stay aloft, fighting each other to stay alive.

But Zipacna was no match for the combined might of the god and his Nightkeepers.

The demon faltered and keened a dying cry, and as

he did so, golden mist expanded and wrapped around both of the creatures, enfolding them, then beginning to rotate, spinning faster and faster, creating a vortex of energy that sucked them inexorably down, toward the mouth of the sacred tunnels.

"Leah," Strike said, his voice going urgent. "Pull out."

But she was caught up in the vortex, caught up in the power and the golden light as the feathered serpent trumpeted victory and the winged crocodile Zipacna fought his fate, fought the barrier that sucked him in, seeking to bind him to hell.

Strike grabbed her and shook her. "Leah. Break the connection before he takes you with him. Remember what almost happened with Anna and the *nahwal*!"

He was right, she realized as she tried to sever the Godkeeper bond and Kulkulkan resisted, taking her with him as he morphed to an insubstantial form and raced through dirt and rock, headed toward the Nightkeepers' sacred chamber, and the intersection beyond, which glowed golden on one side and shimmered with lightless black on the other. She could feel the god's joy in dragging the struggling demon toward the dark side, and his thrill in being free of the skyroad. His longing to return to the sky, bringing her power with him.

"No!" Leah cried, and with an effort of will she wrenched away from the god, breaking the connection and yanking her soul back, fighting for the life she'd just found, the love she'd never expected to have. "Let me go!"

A detonation rocked the earth beneath her feet as she slammed back wholly into herself. She fell, but she didn't hit the ground, as strong arms swept her up and held her hard. Recognizing the arms, the man, she returned his embrace, burrowing in and trembling hard as reaction set in.

But she wasn't the only one trembling, she realized. The earth was heaving beneath her, surging and groaning as though Zipacna were fighting the barrier's hold, struggling to break free. Moments later, the cave mouth leading to the hidden tunnels collapsed with a roar, belching dirt and debris in the moonlight.

Then everything went still. The earth quit moving and the buzz of power drained.

The Nightkeepers stood staring dumbly, some at the cave-in, some at the sky. But there were no winged crocodiles, no feathered serpents. Just the Yucatán night. The world had gone utterly normal.

"Holy crap," Strike said.

Leah levered away from him, beamed up at him, and started laughing, and her laughter became a whoop, a victory cry. *"We did it!"*

She was elated to be alive, to be victorious. To be in love.

"Thank you," she said, kissing him until neither of them could breathe. "I love you."

"Goes both ways," he said between kisses, holding on to her and squeezing so hard she thought she might break, though she never wanted him to let go. "You save me; I save you. That's the way it works from now on."

Then they were being mobbed by a sudden surge of cheering bodies, young and weary, but battle tested now, and victorious. Leah laughed with joy as she was variously hugged and backslapped, and returned the favor, aware of the sting in her palms and the aches everywhere else and the fact that none of that mattered just then. They'd won—for now. They could take a breath. Step back. Regroup. And figure out what came next. Most important, they'd do it together, as a team. As the Nightkeepers.

She bounced off Strike in the scrum, laughed, and latched onto him as an anchor. As she did so, she saw a flash of black where there hadn't been any before. She froze.

Flipped her wrist. Stared.

"Holy shit," someone said. She didn't think it was her.

There were three marks on her forearm where the scar had been. One she recognized from her research: *jun tan. Beloved.* The mark of a mated Nightkeeper. The other she recognized from Strike's arm: the royal *ju.* The third was unfamiliar, but there was no mistaking the flying serpent.

Strike, when he flipped his arm, was wearing the beloved mark too.

He smiled, his eyes for her alone. He touched her marks one by one and whispered, "Godkeeper." The flying serpent. "Queen." The royal mark. And when he got to the third mark, the beloved, he said simply, *"Mine."*

EPILOGUE

Twenty-four hours later

Exhausted from a restless night plagued with half-remembered dreams of dragons or some such shit—like he hadn't outgrown D&D years ago—Lucius mainlined about a gallon of instant coffee and dragged his ass onto campus and up the stairs of the art history building. Halfway down the hall to his office, he stopped dead when he saw that Anna's door was open.

His heart picked up a beat, as hope that she'd come back warred with the fear that admin was clearing out her desk, making it final. Holding his breath, he stepped into the doorway . . . and exhaled on a slap of relief when he saw her sitting at her desk.

She looked up, and her lips curved in greeting. "Lucius."

"Welcome back," he said, grinning with a kick of pleasure as his world realigned itself.

"It's good to see you." The words seemed a little too careful, but he could only figure she was trying to discourage him from asking how she was, where she'd been, where she was living—with the Dick or somewhere else?—and whether she was staying. *Talk to me,* he wanted to say. *Tell me what's going on and how I can help.* But he'd left a dozen voice-mail messages to that effect on her cell, and her lack of response had been answer enough.

"So . . ." she said into the sudden quiet. "Did I miss anything important? Any good university gossip going around? Aside, of course, from the rumors about me having a nervous breakdown and checking into a mental ward."

"Actually," he deadpanned, "you're a closet meth-head and you went for rehab. Sheesh. Keep up, will you?"

"Great." She rolled her eyes, but the tension between them relaxed a notch.

"There was something a little weird you missed," he said. He'd only half paid attention to the buzz because he'd been worried about her, but he didn't think she needed—or wanted—to hear that. "Seems like Ambrose Ledbetter's dropped off the face of the earth."

"Really?"

Again with the too-careful tone, but he didn't have a clue what it meant. Since she seemed interested, though, he continued, "Yeah, really. Granted, he goes off the reservation for months at a time, but it turns out there's a daughter—maybe a goddaughter? I'm not sure, exactly. Anyway, she says he's supposed to check in with her once a week, and he missed his last two calls. Sure enough, when she went down to look for him, no Ledbetter."

"Who—" She broke off. "Never mind." She flipped through some papers on her desk, and as she did so, he saw a flash of yellow at her throat, where an unfamiliar skull-shaped pendant hung on a delicate chain. "I've got to get out from underneath some of this backlog, but let's do lunch. Sissy Burgers?"

He grinned, and more of the tension uncoiled. "Yeah, that'd be good." He lifted a hand and sketched a wave. "Catch you then."

Twenty minutes later he was on his way out the door when the lab phone rang. Figuring Anna would get it, or Neenie, he kept going, but it rang again. Grumbling, he detoured to the closest handset and answered. "Mayan Studies."

There was a pause; then a soft voice said, "Is Anna Catori there? This is Sasha Ledbetter returning her call."

Lucius should've said he was sorry about Ambrose. He should've said no, Anna had stepped out, but he could take a message. Something. Anything. But he didn't. He just stood there, vapor-locked by the sound of her voice, which was weird, because it was just a voice, and there was no reason for it to reach inside him and squeeze a hard fist around his heart.

"Hello? Are you there?"

"Yeah," he squeaked, going soprano. "Yeah, sorry. Bad connection. Um, Anna's not here." At least, she hadn't answered the phone. "Can I tell her you called? Is there a number where she can reach you, like a cell or something?"

Okay, that was even borderline slick, he thought as she rattled off a number and he jotted it down on his palm. "I'll give her the message."

"Thanks," she said softly. Then she hung up, leaving him staring at the handset, wondering why it felt like the world had just tilted beneath his feet.

The night after the autumnal equinox, once the sun was down and the barbecue was long gone, came the time that Rabbit had been dreading. Red-Boar's funeral.

It wasn't that he didn't want to give the old man a proper send-off. It was more that he wasn't sure he could do it right. The ceremony Jade had found in the archive said the torchbearer was supposed to say goodbye with "a heart full of grief and regret, and thanks for the one who was lost." Which sounded great in theory. And yeah, he could find the grief and regret, and maybe even the thanks, but there were all sorts of other emotions tangled up alongside, emotions he wasn't sure the old man needed with him when he set off on his journey.

But Rabbit was the last of the bloodline. The torchbearer's role fell to him.

So when Strike signaled that it was time, Rabbit led the others to the coffin they'd made of ceiba wood and placed near the life tree, at the drip edge, where Red-Boar's ashes would mix with the others' and sink into the root system of a tree that shouldn't be able to grow where it was growing.

Nate, Sven, and Michael stood together, with Alexis and Jade opposite them, coexisting in uneasy accord. Brandt and Patience stood rock-solid, their unity an almost palpable force, while Strike and Leah were together at the foot of the coffin, surrounded by a faint halo of golden light Rabbit hoped would wear off soon, because it was freaky. The gathered *winikin* formed a second ring around the coffin.

Rabbit took his place at the end of the simple wooden box and tried to think of something to say, just like he'd been trying on and off all day. But none of it seemed right, so in the end he said simply, "Safe journey, old man."

Then he palmed his father's knife, which he now wore on his belt, and welcomed the bite of pain from the slash. When blood welled, he let it fall onto the coffin.

Without the need for any spell casting, the droplets burst into flame where they fell. The wood caught greedily, the fire fueled by the magic Rabbit felt flowing through him like water, magic he hadn't consciously called, magic he wasn't sure he could control.

Within two minutes, the heat had driven the others back. Within five, the coffin and the body within it were gone, leaving behind only a smudge of ash that stirred in the desert wind, blending with the darkened soil nearby.

Eventually the others drifted away.

Alone, Rabbit tried to feel peace but found only anger toward a father who'd never been what he needed. Tried to find forgiveness, and saw only the darkness around him. The angry part of him, the part he could mostly control now even as it grew stronger and started to press, rose up in him, urging him to leave Skywatch.

I need to be by myself for a while, he thought. *The pueblo. I'll go to the pueblo.* It wasn't quite leaving, wasn't quite staying. And there, sometimes, he found the peace that escaped him.

But when he turned to go, he realized he wasn't alone, after all. The twin boys, Harry and Braden, stood behind him, unusually silent. Harry held out a hand. "Rabbit come," he said, though unlike his more brazen twin, he rarely spoke.

"You guys go on," Rabbit said. "I'll see you later."

But the kid didn't move, just stood there with his hand out, staring at Rabbit like he knew what was going on inside him, like he understood somehow. "No cliff. Rabbit come."

A chill shivered through him. "How did you—" He broke off as a touch of gold sparkled in the air between them. "Okay," he said after a moment. "In we go."

He followed the twins into the mansion, away from the darkness.

It was late before things wound down and Strike finally found an opportunity to slip away with his woman. Okay, so he sort of interrupted her midsentence, picked her up, slung her over his shoulder, and cavemanned it down the hall to the royal suite, but who was counting?

She squealed and squirmed, drumming her fists on his kidneys, but they both knew she didn't mean it. If she had, he'd be flat on his back and gasping for air. Which was pretty much where he ended up the moment he got the suite doors closed, because she braced her feet on the wall and used the leverage to overbalance them both onto the carpet, then went to work on him with her hands and mouth the moment they were down.

Not that he was complaining in the slightest.

He fisted his hands in her long blond hair, holding her in place above him as he kissed her hard and hot, which didn't do a damned thing to take the edge off the horns that'd been riding him since they got back to the compound. *Mine*, he thought fiercely, and again, *mine*.

It wasn't just the magic of the god, though they both felt it, a kernel of gold at the base of their souls, something they could draw on when they needed it in the months and years to come. They'd won only a single battle. The war was yet to be joined. It wasn't just the relief of having her still there, either, though that was huge. The thought that he could've lost her had him sliding his hands down her shoulders to her waist and drawing her snug against the hard ridge in his jeans. And it wasn't just the total turn-on of wearing their matching marks, the beloved marks.

It was her. Leah. His woman. His love. There were no guards between them, no barriers. There were only the two of them.

"I love you," he said when they came up for air.

"That's convenient, 'cause I love you back." With a lithe twist, she slipped out from underneath him and came up with her fingers wrapped around his belt. Tugged him toward the solarium. "Come on. Jox finally gave up and moved a bed out under the stars. We've got a box spring and everything."

"No shit?" Strike laughed. "There might be some romance in the old guy's soul after all." But he pulled her farther down the short hall. "I've got a better idea."

The torches came up when he opened the door to the small ritual chamber, and the air smelled of *copan* even though he hadn't burned any. Leah flowed past him, shedding clothes as she went, so she was naked by the time she turned and hiked herself up on the *chac-mool*, put one foot up onto the poor guy's head, and crooked a finger at Strike. "I like your thinking."

He went to her, putting his feet in the red outlines on the ceremonial mat, and fitting the rest of his body exactly where it was meant to be—up against his woman. His queen. And when they kissed and the torches dimmed, and he glanced into the obsidian mirror behind the altar, he saw only the strong, delicate curve of Leah's spine, and her face in half profile as she turned it into his neck and breathed him in.

The ghosts, and the past, were gone, leaving them to live the future yet unwritten.

Together.

Read on for a sneak preview
of book two in the Final Prophecy series:
DAWNKEEPERS

Bidding on the thirteen-hundred-year-old Mayan statuette started at two grand and jumped almost immediately to five. At fifty-five hundred, Alexis caught the
spotter's eye and nodded, then leaned back in her folding chair, projecting the calm of a collector.

It was a lie, of course. The only things she'd ever
collected were parking tickets at the Newport marina.
She looked the part, though, in a stylish navy pinstripe
pantsuit that nipped in at the waist and pulled a little
across the shoulders, thanks to all the hand-to-hand combat training she'd gotten in recent months. Her streaky
blond hair was pulled back in a severe ponytail, and she
wore secondhand designer shoes that put her well over
six feet. A top-end bag sat at her feet beside a matching
folio, both slightly scuffed around the edges.

Understated upscale, courtesy of eBay.

In her previous life as a private investment consultant,
the look had been calculated to reassure her wealthy
friends and clients that she belonged among them but
wouldn't compete, wouldn't upstage. She'd played the
part for so long prior to last year's *Oh, by the way,
you're a Nightkeeper* revelation that it'd been second nature to dress for this gig. But as bidding on the statuette
topped sixty-five hundred and Alexis nodded to bump it

to a cool seven grand, she felt a hum of power that had been missing from her old life.

I have money now, the buzz in her blood said. *I deserve to be here.*

It wasn't her money, not really. But she had carte blanche with the Nightkeeper Fund, and orders not to come home empty-handed.

"Ma'am?" said a cultured, amplified voice. It was the auctioneer now, not the spotter, which meant the dabblers had dropped out and he had his two or three serious bidders. "It's seventy-five hundred dollars to you."

She glanced up at the projection screen at the front of the room. It showed a magnification of the statuette, which rested near the auctioneer's elbow, top-lit on a nest of black cloth.

Described in the auction catalog as "a statuette of Ixchel, Mayan goddess of rainbows and fertility, carved from chert, c. AD 1100, love poem inscribed in hieroglyphs on base," the statuette was made of pale green stone that'd been carved with deceptive simplicity into the shape of a woman with a large nose and flattened forehead, her conical skull crowned with a rainbow of hair, and her large hands cupping the swell of her pregnant belly. She sat upon a stone, or maybe an overturned bowl or basket, and that was where the hieroglyphs were carved, curved and fluid and gorgeous like all Mayan writing, which was as much an art as a form of communication.

Love poem, Alexis thought with an inner snort. *Not.* Or rather, it was eau-de-Hallmark read one way, but according to Jade's research back at Skywatch, if they held the statuette at the proper angle under starlight, a new set of glyphs would show up, spelling out one of the demon prophecies.

Aware that the auctioneer was waiting on her, Alexis said, "Ten thousand dollars." As she'd hoped, the advance jumped the bid past fair market value by enough to make her remaining opponent shake his head and drop out. The auctioneer pronounced it a done deal and she felt a flare of success as she flashed her bidder number, knowing there would be no problem with the money.

The Nightkeeper Fund, which had—ironically—been

seeded in the eighteen hundreds with the proceeds from her five-times-great-grandparents' generation of Nightkeepers unwisely selling off the very Mayan artifacts they were scrambling to recover now, had been intended to fund an army of hundreds as the 2012 end date approached. That, however, was before the current king's father had led his warrior-priests into an ill-fated battle with the demons and wiped out most of their culture. Only a few of the youngest Nightkeepers had survived, hidden and raised in secret by their *winikin* until seven months earlier, when the intersection connecting the earth, sky and underworld had reactivated from its two-decade dormancy, and the king's son, Strike, had recalled his people.

Yeah, that had been a shocker. *Alexis, dear, you're a magic-user,* Izzy had pretty much said. *I'm not your godmother, I'm your* winikin, *and we need to leave tonight for your bloodline ceremony and training. And, oh, by the way, you and the other Nightkeepers have a little over four years to save the world.*

According to the thirteenth prophecy, since Strike had refused to sacrifice the human woman who became his queen, the countdown to the end-time had begun in earnest. Info from their archivist, Jade, indicated that they'd passed into the four-year cycle during which seven of the *Banol Kax* would come through the intersection one at a time, each on a cardinal day, and seek to perform a task described in the ancient Mayan legends. If the task was fulfilled, the demon would return to the underworld, Xibalba, and the barrier between the worlds would thin to a degree determined by the demon's power. If the task was blocked, however, the demon would be destroyed and the barrier would strengthen by the same amount. That was what had the Nightkeepers hustling to find the seven statuettes that were supposedly inscribed with star-script prophecies that apparently explained how to defeat each of the demons.

Make that six statuettes, Alexis thought, grinning. *Because I just bagged Ixchel.*

"Excuse me, please," she murmured, and rose, snagging her folio and bag off the floor.

She stepped out into the aisle while the discreet auction house employees whisked her statuette off the podium and set up the next lot, and the auctioneer launched into his spiel. When she reached the temporary office the auction house had set up in the hallway outside the big estate's ballroom, she unzipped the folio and watched the cashier's eyes get big at the sight of the neatly stacked and banded bills.

She handed over her bidder's number. "What's the total damage?"

"Let me check," he said, but his eyes were still glued to the cash.

The two items she'd bought—the statuette and a Mayan death mask that had been an earlier impulse buy—wouldn't be the biggest deals of the day by far, but she'd bet they'd be among only a few handled in paper money. Granted, she could've done the remote transfer thing, too, but she quite simply loved the green stuff. She loved the feel and smell of cash, loved what it could buy—not just the things, but the respect. The power.

And no, it wasn't because she'd been deprived or picked on as a child, as *someone* back at Skywatch had unkindly suggested. Nor was it a reaction to the idea that the world was four years away from a serious crisis of being, as that same someone had offered, or a rejection of destiny or some such claptrap. In fact, she'd decided it was simple biology.

The Nightkeepers were bigger, stronger and more graceful than average humans, pumped with charisma and loaded with talent. At least most of them were. Alexis had somehow gotten the bigger and stronger part without the grace, and while she'd worked long and hard to camouflage the klutz factor, and most days managed to control her freakishly long limbs, the effort left her pretty low on charisma. So far she was decidedly average in the talent department, too, having gotten the warrior's mark, but no inherent magical talent beyond the basics.

Ergo, her enjoyment of the occasional power trip. She liked living as large as possible. So sue her.

"This might take a minute," the cashier said finally,

looking away from the cash to bang a few keys on his laptop, and scowling when the thing bleated at him. "The network's being all glitchy today. I don't know what's wrong with it."

"No rush." She flipped the folio shut and turned away, figuring she'd use the brief delay to check in, which consisted of powering up her phone, text messaging Izzy that she had the statuette and was headed back to Skywatch, and then powering off the unit without checking her backlogged messages.

She wasn't in the mood for the chatter, hadn't been for a while. That was a big part of why she'd jumped on the chance to fly out to the California coast for the auction. The quick trip had given her a chance to breathe air she wasn't sharing with the same Nightkeepers and *winikin* she'd been cheek-to-jowl with for the past half year. Besides, she could guarantee the messages on her cell were nothing critical, because she wasn't in line for the important assignments yet. Strike had his advisers— Leah and the royal *winikin*, Jox. The three of them handled the heavy-duty stuff, and delegated the lower-impact jobs.

For now, anyway.

Alexis had her sights set higher. Her mother, Gray-Smoke, had been one of King Scarred-Jaguar's most trusted advisers, holding political power equaled only by that of her nemesis and coadviser, Two-Hawk. That pretty much figured, because Two-Hawk's son was Alexis's personal nemesis, i.e., the *someone* who'd been driving her pretty much nuts over the past few months, ever since he'd dumped her ass right after the talent ceremony, and then acted like it'd been no big deal for them to go from burning up the sheets to a quick nod in passing.

Damn him. And damn her for falling right back into old habits just as she was starting her new and improved life.

"Ma'am? You're all set." The cashier held out her paperwork. "I have a couple of messages for you, too. She said it was important."

"Thanks." She took the slips, glanced at them and

tucked them into her pocket. Just Izzy mother-henning her. The *winikin* would've gotten the text message by now, so they were square.

A security guard set a metal case on the table and flipped it open so she could see the statuette and the death mask nestled side-by-side in a shockproof foam bed. At her nod, the guard shut the case and slid it across the table to her, rumbling in a basso profundo voice, "Dial the numbers to what you want, and hit this button." He pointed to an inset red dot. "That'll set your combination. If you don't want to bother, just leave it all zeros and it'll just act like a suitcase. Got it?"

"Got it." A whim had her dialing in a string of numbers and hitting the red button, and there was something satisfying about hearing the click of the locks engaging. When they did, the readout zeroed, which she thought was a nice touch.

Once outside, she found herself under the clear blue sky of a perfect February day in NorCal, the sort that made her wish she'd opted for the convertible when she'd rented her car. But it'd been drizzling when she landed, so she'd chosen a sporty silver BMW that hugged the road like a lover. Convertible or not, the silver roadster ought to be automotive muscle enough to entertain her on the way back to LAX.

Sure enough, once she was on the road with the metal case in the passenger seat beside her, the feel of engine power and smooth leather lightened her mood, sending a victory dance through her soul. She had the statuette, and she wasn't technically due back at Skywatch for another day. There was a sense of freedom in the thought, one that had her cranking the radio to something loud and edgy with a heavy backbeat as she pulled onto the narrow shoreline drive that led away from the lavish private estate that was being sold off piece by piece to settle the owner's debts.

Alexis had thought it a stroke of luck that the sale had come up just as they'd started tracking down the lost artifacts, but Izzy had reminded her that there wasn't much in the way of actual coincidence in the world. Most of what people thought of as happy accidents were the will of the gods.

The thought brought a quiver of unease.

"They're just dreams," she told herself, sending the BMW whipping around a low-G curve that dropped off to the right in a steep embankment and a million-dollar view of the NorCal coast.

Still, dreams or not, she didn't like the way the nightmares had stuck with her over the past few months, or how they kept changing, evolving, each time showing a new detail of the same scene. In it, she wasn't sure if she was herself or the mother she'd never known, wasn't sure if the shadowy figure of a man wearing the hawk medallion was supposed to be Nate or his father. She knew only that they were in the barrier, locked together, calling on strong, terrible magic. The dream always ended with a flash of light, and she awoke, drenched in sweat, her heart pounding as tears of loss poured down her cheeks.

"I'm not a seer, damn it." Needing to prove it yet again—to herself, to the gods—she unbuttoned her right sleeve and shoved it up to her elbow, baring her forearm. On the inside, just beyond her wrist, she wore two marks: the curling *b'utz* glyph representing the smoke bloodline, and three stacked blobs of the warrior's talent mark that had given her increased reflexes and strategic thought, along with a power boost and the ability to call up shields and fireballs. "See? No *itz'aat*'s mark. I'm not a seer, and those are just dreams."

And if she told herself that a hundred or so more times, she thought as she yanked down her sleeve, it might even play like the truth.

"Damn it," she muttered, and hit the gas too hard going into the next curve, which was a blind turn arcing along a sheer cliffside drop. Easing off and shaking her head at herself for getting all tangled up when she was supposed to be enjoying the satisfaction of a job well done, she nursed the car around the corner—

And drove straight into a wall of fire.

She screamed and cranked the wheel as flames lashed

at the car, slapping in through the open windows and searing the air around her. Worse was the power that crackled along her skin, feeling dark and twisted.

Ambush!

Her warrior's instincts fired up; she fought the urge to slam on the brakes and hit the gas instead, hoping to punch through the fire, but it was already too late. The car cut loose and slid sideways, losing traction when all four tires blew.

Heart pounding, she fought the wheel, fought to not inhale. Smoke burned her eyes and throat, and the exposed skin of her wrists and face. Then she was through the fire magic and back on the open road, but it was too late to steer, too late to correct even if she could without rubber on the rims.

Alexis screamed as the BMW hit the guardrail and flipped.

JESSICA ANDERSEN

DAWNKEEPERS

A NOVEL OF
THE FINAL PROPHECY

*The brand-new series that combines
Mayan astronomy and lore with modern,
sexy characters for a gripping read.*

In the first century A.D., Mayan astronomers predicted
the world would end on December 21, 2012. In these
final years before the End Times, demon creatures of
the Mayan underworld—The Makols—have come to
earth to trigger the apocalypse. But the descendants of
the Mayan warrior-priests have decided to fight back.

**"Raw passion, dark romance, and seat-of-
your-pants suspense, all set in an
astounding paranormal world."**
—#1 *New York Times* bestselling author J. R. Ward

Also Available
Skykeepers

AVAILABLE NOW

STORM OF VISIONS
The Chosen Ones

Christina Dodd

Jacqueline Vargha has always run from her gift.
Until Caleb D'Angelo forces his way into her life
and insists she take her place as one of the
Chosen. She flees, he pursues, but she can no
longer deny her visions, or the dangerous man
who is her downfall...and her destiny.

"Dodd writes with
power and passion."
—#1 *New York Times* bestselling author
J. R. Ward

**Available wherever books are sold or at
penguin.com**